KT-362-419

A DIFFERENT KIND OF EVIL

Andrew Wilson is an award-winning journalist and author. His work has appeared in a wide variety of publications including the *Guardian*, the *Washington Post*, the *Daily Telegraph*, the *Observer*, the *Sunday Times*, the *Independent on Sunday*, the *Daily Mail*, the *New Statesman*, the *Evening Standard* magazine and the *Smithsonian*. The author of five acclaimed works of non-fiction, he has also written two novels, *The Lying Tongue* and *A Talent for Murder*.

Also by Andrew Wilson

FICTION

A Talent for Murder

The Lying Tongue

NON-FICTION

Alexander McQueen: Blood Beneath the Skin

Mad Girl's Love Song:

Sylvia Plath and Life Before Ted

Shadow of the Titanic: The Extraordinary

Stories of Those Who Survived

Harold Robbins: The Man Who Invented Sex

Beautiful Shadow: A Life of Patricia Highsmith

A DIFFERENT KIND OF EVIL

ANDREW WILSON

A Different Kind of Evil is not authorised
by Agatha Christie Ltd

**SIMON &
SCHUSTER**

London · New York · Sydney · Toronto · New Delhi

A CBS COMPANY

First published in Great Britain by Simon & Schuster UK Ltd, 2018
A CBS COMPANY

Copyright © Andrew Wilson Media Ltd 2018

This book is copyright under the Berne Convention.
No reproduction without permission.
® and © 1997 Simon & Schuster, Inc. All rights reserved.

The right of Andrew Wilson to be identified as author of this work
has been asserted in accordance with sections 77 and 78
of the Copyright, Designs and Patents Act, 1988.

1 3 5 7 9 10 8 6 4 2

Simon & Schuster UK Ltd
1st Floor
222 Gray's Inn Road
London WC1X 8HB

www.simonandschuster.co.uk
www.simonandschuster.com.au
www.simonandschuster.co.in

Simon & Schuster Australia, Sydney
Simon & Schuster India, New Delhi

A CIP catalogue record for this book
is available from the British Library

Hardback ISBN: 978-1-4711-4825-5
Trade Paperback ISBN: 978-1-4711-4826-2
eBook ISBN: 978-1-4711-4828-6

This book is a work of fiction. Names, characters, places
and incidents are either a product of the author's imagination or
are used fictitiously. Any resemblance to actual people living
or dead, events or locales is entirely coincidental.

Typeset in the UK by M Rules
Printed and bound by CPI Group (UK) Ltd, Croydon, CR0 4YY

Simon & Schuster UK Ltd are committed to sourcing paper
that is made from wood grown in sustainable forests and support the Forest
Stewardship Council, the leading international forest certification organisation.
Our books displaying the FSC logo are printed on FSC certified paper.

To my parents

A DIFFERENT KIND OF EVIL

Chapter One

As I felt the ship tilt and roll I looked out of the porthole to see a hidden horizon, the skyline obscured by the dirty smudge of a black storm cloud. I sat up and took a sip of water, trying to swallow down the feelings of nausea as well as wash away unpleasant memories of bad times at sea.

Perhaps a little fresh air would do me good, I thought, as I swung my legs over the edge of the bed. I checked myself in the looking glass, tidied my hair, quickly threw on some clothes and, as I knew it would be cold outside on deck, picked up the Paisley shawl that my friend Flora Kurs had given me and draped it across my shoulders.

I listened at the connecting door that led through to the cabin where Rosalind and Carlo were sleeping. All was quiet and I decided not to disturb them. I knew from previous experience that if we were in for a rough crossing, it would be best if my daughter and my secretary were able to sleep through it.

I made my way down the corridor, placing a hand on the

wall to steady myself. *Oh, please let this not be another Madeira.* On that journey, the outward leg of the Empire Tour, the trip around the world that I had taken with Archie, I had suffered such terrible seasickness that at one point I thought I would die. In fact, a fellow passenger, a lady who had caught a brief glimpse of me through the open door, had asked the stewardess whether I had actually passed away.

Although that made me smile now, at the time I had not found the observation amusing. I had had to be confined to the cabin for four days and, like a sick dog, had brought back anything I had swallowed. I had tried everything, but nothing did any good. In the end, the doctor had given me what he said was liquid chloroform, and after twenty-four hours without food, Archie fed me with essence of beef directly from the jar. How fine that had tasted! I knew my husband hated illness of any kind and the sight of him offering me a spoon of the dark, viscous substance had made me love him all the more.

That love had gone for good now, at least on his part. The crisis at the end of the last year had finally squeezed the life out of our marriage. Archie had gone back to live at Styles, with a view to selling the house, while the new woman in his life, Nancy Neele, had left the country. Her parents had not wanted her to be caught up in the scandal I had caused with my disappearance and had ordered her into temporary exile. I had heard, however, that on her return from her travels she and Archie planned to marry. The word divorce sounded so brutal, so ugly, and although I did not like the idea of it – with all the stigma and shame that accompanied it – I knew that it was something I would have to endure.

It is as inevitable as the force of the sea, I thought, as I stepped onto the deck. The wind was beginning to whip up the water, sending its surface into a fury of white. A fine spray of sea mist left its moist trail on my face, and as I ran my tongue over my lips, I tasted salt. After leaving Southampton we had sailed through the English Channel headed for Portugal. Although I had been prepared for a spot of *mal de mer* as we sailed into the Bay of Biscay, the sea had actually been as calm as a duck pond. It was only after leaving Lisbon and travelling south that we encountered the bad weather.

I held on to the rail as I walked along the deck, straining my eyes towards the distance. Somewhere out there was my destination: Tenerife, one of the Canary Islands. John Davison, a man I had met at the end of last year, had finally persuaded me to help him investigate the murder of one of his agents, a youngish chap called Douglas Greene. I had tried to resist his pleas to work with the Secret Intelligence Service – in fact, I remember to begin with I thought the whole thing had been nothing more than a silly joke – but after the deaths of Flora Kurs and Davison's friend Una Crowe I felt duty bound to help. Neither woman would have died had it not been for me. How could I say no?

And there was something very queer about the circumstances surrounding the murder of Greene: Davison had told me that the agent's partly mummified body had been found in a cave on the island. At first sight, it appeared as though Greene's corpse had been covered in blood, but on further examination it was determined that the glossy red sheen covering his flesh was in fact the sap from a dragon tree, native to Tenerife. Bizarrely, all of his own blood had been drained from his system, but there was no trace of it on the dry earth in the cave or nearby.

When Davison related this to me I could hardly believe it. But I knew, perhaps better than most people, that evil really did exist in this world. The way some people talked about crime astonished me – as if a sadistic murder or violent sexual attack could be blamed on a dreadfully unhappy childhood or a certain background. No, I was certain that some people were born, not made, evil. Those that disagreed with me, I am afraid, were nothing more than blinkered idealists who could not face up to the brutal realities of human nature. I had stared wickedness in the face, in the form of Dr Kurs, and I would never forget it; one could literally smell the stench of evil emanating from him. His scheme to manipulate me into committing a murder, which necessitated that I disappear from the view of family, friends and the world, had driven me to a point of utter distraction and despair. I doubted I would ever be the same again. Certainly, my dreams were still haunted by the horrors of those eleven days in December of the previous year. When I closed my eyes I saw the faces of Una Crowe, that poor young girl who had been determined to follow my trail, and Flora Kurs, the ill-fated wife of my tormentor who had sacrificed herself for me.

I looked out to sea once more and watched the sky blacken in the distance. As a child living in Devon, I would spend hours watching the shifting waters of Torbay, the changing colour of the sea and sky, the reflection of the clouds upon the waves. I would imagine what lay over the horizon, the far-flung countries with their exotic climates and strange people, and try to picture my future. I don't think I ever dreamt that I would be a writer, much less get involved with working for a government agency. It all seemed so fantastical somehow, and yet it was true.

Davison had told me – what was it? – that I had a first-rate brain, or some such nonsense. I surmised that it had more to do with the fact that the division he worked for was extremely short on women. And surely no-one would ever suspect a slightly socially inept, middle-aged lady of anything? I could move about in an almost invisible state, asking questions, listening to confidences. I could simply serve as an extra pair of eyes and ears. Before embarking on the journey Davison had stressed the importance of never placing myself in a dangerous situation. The murder of his friend Una still weighed heavily on him. He was taking no chances this time, and he had insisted on accompanying me on the journey to Tenerife. However, while on the SS *Gelria* – the ship that would take us from Southampton to Las Palmas, before it continued on its journey – and also in Tenerife, Davison would travel under an assumed name: that of Alexander Blake. It would be simpler and more straightforward, he said, if we pretended to meet for the first time on the ship.

I had intended to leave my daughter Rosalind behind, under the care of my sister at Abney Hall, on the outskirts of Manchester, but when I mentioned to her that I might have to go away again she became terribly distressed. At seven and a half, she was old enough to understand something of the miseries of the adult world and, no doubt, the thought of my absence brought back the horrors of the previous year: the sight of uniformed police, the strained atmosphere in the house, the worried looks on the servants' faces; the anxiety that she might see the front page of a newspaper or hear a newsboy's ghoulish call. Also, I don't think she had ever quite forgiven me for abandoning her for almost a year on my world tour in 1922. And so I had reluctantly accepted that my daughter would have to accompany me to the Canaries. She would be looked after by Carlo and I would make sure she did not come to any harm. It had taken me some time to persuade the family, and those fussing doctors, that a holiday would be beneficial – they worried about the difficulties of travel, the water, the foreign food – but finally they relented. A few weeks in a balmy climate would soothe my nerves and restore my spirits.

Just then a blast of icy wind forced me to hug the shawl tighter across my shoulders. The fresh air had done me good, but the cold was getting too much. Just as I went to return to my cabin, I heard what I first thought was the high-pitched cry of a gull. I stopped and gripped the rail. The sound split the air again, the unmistakable scream of a woman that seemed to be coming from the back of the ship. I ran from the front of the boat along the empty deck towards the stern. I looked around to enlist help, but there was no one to be seen. I heard my breathing – fast, shallow and full of panic – as I ran, but by the time I got to the stern, the screams seemed to have stopped. Instead, I saw a heavily-set, dark-haired woman standing on the very back of the ship, staring into the sea. A few feet away from her stood another woman, a thin blonde, who on seeing me took a tentative step towards her companion.

'No, Gina, don't,' said the blonde-haired woman, stretching out a hand. 'I know you hate me, you hate us both probably, but really it's not worth it, *we're* not worth it.'

In response to this, the brunette climbed over the railings onto a narrow ledge, holding on to the wooden balustrade with both arms.

'Please, no,' I shouted into the wind, unsure whether the woman could hear my words. 'What's your name?'

I turned to her friend, the beautiful blonde whose face was wet with tears. 'Gina, did you say? Is that what's she's called?'

'Yes, it's Gina all right,' she said. 'She somehow stowed away on the boat. She's been missing in England, no one knew she was here. She discovered, well, that her husband, Guy—'

I didn't hear the rest because at that moment a terrific gust of wind blasted in from the sea, forcing me to take a step back. Big fat drops of rain began to lash down from the ever-darkening sky.

'Have you tried to get help?' I shouted. 'Sorry, who are you?'

'Miss Hart. No, I got up early to have a walk around the deck. I just chanced upon her and there was no one around. That's when I started to scream. I didn't know what else to do.'

'Are you close to her?'

'We were – once. But I'm sure she must hate me now. You see, Guy, that's Mr Trevelyan and I, well—'

I began to understand the sorry state of affairs. Guy had obviously been carrying on with Miss Hart behind his wife's back. Just like Archie had deceived me with Miss Neele.

I turned away from Miss Hart as I tried to mask my contempt.

'Gina, listen to me,' I said, slowly moving towards her. 'Tomorrow, everything will seem very different, I can assure you. I found myself in just the same situation and at one point I even thought of doing – well, something stupid. But it is extraordinary what time, and a little perspective, can do. Of course, you feel like everything is worthless, but it is not the case. You must have a great deal left to live for. I'm sure you have friends, family, a favourite aunt or grandmother, a pet who adores you.' I thought of the feel of my dear dog Peter's soft head and the deliciously awful stench of his breath. 'Your life is precious. You may not think so now, but it is, especially to those close to you.'

Gina seemed to be on the point of turning around and looking at me and perhaps even climbing back over the railings. But then from behind me I heard Miss Hart scream once more. This time, the noise was low and guttural, primitive almost.

'Gina! No! Please don't!' she shouted, launching herself forwards. 'Not now. Not after everything!'

'Miss Hart, no!' I hissed. 'Please, stand back.'

I tried to stop Gina, attempted to calm her, but it was

8

all so quick. She raised her arms and stood very still for a moment, before she started to sway ever so slightly as if she had given her body over to the force of the wind. And then, like an overweight ballerina, she moved as if she were about to fly, lifting her arms high above her head and then letting them drop to her side. Just as Miss Hart, in a panic, shunted forwards, a desperation in her eyes which reminded me of the look of an animal in the slaughter-house, Gina raised her arms in the air once more and with a graceful movement she jumped off the ship. As I ran towards her I knew there was little point, it was too late. But there was something inside of me – something which I was sure lives inside all people who count themselves decent and good – which propelled me to try and grab her. Instinctively, I thrust my hands out, but there was nothing to hold on to, only mist and rain and wind, the spray from an angry sea, and a darkening sky. I craned my neck to look over the railings, but there was no sign of Gina. She must have been dragged under in the wake of the ship.

'We need to see if we can rescue her,' I shouted, but to no response. I turned to see Miss Hart standing there, the life sucked out of her. 'Miss Hart. Quick. Go and get help. Find an officer.'

'Yes, of course, you're right,' she said, gradually coming back to her senses. 'Yes, it's worth a shot.'

As she turned and ran along the deck, I kept hoping to catch a glimpse of Gina in the water behind us. I called her name, even though I knew that the fierce roar of the wind and the sea would drown out my feeble voice. I was completely soaked through to my skin and my eyes were full of water, a mix of raindrops and tears. I imagined the poor girl in the water, gasping for air as her lungs filled up with salt water.

A memory came back to me from years ago when I had been swimming in the Ladies' Bathing Cove in Torquay with my nephew Jack. I had set off with the little boy on my back – he was not yet old enough to swim for very long by himself – towards the raft that lay anchored in the bay. As I swam I noticed that the sea had been possessed of a strange sort of swell and, with the weight of Jack on my shoulders, I started to take in quite a bit of water. I felt myself going under and told Jack to swim to the raft. As I drifted out of consciousness I didn't have a life-flashing-before-one's-eyes experience. Neither did I hear the strains of stringed instruments or soothing classical music. There was simply a feeling of terrible emptiness, of utter blackness. The next thing I knew I was being tossed into a boat – which also rescued little Jack – and, on the shore, a man laid me out on the beach and started to work the water out of me.

Gina would not be so lucky, I was sure. But we had to try. Where was that woman? Why hadn't she managed to find help? Just then I saw Miss Hart come running with a man dressed in a smart blue uniform, who introduced himself as first officer William McMaster.

'Please, over here,' I said. 'A woman just fell off the ship. Can you stop it?'

The officer leant over the stern and cast his expert eye over the surface of the water. As he turned to us the grim expression on his face said it all.

'Yes, we certainly will,' said McMaster. 'I'll go and tell the captain now, but I'm afraid there is little hope. She would have been dragged down deep into the ocean. Even an Olympic-class swimmer wouldn't be able to survive, I'm afraid.'

'I see,' I said, bristling at his pessimistic attitude. 'But we must do everything we can to make sure.'

'Of course. And if you could please go back inside. We're expecting some rather rough weather in the next few hours, so we will be locking the doors that lead to the decks.'

'And if the poor girl did not survive,' I said, 'what are the chances of recovering her body? It seems only right we should give her a decent funeral.'

Miss Hart let out a quiet cry and dropped her head forwards as she tried to stifle a sob.

'We'll do everything in our power to find her. But I am afraid that the weather and the sea are our enemies. We mustn't delay any longer. Please follow me inside.'

We trailed after McMaster like two mourners after a burial on a wet afternoon, our heads and spirits low.

'Before I go and see the captain, could you give me your names?' said the officer, taking a small notebook from the inside pocket of his jacket.

'Mrs Agatha . . . Christie,' I said, slightly hesitantly, fingering my wedding ring and wondering whether I would carry Archie's name for the rest of my life.

The officer raised an eyebrow. Perhaps he had read one of my books – or, more likely, he had seen something in the newspapers relating to the scandal surrounding my disappearance the year before. Would I ever be free of that?

After noting my name he looked towards the beautiful blonde standing next to me.

'I'm Miss Helen Hart.'

The name sounded familiar.

'Thank you. I'm sure the captain will want to talk to you later. And I'll let you know if we spot anything, anything at all.'

'Thank you, officer,' I said.

'How awful,' I said. 'What a dreadful thing to witness. You must be terribly shaken. Had your friend been standing there long?'

'I'm not sure,' said Miss Hart, brushing a strand of hair from her eyes. 'I'm absolutely soaking, aren't you?'

'Yes,' I said, looking down to see the water puddling on the carpet beneath our feet. 'Why don't we change into fresh clothes and perhaps we can have a talk in the library. I doubt there will be anybody there at this time of day.'

After we had agreed to meet in half an hour, I returned to my cabin. Carlo and Rosalind were still sleeping. I ran a basin full of hot water and proceeded to wash. I dried my hair with a towel and brushed it, but it still looked a fright; it would have to be covered up with a hat. Just as I was dressing, Rosalind ran in from the adjoining cabin, intent on telling me about a dream she had had.

'I lost Blue Teddy, Mummy, I couldn't find him anywhere. It was horrible.'

'How upsetting for you, darling. But it was only a dream,' I said, stroking her hair.

'I know. Thank goodness. I should so hate to lose him.

What on earth would he do without me?' She paused and looked at me as if she had seen me for the first time. 'What kind of dreams do you have, Mummy? Do they make you sad?'

'Sometimes,' I said, remembering some of the horrific visions that had recently interrupted my sleep, often culminating in me sitting up in bed in a cold sweat. 'But then, I always tell myself not to be so silly as it's all make-believe.'

'Dreams are such funny things, aren't they?'

'Indeed they are,' I said, smiling. 'Oh look, here's Carlo.'

'Good morning,' said Carlo. 'I woke up because I felt the ship slow down. Did you feel it too? In fact—'

She broke off to walk over to the spray-streaked port-hole. 'I'm sure the ship has stopped. Yes. Look – we aren't moving. And it's terrible weather too.'

I knelt down and kissed Rosalind. 'Darling, why don't you go and see if Blue Teddy is all right? I'll come and dress you in a moment.'

As I closed the connecting door I told Carlo of the events of the morning.

'How awful,' she said. 'And how awful too that you had to stand by and watch it all. Are you sure you don't need to rest? You know what the doctors said.'

'No, if I lie down I'll most likely start to feel seasick again. That's why I got up early, to have a breath of fresh air.'

Carlo looked pensive and serious before she said, 'She must have been driven to despair.'

'I suppose she must, yes.'

'And it seems as though this other woman, Miss Hart, was having an affair with the poor lady's husband?'

'Yes.'

'A familiar story.'

'Indeed,' I said, glancing at my watch. 'In fact, I'm due to talk to Miss Hart now.'

'Have we met him on board – the husband? What did you say his name was?'

'Guy Trevelyan. No, I don't believe we have.'

'Perhaps he was with that rather fast set we saw across the dining room last night. The ones making all that noise after dinner.'

I thought back to the previous night. As an ear-splitting guffaw had cracked the air, I remembered looking askance at the group of young people in such high spirits at the far corner of the first-class dining room. Did they really have to be quite so loud? Perhaps it had been sourness or middle age or my own particular circumstances – whatever the reason I am sure I had not laughed like that in years – but I had cast a rather disapproving stare across the room and in the process I had met the amused eyes of a handsome, dark-haired man sitting next to an elegant blonde, who I now knew to be Helen Hart.

When I opened the door to the library Helen Hart was standing by the far shelves, her back to me.

'I must say they've got a rather poor show of books. Not that I would read any if they had a better selection. Have you seen them?'

'No, I'm afraid—'

'Oh, I'm so sorry, I didn't hear you come in,' she said. 'I was talking to Mr Trevelyan.'

A tall, rugged-looking man stood up from one of the green leather armchairs. As he walked towards me I noticed that the mischievous glint in his eyes that I had seen last night had been extinguished; now his demeanour was serious and melancholic.

'Guy, this is Mrs Christie, the lady I told you about,' said Helen. 'She tried to help with—'

'I'm so grateful for everything you did this morning, I really am,' he said. 'Such a dreadful business.'

'I'm sorry I couldn't do more,' I said to Mr Trevelyan. 'Have you spoken to Mr McMaster?'

'Yes, he came to my cabin a little while ago. I'm afraid there is no sign, no sign whatsoever,' he said. 'The captain is going to hold the ship here for the next few hours to make sure, but I think that's more out of respect than any-thing else.' His handsome features, so dazzling at dinner the night before, looked a little worn around the edges and shadows had appeared beneath his eyes. 'Poor Gina. If only—'

'You can't continue to blame yourself, Guy,' said Helen. 'Yes, I know, well, we hardly behaved like saints, but Gina was always a bit unbalanced, wasn't she?'

'What do you mean?' I said gently.

'Please let's not go into all of that now, Helen,' said Guy. 'All I know is that I feel we've driven the poor woman to her death.' His dark eyes filled with tears and he bit into his knuckle to prevent himself from breaking down.

'Darling, you know that's not entirely accurate,' said

Helen, placing a hand on his shoulder to comfort him. As she did so I noticed her large, strong-looking hands. Her short nails were not painted and around the cuticles there lay a dark substance that looked like ingrained dirt.

I realised then how I knew her name: I had seen an exhibition of her sculpture – strange, primitive figures, fragmented naked torsos and the like – at a gallery in London. I recalled being quite shocked by some of the imagery – it was certainly powerful stuff – but one could not deny that Miss Hart had the ability to tap into the deepest parts of the human psyche. I also remembered feeling more than a little jealous of her talents. At one point I had had the very stupid idea of becoming a sculptress myself. I had even taken some lessons, before being forced to admit that I was a hopeless case.

'I'm a great admirer of your work, Miss Hart,' I said, trying to lighten the mood.

'Really?' she said, her blue eyes shining.

'Yes, I saw your exhibition at the Pan Gallery early last year. I can't say I understood it all, but I certainly believe you have an extraordinary ability to capture the essence of things.'

'Well, isn't that lovely of you to say so. Isn't that wonderful, Guy?' she said. 'I recognise your name, but I'm afraid I haven't read any of your novels. Reading is not my forte. I can see things – forms, colours and suchlike – but I must be allergic to the written word. You must think me terribly stupid.'

'Not at all, Miss Hart,' I said. 'In fact, it's always

something of a relief to talk to people who haven't read my books.'

'I know, why don't you join us for dinner tonight,' said Miss Hart. 'And by the way, please call me Helen.'

'Yes, of course,' Trevelyan said flatly. Helen looked at him sternly. 'Yes, please do,' he said, more brightly and with greater enthusiasm. 'I'm so sorry, Mrs Christie. I still can't quite believe it – that Gina is dead.'

'I know, a sudden loss is bad enough, but a death of this nature something quite different,' I said. 'I'm sure she would not have suffered,' I added, not quite believing it myself. 'It would all have been over in an instant.'

'I suppose that is one thing we should be grateful for,' said Trevelyan. 'But I just can't understand it. The last thing I knew she had bolted from our house in Brook Street. She didn't leave a note or anything. I thought she would spend the night with one of her Mayfair girlfriends and the next day she would return. It's a pattern I had seen on many occasions. Our marriage was far from a smooth one, you see.'

'And you say she was – well, she had a rather temperamental nature?'

'That's putting it mildly,' said Helen.

'Please, Helen, you don't know the strain that Gina was under.'

Helen looked down, duly admonished, and let Trevelyan continue. 'Yes, it's true that Gina had a nervous disposition. She'd seem quite normal for a while, weeks at a time, and then, for no apparent reason, she would fall prey to an awful kind of mania. She would be up all night dancing or talking or walking the streets. She said she had the most extraordinary energy, creative energy. She once told me she had written a novel in the course of one night, but when I picked up the notebook I found it to be full of gibberish, nothing more than a few nonsensical phrases and obscenities. And then, with the same kind of suddenness, she would take to her bed, crying for no reason, threatening to harm herself, to do herself in. It was terrible, truly terrible to witness.'

'And when, may I ask, did your wife disappear?'

'It was on New Year's Day. We'd had quite a party at the London house. Too much drink, too much ... of everything. Perhaps Gina had seen something at the party, or suspected something. But the next thing I knew, she'd gone. I contacted the police, of course, and they issued a statement to the press – there were posters, searches, the lot. But nothing.'

'She didn't know about you and Miss Hart?'

'I don't know. Helen wanted me to tell her, but it never seemed the right time. Either Gina was in one of her periods of high-spirited ecstasy or she was in the grip of a terrible depression. There was never anything in-between.'

Helen Hart sighed, an expression that spoke of a dozen unsaid sentences, a hundred suppressed wishes.

'There's no point sighing, Helen,' said Guy, his voice rising. 'What was I supposed to do? Tell my wife we'd been having an affair? Did you really want me to drive her to her death?' His eyes stretched wide with anger and his voice cracked with fury. He strode purposefully across the library, opened the door and turned back. 'Is that what you wanted? Well, you've got your wish at last. I hope it makes you happy.'

With that he slammed the door and left us standing there, staring at the elaborate patterns in the Turkish rug beneath our feet.

'As you can see, Mrs Christie, Guy has been left in a state of shock,' said Helen, the china-white skin on her neck now a mass of red blotches.

'Grief does affect people in all sorts of different ways,' I said, trying to smooth over the acute embarrassment felt, no doubt, by both of us.

'Oh, please don't feel sorry for me,' she hissed. 'In fact, I'm pleased the bitch is dead.'

The statement – both the words and the way it was expressed – so shocked me that I was unable to utter a single word.

'I know it's a truly awful thing to say, but I am. She's out of our life for good now.'

Chapter Two

In preparation for the storm, the doors to the decks were temporarily locked. We were a floating island, cut off from the world, with a dead body left at sea.

The majority of the passengers retired to their cabins, and in the course of the morning a steward knocked on my door and handed me a note from Guy Trevelyan thanking me for my kindness. He suggested that, because of the bad weather, we postpone our dinner that night – in addition to the queasiness he was suffering, he doubted whether he could face the pitying stares of his fellow diners. Instead, he invited me to a small dinner in one of the private dining rooms the following evening. He would get together a few interesting passengers and he hoped that, by accepting the invitation, I would go some way to forgive his abrupt behaviour. I sent back a brief letter of acceptance and then lay on my bed, knowing that I would not sleep.

I kept thinking of Gina Trevelyan and the graceful way she had stepped off the ship to her death. I knew from what I had read in the newspapers that the girl was a very rich young lady indeed, an heiress to a huge fortune built up by her late father, a manufacturer of fertiliser. I had not heard of her recent disappearance, as I had rather given up on the news of late. The doctors had advised against it, in case one of the rags printed something relating to my own disappearance the previous year.

I supposed Gina must have witnessed or heard something about her husband's affair at the New Year's Eve party in Brook Street. Perhaps she had continued to follow him and his mistress, watching them steal into restaurants, hotel rooms, even her own home. She must have learnt that they had booked passage on the *Gelria* to Tenerife and had decided to sneak on board as a stowaway. But had something occurred on the ship that forced her to take her own life? Had Helen, who did not make much effort to hide her antipathy towards Gina, discovered her and told her in no uncertain terms that she wished her dead? Or had Gina simply wanted to stage a final exit that she hoped would bring about the collapse of the relationship between her husband and Helen? There were some who, I knew, accused me of doing the same thing, orchestrating my own disappearance so as to cause a public scandal that would then lead to the separation of Archie and Miss Neele. Of course, I would have to live with these slurs and lies, knowing that I would never be able to reveal the truth about how Dr Kurs had tried to use me to commit a perfect murder.

I could not dwell on the pain of last year. To do so would only bring more hurt and sorrow. Too much time to think was, I knew, not always a good thing. That was another of the reasons why I had agreed to Davison's scheme to join him in the Secret Intelligence Service. Perhaps now, when everyone was closeted in their cabins, would be a good time to seek him out. Lying down was only making my seasickness worse; surely it would be better to be up on one's feet, doing something. Carlo and Rosalind had retired back to their beds – there was not a sound coming from their cabin – and so I quietly closed the door and made my way down the corridors. I looked around me – nobody was in sight – and knocked gently on Davison's door.

'Oh, hello, Mrs Christie,' said Davison, running a hand through his ruffled blond hair.

'Am I disturbing you? Sorry, if you'd rather . . .'

'No, please do come in,' he said, opening the door to let me pass. He also checked the corridor to make sure my entrance had not been seen.

'I couldn't lie on my bed a moment longer. I was feeling dizzier and dizzier and the room kept spinning around. How are you feeling?'

'Not too bad, but I must admit I have just taken a brandy. Would you care for one?'

'No, thank you.'

'Of course, I should have remembered that you take no alcohol. And I don't suppose you fancy your favourite drink? Milk and cream?' he said, smiling.

The thought of it turned my stomach.

'Please don't, Davison. If I could just sit down.'

Davison's suite was larger and more luxurious than my own. In addition to a bedroom, it had a sitting room and a larger porthole, next to which were two armchairs. On a small table was a decanter of brandy and a siphon of soda water.

'Now, what's all this I hear about a suicide?' asked Davison, handing me a glass of the water.

'It was just too awful,' I said as I started to relate the events of the morning.

'And you saw all of this happen?' Davison asked.

'Well, most of it,' I said, sipping the water. 'The strangest thing was the complete lack of fear on the part of Gina Trevelyan. As she lifted her hands from the railings she looked like a dancer stepping onto the stage. If it hadn't had been so horrific, I could almost describe her death as beautiful.'

'That does sound peculiar,' said Davison, his eyes darkening. Was he thinking about the way Una Crowe had died? Her death had been anything but beautiful. 'And I take it there was no sign of the body?'

'According to Mr Trevelyan, the crew did their utmost to find her, but of course in this weather they couldn't risk launching a lifeboat.'

'No, very wise,' he said, as he looked outside the window to see the waves, seemingly as tall as buildings, crashing onto the side of the ship. 'My steward said it's going to clear up by the end of the day, but one would never think so. Funny, when he told me that they were locking the doors to the deck, I did think how an ocean liner would be the perfect setting for one of your books. A closed community, a gruesome murder, a number of suspects all of whom have dark and deadly secrets.'

'The idea had crossed my mind,' I said, casting him a half-smile. 'You should try your hand at writing yourself. You'd probably have more luck with it than me at the moment. I've got the blasted *Blue Train* novel to finish.'

'Maybe you'll find some inspiration in Tenerife.'

'That's what I wanted to talk to you about. I've read your notes about our business there, but there are a few things I'd like to go over.'

'Very well.'

'So you say Douglas Greene had been found in a cave, his body in the early stages of mummification?'

'Yes, that's right, poor chap,' he said, his voice cracking slightly. 'He was one of the brightest young men: ex-Cambridge, athletic, fluent in Spanish, in fact he could speak half a dozen languages. Awful thing to happen. I had to go down to Devon to break the news to his parents. Mother, the county type, tough as old boots, took it in her stride, but his father suffered a complete nervous collapse afterwards. Of course, I kept the most gruesome details from them.'

'And what was he doing out in Tenerife? Obviously not there for his health.'

'He was sent because we had reason to suspect that there was someone on the island with Bolshevik links.'

'How long had he been in the cave for?'

'Difficult to say precisely, but about five months. He'd been reported missing by the Spanish woman who cooked and cleaned for him. I think people assumed he must have moved on to another island.'

'Do we know how he died?'

'The doctor who examined the body could not say for certain, but it looked like he had been struck by a blunt instrument to the back of the head.'

'I see. And who discovered the body?'

'Professor Max Wilbor. He's an archaeologist and anthropologist who specialises in the forgotten culture of the Guanches, the people who lived in the Canaries from around 1000 BC. He was snuffling about one of the caves near the coast, looking for bones and suchlike when he came across Greene.'

'And Wilbor is still there? In Tenerife?'

'Yes, as far as we know. As you may have gathered, there is not much of a police force on the island, nothing like we have in England. In fact, the whole setup is very basic. Charming, but quite primitive.'

'I take it this is not your first visit?'

'No, I went in September of last year to see a friend – well, the friend of a friend who has a house there. The climate, as you know, is especially good for invalids, those suffering from tuberculosis, asthma, lung disorders and the like. There is quite an English community in the Orotava Valley. In many respects, it's like a warmer, more tropical version of Bournemouth, or Torquay.'

'With the added benefit, if you can call it that, of having a volcano,' I said, smiling. I remembered seeing the snow-topped magnificence of Mount Teide as I sailed to South Africa out on the RMS *Kildonan Castle* five years ago. That had been a voyage of discovery, a voyage of happiness, one I had made with Archie. I had played quoits and bridge, took part in the daily sweep – I recalled

the childish thrill I had felt when my number came up! –
and danced with my husband. But even though it was
tempting to do so, one could not live in the past: that
way madness lay. 'And do you have any suspects?' I said,
getting back to the main point of the conversation. 'For
Greene's murder?'

'As a matter of fact, we do,' said Davison, taking a deep
breath. For a moment I thought he had lost the power of
speech.

'What's wrong?'

'Forgive me, I'm just trying to think how best to express
what I have to say.'

Davison's sharp, intelligent grey eyes flickered. He
pursed his lips. He started a sentence, hesitated, tried
again and then gave up.

'Please, Davison. You should know me well enough by
now. I'm the least shockable person you're ever likely to
meet.'

'Yes, and that is one of the reasons why you are so
eminently suited to this kind of work. However, there's
something that you need to know that – well, that is more
than a little delicate.'

'Don't hold anything back from me, please. I can assure
you that while my physical constitution may be a little
shaken at the moment due to the movement of the ocean,
my mental facilities have not been affected.'

'It concerns one of the permanent inhabitants of
Orotava, a gentleman by the name of Gerard Grenville.
Have you heard of him?'

'No, should I have done?'

'Not necessarily. It's just that he has a certain reputation in some quarters. You see, he is an occultist.'

'Like that unscrupulous fellow Mr Crowley?'

'Yes, indeed,' said Davison.

'Is that all?' I said, laughing. 'I believe my mother had psychic abilities – her instincts about people and places were quite uncanny – and I've always been interested in that side of things myself.' I thought of some of the supernatural short stories I had written for *The Grand Magazine*.

'But Grenville is, I am afraid, of an altogether darker strain of character.'

'Go on.'

'We've had our eye on him for quite some time. It seems he was attracted to the island of Tenerife because he wants to set up some kind of base for people of his ilk, occultists and those interested in the black arts. He is intent in creating a community of like-minded souls. I got hold of some of his pamphlets a while back, and it makes for rather uncomfortable reading, to say the least. For instance, there are some magical rites that involve certain ... acts,' he said, coughing.

'I see, but isn't that all part and parcel of the charade? Don't they just use the pretence of magic as an excuse to indulge in particular practices that are considered immoral? And what has that got to do with Greene's murder?'

'I was about to come on to that,' said Davison, blushing slightly. 'Before Greene died he wrote a lengthy report about Grenville. He had a source inside Grenville's house, a young Spanish man, José, who informed him that the occultist's ultimate aim was to try and release the spirit of evil from Mount Teide.'

'The evil in Mount Teide? What on earth did he mean?'

'Well, it seems the Guanches, the aboriginal people, worshipped an evil spirit, Guayota. According to local legend, this Guayota was locked up inside Teide for various misdeeds, including the kidnapping of the sun god figure Magec.'

'But as you say, that's the stuff of legend, of mythology.'

'Yes, but according to testimony provided by José, and related to us by Greene, Grenville intends to try to free Guayota from Teide. We don't know how, but there was some suggestion that the ritual might involve, well, a human sacrifice.'

The horror of it all began to make sense. 'So you think Greene was killed as part of some kind of ritual? Grenville needed his blood?'

'Exactly. Every last drop had been drained from his system.'

'But it seems so unreal. Surely it can't be possible?'

'That's what we thought at first when we got Greene's report. Thought the poor chap was suffering from too much sun to the head. But then the discovery of his body – and the condition of his corpse – made us think again.'

'How utterly horrible,' I said. 'I don't think I've heard anything like it. But what do you want me to do?'

As Davison hesitated I felt an uneasiness rising inside. The wave of nausea was nothing to do with the motion of the boat or the swell of the sea.

'We want you to try to find out more about Grenville and his plans.'

'And how do you expect me to do that?' I asked.

'He has a daughter, Violet, who lives with him. She must be twenty-three or twenty-four years of age now. Her mother died giving birth to her. See if you can get close to her. Perhaps she will open up to you, tell you things. See if you can find any evidence that links Grenville to the crime.'

'If you think I'm going to become an out-and-out devil worshipper you can think again,' I said with an air of mock seriousness.

'Don't worry – even we have our limits,' said Davison drily.

'I know it's no laughing matter, but it does sound absurd, you must admit,' I said.

'I wish it was,' he said sourly. 'A man from our service has died and his body has been defiled in a most unpardonable manner. Whoever did this needs to be brought to justice. Who knows, perhaps Grenville's unholy wish has been granted – it seems that evil has already been released from the mountain.'

Chapter Three

A shadow lay over the superficial sparkle of the dining table, with its dazzling display of fine cut glass, glittering silverware and hothouse flowers. The shadow that darkened the private dining room was the one cast by Gina Trevelyan's suicide. Each of the six people around the table was thinking of the death, but understandably no-one wanted to bring up the subject.

The conversation had been awkward and stilted until Mrs Brendel, a friend of Guy Trevelyan's mother, started to talk about how she had survived the sinking of the *Titanic*. With her liver-spotted skin and mane of grey hair I estimated her to be in her late sixties and I felt a little insulted to think that Trevelyan had invited her as my companion for the evening. Surely I wasn't an old maid quite yet, I thought to myself as Trevelyan gestured to me to sit by her.

The storm had reminded Mrs Brendel of the disaster, and although that ship had gone down fifteen years pre-viously, she said the motion of the sea and the groaning noises emitted by our ocean liner had brought it all back to her.

'My trunks of beautiful gowns – and oh, my jewels, my pretty jewels – all at the bottom of the sea,' she said, her bony hand rising to her throat. Her fingers played with a long string of pearls that were draped around her wizened neck as if to reassure herself that at least she had some of her finery left. 'To think of them there, the playthings of fish and stingrays and suchlike. My diamonds used to light up the best salons in Paris. And now they are covered in slime.'

The table fell silent as the diners turned to Mrs Brendel to hear more. As she spoke, the elderly lady's face lit up with a kind of theatrical glow and I suspected that the stories she began to relate had been told many times before.

'It must have been a truly awful experience,' said Daisy Winniatt, the young wife of the bespectacled writer Howard Winniatt, who sat on the other side of her. 'I can't imagine it.'

'Dreadful. Absolutely dreadful.' Mrs Brendel was in her element. 'I was bringing back samples of the very best fabrics and gowns from Paris. I had twenty or so trunks stuffed with chiffons and silks, all from the top couturiers, you understand. I tried to make a claim, a substantial claim, oh yes, the document ran to something like twenty or so pages, but the White Star Line simply would not pay up.'

'"Those are pearls that were his eyes",' murmured Mr Winniatt, as he scribbled into a notebook by his side.

31

'Are you talking about your wife's pearls?' asked Mrs Brendel. 'Those are very beautiful, my dear.'

'Thank you,' said Daisy, her fingers gliding over a strand of what looked like extremely precious jewels.

'No, it's a line from *The Tempest*,' said Mr Winniatt.

'Of course,' replied Mrs Brendel. 'I once saw a tremendous *Tempest* directed by Herbert Beerbohm Tree at Her Majesty's. Did you know he used to live in the theatre? He built a banqueting hall for himself beneath the magnificent dome. Oh yes, his *Tempest* was terribly exciting. There was a battered old ship on the stage, very realistic. One could almost feel like one had been shipwrecked on a desert island. In fact, that's exactly how I felt when the storm started to lash the ship yesterday. I couldn't believe that it was going to be the *Titanic* all over again. I couldn't bear to lose my jewels, no, not again. Oh, those waves and that dreadful sea . . .'

As she twittered on and on, Mr Winniatt continued to scribble into his journal, an act that finally drew her attention.

'What's that you're writing?' Her question did not elicit a response. 'Mr Winniatt, may I ask what you are doing?'

'I'm sorry, I should have made myself clear,' said the small, thin man, pushing his wire-framed glasses farther up the bridge of his nose. 'I'm a writer.'

'Like Mrs Christie here,' she said, turning her head towards me.

'Really?' Mr Winniatt looked over to me. 'What kind of books do you write?'

'Oh, detective stories, thrillers and such like,' I said, smiling.

'Would I have heard of any of them?'

'My most recent was *The Murder of Roger Ackroyd*,' I said. His face remained expressionless.

'It's extraordinary what is written nowadays,' said Mr Winniatt, addressing the whole table. 'And also the kind of people who are published never ceases to amaze me.'

It took me a moment before I realised that the insult had been levelled in my direction. As I did so, I felt the smile melt from my face and a flush come to my cheek. I didn't know quite what to say. Luckily, Mrs Brendel continued with her chatter.

'Soon Puerto Orotava will welcome us,' she said. 'It is so very good for the constitution, I hear. I felt so awful yesterday, I just couldn't get out of bed. But despite that dreadful storm, I'm so pleased I decided to come – oh yes, it was all done on the spur of the moment, at the very last minute. When Mary Trevelyan told me that her son was sailing for the Canaries I thought what a wonderful idea. And you don't mind that I'm here, do you?' Mr Trevelyan gave something of a strained smile. 'I promise to make myself scarce when we get to the island. Imagine how they must be suffering from the cold back in dreary old England. Winter for another few months. But the pros-pect of Tenerife with its sunshine, and those flowers! I'm so looking forward to seeing the more exotic specimens I've only ever seen in botanic gardens – the hibiscus, the bird-of-paradise.' As she paused to take a breath she saw Mr Winniatt scribbling in his notebook. 'But why do you have to write at the table?' she asked him. 'Can't you wait until – I don't know, until you are at your desk or in a comfortable chair on deck? Or is it a case of writing when inspiration strikes?'

'Oh, no,' said Mr Winniatt. 'I don't believe in that sort of nonsense. I believe in trying to capture the moment. I'm writing a new kind of book, one that is free from the artificial constraints of narrative.'

I found Mr Winniatt's pronouncements more than a little pompous and self-regarding, but I kept my views to myself.

'I don't quite understand,' said Mrs Brendel, spooning some turtle soup into her mouth.

'I'm working on an epic oral history, a mass of detail gathered from real life. I want to reproduce life in all its light and shade. I want to capture truth, what people say and how they say it. It's experience, but experience that is vivid and bright and real, experience unmediated by the author, experience free from the contaminants of the story.'

Mrs Brendel blinked. 'So correct me if I am wrong. What you were writing down were the words that I had just spoken?'

'Yes, that's right.'

'Howard has already amassed a book that is approaching something like two hundred thousand words,' added Mrs Winniatt. 'And it's really rather interesting. Other people's lives make for the most fascinating reading. He never goes anywhere without his notebook, do you, Howard?'

'I see,' said Mrs Brendel, ignoring her. 'How clever you are, Mr Winniatt. I've always wanted to write a book. A memoir of my experiences on that fateful ship, but I've never found the right person to help me with the task. That is, perhaps, until this evening.' Her eyes began to mist over and, as she began to relate more details of the sinking, her voice took on the distinctive timbre of melodrama.

Although she might believe that in Mr Winniatt and his notebook she had found the perfect repository, I feared for Mrs Brendel's portrayal in the resulting publication. In fact, I doubted the whole premise of the project, but again continued to play the part of the quiet observer, nodding my head when appropriate, adding the occasional 'Yes, indeed,' and 'That is most interesting,' when necessary. But, of course, Mrs Brendel needed little prompting.

'One thousand five hundred souls perished that night, and I'm sure their spirits must haunt the spot where the ship went down,' she said. 'How could they not? Energy does not simply disappear.'

'Do you believe in the spirit world, Mrs Brendel?' asked Helen.

'Oh, yes. I've been to a number of séances and I have no doubt that there are things that exist which we can barely comprehend.'

'My mother certainly thought so,' I interjected. I explained about my mother's sensitivity, her uncanny ability to foresee certain events, her talent for reading people and situations.

'And I believe you've inherited your mother's gift,' said Mrs Brendel, taking my hand.

'I'm not so sure,' I said, thinking to myself how I had not predicted the calamitous events that had hit me the previous year.

'But then you must meet Gerard Grenville,' said Miss Hart. 'He has a house on the island and lives there with his daughter, Violet.'

I stopped myself from showing too much curiosity, instead letting Mrs Brendel take the lead.

'Surely you don't mean—?' Her voice broke. 'But I've heard such awful things about him. Apparently, as a boy he killed one of the family's kittens after he devised nine horrible ways for it to die in order to test whether a cat really did have nine lives.'

'Perhaps you shouldn't believe everything you hear,' said Guy.

'But who could do such a wicked thing?' she asked.

Mrs Brendel's eyes widened as she contemplated the reputation of the sinister Mr Grenville. 'And what's he doing in Puerto Orotava? Is he really a devil worshipper, as they say? Does he really eat cake made out of the blood of chickens?'

Mr Winniatt did not let Guy Trevelyan answer, but interrupted with his own observations. 'I read that he believes ordinary morality is only for ordinary people. I must say, I have a certain amount of sympathy with him on that score, on a purely intellectual level, of course.'

'Did he not once perform a magic rite inside the Great Pyramid of Cairo?' asked Mrs Brendel.

'I believe he's conducted various experiments at several places around the world,' answered Guy. 'You know of his reputation as one of our best mountaineers. I think Teide is what drew him first to Tenerife.'

'Oh, let's not talk any more about him,' said Mrs Brendel. 'The very idea of him sends shivers down my spine. And I must say, I have no desire, no desire at all, to meet him. And if I were you, Guy, I would avoid any further contact with him. Of course, there were certain people on the *Titanic* who one felt were omens of ill fortune. I remember one man . . .'

The dinner continued – we enjoyed a fillet of brill, a sirloin of beef and a delicious apple charlotte accompanied by great dollops of cream – with Mrs Brendel's mono- logue dominating the table until Helen began to tire of the subject. As I looked across at her, I noticed a spark of devilment in her eyes that unsettled me.

'Mrs Brendel,' she said, interrupting the elderly lady, 'it does sound quite dreadful. You were one of the fortunate ones in being rescued, but so many people died. I believe the majority didn't drown, but died from the effects of the freezing water.'

'Yes, poor souls. As I sat there in the lifeboat I could hear their unholy cries. It sounded just like—'

'And I suppose some passengers must have decided to jump off the boat before the very end.'

'Some people were driven to desperate measures, yes.'

'Just like poor Gina,' said Helen. The words sent an icy chill over the table. 'I can't stop thinking about her. Down there, in the sea.'

'Helen, you're upset, I know,' said Guy, gently, placing a hand on hers, 'but really it's not the time or the place for this.'

She turned to him, her arctic blue eyes shining wildly.

'But when would be the best time? The inquest? How can there be a proper inquest when there's no body? She's down there now, in the sea, bait for every passing—'

'Helen,' hissed Guy. 'Please, do try and control yourself.'

'I suppose that's what you used to say to Gina, is it? "Darling, do try and pull yourself together now,"' she said, imitating his voice. 'And look what it did for her, the poor wretch.'

Guy looked down, stung by the insult. 'I think it's best if we call it a night,' he said, standing up. 'I'm sorry, but please excuse us. We're both still suffering from the shock of yesterday.'

'Yes, quite understandable,' said Mrs Brendel, a sentiment which was echoed around the table.

He reached out to take Helen's wrist, but as he did so she resisted. Guy continued to maintain his grip, but then Helen wrenched away her arm with such determination that, as she freed herself, she was forced to take a step backwards to steady herself. In that moment, her other arm brushed against a glass of red wine belonging to Mr Winniatt, who had been seated on her other side. The dark liquid tipped over onto the white tablecloth, and splashed onto the pages of Mr Winniatt's open notebook. The cries of astonishment, apology and anger came all at once.

'Oh no!' said Mr Winniatt, immediately using a corner of his white napkin to try and remove the spots of wine from the pages. 'My notebook! My words!'

'I'm so sorry,' said Guy. 'Please let me help.'

'No, I'm sure we can manage,' said Mrs Winniatt, as she used her own napkin to try to clean the book.

'Look, you're making it worse!' snapped Mr Winniatt, as a great arc of blood-red liquid smeared across the pages of his journal. There was desperation in his voice. 'The ink is smudging, the words are disappearing.' I couldn't help but feel more than a little pleased.

Helen's face was mask-like, a portrait of misery. 'Stop it!' she screamed, taking up a glass from the table and smashing it onto the parquet floor. The effect was instant. Each person froze – no-one dared so much as breathe – as we listened to Miss Hart's violent outburst.

'They're just words. Nothing but empty words. Can't you see that? It's just a form of glorified dictation!'

Mr and Mrs Winniatt looked down, embarrassed and hurt. From Mrs Brendel there came a sharp intake of breath. Perhaps Helen realised she had gone a little far, because she then softened her voice.

'I'm sorry, but a woman jumped off the ship yesterday. She was driven to it, the poor thing. Driven to it by us, by me.' She looked around her with an air of astonishment, as if the shards of glass that glittered on the floor had been the result of a stranger's sudden intervention. 'I've lived with this long enough, but I can't go on. I'm afraid I'm going to have to go to the captain. I simply can't take it anymore. I have to confess. I killed Gina Trevelyan.'

Chapter Four

Helen's announcement acted like a sinister little explosion, disturbing our psyches and dispersing us to separate parts of the ship. Guy immediately fled with Helen, and the Winniatts returned to their cabin to continue arguing about the management of the wine stain on the notebook. Mrs Brendel, misreading my confusion for distress, ordered me to accompany her to her cabin for a stiff drink. I relented, knowing that she would be able to tell me more about the background of Guy Trevelyan and his unfortunate wife.

'Now, I must insist,' she said, as she sat me down in one of the armchairs. 'You must take something rejuvenating. Whisky or brandy?'

I shook my head. 'I'm afraid it doesn't really agree with me,' I said.

'A little *eau de vie* then?'

I let her pour me a small glass of the colourless liquid. 'Spirits do the world of good after shock, and I can see that you've had quite a shock,' she said. 'When I was hauled onto the *Carpathia* – oh, the indignity of it – after a night spent out in a flimsy lifeboat in the middle of the freezing Atlantic, I was given a glass of brandy. Warmed me and restored me in a matter of minutes. In fact, I believe it would be a good idea to have one now. I don't normally partake of alcohol, but there are some occasions when I'm afraid it has to be prescribed for medicinal purposes. In fact, it's the only way I'm managing to make this sea voyage at all. I'm sure my doctor would approve. Yes, that whole nasty scene at dinner unsettled me as it did you. Now, take a sip.'

I raised the glass to my lips, but the strong alcoholic vapours were more than enough for me. As I pretended to take a small sip, the liquid burnt my lips.

'You'll begin to feel better in a moment or so,' she said, swallowing a large mouthful of brandy. 'Really, I didn't know where to look. Such an awful scene. And we were having quite a delightful evening, don't you think so? I do hope Mr Trevelyan won't blame me for the upset.'

'I'm sure he won't,' I said.

'When Miss Hart said that thing about killing Gina, I turned to you and saw the colour drain from your face,' she continued.

'Yes, it left me rather puzzled.'

'Puzzled? How?'

I stopped myself from telling her my real thoughts – about how the day before, Helen had confessed to me that she was pleased that Gina Trevelyan had died and how this seemed to contradict her most recent confession of guilt about the woman's death.

'Well, I was there when it happened,' I said. 'I saw the whole thing. There was no way that Miss Hart could have had any direct hand in Mrs Trevelyan's death. She didn't push her. She didn't encourage her to step off the ship. I was a witness, I saw it all. If anything, it looked as though Miss Hart was doing everything in her power to stop Gina from throwing herself off.'

'So you think that Miss Hart was just being a little over dramatic?'

'Yes, the pangs of a guilty conscience.'

'I see what you're suggesting,' said Mrs Brendel, her grey eyes sparkling.

I paused and let the woman talk. The delight at being able to impart the information lit up her face. 'Of course, everyone in London knew about the affair between Guy and Helen.' Mrs Brendel took another gulp of brandy. Her face looked quite flushed now, but her eyes were bright. 'It was no secret. And those of us who knew Guy could, I am afraid, hardly blame him. Gina was the most difficult woman to live with. Mentally unstable, you see. Poor Guy didn't know the half of it when he married her, as it seems her father and mother thought it best to keep it from the Trevelyans. Oh, you should hear Mary – that's Guy's mother – on the subject!'

'I see,' I managed to say, as Mrs Brendel took a quick breath and then continued.

'To begin with, it seemed as though Guy could manage her eccentricities, her moods and suchlike. And of course, the money made his life all the more bearable. The Trevelyans are quite a grand family; well, they have a name, but the money dwindled with each passing generation. Their mines in Cornwall are not what they were. Not much demand for tin, of course. You should have seen poor Mary having to make do and mend after the death of her dear Albert. We all tried to help her, but Mary is a proud soul. And Guy's work as a geologist at the university in London didn't pay very much.'

'So Mr Trevelyan married Gina for her money?'

'Oh, I wouldn't express it in quite such bold terms.' Mrs Brendel looked at me with an air of surprise and astonishment, the implication being that I was the one with a love of gossip and tittle-tattle. 'Anyway, after the death of Gina's parents her illness became steadily worse. It became too much for poor Guy to deal with. He sought out the help of experts, psychiatrists, but none of them could do much good. It was during one of these periods, when Gina had been confined to an institution for a time, that Guy came to know Miss Hart. I understand that he met her at the opening of one of her exhibitions. I still can't believe Gina is dead. But I suppose, at the end of the day, it's a mercy.'

I tried to stop myself from sounding taken aback. 'A mercy?'

'Well, Gina's mental state was becoming nothing short of a curse. She could see no way out. Perhaps she did the right thing.'

'I'm not sure about that,' I said. Suicide, I believed, often served as a slow, subtle form of murder, poisoning the lives of those left behind. I was about to cite the example of how Gina's death had started to eat away at Helen and Guy, but stopped myself. Instead, I said, 'But what of Gina's relatives and friends?'

'As I said, her parents are dead and she was the only child. And I think after she married Guy she became so dependent on him that she didn't need any friends.'

'I see,' I said, thinking for a moment. 'And what did she look like? Gina, I mean.'

'Oh, she used to be such a beautiful girl with a lovely figure and moved like a ballerina.'

That explained Gina's delicate movements in the moments before her death.

'In fact, I think she had once toyed with the hope that she might enjoy a career as a dancer. It didn't come to anything though, because she put on a great deal of weight. Can't blame the poor girl, what with all her problems.'

I knew about dashed hopes and broken dreams. Not only had I abandoned the idea of being a sculptor, but I had been forced to acknowledge that I would never be any good as an opera singer or a concert pianist. My teachers had told me that I had some talent, but I just could not cope with the pressure of being on stage, in front of an audience, with all those people staring at me.

'Look, you haven't touched your drink and you've gone all pale again, my dear,' said Mrs Brendel, studying my face. 'If you're not going to have the merest sip of that *eau de vie* – and I can see that you are not – then I think you need some night air. The sea has calmed now, and I believe the storm has passed. What do you say to a stroll around the deck?'

'Yes, a very good idea,' I said.

As we stepped outside into the velvety blackness of the night I noticed that the air had lost some of its cold edge. We were definitely beginning to pass into warmer climes. After the damp and darkness of England I was yearning for sunlight.

Mrs Brendel took my arm in hers and, as we began our promenade beneath the stars, she started to narrate a now all too familiar tale. 'It was a beautiful night when the ship went down, very cold, but beautiful, the sky full of stars ...' I let her voice drift over me as we walked. I thought about the final moments of Gina Trevelyan and tried to imagine her desperate state of mind. I also wondered about the practicalities of a death at sea. In whose jurisdiction had the suicide occurred – Portugal, Africa – or did the sea sit in a no man's land, a kind of limbo? And which authority would take charge of the investigation, if indeed an investigation was ruled necessary?

'You've gone very quiet again, my dear,' said Mrs Brendel, withdrawing her arm from mine. 'I'm sorry, I do hope I wasn't boring you.'

'Oh, no, not at all. All very fascinating and I would love to hear a great deal more about that night and how you suffered from the loss of so many things. But I must admit I was just thinking about Mrs Trevelyan's death.'

'In what regard?'

Just as I started to outline my concerns, I saw the shadow of a tall, dark-haired man approach us. The light from a deck lamp revealed the figure to be Guy Trevelyan, his face a mask of barely contained anger. Mrs Brendel stopped and reached out her hand in a gesture of compassion.

'What is it about women?' he snarled, brushing her fingers from his overcoat.

'Guy, I know you must be terribly upset, but—'

'But what? My mother's just as bad. All of you are,' he said, turning his gaze to me. His eyes were full of dark fury.

'Guy, I don't understand,' said Mrs Brendel.

'Oh, you will in time,' he said. 'I'm sure it will all become clear in due course. A cobra. A Himalayan she-bear. A squaw from the Huron or Choctaws.'

'What are you talking about? You're beginning to frighten me now, Guy. Do you need to see the doctor?'

'No, I've just come from him,' he said dismissively. 'He's given Helen a sedative.'

'Yes, probably a good idea,' she said. 'I'm sure that tomorrow when she wakes up she will be able to put everything into perspective. You've both had such an awful shock.'

'Waking up tomorrow,' he said, his voice beginning to crack. 'That's something that Gina will never be able to do.' His black eyes filled with tears. 'Speech that drips, corrodes and poisons!' he whispered, as he pulled the collar of his coat up around his face and disappeared down the deck into the night.

'Oh, dear, I couldn't make head or tail of it, could you, Mrs Christie?' said Mrs Brendel. 'He's reduced to talking utter gibberish. I do believe the death of his wife has unbalanced his mind. Oh, poor Mary. This is the last thing she needs – a son who has lost his wits.'

I knew my Kipling. 'I don't believe he has, Mrs Brendel.'

'You don't?'

'No, not for one moment.'

What was that line about the basking cobra? Something about how the male of the species avoided the careless foot of a man . . .

'But his mate makes no such motion where she camps beside the trail,' I quoted. 'For the female of the species is more deadly than the male.'

Chapter Five

We approached the island of Grand Canary just as dawn was breaking, the sun casting a light pink glow over the barren mountains that rose up from the backbone of the island. The port of Las Palmas was situated on a headland that stretched out into the ocean like a clenched fist, railing its anger against the world like a fierce god from a Greek myth.

At first sight, the island did not look like the sub-tropical paradise that I had been promised – were the islands not supposed to have been the site of the Elysian fields? – and I felt a sting of disappointment. A memory came back to me from my childhood when my parents had taken me to a village situated at the foot of the Pyrenees. My father had led me out onto the terrace of the hotel and, with a great flourish, had presented a vista of snow-covered mountains. In my imagination I had constructed a more sublime view, one that had the power to thrill, even terrify me. The real view did not live up to my wild expectations and I never forgot that crushing sense of anticlimax and the guilt I felt afterwards at my lack of enthusiasm. Despite my disappointing first impressions of Grand Canary, after six days at sea I was ready to leave the *Gelria* behind. One could endure only so much deck tennis, quoits, shuffle-boarding, and 'horse', 'dog' and 'frog' racing – the animals being crafted from wood. I was not the sporty type and the death of Gina Trevelyan had cast a pall over the games. I was desperate for the feel of firm ground beneath my feet and keen to start my investigations into the murder of Douglas Greene.

While the majority of the other passengers disembarked, the Captain had asked me, Helen Hart, Guy Trevelyan and William McMaster to stay behind to answer a few questions relating to the suicide at sea. I told Carlo that if she and Rosalind waited for me at the hotel in the port I would be with them promptly, while I reassured my daughter, who was showing signs of anxiety at the possibility that I might be late, that we would certainly not miss our connecting boat to Santa Cruz, the port of Tenerife.

As we waited in the library, we tried to make small talk about the change in the weather, our delight at being in warmer climes, and what we had planned over the course of the next couple of weeks. Miss Hart and Guy Trevelyan – both of whom seemed to have relaxed a great deal – informed me that they were going to stay in Helen's house by the sea. Helen hoped to work on some pieces of sculpture over the winter in preparation for another exhibition in London. Mr Trevelyan wanted to continue his study of the volcanic rocks of the island and find some samples which he could take back to England. Mr McMaster, of course, had no such leisurely plans; later on that day the boat would sail on to Pernambuco, Rio de Janeiro, Montevideo and Buenos Aires.

At the sound of the door opening we turned our heads to see a handsome man with unusually pale colouring for a Spaniard. His hair was blond, his skin the colour of cream and his eyes were a piercing blue. He walked towards us, removed his hat and introduced himself as Inspector Artemi Narciso Núñez.

'Good morning, ladies and gentlemen,' he said in an accented but nevertheless fluid and clear English. 'As Captain Hewitt informed you, I'm here to ask you a few questions about the unfortunate death of Mrs Trevelyan. First of all, I'd like to talk to each of you individually – I believe the Captain has set aside a private room for that purpose – and then once I've finished, if I could ask you to accompany me as a group to the scene of the accident. I promise you I will be as quick as I can, as I am sure you are all keen to disembark and carry on with your journeys.'

He led each of us out in turn, during which time the remaining group in the library fell into silence. When the Inspector's assistant called my name and led me down the corridor I felt my cheeks begin to blush slightly. As he thanked me once again and gestured towards a chair I realised why: Núñez had a dimple in his chin just like Archie.

'First of all, Mrs Christie, I must confess that I am a great fan of your books,' he said. 'When I was in

England – I spent some years in London as a student at the university – detective fiction is all I read. They were one of the ways I learnt English.'

'Well, I'm sorry if I set you a bad example,' I said, smiling.

'Not at all. Perfectly succinct – that is the right word? And wonderfully readable. *The Murder of Roger Ackroyd* – now, that is a story!'

That had been Dr Kurs's favourite book too. 'Thank you,' I said, trying not to think of him.

'There's no need to feel nervous, Mrs Christie. As you know, I simply want to try to establish the facts of what happened. I believe you witnessed the unfortunate incident?'

'Indeed.' I outlined what I had seen. 'But what I find curious is Miss Hart's reaction afterwards.'

'In what regard?'

'Well, it seems a little contradictory. One moment she was telling me that she was pleased that Gina – Mrs Trevelyan – was dead. Then she appeared to blame herself for her suicide. In fact, she said that she was responsible for her death.'

'She tried to confess to the Captain,' said Núñez, 'but I think he saw through her. She may have felt as though she had contributed to Mrs Trevelyan's death, but as your statement proves she actually tried to stop her. And, of course, I am not here to stand in judgement on a person's morality, or otherwise.'

'Quite right,' I said.

'Of course, an affair of this kind often has consequences,

especially for those with delicate constitutions. I believe Gina Trevelyan suffered from a nervous disorder that, in the end, consumed her.'

'So I believe. I can only say that, at least at the very end, she seemed content and happy. The way she stepped off the ship implied that she was not afraid of death or what lay ahead of her. Such a graceful step.' I paused. 'And there has been no sighting of her body?'

'None whatsoever, I'm sorry to say,' said Núñez. 'Can I ask if you knew Mr or Mrs Trevelyan back in England?'

'Of course, I'd read about Mrs Trevelyan, but I've learnt a great deal from Mrs Edith Brendel, a fellow passenger. She's a friend of Mr Trevelyan's mother. I'm sure she will be only too happy to help you,' I said.

'Why do you smile?'

'Oh, it's just that Mrs Brendel likes nothing better than an audience. When I told her that I was going to be questioned by the police she became quite indignant. "How shortsighted of them not to ask me!" Anyway, I'm sure she would be more than delighted to give you some background information.'

'Thank you.' Núñez stood. 'You've been a great deal of help.'

'I wish I could tell you more than what I saw,' I said.

'It must be frustrating at times for you.'

I was rather taken aback by the directness of his statement. 'I'm sorry, I don't think I understand.'

'As an author you are used to being in control, having all your characters in your head. But when you come across an instance such as this, it must be frustrating that you do not know the full story behind it. Forgive me, I know I am probably expressing myself badly.'

'I could not have put it better myself,' I said, deciding to place him at his ease. I had something I wanted to ask him. 'I suppose the crime on the islands is very sporadic?'

'It's not like London, if that's what you mean. It's mostly husbands and wives fighting, drunkenness, indecency, the theft of a fishing boat, and so on. Mostly involving – as you would say – the natives of the islands. I believe you are staying at the Taoro Hotel?'

'Yes, that's right.'

'Well, you will have nothing to worry about there. A first rate establishment. And the Orotava Valley is like a paradise. In fact, I will be over there in the next week or so.' He smiled to himself as he said this.

'I'm pleased to hear it.' As I continued I was careful not to lie. 'Of course, I'm interested on a purely professional level to know whether you've had any murders. You see, whenever I travel I make a note of the kind of murders in different countries and cultures, though I know it sounds rather ghoulish.'

'I understand completely, Mrs Christie,' said the Inspector. 'Actually, recently we had quite a difficult case, one that does remain unsolved.'

'Oh, really?'

'This is just between ourselves, you understand. I wouldn't want any of the visitors to the islands to think they have anything to worry about.'

'Yes, of course. I won't breathe a word.'

'Well, a few months ago, a young man went missing. He

was living in a house in the Orotava Valley, had been there for about a year or so. Apparently, he was a pleasant, well-educated man, with a bit of family money behind him. Name of Douglas Greene.'

I did not show that I recognised the name. 'And?'

'He had kept himself to himself, mostly, apart from the friendships he had made with a couple of young local boys. So, when he disappeared people assumed he must have travelled on somewhere else. But then . . .' Núñez hesitated for a moment and his blue eyes darkened. 'Then, a body was discovered in one of the caves, down by the coast, by Martiánez beach. It was difficult to identify, at first, but it turned out the body was Greene's.'

'Why was the body difficult to identify?'

Núñez hesitated. 'I'm afraid it's a little strong, perhaps even for your ears.'

'I worked as a nurse in the war. I've written about murder. Please don't spare me any details.'

'Someone had tried to mummify him and his body had been drained of its blood.'

'How awful,' I said, covering my mouth. Although I already knew the state in which Greene's body had been found, the details were still horrible to hear. 'And do you know who did it?'

'The main person we suspect is a local man, Gerard Grenville – have you heard of him?'

'His name does sound familiar,' I said.

'A self-styled occultist, born in England, who lives in Orotava. Thoroughly amoral type. Has a belief that he is some kind of magus. Unbelievable as it may sound we have heard stories of him planning various rituals, rituals that might require the use of human blood. The problem is we have no proof and the stories may be no more than inventions. The other issue is – well, it's difficult because ...' Núñez looked pained, as though he was uncertain whether to continue speaking.

'Difficult?'

'Oh, just something personal,' he said, deciding to close down further lines of inquiry. 'Anyway, in addition to Grenville, we have another man whom we would like to question. Someone who went missing from the island shortly after we think Greene was killed.'

I felt a bead of sweat begin to break out on my forehead.

'Another well-educated, cultured British man,' he added.

I swallowed, but my throat felt dry, like sandpaper.

'In his thirties. Blond hair, grey eyes. A Cambridge man, I believe.'

'And his name?' I whispered, almost as if I did not want to hear the answer.

'I doubt you would know him,' said Núñez, blinking. 'But if I remember correctly, his name is Davison. John Davison.'

Chapter Six

The sail from Grand Canary to Tenerife was a journey of fragments and isolated images. The blue sea. Clusters of white houses on a barren landscape. Jagged crags and the peaks of desolate mountains.

My attention was drawn inwards as I reflected on what Inspector Núñez had told me. Surely Davison couldn't be a suspect in the killing of Douglas Greene? After all, Greene had been one of Davison's own men. Davison had seemed genuinely upset by the agent's death. He wanted me to help find his murderer. But could Greene have been a traitor? Was he what was popularly known as a double agent? But why would Davison enlist my help if he was the guilty party? It just didn't make sense. And what exactly had Núñez implied? I was sure that he had suggested that Greene's interest in the Spanish boys was something that went beyond simply improving his language skills. Perhaps Davison did not enjoy the intimate company of women either. That would certainly explain why I always felt so comfortable in his presence.

Davison himself had told me that he had visited Tenerife in September. Could he have killed Greene and then returned to England? But when I had first met him, in early December 1926, he had seemed so genial and full of life, a man untainted by the shadows of death; of course, all that changed with Una. In his line of work he must have had to do certain things that would not bear too close inspection. I also knew that he was travelling to Tenerife this time under an assumed name. Was he doing this to avoid capture? Or did he want to try and use his anonymity to bring the killer to justice?

'My dear, you are supposed to be here to relax, not brood upon the past,' said Carlo, reaching out to touch my arm as we sat on the deck. 'Look – look at the mountains! The glorious blue sea! That flock of birds flying past! Breathe in the air!'

Her lilting Scottish voice soothed me a little, but of course I could not reveal the source of my worries. 'Yes, you're right. I was just thinking about what people were doing back home.'

'Archie?'

I nodded.

'Well, he's best forgotten now, isn't he?' She turned to make sure that Rosalind, who was playing with her Blue Teddy with another little girl across the deck, was out of earshot. 'Remember what the doctors said. You're not to put yourself under any kind of strain.'

'Yes, you're right, of course,' I said, taking the sea air deep into my lungs. Carlo knew nothing about the real reason behind my disappearance the previous year, and I intended to keep it that way. 'And poor Gina Trevelyan . . .'

'I know it's hard but you must try and stop thinking about that unfortunate woman's death, God rest her soul,' she said. 'From now on, it's sea swimming, a little light reading, a few strolls around the gardens, good food and plenty of rest.'

'You're forgetting something,' I said, smiling.

'What?'

'A book that has to be delivered.'

'A book can wait, your health cannot, and without it there won't be any new novel.'

'Yes, but I've told Mr Cork that he will have the completed manuscript of *The Mystery of the Blue Train* on my return.'

'I'm sure a few weeks won't make much of a difference.'

'I truly think writing will take my mind off things. It has done in the past, and I don't see why it won't now.'

'Well, if you insist, then yes, we can include a small amount of writing into your daily agenda.' Carlo's eyes twinkled. 'But on one condition. I do the hard work with the typewriter, while you dictate the story to me.'

I had used this method only while sketching out the bares bones of a short story, never on something as large in scale as a novel.

'Very well,' I said. At that moment I caught a glimpse of Miss Hart and Mr Trevelyan disappearing around the corner of the deck. 'Would you excuse me for a moment, Carlo? I'm just going to see if I can find a drink for Rosalind. She must be terribly thirsty.'

'Yes, of course,' she said. 'I'll stay here with her.'

I stood up and walked quickly along the deck, following the couple at a safe distance. They passed through a group of local children and a flap of pale-faced nuns before they came to stop by the rail. I couldn't make out what they were saying and it was too risky to approach them and try to listen at close quarters, so I walked up the deck a little until I found an exit that would take me to the opposite side of the ferry. Within a minute or so I was beginning to edge my way along a length of empty seating that I knew led me towards the spot where Miss Hart and Mr Trevelyan were talking. As I moved closer to them — always making sure that I remained out of sight — I began to make out their conversation.

'I still feel so terrible about the whole thing,' said Helen.

'It's not surprising,' said Guy, with a soft tenderness in his voice. 'It's a terrible shock, a terrible thing for you to witness.'

'I don't know, I feel such a wretch. I wished her dead on so many occasions. I even fantasised about killing her myself, isn't that awful? A drop of poison in her cocktail, perhaps. A gentle push from the top flight of the stairs in Brook Street. God, you must think I'm a monster.'

'Shh,' he said. 'But now we can start to live our lives again, start afresh.'

'Can we? You don't think we'll be damned?'

'Damned? Whatever for?'

'I don't know. I just wondered whether we should have done things differently, that's all. Perhaps helped her see another doctor or sought treatment from an American specialist. I feel we let her down.'

'We couldn't help falling in love, could we?'

'Well, there was a moment we could have stepped back from it all. Do you remember?'

'Yes, I suppose there was,' said Guy. 'But for me that wasn't a choice.'

Their voices fell silent, replaced by the sound of their kissing. I felt my face flushing and I started to edge back the way I came. How shameful of me to listen to such an intimate conversation. They were obviously still trying to deal with the consequences of the sudden death of Gina Trevelyan and I had acted like, I don't know what. What was the worst kind of human being? Like one of those hounds who had stalked me during my most desperate hours. Those men in cheap suits who had called themselves journalists and who had splashed those stories about me across their front pages.

I walked back along the far side of the ferry, feeling thoroughly ashamed of myself. There was nothing more to be learnt from Mr Trevelyan and Miss Hart. I would leave them in peace to grieve and to come to terms with their actions. As I gazed out towards the island on the horizon I wondered what Archie was doing. Was he with that woman? When I disappeared at the end of the previous year, did he secretly wish that I had done away with myself? Did Miss Neele, Archie's new love, in the dark of night, pray that I would never return? And how had my reappearance affected their plans? Carlo, the doctors, my sister, even I myself, had insisted that I should banish the subject from my mind. But I couldn't. It would stay there, like a nasty blood stain that could never be rubbed clean.

Chapter Seven

In contrast to much of the barren landscape of Grand Canary, the northern tip of Tenerife was a lush paradise. As we travelled from the dock by bus towards Puerto Orotava I saw great stretches of banana plantations, fertile terraces and flowers so bright they hurt my eyes. My earlier feeling of disappointment faded away, replaced by a rising sense of anticipation and delight. Then I had to remind myself of why I was here. I was not simply another highly-strung lady seeking rest and recuperation in a fashionable winter resort. I was here to investigate a murder. What was that quote from Genesis? Something along the lines of that out of the earth the Lord had caused to grow every tree that was pleasing to the sight and a good source of food. Indeed, it was true that in the midst of the Garden of Eden stood the tree of life. But even there – even here – lurked evil.

I had been told by my fellow passengers on the *Gelria* that the Grand Hotel Taoro was one of the very best in Europe. As we approached it from the east, it certainly looked imposing, standing high on a hill set a little away from the sea and surrounded by manicured gardens and paths that led down to the ocean. The building formed a U-shape, with the open side facing inland towards more gardens that seemed to run for as far as the eye could see.

'Mummy, look – there's the volcano!' said Rosalind, pointing towards the snow-topped Teide in the distance. Her newly acquired knowledge had been gleaned from a number of illustrated books on the subject stocked in the *Gelria*'s library. Although she couldn't understand all the words, especially the more technical terms, she was enthralled by the idea that we were going to stay in the shadow of the volcano. 'Will it erupt? Will we see lava streams?'

'I shouldn't think so,' said Carlo, smiling. 'I'm sure it's extinct.'

'Oh no, Carlo, you're quite wrong,' said Rosalind. 'There is every chance it could erupt again – once, I think two hundred years ago, it destroyed a whole town near here.'

'Really?' I said, genuinely quite surprised, as I stepped down from the bus. 'But surely we are quite safe?' I looked up at the mountain, which from my reading I knew had been referred to by the Guanches as the 'Peak of Hell'.

'Oh, yes, extremely safe,' said a member of the hotel staff, a man with a German accent, dressed in a pale blue uniform, who stood at the entrance to the Taoro and who had overheard our conversation. 'We've been assured by scientists that there is nothing to worry about from the volcano. My name is Gustavo. Welcome to the Hotel Taoro, the favourite health resort. *Chicos, las maletas.*'

A couple of dark-skinned boys, no more than fourteen or fifteen years of age, also dressed in blue, swiftly took our cases and we, together with Mrs Brendel and the Winniatts, were ushered up a broad flight of steps into the palatial interior. The public rooms were large and lofty; sunlight danced off mirror and marble. Gustavo entered our details into the registration book and then proceeded to tell us about the facilities of the hotel. He was obviously proud of what the Taoro had to offer.

'The hotel is equipped with all modern comforts,' he reeled off. 'There is a private electric plant on the premises. Water is supplied by the Perdomo Spring, which is piped to the hotel and is of the highest purity. In fact, the sanitary arrangements were carried out by certified English plumbers under the supervision of a trained and qualified English physician. We are set within forty-two acres of gardens, which I would recommend you explore. There is an English Church situated within the grounds, also the English Library at the south entrance to the gardens. And if you are feeling adventurous,' he said, directing this towards Rosalind, 'we can arrange ascents to the peak, weather permitting. There is tennis, croquet, sea fishing . . .'

As I dreamt about the pleasures of sea swimming – oh, the thought of water on my shoulders! – I searched for a glimpse of the ocean through one of the windows. The public room faced towards the mountains, not the sea, and so my gaze was drawn to a garden square with a central fountain. Around this there were various colonnaded galleries which were open to the air, and in the very corner

I saw a pale-faced man in a wheeled basket chair being tended to by a pretty, but plainly-dressed girl with mousey brown hair. He took out a handkerchief and coughed into it. He opened his mouth to speak, and said something I could not hear. The young woman looked distressed as she knelt down and clasped hold of his hands.

'Yes, also I should have said that because of its beneficial situation, the hotel does have a number of invalids who come here for the winter,' said Gustavo, following my gaze. 'There is an esteemed doctor, Dr Trenkel, attached to the hotel who speaks and writes perfect English – although he is German I believe his mother was born in England – and also a resident English nurse. Sufferers of asthma, bronchitis and various lung disorders do seem to find relief here. There are some who are cured of their conditions; there are others,' he said, his eyes moving towards the poignant scene on the verandah, 'who are not so fortunate ... Now, if you would allow me and my staff to accompany you to your rooms.'

Gustavo told a couple of his assistants to accompany the Winniatts and Mrs Brendel to their rooms on the first floor – numbers 107 and 117 – while he walked with us up to the second floor. He led us down a long corridor to a suite of rooms, numbers 207 and 208, which were situated on the western side of the hotel, with windows that looked out towards Teide. I would have preferred a sea view, but Rosalind squealed with delight when she saw the peak. She said she would do nothing but sit and stare at the volcano, watching it for signs of eruption. When Gustavo and the boys bearing our luggage had left, Carlo touched me on the arm with a concerned expression in her eyes.

'Grand by name, grand by nature,' said Carlo before she continued in a whisper. 'Are you sure we can afford this?'

'I've just sold a handful of stories to an American magazine that pays a ridiculously high rate.' I didn't tell her the whole truth, which was that Davison's office was meeting most of the cost of our stay on the island. 'And anyway, I thought you said that one's health was beyond price.'

'True, true,' she said, suppressing a smile.

'Talking of health, after that journey I'm in need of a walk. Would you mind if I left you for a few hours?' Núñez had told me that Greene's body had been found in a cave by the Martiánez beach and I was keen to take a look at it.

'No, not at all, I doubt we'll go far,' said Carlo, turning her head to see Rosalind's face pressed up against the glass.

I rinsed my face, changed into a lighter dress and a pair of comfortable shoes, pocketed a box of matches that I had found on one of the tables in the room, and went back down the stairs in search of Gustavo. I told him that I wanted to walk to the sea, and perhaps see the black sands at Martiánez that I had heard so much about.

'Please do not be tempted to swim down by Martiánez,' he said, providing me with directions and a basic map. 'An English man, a very strong swimmer, was drowned only last year. The currents are treacherous and the rocks even worse. If you do want to bathe, there are some rock pools at the far left-hand side of the beach, where you can lie down and let the water wash over you. But remember – no swimming.'

I expressed disappointment – at some point I would have liked to have swum there – and made my way out of the hotel and down a gentle, winding path towards the sea. Instead of taking one of the tracks that led to a cluster of white houses around the harbour I followed a path that passed a charming house called Sitio Litre and then down towards the semi-circular black bay of Martiánez. As I approached, the wind began to pick up and waves dashed against a jagged spur of black rocks out at sea. There was something terrifying about the power of the sea here, something brutal and elemental, not only in the way the waves crashed upon the shore but also in the terrible noise with which they withdrew, sucking a line of black stones back into the water like the rattle of a hundred skulls.

The beach was empty except for a group of Spanish children playing in the rock pools on the far left-hand side of the bay. I skirted along the edge of the bay and started to walk up a steep path that looked as if it led towards the top of the cliff. I stopped to catch my breath, hearing the roar of the ocean below. Wind-beaten prickly pears and various species of cacti, their fleshy protuberances contorted and bent like witches' fingers, clung to the rock face. As I climbed I noticed a dark pocket of a cave above.

I hesitated for a moment before I stepped inside. I noticed that the cave split off into different sections. I chose one of the paths at random, but as I eased myself forwards, feeling the dankness seep out of the walls, the light from the outside world lessened. With shaking fingers, I lit a match and the dim glow cast curiously shaped shadows onto the walls. Just as I began to step farther into the cave I thought I heard something. Just then my match burnt out. My fingers fumbled for the matches, striking one, striking another, but to no effect. One lit, but then burnt the tip of my thumb, forcing me to drop it onto the earth below. Just then I heard, or thought I heard, the sound of footsteps. There was someone inside the cave, walking along one of the other pathways that led back towards the entrance.

'Who – who is it?' I managed to say, my voice rasping with fear. 'Who's there?'

I smelt a sourness that reminded me of the sharp metallic rankness of breath, just like Kurs's fetid breathing – the man who had nearly destroyed me the year before. My hands, desperate now, reached again for the matches, and in a blind panic I felt them falling onto the ground. As I bent down to pick them up, my hands as ineffective as it they had been frozen numb, I heard the sound of footsteps again. As quickly as I could I made my way back towards a point where I could see the front of the cave, but by the time I got there I saw nothing more than a vague silhouette, which then melted away.

I returned to gather the matches, and after placing most of them back in the box, I lit one and then another, repeating the process so that the light illuminated a series of niches that ran deep into the cliff. There was no one here. I was alone. I slowly walked to the entrance of the cave and eased my head forwards. There was no one on the path below, and the beach was still empty save for the cluster of Spanish children playing in the shallow pools. I edged along the path and, taking hold of a branch of an old fig tree growing out of the rock face, strained to look down over the edge of the sheer drop. The scree from the path began to give way, sending fragments of stone falling below. I held my grip and peered over.

There, at the very bottom, back pressed against the undercliff, was a hatless man. I could see only the top of his head – his hair was blond – and the back of his white linen jacket, but I was almost certain of the man's identity. It was Davison.

Chapter Eight

Gently, I eased myself backwards and steadied myself against the rock face. I hurried down the path that led towards the beach, breathless and panting with shock, anger and indignation.

'Davison, Davison,' I called out. 'What on earth are you doing?'

By the time I reached the black sands, Davison had moved away from the undercliff. His face was as implacable as ever, without a trace of guilt.

'What was the meaning of all of that? What were you trying to do?'

'What do you mean?' The tone of his voice, with its rarefied vowels bred and perfected within the privileged halls of Eton and Cambridge, was as innocent as that of a young boy who had yet to experience the sins of the world.

'If you wanted to scare me, I'm pleased to tell you that you well and truly succeeded,' I said, feeling my face begin to redden.

'Agatha – Mrs Christie, I'm not quite sure I quite understand.'

'Up there,' I said, gesturing towards the path, but this was met by nothing but a blank expression. 'The cave.'

'Yes, that's where Greene's body was found.'

'But inside the cave. Standing there silently. It was you, wasn't it?'

Davison remained very still and quiet as he considered what to say next. 'I admit I followed you from the hotel, because I was – I am – concerned about your safety.' He blinked. 'I thought you might take the opportunity to see where Greene's body was found, and I wanted to make sure that you – well, that you didn't get into any danger. But no, I remained down here.'

'So, it wasn't you – inside just now?'

'No, it wasn't. When I heard someone come out of the cave – and I assumed it was you – I pushed myself against the undercliff.'

Could I believe him? After all, I knew he had not given me the whole truth about the circumstances surrounding Greene's death. And Inspector Núñez had told me Davison was suspected of being involved in the man's death.

'I presume that the person must have taken the path up to La Paz at the top of the cliff,' he continued, looking up at the mirador. 'But I can't see anyone there now.'

'Perhaps because the person went down the path and towards the beach rather than up the path to the top of the cliff.'

'But I've seen no one down here.'

'Precisely,' I said.

'Oh my, you're shaking.'

As he took a step towards me, I moved backwards.

'You've had a terrible shock. We must get you back to the hotel. I'll go and see if I can find—'

'No, just stop here, for a moment, please,' I said. 'I need to tell you something.'

'That sounds very serious,' he said.

'Yes, I am afraid it is, rather,' I said. 'When you first tried to persuade me to come out here, I was more than a little reluctant, do you remember?'

'Yes, I do. And I'm very pleased that you agreed. As I said, both my boss Hartford and myself believe that—'

'I should have listened to my instincts and never got involved with your department. It was only because – well, because of what had happened to Flora Kurs and Una. I felt I had to do something, so their deaths were not in vain. That probably blinded me to the reality of the situation. I feel I've made a dreadful mistake. Of course, I will reimburse the cost of our passage on the *Gelria* and the hotel rooms. We'll have to move into a cheaper hotel while we wait for the next boat home. I'm sorry, but there it is.'

'Look, I know you've had a terrible scare. There was obviously someone else in the cave with you just now. I don't know who or what they were doing there. It's understandable that you feel a little anxious after that fright, but—'

I couldn't repress the question any longer. 'Did you kill Douglas Greene?'

The colour drained from Davison's face. 'I beg your pardon?'

71

'Did you murder Greene?'

He remained silent.

'You see, this is exactly why I can no longer continue helping you. I know your department sometimes has to make difficult decisions, sometimes ones that involve life and death. But I cannot—'

'I suppose you must have been talking to Inspector Núñez. Am I right?'

'Yes, he came on board the *Gelria* when we docked to ask some questions about the suicide of Gina Trevelyan.'

'And presumably he told you some nonsense about me being wanted for questioning regarding the murder of Douglas Greene.'

'Yes, that's right,' I said. 'He did.'

'And you believed him?'

'Well, I did wonder why you were bothering to travel under a different name. I thought perhaps Greene might have been a double agent or he was working against the interests of Britain. I'm sorry, I didn't know what to believe.'

'Do you really think that I could have done anything to hurt him?'

Shadows of pain darkened his face and I began to understand. Davison gestured for me to sit by him on a rock and as the waves crashed on the shore he began to tell me something of his friendship with Greene, a friendship that had a deep and intimate connection.

'I think when we first met – this was in London – both of us knew immediately what was going to happen. It was an instant draw, impossible to resist. He was a Cambridge man but a few years younger than myself. Of course, we had to do everything in our power to keep it secret. And I think we both put on an act that we didn't take the friend-ship seriously, that – I don't know – that we'd grow out of it. But we knew, deep down, there was more to it than that.'

'And then Greene got posted out here?'

'Yes, at the end of 1925. There was nothing either of us could do. After all, work came first, both of us knew that. I managed to visit him a couple of times in Tenerife. We had the most delightful, glorious time. We talked about our future, nothing more than silly prattlings, but it made us happy thinking about what might be. And then, early this year, I got the news that Douglas had been killed. That his body had been found in that damnable cave up there. Sorry . . .' His voice broke and tears formed in his eyes.

'I see. But what makes Inspector Núñez believe that you had anything to do with his murder?'

'The last time I came over, in September, I learnt that he had been – well, that he had become rather too friendly with one or two of the Spanish boys. Awful types, really. Only interested in trinkets, bits of spare cash. I suppose I must have become jealous. We'd had a few too many drinks. One of these boys, Diego, came round to the house and I couldn't stand it. We had a blazing row. There were some glasses smashed. An awful scene, one I'm not proud of, and I stormed out. I booked into the hotel and then the next day I took a ferry to Grand Canary, from where I got the boat home. Seems like Douglas disappeared at the same time. When the police started to dig into what had happened, Diego told Núñez about the row that he'd witnessed. Núñez found a letter I'd written to Douglas at his house. I'd always told him to burn my letters, but somehow this one had escaped the fire.'

'So why don't you simply go to Núñez and tell him all of this? About what happened?'

Davison looked at me as if I were a fool. 'Of course, I understand,' I said. 'You're afraid that it would get back to Hartford. That you'd never be trusted again.'

'Yes, and also I'd be a sitting target for every dirty blackmailer out there. But if I can provide evidence of who really killed Douglas then at least that might satisfy the police here.' He stared at me with his kind, intelligent eyes. 'I'm sorry I had to keep this from you. I thought you might think less of me.'

'Not at all, don't be silly,' I said, placing a hand lightly on his arm. 'I just wish you could have trusted me a little more.'

'Yes, it was wrong of me, I'm sorry. Will you forgive me?'

I paused before I turned to him and said archly, 'Well, I was already beginning to regret my decision to leave the Grand. Such a lovely hotel and so very comfortable.'

'Quite right too,' said Davison, smiling. 'A lady on her travels has certain standards to maintain. Now, what do you say to having a proper look at this cave?'

Chapter Nine

Davison took a flashlight out of his pocket and shone it into the dark space. The cave seemed to split into three, with each of its sections stretching farther back into the cliff. I spotted the place where I had dropped the matches – there was still a cluster of them on the ground. Then, as I continued to explore, I found a trail of footprints on one of the pathways that led from the back of the cave to its entrance.

'So it appears that there was someone here after all,' said Davison, shining his flashlight at the ground.

'Did you think I was suffering from some sort of hysterical delusion? Or not telling the truth?'

'No, not at all. But it's always good to find corroborating evidence to back up a story,' he said, bending down. 'But you say you couldn't make him – or her – out.'

'No, only the vague silhouette at the entrance to the cave.'

'But from that impression, would you say it was a man or a woman?'

'I'm sorry, I couldn't be certain.'

We moved on towards the back of the cave, to the spot where, according to Professor Wilbor's testimony, Greene's body had been found. Davison hesitated for a moment before he approached. Although I couldn't see his eyes – Davison directed the flashlight towards the earth – I was sure that they were full of sadness as he gazed upon his friend's last resting place. I bent down and studied the ground for traces of anything left behind, my fingers moving over sharp stones and old pieces of animal bone.

'What a horrible place to die.' Davison's voice was nothing more than a whisper. 'If only we hadn't argued that day then it might never have happened. Who could do such a thing to him? What must he have thought when—'

'There's no use thinking of the past now,' I said, in a deliberately sharp manner. Davison wouldn't thank me if I allowed him to become over-emotional. In fact, I was sure that if I was to witness an honest display of deep feeling he would soon come to be embarrassed by my presence. 'If you want to help Greene, as I'm sure you do, then we need to find a way of working out what happened here.'

'Of course,' he said, covering his mouth with his fist. 'Yes, you're right.'

'Let's check the ground for anything unusual,' I said. 'I'll work on this area here and you do that section towards the back.'

'Good idea.' He knelt down and balanced the flashlight on a rock between us. 'I suppose the police must have looked but as I told you, their methods are basic to say the least. What were your impressions of Inspector Núñez, by the way?'

'Charming,' I said. 'But maybe that was because he said he was a fan of my books.'

'Did he now?'

'He seemed intelligent enough and spoke very good English, I think because he spent some time in London.'

Davison remained silent. 'I'm not having much luck,' I said after a while, a stream of black sand running through my fingers. 'Have you found anything?'

'Nothing but a few old goats' teeth.'

'By the way, how do you hope to keep out of Núñez's way? He told me that he was coming to Orotava next week. I know you're travelling under another name, but surely at some point Núñez will circulate a photograph of you?'

'I will deal with that when, and if, it happens,' said Davison.

'It sounds as though you may have something up your sleeve.'

'Perhaps,' he said enigmatically.

'Well, I won't question you any further, as I know it makes you uncomfortable. But I only hope you feel you can tell me – when the time is right, of course.'

'Of course,' he said. 'I promise.'

'Look,' I said, flinging down a handful of dry sand. 'We're getting nowhere here. Let's try something different. Let's think about the kind of person who did this.'

'Very well,' said Davison, standing up. 'As I said to you

before, from my reading and from what I've heard, this could well be the kind of thing dreamt up by that occultist Gerard Grenville.'

'Yes, that's what Núñez suspects, but if that's the case, why doesn't he just arrest him and have done with it?'

'I suspect that might have something to do with the fact that Núñez is in love with Grenville's daughter, Violet.'

As he described her to me an image of the girl I had seen on the Taoro terrace came into my mind. An angel ministering to a sick, dying man.

'But she's not in love with Núñez.'

'How did you know that?' said Davison, sounding astonished.

'Didn't I tell you my mother had psychic abilities? I suppose I must have inherited them.'

It was delightful to see Davison smile once more. 'No, apparently Violet is in love with Edmund Ffosse,' he said. 'Nice chap. But terribly ill with phthisis.'

'It must be them I saw on the terrace of the hotel earlier. A lovely girl, but she looked so sad.'

'Yes, it probably was her. The Taoro's doctor, Trenkel, is the best on the island. I believe Edmund is one of his patients. Now, after that interlude of trivial island gossip, it's back to the business in hand,' said Davison.

'Indeed,' I said, turning my attention to the cave once more. From my experience it was foolish to dismiss gossip as idle or useless. I knew that sometimes it could provide the clue to the whole thing.

After another half an hour searching we still had not

come up with anything more tangible than a few old coins, the bones of a bird – Davison, something of an expert in these matters, believed it to be a chicken – and an old leather bracelet. Davison had never seen Greene wearing the bracelet and from its appearance it looked as though it had been in the earth for a good few decades.

Davison cleared his throat. 'Did you know that caves like this – in fact probably this one – were used by the Guanches to bury their dead?' he asked.

'Is that true?' I said, standing up and brushing the sand and dirt off me.

'Yes, so Professor Wilbor told me. In fact, if we look closely enough we should still be able to find traces of them.'

Davison withdrew a penknife from his inside jacket pocket and started to pick away at the ground beneath the spot where Greene had been found. Within a matter of moments he had unearthed the tip of an old bone.

My old anatomy lessons came back to me. 'That looks like a femur.'

'Yes, and probably a few thousand years old at that,' said Davison as he continued to attack the soil. 'Dig a bit deeper and I wouldn't be at all surprised if we didn't find a Guanche skull.'

'Perhaps that's for another day,' I said. I was beginning to feel a little breathless and queasy. 'I think it's about time we returned to the hotel, don't you? After all, Carlo and Rosalind will be wondering what—'

'Hello, what's this? How very curious. Bring that other flashlight over and shine it down here,' he said.

I followed his orders, but could make out nothing more distinct than a clump of black earth.

'Can't you see?' he said, as he took out his handkerchief and began to clean the object in his hands.

'All I see is a primitive little clay figurine.'

'It's a representation of Tibicena.'

'And who, pray tell, is Tibicena?'

'The Guanches believed that the island was haunted by a demon that lived in a cave and took the form of an enormous black dog with red eyes.'

'It doesn't in the least bit look like a dog,' I said, as I peered down at the figure with its tiny head and gnashing teeth. It had two arms that looked like the handles of a jug, covered with a series of deep slashes, and in its middle there appeared to be another distorted face or mouth of some kind.

'So you think it could have been buried here by the Guanches?'

'Perhaps. There may be another reason, of course.' Davison bowed his head as he blew on the little statue and then spat on his handkerchief to clean its head, revealing a pair of small and sinister eyes. 'Yes, very intriguing.'

'Are you going to enlighten me?'

Davison did not reply immediately.

'Oh, sorry, I was lost in thought for a moment. You see, the person with the largest collection of Guanche artefacts on the island, if not in the world, is none other than—'

I stopped him before he finished his sentence. 'Gerard Grenville,' I said.

Chapter Ten

Just as we reached the top of the path that led up the cliff we saw the girl I now knew to be Violet standing at the edge of the plateau. Her long hair hung down like a curtain over her face and she stared down at the waves crashing below in a way that reminded me of poor Gina Trevelyan. Surely she wasn't going do anything rash? We were about to approach her to ask if she needed any help when a large, bald man walked down the path of cypresses towards where she stood. His face seemed serious and set in stone.

'It's Grenville,' said Davison, taking my arm and manoeuvring us out of sight behind a large cactus.

We watched as Grenville put an arm around his daughter and comforted her as she sobbed into his enormous chest. It was obvious from the tableau being played out in front of us that Violet had received some upsetting news. Then, in an instant, the tenderness turned to something else, something altogether nastier, as her face flushed a deep crimson, her eyes stretched wide and her voice cracked with anger.

'You just don't understand,' we heard her say, as she spat out the words. 'I love him. I don't care what the doctors have told him. I want to marry him.'

'But he's only got a few months to live, my dear.' Grenville's voice sounded calm. 'You've got your whole future ahead of you. I would be shirking my duties as a father if I allowed you to marry him.'

'We could just marry anyway. You couldn't stop us.'

'Perhaps not. But I doubt Edmund would go against my wishes.'

'What did you say to him?'

'I simply outlined the practicalities of the situation. Edmund is a reasonable enough chap, and I think he saw sense.'

'I don't grasp why you are so against the idea. You know we love each other.'

'Yes, I believe you love him a great deal.'

'And what about your own beliefs? What about all those years of work? Those meetings? Those pamphlets? Don't they count for anything now?'

'Of course they do. But marrying Edmund Ffosse would not be the best course of action for you at this time. I've just spoken to him and I think he's come round to my way of thinking too.'

'And you've always said how there are more things in life than our physical reality, haven't you,' said Violet, sounding desperate now. 'You still stand by that, don't you?'

'Yes, of course I do, but—'

'If you believe that then surely you believe that even after Edmund ... after Edmund is no longer here – in this world – I should be able to continue to love him, perhaps even communicate with him.'

'In theory, yes, but there are certain aspects of—'

'What? Certain aspects of what?'

'Listen, my dear, why don't we go back home and talk about it there?' said Grenville. 'You're in a great deal of distress. You've just heard the news about Edmund's diagnosis and there is an awful lot to take in. Come on.' As he reached down to place a hand on his daughter's shoulder Violet shrugged him off and moved away, taking a step nearer the cliff edge. 'Violet, please calm down. Let's walk back to Mal Pais and we can—'

'Don't touch me,' she said, her eyes flashing wildly now. 'I know why you don't want me to marry Edmund.'

'What are you talking about?'

'Death doesn't hold any fear for me, you know,' said Violet, gesturing towards the sheer drop that lay only a footstep away. 'What was it the Guanche women would say before they jumped off the cliff to their deaths? "Vacaguaré". I'd rather die. That's what I would shout as I went to my death. I'd rather die and be with Edmund than live without him.'

'Violet, please. This is not something we should—'

'You don't think it's appropriate? Are you worried I might cause a scene?' She looked around her, desperate for an audience now, but saw no one. 'Well, that's something you need to ask—'

'I don't understand what you are talking about. The news of Edmund's diagnosis has unsettled you. If you carry on like this, I will have to call Dr Trenkel. You need some kind of sedative, something to calm your nerves.'

'I've never felt more in control in all my life,' said Violet, wiping the tears away from her face.

'I'm going to call Edmund. Perhaps he will help to calm you down.'

'Don't you speak another word to him – not another word, do you hear?'

But Grenville turned his bulky frame and, ignoring his daughter, walked back up the cypress walk towards the green-shuttered house set back from the plateau. I watched Violet carefully, ready to stop her if she took another step towards the edge of the cliff. But she remained immobile, a haunted look in her eyes.

'Is she going to jump?' whispered Davison.

'I shouldn't think so,' I replied. 'Not while Edmund is alive, at least.'

'Should we slip away while we've got a chance? Back down the path to the beach?'

'No, but let's be ready to show ourselves at any moment.'

Violet tidied her hair and dabbed a handkerchief over her face. She looked up towards the house and began to walk in its direction, before she changed her mind and turned towards the town. A minute or so later the door to La Paz, the home of Edmund Ffosse, opened to reveal the pale-faced man I'd seen earlier at the hotel, this time in a wheeled chair, with Grenville behind him.

'Now,' I said to Davison, taking a gentle hold of the bottom of his linen jacket. 'Take my arm.'

'Excuse me?'

'I said take my arm.'

'But—'

'There's no time for questions,' I said, linking my arm with his and moving forwards along the plateau to the house.

As Grenville pushed the wheeled chair towards us it became obvious that the two men were in a state of distress and anxiety. The older man's eyes seemed to bulge out of his ugly face, while the young invalid looked haunted, if not somewhat hunted too. They stopped us as we walked towards them.

'Have you seen the girl who was here a minute or so ago?' Edmund asked us. 'Please tell me you've seen her and that she is all right. I couldn't bear it if she has done anything stupid. Grenville – wheel me to the edge. Look down to see if—'

'Do you mean a young lady with light brown hair? Dressed in a black skirt and white blouse?' I said.

'Yes, that's her,' said Edmund, his black eyes full of pain. 'She's not—'

'When we were coming up from the beach a few minutes ago, I saw a woman on the plateau,' I said. 'But when she saw us she turned her back to us and started to walk towards the town.'

'Are you quite certain?' asked Edmund, as he started to cough. He took out a handkerchief, the corner of which was stained with blood.

'Yes,' added Davison. 'Quite. Why? Is there is something wrong?'

'Oh, no, my daughter was just a little upset,' said Grenville, wheeling Edmund back from the edge of the plateau. I saw the older man's eyes studying every inch of me, taking in a spot of dirt on my dress that I must have picked up in the cave. 'Did you have a mishap down on the path? I know it's quite steep and, in some spots, very narrow. One misplaced step could prove fatal.'

I lowered my head and pretended to be embarrassed. Fortunately, Davison had finally understood the significance of the dissembling.

'You've rumbled us,' he said, blushing slightly. 'Yes, my companion did slip on the path down below. Luckily, I caught her before it was too late.' Davison looked at me with amusement and affection and, keeping up the charade, I met his gaze with a simpering giggle.

It was obvious that Edmund was not interested in pursuing this line of conversation or knowing any more details of the strangers' lovemaking in the remote spot below his house. He only wanted to know more about Violet – what kind of state she had been in, whether we had heard anything she might have muttered to herself, and the precise direction of her movements.

'Sorry, so rude of me,' said the older man. 'I'm Gerard Grenville. I live here on the island with my daughter, Violet. And this,' he added, gesturing to the emaciated figure in the wheeled chair, 'is my daughter's very good friend Edmund Ffosse.'

Davison introduced himself as Alexander Blake, an insurance agent from Southampton, and I, knowing that the best disguise was often oneself, simply told the two men the truth. No doubt they had read about my disappearance – all the world seemed to be acquainted with it – and they had also probably heard about my arrival

at the hotel. I'd had a somewhat distressing winter, I told
them, and, after an attack of nerves, had escaped England
for the fortunate isles. I hoped that the rest and relaxa-
tion, beneficial climate and good company – at this point I
looked at Davison – would restore me to good health.

'Oh my, the famous lady novelist,' said Grenville, his
frog-like eyes widening. 'Or, as you are better known in
our household, the writer of rather fine supernatural short
stories.' He began to question me on some of the silly tales
I had dashed off for magazines like *The Grand* and *Ghost
Stories*. 'Of course, my favourite is *The Woman Who Stole
a Ghost*. I wonder how you got the inspiration for such a
story? And that awful Madame Exe, interfering with a
medium like that. Yes, it's perfectly understandable that
she may miss her dead daughter, but to try and take the
spirit away, this is very dangerous, as you know. In fact, it
once happened to me, when I was taking part in a séance
in Paris. Just as I felt myself being totally possessed – my
guide is an ancient Egyptian spirit ... But listen to me
going on. I'm sure you don't want to hear me talk about
my experiences, all my strange interludes, which you no
doubt regard as—'

'Oh, Mr Grenville, I'm absolutely fascinated,' I said,
interrupting him. 'As a writer I'm always keen to hear such
things, especially from someone with your talents.'

'What have you heard?'

I felt my heart lurch. All I knew was the gossip I had
picked up from the *Gelria*. 'Your particular sensitivities,
your ability to sense things and see things that escape the
rest of us.'

At this, Grenville puffed up his mighty chest. 'Well, if that is the case we must carry on this conversation in a more civilised environment. Would you – and your friend, Mr Blake,' he said, pausing before saying his name almost as if he had seen it written in an italic script, 'like to come for tea tomorrow?'

'Yes, I – rather, we – would like that a great deal,' I said.

'I hope my daughter will have come to her senses by then. She's a lovely girl, just a little highly strung. She's a great fan of your writing too, so I am sure she would be delighted to meet you. Now, do you know where my house is? Mal Pais? Ask at the hotel. It's built on the tongue of a lava flow. They said nothing would grow there, but I think I've proved them wrong. Anyway, you'll see when you come.'

His eyes bulged out of their sockets as he moved a step closer to me. An absurd comment made on the ship about Grenville's fondness for cake made from the blood of chickens came into my mind. My vision began to soften and blur a little. The taste of bile soured my mouth. I leant on Davison, who was still at my side, and I became aware of him looking at me with a concerned expression.

'And despite all the rumours, or what nonsense you may have heard,' Grenville said, smiling and revealing a mouth of rotten, blackened teeth, 'I don't serve cakes made out of chickens' blood.' He stared at me to watch my reaction, a reaction that reminded me of the look a hawk might give a rodent before swooping down and catching it in its talons. 'I'll expect you tomorrow – shall we say half past three?'

I smiled nervously; inside a mass of questions rattled me

and jarred my nerves. Had Grenville murdered Douglas Greene? If so, what was his motive? What was the nature of Grenville's relationship with his daughter? Was he aware that Davison was using a false name? And the most pressing, and indeed the most worrying, of all: as an occultist did Grenville have the ability to tap into my consciousness and read my mind?

Chapter Eleven

'But I assumed he was a fake,' I said to Davison in the taxi back to the hotel. 'I just don't understand how he could have known what I was thinking about.'

'That story about the cakes is one of the more common anecdotes about Grenville repeated in the popular press,' said Davison. 'I'm sure it's nothing more than a coincidence.'

I wasn't sure I believed in coincidence. Of course, odd things happened all the time – strange confluences, surprising but fortunate meetings, odd parallels. But were these things without meaning? Was it simply that some people had the ability to see certain patterns that others would not even notice? Certainly, my mother had been a great believer in the hidden power of the spirit world. She had hinted to me on several occasions that an individual's actions, while seeming on the surface to be a product of his or her willpower or personality or background, could actually be determined by other, more mysterious factors. It would have been easy for sceptics to dismiss her theory as nothing more than the musings of an elderly widow. How much more comforting it was to believe that, at the end of one's life, one was about to join a community of dearly loved souls, rather than face up to the bleaker prospect of eternal non-existence. Yet, since my mother's death, I had felt her spirit close to me. Was this wishful thinking? Perhaps. Could it have been a symptom of my occasional nervous disposition or, that fashionable concept, the unconscious? Indeed it could. Yet I liked to believe that my dear mother was still near, still guiding me. How much I would give to see and touch her again. Tears stung my eyes as I realised just how much I missed her.

'It's been quite a day,' said Davison gently. 'I expect you need a rest.'

'Yes, I think I do. Especially if I'm going to go to this dinner tonight at the hotel hosted by Guy Trevelyan and Helen Hart. I think it's meant as a kind of peace offering towards the Winniatts.' I related the incident on the *Gelria* that culminated in Miss Hart spilling red wine over Howard Winniatt's precious notebook. 'Did you ever meet him during the voyage?'

'No, I don't believe I did.'

'He's a dreadful bore, terribly pompous. A writer. But, of course, a much *grander* writer than I could ever be.' I remembered his comment to me on the ship. As I told Davison about Winniatt the cloud of melancholy I had felt a few moments before began to disperse. A smile formed on my lips and soon both of us were laughing at the absurdity of it all.

'What a fool,' said Davison. 'Who does he think will read his magnum opus?'

'Oh, I'm sure a whole brigade of high-minded literary critics will work themselves into a frenzy at the idea of his unrefined reality, or whatever it is he calls it.'

'Well, I don't think you need to worry about the competition,' said Davison. 'He's not going to steal any readers from you.'

'To be honest, I don't think he'd have them,' I said. 'He'd regard them as not the right sort.'

On the taxi journey back to the hotel we discussed the events of the day, what we had found in the cave, our impressions of Gerard and Violet Grenville and our thoughts about the sad fate of Edmund Ffosse. Davison decided to leave the taxi at the entrance to the hotel's grounds, from where he would walk back to his room at the Taoro.

'After all, we don't want any gossip,' he said.

'You mean any *more* gossip,' I corrected him. 'Did you see the way Grenville looked at the dust and dirt on my dress? I don't know what he thought we had been up to.'

'Well, some misinformation of that sort is always helpful,' he said, pausing. 'Una often accompanied me to various events and dinners.' He turned from me, a sadness in his eyes. He would, I knew, never get over her death. 'Goodbye,' he said.

'I know I'm a poor substitute,' I replied, trying to cheer him up, 'but it's about time I did a little more socialising myself. See you tomorrow.'

In truth, I was not in the mood for company, but I had given my word to Mrs Brendel that I would accompany her to the dinner later that night. On returning to the hotel, I managed to discard my dirty clothes and have a long bath before I saw Carlo and Rosalind, who had spent the afternoon playing in the gardens with a couple of other children who were staying at the Taoro.

'You're never going to die, are you, Blue Teddy?' said Rosalind, as she picked up her favourite toy and gave it a tight hug.

I looked at my daughter with concern. 'What makes you say that, dear?' I asked gently.

'Oh, nothing. Only that Raymond, the boy I met this afternoon, he told me that last year his brother died.'

'Well, I expect that the little boy is very sad,' I said.

'He didn't seem terribly sad,' said Rosalind. She paused and then looked at me with questioning, serious eyes. 'Will you die one day?'

'Yes, my dear,' I said, stroking her hair. 'All of God's creatures have to die. But that doesn't mean that I will ever stop loving you.'

'How can you love me after you're dead?'

'A very good question, but it's a matter of belief.'

'What do you mean?'

'Well, you know Grannie – my mother – died last year.'

'Yes, and you were very, very sad.'

'I was, and in some ways I still am. But she hasn't left my heart and that is all that matters.'

Rosalind blinked as her young mind tried to process what I had just said. 'Have you ever seen a ghost?'

'Well, it depends on what you mean by a ghost.'

'Raymond said that sometimes he sees the ghost of his brother walking into his bedroom at night.'

'It might have been a trick of the light,' I said. 'But don't worry, there's no reason for you to be scared.'

'Did you hear that, Blue Teddy? We have nothing to be afraid of.' And with that Rosalind proceeded to run across the room to show her adored stuffed toy something she had spotted, or imagined she had seen, on the floor.

But were those words true? How would I react if an apparition were to appear to me in the middle of the night? Would I be driven to the edge of madness? Or, were it my mother or father, for instance, would I feel comforted to know that she or he was at close quarters? Just how porous was the barrier between this world and the next? These kinds of questions lay behind many of my most recent ghost stories, like the one that Grenville said he had enjoyed.

An idea for a story began to form at the back of my mind, an image of a young boy, dead for some time, but terribly lonely. What if he, this spirit child, were to yearn for a companion? One day, a family could move into the house where the dead boy had once lived. What might happen then? Would the spirit want to claim the life of another young boy so as not to feel so lonely? I picked up a notebook and jotted down the scrap of the idea, together with some lines of poetry that came into my head. *Where had I heard this?*

> *'What Lamp has Destiny to guide*
> *Her little Children stumbling in the Dark?'*
> *'A Blind Understanding,' Heaven replied.*

Chapter Twelve

The words of the poem haunted me all evening. I too felt like a child stumbling in the dark, searching for a meaning that did not exist. Gina Trevelyan had thrown herself off the ship, her body never found. Douglas Greene had been murdered, his body left to mummify in a cave, and still his killer was at large. Violet Grenville had just learnt that the man she was about to marry had only months to live. Nothing seemed to make any sense. Was this because it was never possible to really know another person? Were we all just figures in some kind of elaborate shadow dance, destined to communicate by a series of superficial gestures?

After dressing for the evening I made my way to the hotel dining room on the ground floor overlooking the gardens. As I looked around the room and saw the faces of the guests sitting around the table – Guy Trevelyan and Helen Hart, Mr and Mrs Winniatt, Mrs Brendel and two new members of the party who had been pointed out to me, the archaeologist Professor Wilbor and his assistant Rupert Mabey – I took a moment to wonder at the meaning of it all. For many, life was chaotic, messy and sometimes without purpose. Perhaps that was why I wrote the kind of books I did, and perhaps why they proved popular with readers too.

'You're looking ever so serious tonight, my dear,' said Mrs Brendel, sitting between me and Mr Winniatt.

'I'm sorry, I was just thinking of something my daughter said to me earlier,' I said.

'Not bad news, I hope?'

'Oh, no, just a silly aside,' I said, not wanting to dwell on it.

'Now, Mrs Christie, what have you been doing today?' asked Mr Winniatt. He had a notebook at the ready, but of course I wasn't going to tell him about the day's events.

'Oh, nothing very much, I'm afraid. I have been enjoying the comforts of the Taoro.'

'But I thought I saw you walking down by the beach, what's it called, the Martiánez?'

What else had he seen? 'Yes, I did take a stroll in that direction. I thought about the possibility of swimming in the sea, but I was warned off by Gustavo.'

'That's quite right, dear,' said Mrs Brendel. 'I would never swim there. I've heard such awful stories about that bay. Of course, it's quite all right to sit in one of the rock pools, but no, I would never venture into the rough waters.'

'Did you by any chance have an encounter, pleasant or otherwise, on your walk?' asked Mr Winniatt, looking up from his notebook with a cruel, hard expression in his eyes.

I knew exactly what he was referring to – he had obviously seen me with Davison – but I wasn't going to give him the satisfaction of a confession.

'Forgive me, Mr Winniatt, I'm not exactly sure what you mean.'

'I must have been mistaken, but I thought I saw you walking in the company of a fellow guest from the hotel.'

What a thoroughly unpleasant man, I thought to myself. The insult he had thrown at me back on the *Gelria* played in my mind, stinging me once more. At my side Mrs Brendel tutted disapprovingly.

'Imagination can sometimes get the better of us,' I said, smiling sweetly, 'especially writers of such rank as you. I'm afraid my abilities are confined to the lowest rung of the literary ladder, while you occupy the very top.'

Winniatt looked momentarily confused before his expression changed to one of supreme self-satisfaction. He was obviously so stupid as not to realise the sarcastic nature of my comment.

'Yes, that is the problem with fiction when it is conceived as nothing but entertainment,' he said. 'The drive for narrative does rather function as a pollutant. And of course, the detective genre is really the lowest of the popular forms.'

'Well,' sniffed Mrs Brendel.

'I wouldn't quite—' I mumbled, reddening, before I was interrupted by a loud and confident voice from down the table.

'I don't know about you, but I enjoy a murder mystery just as much as the next man,' said Guy Trevelyan, who was sitting to the left of the high-minded writer. 'I know, why don't you ask me what I've been doing since I arrived? I'm sure I can give you some interesting information. But some of my stories do involve rocks, I'm afraid, so you'll have to bear with me.'

Guy winked at me as he began to relate to Winniatt what had changed in Puerto Orotava since his last visit, his impressions of certain guests at the Taoro, his opinions on the sculpture of Miss Hart, before he ventured off into the very specific and technical world of geology. I heard mention of such terms as basaltic rock, substrata and fault lines before Mrs Brendel turned her back on Mr Winniatt and began to whisper to me about how she had changed her mind about him. There was no excuse for such rudeness, she said. She would much rather read a proper story with a beginning, middle and end – and detective stories had such clever endings – than a mere reportage of the details of everyday life. What was the point of that? She asked.

'Although I did tell him I would let him record my memories of the fateful voyage, I don't think I will now, not after the way he's behaved towards you,' she said. 'I should think he's just jealous, my dear. So don't pay any attention to him. There was a man on the *Titanic* who was just like him. You should have heard some of the things he said. He didn't survive. Went down with the ship like many of the first-class men. Of course, it was only right that ...' She continued in this vein, telling me more stories of life – and death – on the tragic ship until she looked towards her left with a puzzled expression. 'Oh my, now he's gone and upset poor Guy, after everything he's been through. Really, it's not on.'

Mr Trevelyan's eyes seemed fixed on a point directly in front of him, a glass perhaps or a knife or fork. Noticing a slight chill descend on the table, Miss Hart turned her attention to what was happening.

'Darling, are you all right?' she whispered, quickly glancing at each of us in turn to assess our reactions to the situation. 'Guy?'

Guy did not respond and Mr Winniatt continued to scribble away in his notebook.

Helen slowly stood up from her seat and walked over to the two men. Her hand lightly caressed Guy's shoulder, but her eyes did not look in his direction.

'It's nothing, honestly – just thinking of Gina, that's all,' Guy said, his eyes continuing to look down. 'Would you like to dance?' He stood up and, without giving Helen a chance to respond, led her off towards the ballroom. The Winniatts followed them into the ballroom, leaving me and Mrs Brendel sitting at the table like two old maids. But then, just as I was beginning to lose patience with the elderly woman's prattle, Professor Wilbor came to my rescue.

'Would you care to dance?' asked the Professor, a fat man of late middle age with a red face, a shock of grey, untidy hair, an unkempt grey beard and kindly eyes the colour of stewed gooseberries. It was the last thing I wanted to do but what was the alternative? Yet more *Titanic* talk with Mrs Brendel? I had heard enough about that ocean liner to last me a lifetime. And there were certain questions I wanted to ask Professor Wilbor.

'Yes, I would love to, thank you,' I said, standing and taking his hand. But instead of leading me towards the ballroom to join the rest of the swaying couples, he gestured towards his assistant Mr Mabey. 'What could I be thinking? No, you must dance with my colleague here. May I introduce you to Mr Rupert Mabey, one of the finest young archaeologists in England. I don't know what he thinks he is doing working with a shambolic old fool like me, but there you are. Rupert, this is Mrs Agatha Christie.'

The invitation to dance with me was greeted with little enthusiasm. 'How do you do?' he said in a nonchalant manner.

Mr Mabey was a few years younger than me, and when he stood up I became aware of an air of strong, arrogant masculinity. He was handsome with fine features and dark, slicked-back hair. As he led me towards the ballroom he did not look in my direction, and his manner was detached and reserved.

'How long have you been working with Professor Wilbor?' I asked as we stepped onto the dance floor.

'Two years now,' he said, looking over my shoulder. His style of dancing was just like his personality: efficient, but lacking in warmth or passion.

'It must be fascinating work, studying the Guanche culture. I heard they used to mummify their dead, is that correct?'

'Yes, that's right.'

'Like the Egyptians?' I asked, a question that received only a cursory nod of the head. 'I hope you don't think

I'm ghoulish, but you see I write about crime so, of course I'm very interested in the customs of death, rituals and the like.'

'Really?' He obviously regarded me as nothing more than a sexless, middle-aged matron and he made no effort to disguise his lack of interest.

'And what was the process, if you don't mind me asking?'

His voice was monotonal and completely devoid of emotion. 'The body would be washed. The internal organs would be removed. Certain unguents and aromatic woods would be used.'

'And have you found many mummies in Tenerife?'

'A fair number,' he said.

With each step I looked forward to the moment when we might be released from each other's arms.

'I paid a visit to a Guanche cave today,' I said.

'Yes?'

'The one set into the cliff, overlooking Martiánez beach.'

I felt his arms and shoulders go stiff, and for a moment, I thought that he was about to stop in the middle of the ballroom, release me from his grip and let me fall. He glanced at me with renewed interest, almost as if he was seeing me for the first time, and then continued with the dance. Was it my imagination or had his breath suddenly quickened?

'And what did you find? Any skulls? That's the thing the tourists seem to want.' His tone was harsh and mocking. 'Dreadful how so many of them have been looted. I expect they decorate many a suburban mantelpiece in Croydon or Purley.'

101

'No, no skulls I'm afraid,' I said as if I were terribly disappointed. I hesitated deliberately, letting Mr Mabey wait and suffer. A few beads of perspiration appeared on his upper lip, which was free of a moustache, and about his forehead. Could I also smell the faint aroma of fear about him?

'Did – did you find anything else?'

I didn't answer. 'I heard that a body had been found there recently.'

'Yes,' he said.

'And Professor Wilbor was the one who found it?'

'Indeed.'

'Were you with him that day?'

'I was.'

'It must have been an awful shock for you,' I said softly. 'What with—'

'I'm sorry, would you mind if we sat down?' he said as he stopped moving and unhanded me. 'It's just that I'm feeling a little—'

'No, not at all,' I said, relief washing over me.

He led me along the edge of the ballroom back towards the table. Mrs Brendel had retired to bed, leaving Professor Wilbor by himself. When he saw us approach he looked surprised and a little befuddled.

'Back so early? I thought you were having fun!'

'I'm afraid I started to feel a little worse for wear. Perhaps it was the water I had from the spring at lunch-time,' said Mabey.

'My dear boy, come and sit down.'

'Would you mind if I went to my room? I'm terribly

sorry, but I do feel rather out of sorts.' Mabey did look pale and sickly, and perspiration now covered all of his face.

'Of course, of course. Let me know how you feel in the morning. I can always continue with the dig up by Mal Pais without you.'

After Mr Mabey said his goodbyes I took a seat next to Professor Wilbor. We made small talk about the house in Puerto Orotava that he shared with his younger colleague, the hotel and its history, and the climate of the island, before I started to ask him about his love of archaeology. To see the past come to life was a wonderful thing, he said. To uncover the layers of history beneath one's feet, to be able to visualise the customs and habits of ancient cultures was a joy to behold. I could not agree more, I said, and talked a little of my love for the British Museum. He continued to speak of his fascination for the Guanche culture and his ambition to recover their lost language. He then started to demonstrate how some of the people might have talked, employing a curious series of whistles and strange noises. I let him have his fun, before turning to the matter of most interest to me.

'I hope Mr Mabey will feel better tomorrow,' I said. 'He did seem to take a turn for the worst when I mentioned something about a Guanche cave that I had visited earlier today. The one in the cliff, up from Martiánez beach.'

Professor Wilbor's face turned grave. 'Oh, I see, yes,' he said stroking his grey beard. 'I suppose you brought up the question of the body we found there?'

'Yes, I'm afraid I did. Perhaps it wasn't in the best of taste. Oh, I am sorry if I said the wrong thing.'

'You weren't to know,' he said in a quiet, preoccupied manner.

'Know what?'

Professor Wilbor looked down, seemingly unable to say a word.

'Professor Wilbor – what do you mean?'

He looked confused and then angry with himself. 'Oh, dear. I wasn't supposed to say anything.' His big gooseberry eyes moistened a little. 'What a fool. Why couldn't I just keep quiet?'

'Don't blame yourself, please.'

'Mr Mabey found the whole thing very upsetting; it was he who first found the body, you see,' said the Professor, his hands twitching nervously.

'Of course, very distressing indeed,' I said. 'It must have been horrible to find a body – in that condition.'

'So you know that someone had tried to mummify it?'

'Yes, I do. Terrible. And awful for you to see too.'

'Well, of course it was a horrible shock. It was early morning. We had been working on a nearby cave for a few weeks. We had found some Guanche skulls, some bones, some shards of prehistoric ceramic before we moved on to the one overlooking Martiánez beach. Mabey entered the cave first. He had a lamp and when the light illuminated what was on the ground he took a step back. He was in shock, bent double. I think he was nauseous. He was gesturing to me to take a look. I stepped closer, and that's when I saw it. I shouldn't call it that. It was – or had been – a man's body. I will never forget the expression on his face. You see, many people make the mistake of thinking that mummies are things that have never lived. But as an archaeologist, one always has to have in mind that these fascinating objects were once human, once drew breath like you and I. Sorry, I'm going off at a tangent here.'

'I think that's terribly important,' I said softly. 'But what – what did you see?'

'Oh, the most horrible grimace imaginable. As if the man was still feeling the pain of that initial assault, as if the person who had tried to mummify him had also managed to capture the horror and fear of the moment of death itself.'

'How shocking. Who would do such a thing?'

Professor Wilbor fell silent once more. 'I can't imagine. But of course, if that wasn't bad enough . . . Poor Rupert.'

'Yes?'

'The murdered man's skin seemed to have been covered with a dark, viscous substance. At first we thought it was blood. But then it came to light that his body had been covered with sap from the dragon tree. You see, when the sap comes in contact with air it takes on a reddish colour exactly like blood. Of course, you know this was used by the Guanches to mummify their bodies. But it would never have been applied to the skin.'

'I see.'

'Of course it was a horrible shock for both of us. But when I recovered myself I looked at Rupert and he was still on the ground – crying, sobbing, retching. He was in a real state. Rupert had come in contact with the dead before, so I knew there was something else wrong. The depth of his grief signified something else, something more personal.'

Professor Wilbor cleared his throat and took a sip of water. 'I didn't understand at first, because I didn't recognise the body. But Rupert knew who it was – or rather, who it had been – straight away. You see, Douglas Greene and Rupert Mabey were brothers.'

Chapter Thirteen

'Brothers? I don't understand. No wonder he felt unwell just now. How awful.' I felt a blush rising from my neck to my face. 'How insensitive of me.'

'You weren't to know,' said the Professor. 'Actually, I should say half brothers. They shared the same father, but different mothers. Douglas's father, Patrick Mabey, was a botanist, and thirty or so years ago, on a trip to Tenerife to study the wild fauna and flora of the island, he met a beautiful Spanish woman, Francesca. They had a child, a boy – Douglas – conceived in love, but they never married. Patrick's sweetheart died while giving birth and it was thought best by all concerned that the boy be brought up by Francesca's mother and her other daughters. Patrick returned to England, where he married into a grand Devon family – Lucinda, I believe his wife was called – and a few years later Lucinda gave birth to Rupert. Patrick sent money over to his dead lover's family and, later, paid for Douglas's schooling and education in England at a Catholic boarding school in the north. The two boys grew up knowing nothing about each other.'

'But – but,' I stammered, trying to formulate in my mind the questions that began to ricochet like bullets through my brain. I remembered a comment Davison had made about the reaction of Greene's parents when he had broken the news of their son's death. I had thought it odd that the mother had reacted with stoicism while the father had suffered a nervous collapse. Now it made a little more sense. 'But what about their surnames? Why was one called Greene and the other Mabey?'

'Simple – Greene was a translation of the Spanish woman's surname, Verde. When he was enrolled at boarding school it was thought best to give him an English name.'

'And you say neither one of them knew about the other?'

'No, they had no idea. Douglas was told that his father, an Englishman, had died in a swimming accident, that he had been drowned off Martiánez beach, and that a trust had been set up to pay for his education. There was no one in Tenerife who knew of Patrick Mabey and his relationship with Francesca Verde except for her mother and sisters. I believe that after the death of Señora Verde some years back her daughters moved to Spain.'

'So how did the two brothers find out about each other?'

Professor Wilbor drew out a handkerchief from his top pocket and ran it over his sweating face. As he opened his eyes he looked as though he were waking up from some kind of strange dream. 'Oh, I've said too much already,' he said, nervously. 'Listen to me gossiping. Why I'm telling you all of this I don't know.'

'But—'

At this moment, Guy Trevelyan and Helen Hart returned to the table in a wild heat of laughter, their spirits revived by the dancing. Guy asked the Professor if he would care for a brandy or liqueur and the two men started talking about rocks, sediments and suchlike.

'Mr Winniatt and his damnable questions!' exclaimed Miss Hart, her attention directed towards me. She motioned to a pair of seats, and we settled down to converse. 'I think it's a beastly thing to do, don't you, Mrs Christie?'

I tried not to show my annoyance – after all, I was sure Professor Wilbor had been about to tell me something of importance – and instead asked Miss Hart if she wouldn't mind expanding her point.

'Well, I'm sure you must have been mightily fed up being chased like a fox through the country when you disappeared last year. The last thing you probably want is any more questions about it.'

I felt myself blushing. 'Yes, it was rather exhausting for the spirits. That's one of the reasons I am here. To have a good rest.'

'Is it now?' she said, cocking her head, her blonde hair swinging about her pretty face. She studied me with a penetrating glance, before she continued. 'Earlier, at the table, Guy was terribly upset by something Winniatt said. I don't supposed you heard?'

'No, I'm sorry, but I was talking to Mrs Brendel.'

'He won't tell me, the beast, no doubt trying to protect me,' she said, gazing over at Guy with affection and amusement. She lowered her voice so only I could hear.

'I suppose Winniatt must have asked him something about Gina.'

'It's natural to be upset by such a question. But why don't you ask Mr Winniatt?'

'He's gone to bed, I believe. No doubt to write everything down. For "posterity".' She imitated Winniatt's pomposity in a way that made me smile.

'How do you know the Winniatts?'

'Howard and Daisy? Oh, we met them the first night on the *Gelria*. He may seem quite serious, but I'm certain that underneath that pompous exterior is someone quite wild. I think you find that with some people. They seem one thing, but deep down they are something rather different. Don't you agree?' Again Miss Helen studied me closely, as if she were trying to see beneath my skin or into my brain.

'Yes, I do believe you're right.'

'Do you have a secret side, Mrs Christie?'

'I'm sure all of us do,' I said, brushing a strand of hair back from my face. 'We would be the most terrible bores if we were all just what we seemed.'

'So what's yours?'

I hesitated.

'Oh come on. You know everything about Guy and me. Look at the scene you witnessed on the boat – or rather scenes, I'm afraid. I think it's your turn to spill the beans. Just what is it you're doing here? Guy and I have been debating the real reason. Come on.'

'Well, as you know, I had my fair share of unhappiness in England towards the end of last year.'

'Yes, now what was that about? It all seemed very queer if you ask me. I didn't really believe the nonsense in the newspapers that you had lost your memory.'

'The newspapers did write an awful lot of twaddle about it. But I'm afraid that is the truth of the matter. The doctors thought it was an attack of amnesia brought on by the death of my mother, my inability to write and my, my—'

'Your brute of a husband having an affair with . . . was it his secretary?'

'Not quite, but—'

'But even so, I don't understand how you could lose your memory and yet do the kind of things you did. For instance, when you were in Harrogate—'

I really could not allow her to continue to question me like this. 'I'm afraid the doctors have said it's something I mustn't dwell on. Forgive me.'

'You don't want to talk about it? Yes, I understand. I perfectly understand.' Helen paused as she took out a small mother-of-pearl cigarette case, lit a cigarette, inhaled deeply and blew out the smoke in my direction. 'I must go to bed. So many things to do at the studio tomorrow.' She picked up her jewelled evening bag and stood up. Before walking over to Guy, Helen turned to me and said, 'Winniatt was telling me what he'd seen earlier today. About you and a fair-haired gentleman down towards the beach. Winniatt said he thought he'd seen him on the boat over here. Very romantic, meeting on an ocean liner.'

'Oh no, it's nothing like you think—'

'Don't worry, your secret is safe with me. As you know, I'm in no position to judge.'

As Helen joined Guy and took his arm to walk out of the dining room, together with Professor Wilbor, she looked back at me with a triumphant smile. She had, or so she believed, found out a piece of information that seemed to suggest that I was a woman of her temperament, subject to the same needs, desires and sins of the flesh as she.

'Love has the power to turn us all into criminals,' she whispered with a sphinx-like smile as she said goodnight.

Chapter Fourteen

I woke up feeling as disoriented as I had on the *Gelria*. The tilting motion I had experienced on the ship had returned, but its source was not so much a physical one but something psychological in origin. It was as if some outside force was playing with my perception, undermining what I had assumed to be true. I had to question everything I had previously considered as a statement of fact.

Professor Wilbor's revelation left me wondering about Davison once more. Did he know that Greene and Mabey were brothers? Surely he must have done, as his relationship with Greene had been intimate. But why hadn't he told me? What was he trying to hide? Wilbor, I knew, had felt nervous about revealing so much about the background of the two men, but who was he afraid of? Could it be Grenville? Did the specialist in the black arts have some kind of hold over him? After all, it was interesting that Wilbor never mentioned his name during the course of our conversation. And what of Winniatt? What had he seen? How much did he know about my friendship with the man he took to be a stranger I had met on the voyage over? How could he know of Davison's real identity or the purpose of our mission here? And what of Helen Hart? She suspected something, but hopefully Winniatt's sighting of Davison and me had put her off the scent.

The maid had already delivered my morning tea to my room. As I took a sip, I thought of Helen Hart's parting words as she had said goodnight. They were, I knew, true enough. Love could turn people into criminals; it also had the power to drive us insane. I thought of Violet's reaction to the news of Edmund's illness, and the threat that she would kill herself if she was not allowed to marry him. I pictured poor Gina Trevelyan standing on the side of the *Gelria*, then stepping off the ship into the sea. I recollected the nasty scenes on board the ocean liner, when Helen Hart and Guy Trevelyan were dealing with the grief and guilt and shock brought on by the news of Gina's death. I thought of Davison's love for Douglas Greene and the sadness in his eyes when he thought of the fate of his dear friend. I even allowed myself to run over my feelings for Archie, a man who I had assumed would stay with me until my dying day.

How could love, something supposed to be so magical and transformative, even divine, have the power to wreck lives and turn us into savages?

'Mummy! Mummy! Are you awake?' said Rosalind, bursting through the connecting door. She jumped up in bed with me, her skin smooth, soft and warm after a good night's sleep.

At least this type of love – the pure love a mother felt for her daughter – seemed not to be so prone to the same kinds of problems as those one often saw in relationships based on sexual desire. But then I had encountered mothers jealous of their daughters' beauty, frustrated that they were losing their looks and their allure. I had known a widowed woman consumed with anger because her estranged daughter had married a rich man, while she herself had to face the prospect of a lonely old age in penury. And then there were the fathers and sons! Human relationships of whatever kind were so very complicated and fascinating. That was what made them such good material. Winniatt's insult came back to me. The pompous man knew nothing! I thought of some of the greatest, most critically acclaimed works of Western literature. What were the *Oresteia*, *Hamlet*, *Bleak House* and *The Duchess of Malfi* but brilliantly told crime stories? A line from Webster's play whispered its sinister meaning to me. '*Cover her face; mine eyes dazzle: she died young.*' Beautiful words, yes, but why had they come into my mind?

'Mummy, can I play with Raymond this afternoon?' asked Rosalind from the womb-like space under the blankets.

'Yes, of course darling. You're on holiday and you can do whatever you like.'

'I know he pretends not to be sad, but he must be sometimes. Like his governess, Madame something-or-other – oh, I can't pronounce her name. I think she must be sad. Raymond must miss his brother, don't you think?'

'Yes, I'm sure he does. And it's very kind of you to want to cheer him up.'

'I'll go and tell Carlo,' she said, bolting out of the bed and into the next room.

I proceeded to wash, dress and took breakfast downstairs at a table on the terrace. As I made some notes for my new novel I felt the soft rays of the sun warm my face. In the distance there was Teide, rising up like a shadow of death. I thought of what Davison had told me about Grenville and the rumours about his ghastly scheme. Surely that could not be true? Even though the air temperature was beginning to rise, I shivered. How would I be able to find out Grenville's intentions? Was Violet the key? Would she betray her father? She was obviously quite angry with him for his refusal to give permission for her desired marriage to Edmund Ffosse. If I persuaded Violet to turn against her father, would she reveal everything she knew about the murder of Douglas Greene? Or was there another way? Grenville himself told me that he had admired some of my supernatural stories. Could I convince him that my interest went beyond the literary?

I spent the morning with Carlo. We did a little work – me dictating, Carlo typing – but my heart wasn't in it. Carlo suspected something was wrong – she kept stealing a concerned glance over at me when she thought I wasn't looking – and so I talked about my lack of faith in the new novel. It was true enough – *The Mystery of the Blue Train* lacked something, was it drive, energy, verve? – but of course this was not the whole story. Rosalind also kept interrupting, which didn't help my efforts at concentration. At one point, I'm afraid I rather lost my temper with her – this was when she had burst into my room for the fifth or sixth time in an hour asking whether it was time to go and play with Raymond – and so I sent her away in tears.

'If only I could be here to relax like the rest of the visitors,' I said to Carlo. 'What a heaven that would be!'

'Can't the book wait?' she asked.

'I wish it could. But from now on, we can't depend on Mr Christie to help us.'

'I suppose not,' she said.

'But I'm determined not to give up. I'll finish this book even if it kills me.'

'I wish you wouldn't say things like that,' she said, a serious tone to her voice.

'It's only an expression, Carlo.'

'It may be, but all the same, you don't want to tempt fate.'

'Oh, nonsense,' I said, somewhat irritably. 'Anyway, I think we've done enough for today, don't you? I've got an appointment to take tea. Would you mind watching Rosalind?'

'Of course,' said Carlo, looking down. It was obvious I had hurt her feelings. 'Who are you going to see?'

'No one you know.' The words came out sharper than I had intended. I saw Carlo's wounded expression, and although I tried to explain that they were a father and daughter, residents of the island, not guests of the hotel, the damage had been done.

'Forgive me, Carlo,' I said, tears stinging my eyes. 'I didn't mean to say anything to upset you. It was just that—'

Carlo came to me and wrapped me in her arms as though I were a child. 'I understand,' she said softly. 'It's been hard for you. You're still getting over . . . last year.'

She was, in a way, quite right. But she knew nothing of the true horrors I had been forced to endure. Or, almost certainly, the horrors that were yet to come.

'Thank you, Carlo. I don't know how I would have ever managed without you.'

Chapter Fifteen

I carried a vision of Carlo's angelic face with me as I walked through the hotel grounds towards Mal Pais. I kept telling myself that Grenville was nothing more than a showman, albeit a sinister one, and he really didn't possess any dark powers or occult abilities. But the anxious look Gustavo gave me when I asked at the hotel desk for directions to the house worried me, as did the fragments of conversation that I recalled between Grenville and his daughter.

I had attended a séance or two, and had sat at a table when a ouija board had been used, but part of me had always been sceptical about so-called mediumship. All that theatricality: the dimmed lights, the banging on tables, the strange voices. And yet, and yet ... could there be something in it? I was certain that some people, such as my mother, were more instinctive than others. But she had been a sincerely good person. What if a person had these talents, then used them in the name of evil? That was a truly frightening prospect.

I had arranged to meet Davison at the gates of Mal Pais, but was in no mood to see him. How could he expect me to help him investigate a murder when I was not in full possession of the facts? I thought back to the excruciating moment in the ballroom when I had been dancing with Rupert Mabey. I took a few deep breaths, but my anger would not dissipate. First of all, Davison had kept back the secret that he had had a close relationship with Douglas Greene. That was, I acknowledged, understandable. His reputation, his very career, was at stake. If that information fell into the wrong hands, such as unscrupulous blackmailers, or even the so-called right hands, such as the police, he could face prison and ruin. But this? Why keep the connection between Douglas Greene and Rupert Mabey a secret? I would have to say something to Davison, even if it meant a rupture in our friendship.

After walking through the manicured grounds, I passed into a section of garden that seemed to have been allowed to grow wild with prickly pears, cacti, fig trees and low-lying palms. A path here led up to a tall iron gate, the entrance to Mal Pais, where I saw Davison waiting for me. I did not meet his eye and refused to greet his smile.

'Agatha, are you all right?'

'Yes, I'm very well, thank you,' I said coldly.

'Oh dear, what have I done wrong?'

There was no point in sulking. I had to say something. 'When were you going to tell me that Douglas Greene and Rupert Mabey were related? That they were half-brothers?' I deliberately kept my voice low so as not to be heard by anybody who might be lurking nearby.

His face became serious. 'I see. You've found that out already, have you?' Davison also spoke in a whisper.

'Yes, what did you take me for?'

He didn't answer.

'Look, as far as I'm concerned,' I went on, 'I can travel to Santa Cruz tomorrow and wait for the first available boat to take me back to England. I don't need to be here. I've got work to do, a book to finish. I can't afford to waste my time.'

'I'm sorry. I should have told you.'

'But why didn't you? Perhaps you've got something to hide after all.'

'You know that's not the case,' he said, his face reddening slightly. He took a deep breath as he ran his fingers through his blond hair. 'The truth is, I wanted you to come to this situation with a completely fresh perspective. I didn't want you to be blinded by certain things that I thought might obscure your perception of the case.'

'I would have thought this was essential to the understanding of the crime. It was quite embarrassing. I was dancing with Mr Mabey and started prattling on about how I had visited a Guanche cave. I knew that the Professor had discovered the body and I started to ask Mr Mabey about it. The poor man turned white and had to leave the ballroom and return to his room. I felt so stupid, so callous and unfeeling.'

'Yes, but there's something I didn't tell you on purpose, something that—'

At that instant the gate opened to reveal the great bulk of Grenville standing there with his arms spread wide in

121

welcome. A huge smile cut into his face, showing off his rotting teeth.

'*Buenas tardes y bienvenidos,*' he said in a perfect Spanish accent. 'Please come in.'

He gestured for us to step inside the gate. We smiled a little awkwardly – had he heard our whispers? – and entered an enormous walled garden. My first impression was of a tropical paradise, a botanic garden with tall, fleshy plants that stretched up to the sky, ridiculously gaudy flowers and unusual exotic specimens I had never seen before. Butterflies the size of small birds fluttered around the garden, and the deep hum of insects vibrated in the air. Grenville witnessed our astonishment, a reaction that obviously pleased him.

'Yes, it's quite extraordinary I'm sure you'll agree,' he said, leading us down a path, past some clusters of white and pink oleander bushes. 'When I first arrived on the island, fifteen or so years ago now, this was nothing but a patch of barren earth. *Mal Pais.* Bad land.'

'You must have worked terribly hard to achieve this,' said Davison.

'I did. I cleared away the top layer and imported some soil. But do you want to know what the secret is?'

We looked expectantly at him. 'Blood and bone, blood and bone.' He watched for our reactions. When we didn't say anything, he added, 'That in itself is not unusual. However in this case . . .' But he left the sentence hanging for full effect. 'Yes, a great deal of planning and, of course, cultivation.' He stopped to finger the leaves of what was called a Carissa plant. 'We have a wide range of delightful varieties here.'

As he pointed around the beds, which seemed to have been arranged according to some sort of pattern, Grenville recited the names of the plants: cardoon, angel's trumpet, the calla lily, lantana, poinsettia, henbane and hemlock. I remembered how Socrates had been killed. It was this, the last name in Grenville's list, that caused me to come to the slow realisation of the true nature of his seeming paradise. Grenville had created a garden full of evil.

'I see, Mrs Christie, that you understand something of the characteristic of these plants,' he said, watching me closely.

'Yes, I think I do. All of the plants have the capacity to cause some degree of harm to the human body.'

'Exactly so,' he said. 'For instance, hemlock, or at least this species, *Conium maculatum*, acts very like curare on the human nervous system, causing muscular paralysis and death due to lack of oxygen to the brain and heart. The ingestion of six or eight leaves would be enough to lead to death. Isn't that fascinating? I know, just by reading your books, that you have a great deal of knowledge on the subject and I was keen to share my little hobby with you.'

'Yes, thank you,' I said, trying not to look too horrified by what I saw. 'Quite fascinating.'

'And look, the dear *Ricinus communis*,' he said, referring to what I knew to be the castor oil plant. 'It looks so harmless. And indeed, the castor oil produced by its seeds is considered to be a tonic for small children, invalids and the like. But its seed also contains ricin. Eating, or I should say chewing, the innocent-looking seeds results in a burning sensation in the mouth and terrible stomach pain.

Subsequent effects include severe dehydration and a drop in blood pressure, followed by seizure and death with three to five days. Oh yes, a very powerful little plant indeed.'

He gazed around with pride. 'I suppose you could call this a poisoner's paradise,' he said. 'I've got everything I need here to protect myself and those I love. Not that I would go to such extreme measures, you understand. But it's nice to know it's here – just in case.' I thought of my own little set of poisons, which I had secured away safe and out of sight in a locked suitcase at the hotel. I hoped I would never have to use them again.

Grenville continued to lead us through the elaborate paths of the garden, up a steep path and onto a rocky out-crop. From here, we looked down onto a cluster of dragon trees, their top branches splaying out to form an impressive umbrella-shaped canopy.

'A wonderful display of the *Dracaena draco*,' said Davison. First his expertise on Guanche civilisation. Now his knowledge of botany. Was he an expert on everything? 'And, of course, the "blood" from the dragon tree has been put to many different uses over the years.'

I knew what Davison was up to. Greene's body, after being drained of its own blood, had been painted with the red sap from the tree. I watched Grenville to see if he reacted in any way, but his toad-like features did not register any sign of distress.

'Yes, I believe it's been used to treat watery eyes, minor burns, dysentery, the spitting of blood and suchlike, so the garden is not just full of things that do harm,' said Grenville. 'Of course, I harvest it for my own purposes.

I've tried it as an ink, very good for inscribing magical seals and talismans. And it also seems to increase the potency of certain spells.'

He looked first at Davison and then at me. 'I hope what I say doesn't shock you? I'm sure both of you are sophisticated and educated enough to understand the subtleties of what I do. Some of the things that have been written about me have been complete fabrications, indeed libellous. Of course, I could have sued the various publications and individuals, but to do so would only admit to a form of bourgeois thinking that is against my general ethos, don't you think? Anyway, why don't we go inside, have tea and we can have a nice chat? Violet isn't here, but I expect her back very soon.'

We followed him along a walkway lined with palms and towards an enormous house. It was Spanish in style rather than English, with a series of arches that ran the length of a verandah, and, on its first and second floors, a number of elaborately carved wooden galleries decorated with various pots containing brightly coloured flowers. Grenville led us through the doorway into an open courtyard paved with white marble, in the centre of which stood a tall, thin palm tree. The two levels of galleries, with a series of columns, had been created from dark wood into which a number of scenes or tableaux had been carved. In pots around the courtyard stood exotic plants, including the vivid bird-of-paradise with its bright orange and violet flowers, and another plant which boasted an almost obscene display of open fleshy redness twinned with a bright yellow stamen.

'I see you admiring my collection of *Anthurium andraeanum*,' said Grenville. 'A thing of strange beauty, don't you think? The flamingo flower with its red ovate spathe and then the erect yellow spadix, a plant combining certain elements of the female and the male.'

'What an extraordinary house,' I said, changing the subject.

'Thank you,' said Grenville. 'It mostly dates back to the late seventeenth century. The beams are of Canarian pine, the ceilings and columns carry some very interesting detailing. But that's for another day. I want to know more about your fascination for the supernatural, Mrs Christie. Please sit down.'

He gestured towards four basket chairs that had been arranged in a loggia formed under the first floor. An elderly Spanish woman, thin and pale and careworn, brought in a silver tray of tea things.

'How did your interest begin?' he asked, his eyes fixed on mine.

I began to talk about my mother and her psychic gifts, her uncanny ability to know what those close to her were thinking. I recalled how I had started to read the stories of May Sinclair, and how I had tried to write tales in a similar manner. But then I also told him about a friend I had had, Wilfred Pirie, who had tried to indoctrinate me in the wisdom of theosophy, which I had found nonsensical. Pirie had related to me stories about two young women who were mediums. Some of the anecdotes about them were too ridiculous to be true and, as a result, I lost all respect for him.

'Whereas you, Mr Grenville, I believe you have something very special,' I said. 'From my briefest of meetings with you I feel that you have a gift.'

'Thank you, my dear,' he said. 'And I feel the same about your abilities. I can sense that you have a great store of psychic energy that has not yet been fully tapped.'

'Do you think so? Well, I wouldn't know where to start.'

'Everyone has these reserves, even you, Mr Blake,' he said, smiling at Davison. 'And really it's just knowing how to build and strengthen and sharpen the sense. I can help you if you like.'

'Could you? I wouldn't want to take up any of your precious time.'

'Not at all, Mrs Christie. It would be a pleasure. In fact, if you have got nothing planned we could even start now.'

'I'm not sure if we—' said Davison, looking distinctly uncomfortable.

'I don't think I need to get back until six o'clock,' I said.

'Very well. If you will excuse me for a moment, I'll go and bring my Tarot cards.'

With some effort, he pushed himself out of the chair and crossed the courtyard and up the stairs to the first floor.

'What are you thinking of?' hissed Davison.

'You said yourself that if we are ever going to discover who killed Greene we must find out more about Grenville. I need to get close to him.'

'Yes, I realise that, but is this the right way to go about it? I'm not sure I trust him.'

'Of course you don't trust him. Neither do I. But how else—'

At that moment I saw Grenville's huge form appear at the top of the stairs. His dark eyes flashed with an excitement bordering on the manic.

'Now, this set of Tarot cards is incredibly powerful, very potent energy indeed,' he said as he descended. 'It was said, when I bought them from a dealer in Paris, that they were coloured with the blood of several virgins.' As he walked towards us, he watched us carefully before he burst into laughter. 'Sorry, that's just my odd sense of humour, you'll have to forgive me. No, the cards were coloured with nothing more than dead animal and vegetable matter, the cochineal beetle, the dragon tree and suchlike.' He paused as he looked at me and then Davison, and then continued, 'Actually, Mrs Christie, I think this would work much better upstairs, in one of the private rooms. The courtyard is just too light and open. We need an enclosed space to concentrate your energies. If you could please follow me.'

'Of course,' said Davison, rising from the chair.

'I would be grateful if you would remain here, Mr Blake,' said Grenville.

'I'm not sure whether—' said Davison.

'Don't worry, Mr Blake, I'll only be upstairs,' I said, interrupting him.

'Are you quite certain?' he said. The words did not convey the depth of Davison's concern, but the anxiety that darkened his eyes certainly did.

'Yes, I'll be quite all right,' I said breezily, as I followed

Grenville towards the stairs. Inside, I felt my heart begin to beat faster, my stomach turning to liquid.

'We won't be long, only half an hour, or so,' said Grenville. 'Please help yourself to some more tea. And feel free to look around the house and garden too. I've got a good collection of Guanche figurines and ceramics in the library that you may find intriguing.'

'Thank you,' said Davison.

'Now, if you come this way, Mrs Christie,' said Grenville. 'I think you'll find the experiment most interesting.'

I followed him up the stairs to the first floor and along the open gallery, with its thick floorboards darkened by age. We passed a large drawing room, full of baroque paintings and blackened mirrors, and entered a study with walls the colour of blood. Grenville gestured to one of the chairs around a small baize table. As I sat down I noticed that on the walls were a number of woodcuts and engravings of beasts with cloven hooves, ravens, skulls and other representations of the occult arts. In the corner of the room stood Grenville's desk, covered with papers.

Grenville cleared his throat. 'I'd like you to take a number of deep breaths and clear your mind of any worries and concerns you may have,' he said, still standing. 'Now, close your eyes.'

I did as he wished, trying to forget the images that flashed through my mind like a horrible *tableau vivant*: the shadowy figure I had encountered in the cave; the mummified body of Douglas Greene; the sight of Gina Trevelyan throwing herself from the ship; the spectacle of poor Violet Grenville ministering to Edmund Ffosse; the dangerous beauty of Grenville's poison garden and those horrific portrayals of Satan that hung on the walls of the study.

'Yes, that's right, a few more deep breaths,' said Grenville. I then felt a light touch on the top of my head, which I presumed to be Grenville's hand resting on my skull. I heard him breathing behind me and felt, or at least imagined I felt, the light brush of his thigh against my shoulder.

'I'm going to pass you the Tarot pack now – hold out your hands.' A moment later I felt the cards in my palms. 'We will start simply. Shuffle the pack and continue to clear your mind. Then ask the Tarot a question and, after placing the cards on the table, cut the pack with your left hand. Yes, that's right, the table is just a little to your left.' I did as he said and, even though I had my doubts, asked the question to myself: 'Who is responsible for the murder of Douglas Greene?'

'Then, with your right hand, take a card from the pack,' said Grenville. 'Now you can turn— '

Just then Grenville's words were interrupted by shouts of distress from downstairs.

'Help! Father! Father!' It was Violet's voice.

I dropped the card, opened my eyes and followed Grenville as he bolted from the room. We ran down the gallery and saw Violet being comforted by Davison at the entrance to the house. She was in a terrible state, crying, gasping for breath, unable to get out her words. Her eyes were wide with terror, her face was even paler than normal and her hands were shaking.

'Darling, what is it? What on earth is the matter?' Grenville ran towards her.

'It's – it's all too horrible, I can't—'

'Just calm down now, take a few deep breaths,' he said.

Her desperate, frantic eyes jumped from her father to Davison to me and to the Spanish maid, who had heard the commotion.

'I've seen something, something in the – the—,' she said before her voice fragmented.

'Take your time, darling,' said Grenville. 'Come and sit down. Oh, you're shaking. Consuela, *la botella de cognac, por favor.*' The maid disappeared to fetch the brandy.

'It was in – in the *rambla*. I was walking home from La Paz. It was when I was passing over the bridge. Something caught my eye. Something red. I looked down into the barranco. I wasn't sure what it was to begin with. I knew there was something not right, but I didn't know what. I just couldn't take it in.'

'Violet? What was it?' asked Grenville.

'Blood on the rocks,' she said, taking a sip of the brandy that the maid poured for her. 'And a shape, a body.'

'Who was it?' asked Davison. 'Did you manage to see?'

'No, as soon as I saw it I ran here. I didn't know what else to do.'

'Was it a man or a woman?' asked Davison.

'A man,' she said.

'Do you think he might still be alive?' I asked.

The girl did not respond. Instead, she gazed in front of her with a horrified expression as if the body lay on the ground by her feet.

131

'Violet, listen to me,' I said. 'It's very important. We may still be able to save the person's life. Do you think the man you saw is still alive?'

'He may be, but I'm not sure. There was so much . . . the redness on the rocks. Oh, Father!' She burst into tears and Grenville cradled her in his arms.

'Quick, we must do everything we can to try and save him, if it's not too late,' I said. 'I trained as a nurse in the war, so I may be able to help.'

I turned to Grenville. 'Can we borrow your car?'

He hesitated for a moment. 'Yes, but—'

'Thank you. Violet, you must come with us, and tell us where you saw this . . . accident.' I suspected it was anything but an accident, but this was no time for accusations of murder. That could come later.

'Do I have to? Oh Father, it was so horrible. Couldn't I—'

'Violet, I think you should do what Mrs Christie suggests,' said Grenville. 'Don't worry, I'll come with you.'

'And could you ask your maid to fetch the doctor from the hotel? Would he know where to find us?'

'Yes, of course, I'll give him directions, but he should know the spot all right,' said Grenville.

'Quickly,' I said. 'We may only have a matter of minutes, if that.'

Grenville, Violet, Davison and I all jumped into the car. But when Grenville tried to start the vehicle nothing happened.

'Damn,' he said. 'This Ford has always been temperamental, but it would have to be now.' He jumped out and started to hand-crank the car, but nothing happened. 'Blasted thing! Come on!'

I felt the sweat prick the back of my neck. 'How far is it? Violet, how far from here?'

'About ten minutes on foot,' she said.

Grenville continued with the hand cranking, but again the car did not start.

'Let's go,' I said, taking hold of her arm and pulling her out of the car. 'Show me.'

'But—'

'Come on,' I said, digging my fingers into her wrist.

'Father—'

'I'll meet you down there,' said Grenville. 'And if I get the car moving, I'll pick you up. Do what Mrs Christie says.'

We started to run along a dusty track that led from Mal Pais, along the back of the grounds of the Taoro, towards an abandoned onion seed farm.

'Was there any sign of breathing?' I said. The afternoon clouds had started to dissipate, and the sun beat down onto the back of my neck. My face felt flushed and lines of perspiration were soaking into my clothes.

'Not that I could see,' said Violet. 'But I was only look-ing from the bridge. Do you think I should have gone down into the *rambla* to help? Could I have saved him? Oh, but I couldn't. You'll understand, when you see.'

Gasping for breath, we arrived at the wooden bridge, our faces red and our clothes dusty and stained. I looked around me. There were no houses in sight.

'Where was—'

I stopped in mid sentence. Looking down from the bridge, I saw a trail of blood splattered against the rocks below. A few feet farther down into the dry river bed, surrounded by a clump of white wild oleander, lay what looked like a dummy wearing a soiled linen suit.

'Oh, my word,' I said as I started to ease myself down the side of the *rambla*. 'You stay up here in case the doctor arrives,' I shouted back to Violet.

The rocks were sharp, and some of them cut into my hands. At one point I slipped, ripping my skirt and bruising my thigh. I strained my eyes towards the crumpled heap below, watching for signs of life. As I approached, my training as a VAD nurse came to the fore. I had seen some truly horrific sights in the war, so I assumed nothing would shock me. It was then, as I was able to get a closer look at the body, that I understood Violet's words about her mind not being able to comprehend what she had seen. I too felt the same thing. There was something not right about what lay here, in this ugly heap, on the rocks.

I moved quickly, finding an arm to check for a pulse. There was nothing. I was too late.

I began to study the top of the body. The head was turned away from me and it was obvious that a great deal of blood had been lost. As I moved around to examine the face I gasped in disbelief. The corpse was that of Mr Winniatt. And sticking out of his right eye was the bloodied spike of a bird-of-paradise flower.

Chapter Sixteen

'Is there any hope?' called out Violet from the bridge.

'No, I'm afraid not.'

'Who . . . who is it?'

'It's a guest at the hotel, Mr Winniatt,' I shouted. 'Did you know him?'

'No, no I didn't. How awful. Do you think it was a terrible accident?'

I did not respond. I looked down at the body. There was nothing I could do to bring back the life that had been taken, but I still felt the overwhelming urge to give Winniatt respect and dignity in death. I would have liked to have reassembled the bent, twisted limbs in a way that I thought fitting, but I knew that the Inspector would want to see the body in its original state. I couldn't even close the poor man's eyes.

In the distance I heard the sound of an engine.

'That's Father,' Violet called down. 'He must have managed to get the car to start.'

I had not particularly liked Mr Winniatt, what with

his talk of high literature and his project to document experience in an unmediated form. What was it that his wife had said? 'Oh, he never goes anywhere without his notebook.' Without thinking I stretched out my hands and began to look through the pockets of his blood-splattered linen jacket. I did the same with his trouser pockets, but still nothing. On the ground near the body were a pair of shattered spectacles, a copy of a German novel called *Der Zauberberg*, a bookmark, a fountain pen, a handful of Spanish coins and a photograph of Daisy Winniatt, its top right-hand corner torn. Despite my feelings for him, the sight of the dead man's belongings brought tears to my eyes.

'Mrs Christie? Mrs Christie?' It was Grenville from above. 'Violet says we're too late to save him. A guest from the hotel?'

'Yes, I'm afraid so,' I shouted.

'What a terrible accident,' he replied.

I thought of the clump of bird-of-paradise flowers I had seen in Grenville's garden earlier.

'Could you send Mr Blake down?' I asked.

'Of course,' shouted Grenville.

A moment later, Davison steadied himself as he descended the slope into the *rambla*. His first thoughts were for me.

'Are you all right?' he asked, his kind eyes searching my face.

'Yes, but . . .'

We both looked at the terrible sight that lay before us. I pointed out the head injuries, the bird-of-paradise flower, the fact that Mr Winniatt's notebook was missing.

'I don't understand it,' whispered Davison. 'First Douglas in the cave. And now, Winniatt, like – like this. It seems so random, yet—'

'I don't think so,' I said.

'Everything points to Grenville, doesn't it? That stuff about the car not starting was nonsense. After a couple of attempts I told him that I would give it a go. He reluctantly agreed, and when I tried the car started like a dream.'

'So you think he was trying to delay us finding the body? In case Winniatt was still alive and could tell us something?'

'It certainly looks like it. What are we going to do?' said Davison anxiously. 'I suppose now it's only a matter of time before Núñez arrives on the scene.'

'Which means that—'

'That I'm going to have to make myself scarce, I'm afraid.' He paused. 'Agatha, I don't like this, not one bit. I couldn't live with myself if any harm came to you.'

I couldn't bring myself to say that I would be all right, that no harm would come to me. Instead, I asked, 'How much time do you think we have before Núñez arrives?'

I looked up at the bridge. Grenville and Violet were staring down into the dry river bed, but I was certain they could not hear us.

'It depends where he is on the island. But half a day at the most.'

'What will you do?'

'I know a little *hostal* in Icod de los Vinos. I'll go there. Let me tell you where it is in case you need to get hold of me there.'

The sound of small stones falling down the bank made me look up. Grenville peered over into the *rambla*.

'Do you need me to do anything?' he shouted.

With his great bulk, Grenville could easily pick up a large rock and hurl it down, crushing our heads or fatally injuring us. Davison obviously had the same thought.

'We need to get out of here,' he whispered to me before shouting up to Grenville, 'Could you go to the hotel? We should fetch the doctor and inform the police.'

After giving me details about his *hostal* in Icod, Davison helped me climb back up to the bridge, where Grenville was waiting with a large, outstretched hand. I looked down at my clothes covered in dust, dirt and even a spot or two of blood.

'I just don't understand it,' said Grenville. 'Do you think he fell? Or do you think he intended to die? Perhaps there was something in his life that was making him unhappy.'

'That's for the police to decide,' said Davison. He kept the description of the body brief, and did not mention the detail of the bird-of-paradise spike projecting from Winniatt's right eye.

'Yes, I see,' said Grenville, as he helped Violet, who was still weeping, into the car. The engine started promptly. 'When all this is over we must get back to our little experiment, Mrs Christie.'

'I'm sorry?' I couldn't help the look of surprise from stealing across my face.

'Yes, indeed, I believe you must have a great deal of

untapped energy,' he continued. 'Didn't you see the card that you had selected from the Tarot pack?'

I replied that I had not.

'It showed a figure, a skeleton dressed in armour, riding a white horse.'

'And its meaning?' I asked.

'The triumph of death,' he said.

Chapter Seventeen

After Grenville and Violet had left the scene of the crime we stayed with the body until Dr Trenkel and a couple of porters from the hotel arrived. We informed Trenkel, a steely type with cold Germanic good looks and ice-blue eyes, of what we had found. No, we had not touched the body, we told him, except for checking for the pulse. Trenkel could not say for certain how long Winniatt had been dead, but he estimated it to be in the region of four to seven hours. He told us that he would break the tragic news to Mrs Winniatt and would communicate all the necessary details to Inspector Núñez, who had been summoned and would no doubt want to question us at our convenience.

'Núñez is going to have a shock when he finds that one of the witnesses has disappeared,' said Davison as we made our way back to the hotel. 'I suppose it will be only a matter of time before he puts two and two together and realises that Mr Alexander Blake is none other than the man he suspects of killing Douglas Greene.'

'Yes, but I can't see what else you can do – apart from turn yourself in, that is.'

'Now, we don't have much time,' he said. 'As soon as I get back to the Taoro I'll leave for Icod. And there are certain things you need to know, things that I didn't tell you.'

'Such as the fact that Greene and Mabey are brothers?'

'Yes, and there's more. You see, we've suspected Rupert Mabey of being a Bolshevik agent for some time. The last time he was in England he met someone who works for a joint-stock trading company called Arcos. The name may not mean anything to you, but we believe that Arcos – the All-Russian Co-operative Society, based at 49 Moorgate – is a front for a range of highly subversive activities. Perhaps Douglas found out something about Mabey, something that linked him to the Soviets.'

'I see,' I said. 'So you think that Mabey could have killed Greene?'

'It's certainly a possibility,' he said. 'When I came over to Tenerife last year I felt it was my duty to tell Douglas about his blood link to Mabey. Of course, to begin with he didn't believe it, thought it was some surreal game I was playing, but then he realised I was telling the truth. He asked me how long I had known about the connection and he was – quite rightly – angry that I had kept the information from him.'

'But would Mabey have gone so far as to kill his own brother?'

'I suppose he would never have thought of him like that. And agents have done worse things.'

141

What an empty world Davison inhabited. Was it all worth it? All those killings and double crosses and betrayals. For what? King and Country. Yes. And freedom. But still . . .

'Look, I wouldn't mind in the least if you decided that this was all too much,' he said. 'I know you have your life, your daughter, your own work. Hartford, back in London, would completely understand.'

I thought of the delicious prospect of bundling up Rosalind and taking her back on the first boat to England. I would see the old familiar face of Torquay with its creamy villas and seven hills and lovely bays. I could walk where my mother and father had once walked, where I had played as a child, where I had learnt to read and tell stories, where I had been bathed in happiness.

But what would happen to Davison? He would no doubt be arrested for the murder of Douglas Greene, perhaps even that of Winniatt too. Even if he escaped that charge, evidence of his intimate friendship with Greene would get back to his seniors and he would face certain disgrace. Recently he had lost his best friend, Una, and his closest companion, Greene. I would not fail him now.

'My mother brought me up better than that,' I said. 'No, I've given you my word and my word is never broken.'

'Thank you, Agatha,' he said, his voice breaking. 'I won't forget this.'

We parted before we entered the Taoro's grounds. Inside, I tried to slip upstairs to my room unnoticed, but Helen Hart and Guy Trevelyan spotted me.

'Oh my goodness, Mrs Christie, what on earth has

happened to you?' shrieked Miss Hart, looking at my dishevelled appearance.

'Are you all right?' asked Trevelyan.

I told them that I had suffered a fall while riding. Of course the news would leak out soon enough, but I could not face the inevitable series of questions that would accompany the truth. I just hoped I did not meet poor Daisy Winniatt, as I was sure I would not have been able to lie to her. Fortunately, I managed to enter my room unobserved; even Carlo and Rosalind were out. I undressed rapidly and ran a bath, scrubbing my skin hard with soap to erase the stench of murder.

Davison had packed his things and left the hotel before the gong sounded for dinner. The noise, instead of promising the delights of the evening, only struck fear into my heart. With Davison gone I had nothing but my wits to protect me. Thank goodness I had brought my secret leather pouch containing the selection of poisons. As I walked through the corridors of the hotel I recited some of the names silently to myself – *aconite, belladonna, cyanide* – an alphabet of death that, in a strange way, soothed my spirits.

Chapter Eighteen

Another dinner marred by news of death. There were two empty spaces at the table: those belonging to the late Mr Winniatt and his wife Daisy, who remained under heavy sedation in her room. Professor Wilbor had raised the idea of trying to get a couple of acquaintances to take their places, but it was decided that this would not do. And no matter how hard we tried to change the subject, the talk always ventured back to the strange manner in which Howard Winniatt had died.

'I just can't understand it,' said Mrs Brendel, who was in her element. 'Do you think he fell? Or did someone push him? How awful if he was murdered. But who would want him dead?'

'It's a matter for the police now,' said Professor Wilbor. 'Don't you agree, Mrs Christie?'

'Oh, yes, indeed,' I said. It had been announced that Inspector Núñez would arrive later that night.

'Can you go over it one more time, my dear?' asked Mrs Brendel. 'I really do fail to picture it.'

'I think Mrs Christie is still recovering from the shock of the discovery,' said the Professor. 'Isn't that so?'

As I nodded in agreement and took a sip of iced water, I saw Helen Hart's blue eyes flashing. What kind of mischief would she start to make now?

'Witnessing a death like this is just beastly, is it not?' said Helen. 'When I saw Gina do . . . what she did, I simply fell to pieces. Well, you saw me. I was hysterical with shock. I didn't know what I was saying, or doing. I think I talked nonsense for the whole second half of the journey on the *Gelria*. Wasn't that right, Mrs Christie? You saw the kind of state I was in.'

'Well, each of us is affected by grief in different ways, of course,' I said gently.

'And by the way, I heard that you made the discovery with this mysterious man of yours you've been keeping secret,' she added.

'To be accurate, it was Violet Grenville who discovered Mr Winniatt. My recent acquaintance Mr Blake came along with Mr Grenville in the car.'

'I see. And where is he now?' asked Helen.

'I believe he may have moved to another hotel. Somewhere on the south coast,' I said, lying. I knew that Davison had travelled fifteen or so miles westwards.

'That's a shame for you. Howard said you were quite chummy. Never mind, these things can't be helped.' She gulped back some more white wine and called the waiter for another bottle to be served. 'Poor Howard. We'd only just met him, but of course we'll miss him. What with his devotion to the higher arts. Now, I wonder what's become of that notebook? I wonder if Daisy has had any thoughts of publishing the magnum opus?'

'I would have thought it would be a little too soon for that,' said Guy Trevelyan.

'Do you think so? Yes, I suppose you are probably right,' replied Helen. 'Perhaps I'll create a piece of sculpture in memory of him. Isn't that the most fabulous idea? I can just see it now, fashioned from white marble. Of course, it wouldn't be a mere conventional representation of the man. It would have to be fitting to Winniatt's literary aspirations and ambitions. What about a sculpture of something approaching the form of a full stop? Or would you say a semicolon?'

She then fell into a discussion with Guy, while I attempted to strike up a conversation with Rupert Mabey. He was not well disposed to me and did not make discourse easy.

'I feel I need a little distraction to take my mind off today,' I said. 'Tell me, Mr Mabey, what have you been doing?'

'I've been helping the Professor with the work on a burial site near Mal Pais.'

'So you too were in the area today? That's not very far from the *rambla*.'

'Yes, that's right.'

There was a silence while Rupert Mabey lit a cigarette.

'But you didn't see anything odd or untoward?' I asked.

'I thought you said you wanted to take your mind off what happened?' His tone was mocking, cruel even.

'Yes, of course, you're right.'

His rudeness forced me to turn to my other neighbour at the table, Mrs Brendel. Despite warnings from Professor Wilbor I could tell she was only too keen to ask me more about the gruesome discovery. To prevent her from doing so I started to quiz her about what she knew about Gerard Grenville.

'Oh, I wouldn't be surprised if it was him who was responsible,' she growled. 'He's a demon incarnate, that one. The things he gets up to simply cannot be repeated.'

'What kind of things?'

'Oh, you don't want to hear,' she said, murmuring about certain illicit acts and Satanic rituals.

'And who told you all of this?'

'I've seen it in black and white, in the newspapers. It makes for shocking reading, I can tell you.'

'Don't you think it's all a bluff?' I said. 'From my experience, I doubt the whole enterprise – contacting the dead, table turning, nothing but nonsense.'

'My sweet innocent child, I think it best if you continue to believe so,' she said, patting my hand. 'However ...' and she launched into a long story about the daughter of a friend of a friend who had inherited a pearl necklace, not knowing that its original owner had been strangled while wearing it.

The dinner dragged on until Helen Hart decided that she would like to take the night air. She enlisted Mrs Brendel and me to accompany her, leaving Professor Wilbor, Rupert Mabey and Guy Trevelyan to take brandy and cigars in the library.

As we were strolling along the terrace, past a low-lying

hedge of neatly shaped oleander, I suddenly had an idea. I pretended to shiver and asked to be excused for a moment, telling my two companions that I wanted to fetch my shawl from the hotel. I ran up the stairs, remembering the number of the Winniatts's room: 107. I listened at the door for a moment, gently knocked in case the doctor was still in attendance, and quietly tried the handle. It was open. Trenkel must have just stepped out for a few minutes and I knew I did not have long. I quietly slipped into the room. The layout was similar to my own room, so I could find my way around easily in the dim light cast from a single lamp in the far corner. Daisy lay in bed, a small figure who seemed bereft and alone in an enormous four-poster, her breathing shallow, her face as pale as death itself. It seemed as though the doctor had given her a generous dose of sedatives; I was certain that she would not wake up until the morning.

Daisy had said that night at dinner on the ship that her husband always carried his journal with him, yet it had not been found on his body. So where was it? Had he, for some reason, decided to leave it behind at the hotel? Or had someone taken the notebook from the corpse after they had murdered him? Perhaps I would find a clue here in their room.

I crept over to a chest of drawers on which Howard Winniatt's possessions were still laid out: a bottle of hair oil, a fountain pen and ink, a set of combs and brushes, a hip flask, a few novels (most of which I had never heard of) and some notebooks. I picked up each in turn, but the pages were blank and empty, waiting for Winniatt's words. Now, of course, they would never get filled with the lives of others. Perhaps that was for the best, I thought to myself. I searched through Winniatt's drawers, blushing as his socks and underclothes passed through my hands. I felt no better than those fiends who had pursued me and hunted me down at the end of last year. I had to tell myself that I was doing this not to produce a form of perverted entertainment, but to help solve the murder of an innocent man.

I turned my attention towards a half-unpacked leather case that stood in the corner. Inside, there were some well-thumbed copies of a literary journal, some starched handkerchiefs, a snake's nest of ties and, yes, a black note-book. I was about to turn its pages when I heard a noise at the door. The handle started to turn. The room had been fitted with the same wide wardrobe as mine, and without having time to think I opened the door and slipped inside. I pushed myself between Daisy's gowns, their flimsy fabrics playing and dancing across my face, squatted down and drew my knees towards my chest. At the very last moment, I managed to stretch out my arm, pull the small key from the lock and then close the door. I rearranged myself so I could peer out of the tiny lock.

I heard a figure cross the room and then silence, fol-lowed by the sound of someone humming to himself. I saw nothing more than a man's legs and waist, dressed in a dark suit. He walked over to the bed and stood by Daisy. It had to be Trenkel, the doctor. He waited by her side for a minute or so, before he walked back around her bed towards the door. I heard the sound of a key turning in the lock. What did he intend to do? Did he know that I was in the wardrobe? Or were his intentions even more sinister?

I saw his form pass by the front of the wardrobe and lost him for a minute or so. Everything went quiet and then I heard the sound of humming once more. I recognised the tune. What was the name of the popular song? The humming became louder and, in an instant, my sight line went black. Trenkel was standing directly in front of the wardrobe. Only a few inches of wood separated him from me. I tried to stifle my breathing, but with each moment I felt as though I was about to choke. Then, just as I could stand it no longer, he stepped away from the wardrobe and moved towards the bed. I had to suppress the urge to exhale loudly, and used one of Daisy's dresses to cover my mouth as I breathed out.

Trenkel placed a hand directly over Daisy's face. Oh please, no. At what moment would I have to make myself known? If he was to attempt to do something despicable to the sleeping woman I would, I knew, have to stop it. But how would I explain my own odd behaviour? The fact that I had stolen into the Winniatts's room, and hidden in their wardrobe? I couldn't think about that at this moment. The main thing was to prevent a horrible assault on an unconscious woman. I raised my hand towards the door and was about to push it open and emerge into the room, when Trenkel moved away from Daisy. I watched through the lock as he walked from the bed towards the dressing table. He stopped, opened a jewellery box, and fingered what looked like a brooch and a ring. He picked up a strand of pearls and carried them over to the lamp in the corner of the room where he inspected them. Then he returned to the dressing table, closed the jewellery box, and slipped the pearls into the inside pocket of his jacket. He went to check on Mrs Winniatt once more before he walked back across the room, unlocked the door and disappeared.

I waited a minute before exhaling deeply and noisily. I pushed open the wardrobe door and climbed out. I went to check on Mrs Winniatt to make sure that Trenkel had done nothing to harm her, examined the jewellery box, which was full of valuable pieces, and then returned to the suitcase. I pulled out the notebook, which seemed to have been written by Howard Winniatt, and then slipped out of the room.

Chapter Nineteen

I sent word down to Mrs Brendel and Miss Hart that the day's events had taken their toll and I had retired to bed. Carlo and Rosalind were already asleep and so, after undressing, I was free to read Howard Winniatt's notebook. A quick glance told me that this journal was not the most recent, as it contained only reproductions of conversations and incidents up to the moment of our disembarkation at Grand Canary. A large section focused on the voyage on the *Gelria*.

As I flicked through the journal, written in a small, ordered hand, my own name jumped out at me. Winniatt related some of the snatches of conversation between Mrs Brendel and me, as well as a few choice words of his own. 'Successful, no doubt, but writes books of the lowest kind,' and, 'Apparently the creator of a Belgian detective of some note and fame, but as I see it Mrs Christie deals in cliches and types.' Another entry made me smile, 'Not unattractive per se, but very middlebrow.' But then he had added underneath, 'She grew up in Torquay, which perhaps explains it.' What was wrong with Torquay? I felt angry on the town's behalf. After all, my birthplace had attracted its fair share of artists, royals, society figures, even Mr Wilde himself. Henry James had taken tea at my parents' house, as had Kipling. And then there were all the scandals – divorces, embezzlements, even the occasional murder – of which Mr Winniatt had known nothing. For all his bohemian friends the unfortunate Winniatt must have been a very blinkered man indeed.

Nevertheless he had taken the trouble to record, in detail, conversations with all sorts of people on the *Gelria*, men I had never seen, crew members I hardly knew existed. Here were snapshots of hidden lives, transcriptions of interviews with engineers, cooks, boilermen, restaurant staff and porters. How any of this would ever make a book was anyone's guess. I doubted any publisher would take it on, but then perhaps Winniatt, funded by his wife's fortune, had considered financing publication himself. I continued to read into the early hours, learning many details of ship life. I was particularly gripped by a section on death at sea, the conversations prompted by Gina Trevelyan's suicide. One crew member told Winniatt of an incident in which a steward had been found dead in an empty swimming pool. Scotland Yard had suspected foul play, so they had ordered the officers to keep the body cold. It was decided to place the corpse in the ice room, but because they were afraid the body might freeze to the deck, the crew were told to turn the body every twelve hours. The boat-swain related the rituals surrounding death and burial at sea. Normally a corpse would be placed in a canvas bag, which would be sewn up, with a final stitch through the body's nose to prevent it from slipping around inside the bag. Before the burial ceremony, the body would be draped with an ensign, and the exact time and location would then be recorded in the ship's log.

I went on to read about the work of the liner's photographer, who would often have to create makeshift darkrooms from lavatories, ironing rooms or laundries. Sometimes hot water would gush out of both taps, causing the negatives to 'reticulate' and be destroyed. In high temperatures, a strong hardening bath would have to be used to stop the emulsion from slipping off the photographic film. I read about the experiences of the waiters, pursers and porters, two of whom had carried Guy Trevelyan's trunks on board. Winniatt had described the men as having faces as red as beetroots, a not particularly original metaphor for someone who held himself in such high esteem as a writer. I scanned over the testimony of one of the officers who related how, when a ship entered tropical climes, the crew would change from their blue uniforms to white.

All this detail, while superficially interesting, told me little about why someone would want to murder Winniatt. The real reason, I suspected, would have been found in the contents of Winniatt's last notebook, which the murderer had no doubt taken from his jacket pocket after his death. Had Winniatt written or witnessed something that would implicate Grenville in the murder of Douglas Greene? Or had the two men known each other in the past? Was there some hold Winniatt had over Grenville, a bond that could be broken only by murder?

Rupert Mabey had told me that he had been in the area earlier that day near where Winniatt's body had been found. Could he have had a motive for wanting him dead? Could Winniatt have stumbled across evidence to show that Mabey had killed Douglas Greene, his own brother? And what did Daisy know about any of this? Had Howard Winniatt let anything slip to her, some seemingly insignificant detail, that might help shed some light on the strange series of events? Or were the two deaths – those of Douglas Greene and Howard Winniatt – not connected at all? And how did Dr Trenkel fit into all of this?

As I turned out the light, unable to sleep, the questions kept running around my mind, chasing each other in an interminable greyhound race. I closed my eyes, but I kept seeing the horrific image of Winniatt's broken body lying in the dry river bed. It seemed as though someone had either killed him by a hard strike to the head and then thrown him over into the *rambla* or they had sedated him and finished him off with a series of vicious blows down there by the rocks. And then there was the violent, theatrical flourish of splicing his eye with a spike of the bird-of-paradise flower. That had been a truly horrible touch. But what did it all mean?

Chapter Twenty

Inspector Núñez lost no time in beginning his enquiries, taking over a corner suite at the Taoro for the purpose of his investigations. The next morning he called in people one by one, beginning with Guy Trevelyan and Helen Hart, other guests such as Mrs Brendel, and then finally Gerard and Violet Grenville. Reliving the discovery of the body had been a difficult process for the girl; when she emerged from Núñez's room she was being supported by her father.

'Núñez was as kind and gentle as he could be, but even so, it was hard for Violet to talk about it all,' Grenville said as he helped his daughter into one of the chairs that had been placed outside the room. He turned to me and said in a whisper, 'Of course, you know the Inspector is in love with her. But she gives him no encouragement. No encouragement at all.' He looked down at his daughter with a tender expression. 'A truly awful thing for you to witness, my dear. I'll give you something for the shock when we get back home.'

Violet did not speak.

'And of course a terrible shock for you too, Mrs Christie. I say, why don't you come over to Mal Pais for some dinner later? I also thought about inviting Mr Blake, but he seems to have disappeared.'

What did Grenville suspect? I had to think quickly.

'Yes, he was greatly distressed about the discovery of Mr Winniatt's body, and unfortunately the incident forced him to remember something in his past which he has been trying to forget.'

'I'm sorry to hear that.'

'I believe his younger brother died in rather suspicious circumstances. So he has checked into a hotel in a different part of the island. He needed a change of scene.'

'How tragic,' said Grenville. 'But we would be so delighted if you would join us. I know Violet here would appreciate a little female company, wouldn't you, dear? It's the least I can do to thank you for helping as you did.'

'Yes, that's very kind of you,' I said, trying to force a smile.

At that moment Núñez's assistant opened the door and asked me to enter the suite. The Inspector had established himself behind a huge mahogany desk with what appeared to be two of Winniatt's notebooks in front of him. I knew there were none on his body, and no other ones visible in his bedroom apart from the one I had taken. Had Núñez found the missing journal? I was conscious that I must return the notebook I had taken to Daisy's room; it nestled in my handbag, waiting for an opportune moment.

'Please take a seat, Mrs Christie,' said Núñez. 'I see that

you are wondering about Mr Winniatt's notebooks. Yes, very astute of you.'

'I was just thinking whether they might offer a clue to the murder.'

'My thoughts exactly,' he said. 'Unfortunately these two date back to his time in England before he left. It seems as though the book he was using at the very end of his life has gone missing.'

'Mrs Winniatt did say that her husband carried it on his person at all times. I trust it wasn't found on his body?' I asked.

Núñez raised an eyebrow. 'No, it wasn't,' he said.

'And have you questioned Mrs Winniatt about whether she knows what could have happened to it?'

'I went to talk to Mrs Winniatt, but unfortunately she is not responding to my enquiries.'

'I suppose she must still be sedated,' I said. The image of Dr Trenkel standing over her lifeless body flashed into my mind. For a moment, I considered telling the Inspector about the theft of her pearls, but something told me to hold back this piece of information. Perhaps I would need to use it later.

'She was a little groggy, yes, but I also got the sense that she is still in a state of shock. Of course, it doesn't help that she is faced with having to talk to an official-looking man first thing in the morning. In fact, I was wondering if you wouldn't mind going to talk to her. I think she would respond better to another woman.'

'I'd be happy to, if you think it might help. She must be absolutely devastated and needs some time to take in the horrible news.'

'Of course, the murderer could be on the other side of the island by now,' said Núñez, watching me closely for my reaction. He had obviously learnt that the man he knew as Alexander Blake had left the hotel.

'I'm sure time is of the essence,' I said without flinching. 'Would you like me to go and talk to her now?'

'Yes, if you don't mind,' he said, standing up and walking me to the door. 'Anything she might be able to tell you about her husband's movements yesterday and any ideas about who she suspects could have done this would be very helpful.'

Núñez accompanied me along the corridor to room 107. He asked that I join him back in his suite when I had finished. I knocked gently and then entered to see Daisy, dressed in her nightgown, sitting in bed. Her face was a ghastly colour, almost as if she herself were on the point of death, and her eyes were lifeless. She did not meet my gaze as I walked towards the bed, but instead stared blankly ahead.

'My poor dear,' I said, taking her hand. 'What a terrible shock for you.'

'Yes,' she said in a whisper. 'I can't believe it.'

There was little use in expressing platitudes. Personal experience had taught me that the recently bereaved do not want to know how time is a great healer, how a loved one now rests in a better place, and how the best are always taken first. I still longed to see my mother, who had died in April of the previous year. Perhaps Grenville's wild ambitions as an occultist were really just a perverted extension of this urge to unite the dead with the living. 'An awful thing to happen,' I said. 'But the most important thing is to find the monster who did this to your husband.'

Again there was no response. 'You do realise that there is evil in the world, don't you my dear,' I said in a very soft voice. 'And we must not allow it to triumph. No, that would be very wrong. And I think the person who did this to Mr Winniatt must have been very evil indeed.'

As her eyes met mine I saw the depths of pain that raged inside her. 'Who would do such a thing?' A wave of grief wracked her body.

I let her cry for a minute or so, holding her hands as she did so. 'That's why you must help the police,' I said. 'If you don't mind, the Inspector has entrusted me to ask you a few questions. Would that be all right, my dear?'

As she wiped her eyes and nose with a saturated hand-kerchief, I took out my own and passed it to her.

'Thank you,' she said. 'I'm certain I don't know any-thing.'

'Well then. Let's start with what you remember of yes-terday. In what kind of state of mind was Mr Winniatt?'

'He was in a very good mood,' she said. 'He was feeling confident of his book, or books, I should say, as you know he did see them as part of a larger series.'

I smiled encouragingly. 'Yes, such a very good idea,' I said. 'Did you know what he had planned for the day?'

'We had breakfast here, which was lovely as usual, and then he told me that he wanted to explore a little around the hotel grounds.'

'What did he do after that?'

'He left the hotel at about ten o'clock and said that

he wanted to note down some impressions of the island, of the wildlife, the gardens, and I suppose he must have walked towards the dry river bed.' At the mention of this place, Daisy's eyes filled with tears once more. 'But, Mrs Christie, who could be so cruel? The police told me about the way he had been killed, and what they had found . . .'

Daisy covered her mouth with a handkerchief. 'I'm sorry, would you please excuse me?' She jumped from the bed and ran towards the bathroom, from where I heard the sounds of retching. I seized the opportunity to open the suitcase and place the notebook that I had stolen back inside.

'I know, so horrible,' I said. 'Which is why it's very important we find this man.'

'Yes, yes,' she said, re-entering the bedroom and trying to regain her composure. 'Would you mind if I retired back to bed? I'm still feeling awfully weak. My head feels so strange,' she said, raising a hand to her forehead. I suspected that the doctor had given her something extremely strong indeed to ensure that she did not stir when he entered her room. I wondered when she would discover the theft of her pearls.

'Did Mr Winniatt ever mention the name Gerard Grenville to you?'

At this her eyes widened slightly. 'The famous occultist? The one you were talking about?'

'Yes, as you know he lives quite near the hotel.'

'I do believe he did say that he would like to make his acquaintance. Do you think that he could be responsible?'

'He may have played some part. Do you know if the two men had ever met before?'

'I don't know. I'm sorry.'

'And what of Violet Grenville?' I asked. 'The daughter? Had Mr Winniatt had any reason to make her acquaintance?'

'I've never heard him mention her name, I don't think.'

'Do you know if your husband expressed any interest in the occult?'

'Oh no, he thought it was a load of hokum,' she said.

'And do you remember if Mr Winniatt took his notebook with him that morning?'

'Oh yes. He carried it with him everywhere, always in his hand or the inside pocket of his suit jacket.'

'Did the police tell you that they could not find it? That they think it is missing?'

'Yes, the Inspector did mention that, but he did take away a couple of Howard's earlier notebooks that were buried at the bottom of one of our cases. Núñez asked me some questions, but I'm afraid I was in no fit state to talk to him.' Her fingers freed themselves from my hands and started to work themselves over and over in a frenzy of anxiety.

'Don't worry. They understand, of course,' I said, taking her hands into mine once more to help calm her down.

'And do you know if the police took all his notebooks and letters with them?'

She hesitated for a moment, unsure of what to say. Her eyes darted back and forth to the drawer by the bed. 'Well, I—'

At that moment, the door opened and Núñez came into

the room. His friendly demeanour had been replaced by a stern expression.

'Mrs Christie, if you could come with me, please?' he said, looking at the carpet.

'Mrs Winniatt was just about to—'

'If you could be so kind as to accompany me back to the suite.'

I felt my heart begin to beat faster and my mouth felt as dry as desert sand. 'Has something happened? What's wrong?'

'There's nothing more to be done here,' he said.

'But—'

'Now, please,' he said.

Daisy, disturbed by the sudden entrance and Núñez's harsh behaviour, started to cry again. 'Don't worry, my dear, I'll come and see you a little later,' I said, squeezing her hand. I left her looking absolutely desolate, a lost child who had just realised she inhabited a cruel and evil world.

Núñez led me out of the room and we walked in silence back to his suite. What on earth had happened? Had he discovered something about the Winniatts? Why did he not want me to stay in the room with her? I felt my face flushing with anger. After all, I was sure that Daisy had been about to tell me something, something relating to a missing journal, something that she had secreted away in the drawers by her bed.

Núñez gestured for me to sit down. I had only left him half an hour ago at the most and yet he seemed like a changed man. The atmosphere in the room was decidedly frosty.

He looked down at his papers with something of a frown. 'You and Mr Winniatt, I believe, were not on the best of terms?'

'Forgive me, I don't understand . . .'

'From what I've just heard it seems as though Mr Winniatt had made some rather cutting comments about you, both on the *Gelria* and here on the island.'

'Let's just say that his and my ideas of what constituted a good book were very different,' I said, trying to force a smile.

'People say that he insulted you, is that correct?'

'Well, some of his comments were a little low, I'll give you that. But I didn't take them seriously, not at all.'

'Really? You did not bear Mr Winniatt any ill will?'

'I know you're not supposed to talk ill of the dead, but some of the things that came out of his mouth were really quite astonishing.'

'And you didn't retaliate in any way?'

'Inspector Núñez, what are you suggesting? You can't seriously believe that I would cosh a man over the head because he didn't like my books?'

'No, no, of course not,' he said. 'But what about your friend, Mr Blake? He seems to have left the hotel.'

I told him the same lie I had told Grenville. 'But he was just a brief acquaintance. Someone I had met on the journey over here. Very pleasant, but I doubt I will see him again.'

'Really? I've been told that you seemed very close indeed. There was also some suggestion that you were upset that Mr Winniatt had seen you in the company of Mr Blake down by Martiánez beach. Is that correct?'

I thought back to the scene that first night at dinner at the Taoro.

'I didn't think it was any of his business, that's all,' I said.

'Well, it's certainly very remiss of Mr Blake to vanish like this. I will have to ask my colleagues here to put every effort into finding him.' He stared at me for a moment without speaking, before he continued, 'You don't happen to have a photograph of Mr Blake in your possession, by any chance?'

'No, I'm sorry, I don't.'

'You see, Mrs Christie, I've just been speaking to one of the guests here who gave me a very good description of this Mr Blake. He is tall, handsome, well educated. Finely cut clothes. Expensive shoes. From what I can gather he doesn't strike me as the type of man who would go into insurance and live in Southampton.'

'Is there such a type?' I asked.

He didn't stop to answer the question. 'Do you remember the man I mentioned to you when we first talked on the *Gelria*? When you asked me about the murder of Douglas Greene? The body found in the cave?'

'Yes, yes, I do.'

'Well, I have reason to believe that the man I was looking for in connection to that case – John Davison – is none other than your friend, Mr Alexander Blake.'

I froze. I had to think quickly to put him off the scent. 'But I don't see how it could be possible.'

'Oh, it could be very possible indeed.'

'But if you say that these two men – Blake and Davison –

are one and the same, why would this fellow risk coming back to Tenerife?'

'That's what I don't know – yet. But I'm certain I will find out.'

'Have you found anything more out about that case? The body of poor Mr Greene in the cave?'

'I am afraid I am not at liberty to say.'

It was obvious Núñez no longer trusted me. He cleared his throat before he asked, 'And did Mrs Winniatt give you any information that might prove helpful?'

'No, I'm afraid she didn't,' I said.

'But I thought you said she was about to tell you something?'

'Yes, I did get the impression that she was on the point of saying something, but that's when you walked into her room.'

'But you don't have any suspicions of what that might be?'

'No,' I lied, determined not to give away more than I had to. 'I'm afraid I don't.'

Núñez cast me a disapproving look, almost one of disgust, before he dismissed me with a flick of the hand. 'I don't like being kept in the dark, Mrs Christie.' The threat in his voice was unmistakable.

Chapter Twenty-one

I left Núñez in a state of nervous agitation, my hands shaking, my mouth dry, my heart beating. The Inspector had treated me as though I were a criminal, someone bent on subverting the natural order of things. If only I could tell him that I was trying to work towards the same ends as he was. There was no point in telling him the truth, partly because I wasn't quite sure of the full nature of the facts myself.

I returned to my room, took out my notebook and wrote down what I knew to be true. In front of me I had assembled fragments of the puzzle; actually, this was not quite accurate. What lay before me were what seemed like pieces of several different puzzles, all mixed up into one unintelligible heap. I did not even know what I should be looking for, what I ought to select from this terrible mess that lay before me.

I tried to plot out the various strands of the narrative as if they were elements of a story. By the initials 'DG' I wrote the names of the suspects and their possible motives for wanting Douglas Greene out of the way. At the top of the list was Gerard Grenville, next to which I added the words, 'killed Greene as part of an occult ritual? Or murdered him because Greene was about to expose him – was Grenville the one with secret Bolshevik leanings?' Below this, next to 'RM', I wrote: 'Motive? Was he the Bolshevik spy or could it be something more mundane: could Rupert Mabey have killed Greene because he wanted to ensure that he was the sole heir to his father's fortune?' Would it be possible to check Mabey's father's will? If Davison had been around this was something that could be arranged. Could I write to his *hostal* and ask him to do this?

To this list I added – in a rather reluctant fashion – the name of Davison himself, who despite his protestations, did have a motive for murdering Greene: he could not risk his friend exposing the true nature of their relationship. The shadow of disgrace, of prison, was a reality for any man engaging in homosexual activity.

Were there any other suspects? What about Dr Trenkel? Had Douglas Greene discovered the doctor's profitable little sideline thieving from his rich patients and threatened to expose his dirty secret?

And what of the other murder, that of Howard Winniatt? Did Daisy Winniatt have a reason for wanting her husband out of the way? Had Howard asked for a divorce? Did he have a mistress, a woman he was prepared to leave Daisy for? It seemed as though Grenville was at the top of the list. The writer may have witnessed something and documented it in his notebook without realising its true significance. Perhaps Winniatt had recorded, in all innocence, some small detail that Grenville knew would implicate him in the murder of Greene. Mabey could have killed him for the same reason. If only I could find the notebook that Winniatt had been using at the time of his death.

By the time I had finished, the pages of my own notebook were full of initials and words, interconnecting circles, complete with a frenzied rash of lines and arrows. Something was being kept from me, I knew; some fact, or more likely a number of facts, without which none of this made any sense. Just as I flung down my notebook in frustration Carlo walked into the room.

'My dear, whatever is wrong? You're looking very tired,' she said as she came over to the desk where I had been sitting. She bent down to pick up my notebook, but I quickly snatched it out of her hand. I had to keep my intelligence work secret from her at all costs.

'This damned book is not working,' I said. 'Sorry, Carlo. But the thing is driving me mad.'

'It's no surprise after what you've been through. And then having to see that body and deal with all of that. It's the last thing you need.' She looked at me with a serious expression. 'Do you think we should leave here? Go to another hotel?'

'I have considered it, but I think that would set a terribly bad example, don't you? It would hardly be fair on poor Mrs Winniatt.'

'Yes, perhaps you're right. I'm trying to think what would be best for you. What about a nice stroll? Rosalind is playing with her friend and if you like we could go down to get some sea air. Walking has always seemed to help in the past. What did you once say? That it helps unknot the knottiest of problems?'

'I wish it were that simple,' I said, sighing. 'No, I think I'm going to have to admit defeat for the moment. Could you ask Gustavo or whoever is down on reception if I could book an appointment with the doctor here?'

'Is it that bad?'

'I'm sure it's nothing. Probably a simple tonic will do me the world of good.'

As Carlo cast me another concerned look I slipped my notebook back inside my handbag and zipped it up. The action forced me to remember the time in Harrogate when I sequestered that poison inside my handbag. Would I have to resort to such measures here? Surely not. After all, I was not being threatened myself, or at least not yet.

An hour or so later, I was standing outside Dr Trenkel's room. As I waited by the door to his office, which was situated on the ground floor overlooking the terraced gardens, I heard the vague murmur of voices from inside. I had been told by the English nurse, who also seemed to serve as Trenkel's secretary, that the doctor was seeing another patient, but an appointment had become free at the last minute because one of his regulars had just died. I looked out to the terrace and saw the shadow of illness lying on the faces of a dozen or so patients, many of whom sat in basket or wheeled chairs, their knees covered by blankets.

They were of different ages and nationalities, but they all had one thing in common: the deathly pallor of their complexions.

The invalids came to the island in the hope that the balmy climate would help relieve them of their symptoms; many of them knew they could not be cured. The island did not have a winter, or so they had been told, and although it was far from cold, today the sun was obscured by a low-lying cloud. The great volcano could not be seen, but – like death itself – was ever present.

I may have been imagining it, but I thought that I could discern a glint in the eyes of one or two of the patients, a certain degree of animation that played across their faces where it had not existed before. Perhaps the news of Howard Winniatt's death had acted on the nervous systems of the invalids as a kind of tonic; after all, they may have reasoned, death had claimed a man in the prime of life, suffering from no discernible illness. Yes, they did have to endure an awfully cruel disease, one that would probably finish them off, but at least they had not been murdered, and murdered like *that*.

The door opened to the sound of low laughter; it was good to know that the doctor, although a thief, had the capacity to instil hope and cheer in his patients. Dr Trenkel, standing behind the wheeled chair of Edmund Ffosse, looked surprised to see me, as did his patient.

'I believe I have an appointment at noon,' I said.

'Oh, I wasn't aware of that,' said the doctor, looking vexed.

'Should I come back later?' I asked, feeling more than a

little embarrassed. I was heavy with the knowledge of the theft of the pearls that I had witnessed the previous night, and for some irrational reason, felt as though I had been infected with the doctor's burden of guilt.

He met my question with another question. 'What's your name?'

'Mrs Christie. I'm staying here at the hotel.'

The answer seemed to satisfy him.

'No, no,' said Trenkel. 'Let me just place my patient into the hands of his good friend Violet Grenville and then I'll be back. Please go inside and take a seat.'

As the doctor wheeled Ffosse down the corridor I stepped into the office and shut the door behind me. The room was bare and clinical, lined with shelves containing classic text books on the treatment of various lung disorders. An odour of something rotten being masked by a cloying antiseptic smell hung in the air.

On Trenkel's desk, ordered and tidy, lay a green file marked with the name of Edmund Ffosse. I looked at the door and then down at the file. What I hoped to gain by looking at the private medical file of Mr Ffosse I did not know, but I opened it anyway. My heart raced as I flicked through the pages of the neatly written report, my eyes quickly taking in words and technical terms about the diagnosis and treatment of tuberculosis. The upshot was that Trenkel had diagnosed Ffosse as a terminal case: he had only a matter of months to live.

How different from the handwriting of the English doctors I had known, the spider crawling out of an ink pot variety. Perhaps all German doctors shared the same precise, steady hand, a product of their supremely ordered, logical brains. Just as I closed the file, Dr Trenkel opened the door and walked into the room.

'Sorry about that, Mrs Christie. Now what can we do for you today?'

I told him that I was feeling rather nervous. I felt anxious and was sure that my heart was beating faster than it should. I gave him a little background information on my state of mind in England, the recent troubles with Archie and the grief I had felt after my mother's death. I informed him that I had been one of the first people to come across Mr Winniatt's body in the dry river bed.

'Let's start with me listening to your heartbeat,' he said, taking out his stethoscope and placing it on my chest. He listened intently for a minute or so before he concluded that yes, my heartbeat did seem somewhat irregular. He proceeded to take my blood pressure and then looked into my eyes. 'And how long have you been feeling like this?'

'Well, I've been feeling a little out of sorts for a while now, but I felt so much worse this morning.'

'I can imagine. Quite a shock for many people,' he said. 'Did you know this man Winniatt?'

'Not very well, but we were on the same ship, the *Gelria*, over from England. It's his poor wife I feel sorry for.' I watched Trenkel carefully as I spoke. 'I went to see her earlier. The Inspector asked me to help him with his enquiries. You see, Mrs Winniatt clammed up in front of him and he thought that she might open up to me. But she is in a terrible state.'

'Yes, I gave her a sedative last night, but of course something like that is only ever a temporary measure. I'm afraid there is no medicine that can cure a loss like this.'

'Indeed,' I said. 'When my mother died I simply fell to pieces. I think I actually lost my mind for a while.'

'That's perfectly possible,' said Trenkel, turning his attention back to my health. 'There's nothing seriously wrong with you, as far as I can tell. What I advise is to try and alternate rest with some form of light exercise. And try not to think about the gruesome discovery you made down there in the *rambla*.'

I hoped the doctor might be able to give me a little more information about how Winniatt had died. I was prepared to use the fact that I had seen him steal Mrs Winniatt's pearls, but this was a last resort; after all, if I used this strategy I would have to explain what I had been doing in Daisy's room. First, I wanted to try and engage some of my feminine wiles: distress, charm and flattery.

'It really was a terrible shock, Doctor,' I said, my hand fluttering up to my neck like a distressed bird. 'To see the body there in that ravine. And the state of it.'

'Yes, a very terrible thing,' he said. 'As I said, best to put it out of your mind, if you can.'

'I have seen some terrible things in my time – I was a nurse in the war, you see,' I said. I knew that this would mean something to the doctor and he nodded in acknowledgment of shared experience. 'But this, it was—'

'I've never seen anything like it,' he said, alluding to the autopsy he had performed. 'To be honest, it was hard for me to take in. Obviously, the head injuries were bad enough, but then this business with the bird-of-paradise flower.'

'Yes, that was one thing I didn't understand. I was only a nurse, and that was many years ago now. Your knowledge is much more profound and your experience much deeper than mine ever was, so I wondered what you made of it all.'

The flattery was beginning to work on Dr Trenkel, whose chest puffed out like a prize pigeon. 'You are too kind, Mrs Christie, too kind,' he said.

'As I was saying, from your expertise would you say that the flower spike was inserted into the eye before or after death?'

'Difficult to say, as I cannot compare it with anything I've seen before, but I think that it was probably done after death.'

'At least that's some comfort to poor Mrs Winniatt,' I said. 'And what of the head injuries? I couldn't work out whether they been sustained as a result of the fall or—'

'Or whether they had been inflicted before the fall?'

'Yes, exactly.'

'From examining the body for the police, I think that Mr Winniatt was killed as a result of falling from the bridge and suffering these very significant injuries to the head.'

'So he fell or was pushed from the bridge?'

'Perhaps, but I don't think so.'

What was Dr Trenkel suggesting? 'But it can't be suicide? Surely you're not implying that Mr Winniatt took his own life?'

'No, no, I'm not saying that at all,' he said.

I tried not to sound too eager to extract the information from him, but it was difficult to keep my voice steady, detached and professional. 'You're not? But then what would cause Mr Winniatt to fall from the bridge into the ravine?'

'I'm not an expert by any means, but I think Mr Winniatt may have been poisoned.'

'Poisoned? By what?'

'I'm not sure yet,' he said.

I ran through a list of poisons in my mind and came up with one name: henbane, something I had seen in Grenville's garden. Yes, that would make sense. The plant had a nasty range of toxic side effects including vomiting, flushing of the skin, confusion, blurred vision, and most relevant in this case, hallucinations.

'Henbane,' I said. 'The tropane alkaloids in the henbane made Mr Winniatt think he could fly.'

'I see you know your poisons, Mrs Christie.'

I explained a little of how I had trained in the dispensary in Torquay during the war. I told him about the pharmacist who always carried a lump of curare in his pocket and a little of how this knowledge had helped me with my books. Of course, there were certain aspects of my interest in poisons that I kept back from him.

'So it seems as though this is one area in which you may have more expertise than I?'

'I'm not sure about that.'

'But this is fascinating. What else do you know about henbane?'

I proceeded to tell him what I knew. I talked a little of a case reported by Charles Millspaugh in a book of his I had read. Nine people ate the roots of the plant. After suffering from convulsions, some of the group experienced speechlessness, while others could only howl, and for three days afterwards they seemed to see everything through a prism of a scarlet hue. Another case, reported by a Dr Stedman, detailed how seven people supped on a broth made from the leaves of the plant. They went on to suffer slavering, delirium and hallucinations, believing that everything around them was on the point of collapse. I had always been particularly struck by the first-person account of Gustav Schenk who roasted some seeds of the plant and then inhaled the fumes. Although he could not remember everything that he had experienced – memory loss was one of the effects of the poison – he wrote that he suffered tremendous pain and a realisation that he was close to death. His limbs felt as though they were separating from his body. At one point he thought he was about to dissolve into thin air, and he related how he believed that he could fly. Perhaps this is what Winniatt had experienced when he stood on the bridge by the *rambla*.

'And then, of course, there is the Crippen case,' I said, referring to the infamous murder of 1910. 'It's thought that's how the doctor finished off his wife Cora – with hyoscine.'

'How very interesting,' said Trenkel. 'I must tell the Inspector how very helpful you've been.'

'I would be more than happy if you claimed the knowledge as your own,' I said, smiling. 'After all, I always think it vulgar for a lady to show off about what she knows, don't you?'

The doctor nodded his head in agreement, failing to pick up on the frisson in my voice as I thought about the secret knowledge I had of Trenkel's own crime. It was powerful information and I had every intention of using it for my own advantage.

Chapter Twenty-two

Everything pointed towards Grenville: the henbane in his poison garden, the proliferation of bird-of-paradise flowers near his house, the proximity of the body to Mal Pais. Grenville could have spiked Winniatt's drink with hyoscine, extracted from the henbane, led him to the bridge, where the man became convinced that he could fly. If anyone had witnessed the scene from afar, it would have looked as though Winniatt had simply jumped off the bridge into the ravine. Grenville could then have stumbled down into the *rambla*, where he made sure Winniatt was dead before adding that ghoulish garland of the bird-of-paradise flower. But what was his motive? Why would Grenville want Winniatt dead?

I left the hotel and walked through the gardens, tracing my way back to the bridge under which Winniatt's body had been found. Standing above the ravine I could still make out the red stains that streaked the dark earth. The splash of blood on the black rocks served as a sign that death, and violent death at that, had visited here.

I closed my eyes and imagined Winniatt's arms reaching up to the sky, his feet moving towards the end of the bridge. I saw the expression of joy on his face, the belief that – yes! – he could fly. The dream that had played in his head as a child, as it did for so many children, had actually come true. He was going to soar high into the air. His body felt so very light, and as he stretched out his arms he likened the weightlessness to the same feeling one enjoyed while swimming. But then, as he stepped off the end of the bridge, ready to arc his way up towards the sun, perhaps even as far as the great mount Teide, the pull of gravity returned. He tried to pretend that he was flying, but he wasn't. He knew he was falling. His body was heavy and he heard a part of himself hit a rock. The pain was indescribable, something far beyond anything he had ever experienced before. Something twisted, a leg perhaps. He heard the snap of bone and vertebrae and felt the crush of skull on rock and then nothing.

I opened my eyes, my mind flooding with confused fragments of memories and images from a parallel narrative. I thought of Gina Trevelyan throwing herself off the ship into the ocean. Was falling into freezing water less or more painful than hitting sharp rock? Winniatt's death, I presumed, would have been instant, whereas Gina may have survived in the sea for a minute or more. I also remembered Davison telling me about the way poor Una Crowe had died. Her feet bound in green tape. Her body found at the bottom of that lonely cliff in Dorset.

Winniatt may not have been pushed off the bridge, but if Grenville had given him a tincture laced with henbane that led him to believe he could fly, then it was murder all the same. If Grenville had done it, what was the best way to prove it? And what could be his reason? This important point was still troubling me. Was it connected to the death of Douglas Greene as I suspected? And if so, in what way? There was no point going to the Inspector with half-baked theories. No doubt Trenkel would tell Núñez about the poison, but how would he ever link Winniatt's death to Grenville? I needed to find some kind of evidence, evidence that could possibly lie within the walls of Mal Pais.

As I walked back to the Taoro I thought about a plan. In order to search the house I would need some time, much more time than a mere dinner invitation would give me. I would have to manufacture a reason to stay with Grenville and his daughter overnight. My brows knitted together as I ran through a list of possibilities, all of which seemed to have some kind of flaw.

'Planning a murder?'

I looked up to see Helen Hart, who had just passed by me as I walked up the grand staircase to my room.

'I'm sorry?'

'You looked so serious and contemplative, that's all. So lost in thought. I assumed you must be working out a murder in your head.'

'Oh, yes, that's right. Sorry, I get so distracted at times.'

'I'm pleased I've caught you. I've just been to see a couple of people here to invite them to a party I'm giving on Valentine's Day. You see, my latest piece of sculpture is about love. It's quite an informal little gathering, but it would be wonderful if you could come.'

'That sounds ... delightful,' I said.

'All of us need something to take our minds off this awful business.'

'Yes, indeed. A terrible thing to happen. Poor Mrs Winniatt, and then there is the funeral to get through too.'

'At times like these, I do think it's important that people carry on. There's so much doom and gloom in the world as it is, why should we contribute more to the great heavy bag of misery. Don't you think?'

I wasn't quite sure I would agree with the way Helen expressed it, but in general I did agree that one had simply to carry on. I remembered a phrase that always used to be quoted in my parents' house when I had been a child.

'*What can't be cured must be endured*, my grandmother used to say,' I said, sounding more like an old maid than ever.

Helen's blue eyes sparkled with mischief, a sign that this was one platitude she would not subscribe to – indeed, I imagined her to be the kind of woman who did not endure anything that displeased her. Her lips pursed to say something amusing, if not cutting, but she obviously thought better of it and simply said, 'So we'll see you at my house at eight o'clock, on Valentine's Day. I'll leave directions for you at the hotel.'

'Thank you,' I said, and carried on up to my room.

From the window I saw Rosalind with her friend in the gardens and Carlo sitting on a bench nearby. The two children were playing with their toys, Rosalind with her Blue Teddy and Raymond with another one that, from a distance, looked remarkably similar. As I watched my

182

daughter play – her mind free from all the horrors and troubles of the world – I wondered why I could not be like a normal mother to her, a woman who devoted all her energies to raising her child. I never seemed to find enough time simply to sit still with her, to feel the soft warmth of her breath on my face, to run my fingers through her hair. I wondered whether she loved Carlo more than she loved me. If she did, I would not blame her, considering that Carlo was the one who spent the most time with her. Perhaps I should not have brought her with me on this trip; after all, it wasn't a holiday, but a job for the Secret Intelligence Service. Davison had assured me that all would be well, that my daughter would be safe, but now with Davison gone who was to say that was still the case? I was facing an enemy whose face was hidden from me, an enemy who could strike at any moment. I thought of Davison's pleas to be careful – he had made me promise that I would not put myself in any sort of danger. Staying overnight with Gerard Grenville was risky, of course, but I could see no other way.

I walked over to the door of my room and locked it. From the bottom of the wardrobe I took out a small leather suitcase and placed it on the bed. I entered the bathroom, smoothed down my hair with a splash of cold water, applied a little powder to my face, and then from the inside pocket of my toilet bag eased out a small key. With this I opened the suitcase and took out the leather pouch containing my poisons. As I ran my fingers over the vials I felt the familiar thrill that came with the knowledge that a single drop of liquid or a couple of grains of powder could kill a man. It went without saying that the sense of responsibility that came with such knowledge was enormous and I knew that I would never use any of them unless it became absolutely necessary. But if I was going to spend the night in Grenville's house I would need some sort of protection.

Of course, some of the chemicals I carried in the pouch could also be used as an antidote to reduce the toxic effect of other poisons. I thought of how atropine, itself a very dangerous substance, could be used to treat the symptoms of gelsemium poisoning. That plant, sometimes called evening trumpetflower, was a common sight in many a garden, and few knew of its poisonous qualities. I had read of how Conan Doyle, in his days as a medical student, had experimented with the stuff, administering a small amount of gelsemium each day, a toxin that had resulted in terrible headaches, depression and diarrhoea. If he had carried on he would have experienced nausea, the paralysis of the muscles of the mouth and throat, delirium, difficulties with respiration and, at some point, death.

But to get back to atropine itself, some believed that it had been used by Cleopatra to dilate her pupils and make her more attractive. In Paris, at the end of the last century and the beginning of this one, certain types of women had used the juice of *Atropa belladonna* for the same cosmetic purposes. It had its deadly qualities too, of course. The clue was in the name: Atropos, one of the Three Fates of Greek mythology. She chose how a person was to die.

Chapter Twenty-three

Before I left for Grenville's house I sent a letter to Davison, care of his *hostal* in Icod de los Vinos. He had assumed that Núñez would start searching for the mysterious Alexander Blake, and so he had made provision to register under the name of Arthur Jones.

In the letter I told Davison that I intended to spend the night at Grenville's house. If anything was to happen to me then he could safely assume that Grenville was guilty. The thought of never seeing Rosalind again, or dear Carlo, or my sister and her family, entered my head. Tears filled my eyes as I remembered touching Rosalind's soft face soon after she had been born. Trying to swallow my fears, I took up the pen again and wrote a short letter to my daughter, outlining how much I loved her. I placed it in my large suitcase, one that the hotel staff would no doubt search in the event of my disappearance. I dashed off a quick note to Carlo, saying that I was spending a night at the house of Violet Grenville. I also wrote down a summary of what I had discovered so far about Grenville, which I addressed to Inspector Núñez, and which I left inside the case, next to the partially completed manuscript of my new novel. What would happen to that in the event of my death? Perhaps it was for the best if it never saw the light of day. Even so, I was slightly irritated at having to leave the book in that rather shoddy state. If only I had a little more time to work on it then I was sure I could get it into a shape to be published. Loose ends, in fiction and in life, did get on my nerves.

I knelt down by my bed and prayed, not only to God but to my mother, who I hoped would be watching over me. I looked back at the previous year when I had been at my lowest ebb, nearly driven mad by the grief of losing her, the shock at discovering Archie's betrayal, the horror of not being able to write, and then the appearance of Dr Kurs in my life. During one of the conversations I had endured with Kurs, the doctor had told me that the experience might actually be the making of me. I had dismissed the suggestion at the time as nothing more than a sick joke. But looking back, Kurs had been right. If I had not encountered him I would never have become involved with Davison and the Secret Intelligence Service. Writing about murder was one thing, but actually helping solve one was something quite different. It was messier and, of course, much more dangerous. But fundamentally it was worthwhile. By working with Davison I hoped to make a difference. As I had told Daisy Winniatt, evil could not be allowed to triumph. I pictured the poor woman in her bed, and recalled the noise of her retching when she had been forced to remember the horrible way in which her husband had died. The image of the bird-of-paradise flower skew-ered through Howard Winniatt's eye flashed into my mind. If Grenville, or whoever had done that, thought they could get away with it then I was afraid they were wrong. Very wrong indeed. I had always been intrigued by the idea of Nemesis, the figure of the avenging angel. Perhaps I could draw some strength from it.

I gathered my things together, placed my note for Carlo on the desk in her room, dropped off the letter for Mr Jones at the front desk and walked out of the Taoro.

As I made my way through the pleasing gardens I breathed in the late-afternoon air, full of the aromas of exotic flowers. The beauty of it was deceptive. I approached Mal Pais with the words of Psalm 23 on my lips. 'Yea, though I walk through the valley of the shadow of death, I will fear no evil.' It was one thing to say the words quietly to oneself, another thing to believe them. I clutched my handbag tightly. Like Grenville, I had my poisons. But would they be enough to protect me?

Chapter Twenty-four

Violet, still pale and troubled, met me at the door of Mal Pais. 'Father's upstairs, he won't be long,' she said, gesturing for me to step inside.

'I'm sure you must be feeling terrible. I know I am,' I said.

'I've never seen a dead body before,' she said, her anxious eyes meeting mine. 'That awful mess, that blood, those rocks.'

'I know. Even though I worked as a nurse and saw some very serious things in the war, it was a horrible sight.'

'Did it look as though the man had suffered? I mean, was his death instant, do you think?'

From Violet's demeanour, it was clear that if her father had killed Winniatt, then she likely knew nothing about the crime. But I had to make sure.

'Well, one hopes so,' I said.

'What do you mean?' Her hands went up to her swan-white neck and then her face.

'In cases such as these, one can never be quite certain,' I said, looking around the courtyard. 'Is there somewhere quiet where we could talk?'

'Of course,' she said, leading me towards a drawing room on the ground floor. 'Please sit down while we wait for Father.'

'I'm sure he wouldn't mind us having a little talk without him. If that's all right with you?'

'Yes, of course,' she said nervously. Her hands ran through her hair, playing with a strand that had escaped from underneath her hat. 'What was he like? The man who died?'

'To be honest, I didn't like him very much. I know it's a terrible thing to say, but there it is.'

'Why not?'

'Oh, let's just say I found him to be a little pompous and opinionated. But that doesn't mean I'm pleased he is dead.'

'Do you have any idea if the Inspector knows who was responsible?'

'Not yet, I'm afraid.'

'It was horrible to have to relive it all. Even though he was very kind and considerate – I know he is rather sweet on me. But still, all those questions he asked me.'

'A necessary evil,' I said. *What a strange phrase*, I thought to myself. Was there ever really such a thing? I believed that evil, true evil, could never be justified. I took a deep breath and moved a step closer to Violet. 'I know you said you didn't know Winniatt, but are you sure you never caught a glimpse of him? After all, what

189

you saw down in the river bed bore no resemblance to the man.'

'Yes, I'm sure.'

'You didn't see him come to the house?'

'No, sorry.'

'Never saw him with your father?'

'What are you trying to say?'

'Nothing, nothing at all. I just wanted to get a few things clear in my head.' I knew Violet's weak point and was prepared, at this stage, to exploit it. 'It's his wife I feel sorry for, of course. Poor Daisy. She is quite beside herself. It's the funeral soon. Of course, I don't need to explain to you how dreadful she must feel. Losing one she cared for so deeply.'

The comment stirred an emotion deep within the girl. She tried to keep her face steady and composed, but her feelings about the imminent loss of Edmund Ffosse could not be contained. Her eyes filled with tears, her lips trembled and then her body was overtaken by a sob that forced her to fall back into a chair.

'Oh my dear, how insensitive of me,' I said, going to her side. 'Calm yourself, now.' I took out my handkerchief and passed it to her. 'I shouldn't have said anything. Coming across Winniatt as you did was shock enough for you. The last thing you need to think about is losing someone close to you.'

The sob consumed her, sending her body into a kind of spasm. I knew the feeling. Sympathy was all very well and good, but I got the impression that Violet was not telling the whole truth. I knelt down by her side and placed a hand on her knee.

'Violet, if you do know something, even perhaps some-thing you regard as insignificant, I would beg that you tell me. Your words could make all the difference. It's hard for you, and you know why Edmund is dying. But try to place yourself in Daisy's position. Imagine if Mrs Winniatt never knew the answers to all those questions that must be racing around her head. Not knowing who killed her husband will haunt her to the last of her days. It will most likely destroy her.'

'Yes, I know,' she cried. 'But it wouldn't be right.'

'What wouldn't be right?'

Violet did not respond and so I continued. 'When we love someone it can be difficult to acknowledge that they may have sides to their characters that are, well, that are not all that we'd like them to be. And, of course, no one is totally good, or totally evil. If your father has ever—'

'Has ever what?' said Gerard Grenville as he walked into the room.

Violet looked suddenly terrified, like some kind of wild animal that had been hunted and cornered, and she bolted from the chair.

How much had Grenville heard? 'Violet was just telling me about your work and I was wondering whether you had ever met a malevolent force, something or someone you regarded as truly evil.'

His big eyes stared at me with an expression of slight surprise, and then, as he considered the question, a look of unmistakable glee spread across his ugly face. 'From this world or the next?' he said.

'Either, I suppose,' I said, trying to steady my nerves.

Grenville cast a concerned look at his daughter, who had turned her back on her father and was now standing by a drinks table in the corner of the room.

'Darling, are you all right? It's this beastly business, isn't it? Perhaps we should go away for a while? What do you think?' He walked over to her and touched her lightly on the shoulder. At this she recoiled, shrinking back as if she had suddenly felt a snake or another kind of reptile caress her skin. 'Violet?'

'No, I'm fine,' she said flatly. 'Honestly, Father, I'd rather just stay here.'

'I thought a trip to Paris might do you the world of good. Or there's always Athens or Cairo.'

At this Violet looked repulsed, as if the mere mention of the names was enough to turn her sick to the stomach. What had she encountered there?

'Another time, perhaps,' said Grenville, patting his daughter on the shoulder before turning to me.

'Now, Mrs Christie, what do you say to a little consultation with the Tarot cards?'

Keen to try and ingratiate myself with Grenville, I nodded my head in agreement. 'You've got so much you can teach me,' I said. 'I really do feel that my visit to Tenerife was meant to be.'

'That's very sweet of you to say so, Mrs Christie. Let's start where we left off, in the study upstairs. And Violet, why don't you go and help Consuela with the food? There shouldn't need to be too much done – it's quite a simple *cena* we have in store for you, Mrs Christie.' He turned back towards Violet. 'I told Consuela that after she has prepared the dinner she may go. I think José is causing her some trouble again.'

I thought back to what Davison had told me about José, the young man who had informed Greene about Grenville's plan to release the spirit of evil from the mountain. The scheme may have sounded quite preposterous, but there had been two murders on the island already.

'Boys can be so troublesome,' I said, as Grenville led me out of the room and towards the stairs. 'I know my sister's young son can be an absolute terror at times.'

'The masculine drive can be an extremely powerful force, often very disruptive.'

'Is that what is worrying Consuela?'

'Well, she wouldn't put in quite those terms, I don't think,' said Grenville, smiling to himself.

'Do you know the young man well?'

'Not very well. He used to work here. He did the odd bit of carpentry, odd jobs, helping out in the garden at times. But I'm afraid we had to let him go.'

'Oh really,' I said in as casual a manner as I could manage. 'Lazy, was he?'

'If only,' said Grenville, opening the door to his study. 'No, José's problem was that he had developed an attachment to my daughter. Terribly embarrassing, of course. Violet wasn't interested, but it all got a little heated. I didn't blame the poor boy. The sexual urge at that age is so very strong and it's only a matter of biology, trying to spread one's seed far and wide. But it was very distressing for Violet, so we had to let José go.'

'I see,' I said.

193

'If that wasn't bad enough, José then started to spread the most ridiculous rumours about me.'

I made a mental note to try and find José.

'I told Consuela that she would have to deal with her son, or she would find herself out of a job too, and I think now he's calmed down,' Grenville continued. 'Anyway, to the matter in hand.'

He turned to me and gestured that I should take my place at the table. He closed the door softly behind us. Although I was nervous, I was not afraid as I doubted that Grenville would do anything while Violet and the Spanish servant woman were in the house. But what would happen when Consuela left for the day?

'I'm very grateful you are taking the trouble to do this, Mr Grenville,' I said as I took my seat.

'Gerard, please. And it's fascinating to witness your raw talents emerge. On your first visit you chose a card that predicted a death. I wonder what you will see today.'

Grenville took out his pack of Tarot cards and began to shuffle them in his large, sausage-like fingers. We went through the motions again, but this time he asked me to close my eyes and select several cards from the pack and then tell him my impressions of the imagery. This was, he said, not a reading, but a simple exercise to strengthen my powers, whatever they might be. Part of me was highly sceptical – after all, how did I know that Grenville had not made the whole thing up? I had not seen the death card; I had only his word for it. Perhaps he had drawn out the card from the pack himself, or if he had indeed murdered Winniatt, then he would have known exactly which card to choose so as to make the maximum impact. Instinct about people, places and certain situations was one thing; yes, most probably I did possess a range of highly tuned sensitivities on that score. But power of clairvoyance? I doubted it very much.

With each of the cards I selected – the Three of Swords (which showed three swords puncturing a heart), the King of Cups (a man enthroned, wearing regalia), the Eight of Swords (a blindfolded and bound maiden on a seashore surrounded by eight swords) – I related my vague impressions of them. On seeing each of the images Grenville nodded, discerning, or at least pretending to discern, significance where I could see none. Then he asked me to close my eyes once more and ask the cards a question. This time I was going to make sure that I saw the card I selected from the pack. Instead of inquiring about the murder of Douglas Greene I asked – again only to myself – about the death of Howard Winniatt. My fingers hovered over the pack, then finally, after a few seconds, I selected one of the cards from down towards the bottom.

'Now, this is interesting, very interesting indeed,' said Grenville, his dark eyes lighting up.

I opened my eyes to see a card showing a man dressed in a white Roman tunic and a scarlet cloak, standing next to a red table on which sat a cup and a pentacle. In his right hand he was holding up what looked like a staff.

'What does it mean?' I asked.

Grenville's fat fingers began to paw the card. 'The Magician, reversed,' he said, turning his gaze towards me with a heightened degree of intensity.

'Reversed?'

'If you draw it out of the pack upside down like this it gives the card a different kind of meaning,' he said, before he paused. He ran his fingers across his fleshy lips. 'Do you mind if I ask what you inquired of the cards?' he asked.

Should I risk telling him the truth? After all, I might gain something by studying his reaction. I blinked, and said in as innocent a voice as I could manage, 'Not at all. I was simply wondering who was responsible for the murder of Howard Winniatt.'

Grenville fell silent and his huge, grotesque face reddened.

'And in this case?'

'I think it best if you choose another card,' he said, taking the Magician and incorporating it back into the pack.

'But why? Have I done something wrong?'

'No, nothing at all, but I sense there's been an interruption in the energy in the room. What I call a false reading. Nothing to worry about.'

'Very well,' I said.

Just as I reached out and started to take another card Grenville said, 'Now, remember, you must close your eyes. And keep your mind blank, if you can.'

As I shut my eyes I heard Grenville get up from his chair and come and stand behind me, just as he had done on the previous occasion. I felt something hardly discernible at the back of my neck, like a feather brushing against my skin. The temperature in the room seemed to increase – I felt my face burning, my cheeks flushing. I took a deep breath and thought about the bloodied, broken corpse lying at the bottom of the dry ravine. Who was responsible for this act of evil? I selected a card, turned it over and opened my eyes. It was the Magician again.

Chapter Twenty-five

'I don't know what was going on in there,' said Grenville, leading me out of the room and back down the stairs. 'Perhaps it's the alignment of the planets at the moment. We will have to try it again at some other time.'

I followed Grenville towards the sitting room, where a tray of drinks had been laid out.

'Now what would you like? We have a local wine, quite strong and not to everyone's taste, but also sherry – or would you prefer a cocktail?'

'I'm sorry, Mr Grenville – Gerard – but I don't care for alcohol.'

'Oh, dear. Well, never mind. What would you like instead?'

'Don't go to any trouble. I'm happy with water.'

'Are you sure?'

'Yes, indeed,' I said

'It's from the spring down by Martiánez beach – such pure, wonderful water,' he said, as he went over to the sideboard and poured me a glass of water from a large ceramic jug. 'The water from the same source the Guanches drank, all those years ago.'

'Is that near where that other body – Mr Greene – was found?' I asked, again trying to sound as innocent as possible.

'Yes, awful business. I don't know what's going on here on this island. All this death.'

'Did you know the man?'

'No. The Inspector did come round and question me about him and I told him the truth – that I had never met him. Until recently I haven't been a very social animal, as I've been busy with my work, trying to build a network of like-minded souls and also the compilation of a definitive dictionary of magic. So much to do when working on a new book. Writing up all the notes, the indexing, and so on. Of course, Violet helps when she can, but her nerves do seem to get the better of her, I'm afraid. Anyway, it's very nearly finished, which is why I'm beginning to see people once more. I'm looking forward to Miss Hart's party on Valentine's Day. I think she mentioned that she had invited you.'

'Oh yes, that will be very interesting. How do you know Miss Hart?' I asked.

'Helen? I think we met in London. I can't quite remember now, but you know how it is. She's a wonderful artist. I've asked her to create a piece for my garden, but it seems to be years in the making.'

'Did you hear what happened on the ship over here? Involving Mr Trevelyan's wife?'

'Oh, yes, just awful. But I heard that she had been quite

ill for some time. In fact, I once saw her at one of those parties in London behaving as though she had lost her mind. Guy had to call in a doctor to sedate her, but it put a terrible strain on the marriage, as you can imagine. I kept telling him he should take her to the Mediterranean or even here, to Tenerife, where the sunshine serves as a form of healing in itself. You see, doctors only really look at the body, when of course there is so much more to health than that, as I'm sure you are aware.'

'Indeed,' I said. What was it my mother used to say? Yes, it was a quote from Eden Phillpotts. "The universe is full of magical things patiently waiting for our wits to grow sharper".'

'A *Shadow Passes*? I'm right, it's Phillpotts, isn't it?'

'How extraordinary, that's right,' I said, genuinely amazed.

'I've got a photographic memory, you see, Mrs Christie. I never forget anything I read. Would you like to see my books?'

'That would be fascinating,' I said as he led me through another sitting room towards the library, part of which held a display of primitive sculptures, Guanche artefacts that he had collected over the years. I strained my eyes to see if I could spot anything that resembled the figure Davison and I had found in the cave.

'They are my pride and joy,' he said, gesturing towards the shelves stacked with a range of esoteric titles dealing with a wide range of subjects. My interest was drawn towards the sections that dealt with the black arts and magic before my eyes moved over to a whole case containing pharmaceutical texts, many of which were devoted to poisons. Grenville saw me studying the books and pulled one out for me to look at.

'Here, cast your eye over this,' he said, handing me an ancient, leather-bound volume. 'What a title! *Directions for the Treatment of Persons Who Have Taken Poison, and Those In a State of Apparent Death.* I would have thought you'd find that most interesting reading, Mrs Christie.'

'Yes, I'm sure I would,' I said, turning to the title page, where I learnt that the book, which was written by M. J. B. Orfila and translated by a surgeon called R. H. Black, had been published in this second edition in 1820. What was Grenville trying to do? Did he know that I suspected him of poisoning Winniatt? Was he playing a clever game of double bluff? Surely he couldn't know anything of the horrors I had endured during my so-called disappearance?

'If you don't believe me about my memory, let us play a little game. Open it anywhere you like and give me the page number and subject. Then I'll tell you what it says, word for word.'

'I've never heard of anyone being able to do that before.'

'It's a trick I learnt in Paris. Go on.'

'Very well,' I said, as my eyes ran through the contents page, past the sections on mercurial, arsenical and antimonical preparations, through to nitre, sal ammoniac, liver of sulphur, preparation of lead, opium, laudanum and poppy seeds to one particular poison that caught my eye. 'Page eighty four, henbane.'

His eyes bulged and his tongue ran lizard-like over his fat lips. His eyes flickered as he began to recite the paragraph, word for word as it was written in the book. 'The root of black henbane has been sometimes confounded with the parsnip and used in soups, which has occasioned very serious accidents; the leaves are also very poisonous.'

I was dumbfounded.

'Don't look so shocked, Mrs Christie,' he said. 'It's actually very easy to do – it's just a matter of training, like everything else in life. And it's actually very interesting that you chose that section to read.'

'Why?'

He broke into a wheezy laugh. 'We're going to have parsnip soup tonight.'

Chapter Twenty-six

The three of us took our places at the wooden dining table, which had been covered in beautiful elaborate lace mats that Grenville said had been made by local women. Consuela entered the room carrying a tureen bearing the soup. As she placed it on the table and lifted off its lid I smelt the distinctive aroma of parsnips. I watched closely as the servant woman spooned out the soup and passed us a bowl each. If the soup had been made from a poisonous root then I was certain that it would affect not only me, but each of us in turn. Grenville watched me as I looked down at the pale brown liquid before me.

'It's one of Consuela's recipes, using chicken stock from one of her own hens and parsnips grown at my request in her husband's *huerta*,' said Grenville. 'Consuela, *gracias por todo*,' he added, dismissing her for the evening. 'Please, you must start before it gets cold.'

I took hold of a silver spoon and lifted a little of the soup towards my mouth, but then stopped. A glint of dark mischief flashed through Grenville's eyes.

'Don't be nervous, Mrs Christie,' he said, turning to his daughter. 'I was teasing her earlier, you see. We had a discussion just now about how easy it is to confuse parsnip with the root of black henbane.' The asthmatic laugh returned to rack his chest. 'Listen to me, if I carry on like this I will have to go and seek out the damnable Dr Trenkel.'

'Father, please don't speak ill of the doctor,' said Violet. 'I think he's worked wonders with Edmund.'

'The less said about that the better,' mumbled Grenville, as he spooned some soup into his mouth.

Violet looked sullen and almost instantly her mood enveloped the table, extinguishing the glint in her father's eyes and forcing us into silence.

'Very wholesome,' I said as I tasted the earthy soup, confident enough to swallow it now that both Grenville and his daughter had done so.

The only sound in the dining room was the slurping of the soup and the ticking of a clock in the corner. I had to do something to bring a bit of life to the table.

'Are you a fan of Mr Phillpotts?' I asked, biting into a piece of bread.

Grenville looked up from his soup. 'Eden? Well, of course, a very fine writer indeed. He had the potential to be a good actor too, but he had a terrible problem with his legs. Couldn't control them apparently. I knew him in London before he moved to the country.'

'I can't quite believe it,' I said, the words getting stuck in my throat. 'He was our neighbour, in Torquay.'

'Do you hear that, Violet? How extraordinary. Yes, a

wonderful writer, and so prolific, I don't know how he manages it.'

'And so kind too,' I said, my face brightening. 'I remember when I was young, around eighteen or so, I went to speak to him about writing. He was ever so encouraging and even read my first effort, dismal though it was.'

'Was that a book about crime?' asked Violet, her mood dissipating as she took a sip of wine.

'No, it was set in Cairo and concerned the choice a woman had to make between two suitors.'

'That sounds promising,' said Grenville. 'Did it have a title?'

'*Snow Upon the Desert*,' I said. 'I'm not sure why I called it that, but of course although Mr Phillpotts was encouraging – he even sent it to his agent – it was never published. I'm sure it had many faults, but its chief problem was the fact that I had chosen to make my heroine deaf. With no conversation or dialogue it became a very boring book indeed.'

Laughter broke out at the table and the mood lightened. For that moment, as I basked in the temporary glory of taking pleasure in making others laugh, I forgot what I was there for. As Grenville and his daughter asked me about how I started writing, and what I planned to write next, I tried to formulate what I needed to do while I was here.

'That's very interesting that Phillpotts helped you in your early days,' said Grenville, returning to the earlier subject. 'He had a very talented daughter, or so I've heard. What was she called?'

'Adelaide,' I replied.

Grenville's eyes seemed to mist over at the mention of the name.

'I went to ballet lessons with her when I was a girl,' I continued. 'And, of course, she is a playwright in her own right now. After the success of *Yellow Sands*, the play she worked on with her father, she wrote one set in ancient Egypt.'

'Yes, a very unusual woman,' he said. 'And wonderful that father and daughter can enjoy such a close relationship. Rather like Violet and me.'

The girl did not say anything, but simply stood up and started to clear away the soup bowls. As she left the dining room for the kitchen, carrying the dishes and spoons on a tray, Grenville turned to me and said, 'Violet's a lovely girl, don't you think?'

Violet returned with a tray of food: potatoes, accompanied by a few small dishes of red and green sauces, a platter of fish and a large salad.

'Would you serve, dear?' said Grenville to his daughter.

I still had to be careful – food like this could carry poison too – and so I asked whether they would mind if I served myself. 'I have a very small appetite, you see. Since arriving on the island my stomach has been a little delicate.'

'Of course,' said Grenville. 'It's a common problem with visitors. But I have the most effective remedy, which I can show you later, if you'd like.'

I nodded my head, but I would resist sampling anything of the sort. The meal continued, with Violet remaining mostly silent while Grenville asked me about my life in

England, my childhood, my parents, and my interest in the supernatural. Of course, I had to embellish my fascination with the occult, but Grenville continued to maintain that I had talents in this direction. In turn, I quizzed him about his beliefs. He told me how he had been fascinated by Arthurian legends as a child – an interest I shared with him – and how he had always felt able to access different planes of reality. He had kept all this from his parents, who had been strict Christians, the puritan type, but at Oxford he started to attend ceremonies that worshipped the goddess Isis and became interested in the Golden Dawn movement. Luckily for him, he added, after the death of first his mother and then his father, he was left a large inheritance – the result of the family's timber trade business – which meant he did not have to take up a profession. He was free to follow where his intellect and spirit of curiosity led him, which was to Paris, where he fell in with a bohemian crowd, and where he experimented with drugs which he believed had the power to liberate the soul from its confines. There he became close to a Spanish-born occultist called Encausse, or Papus as he was generally known.

'So I became a sorcerer's apprentice of sorts,' said Grenville, dipping a small, wrinkled potato into a dish of red spicy sauce that he told me was called *mojo*. 'Papus taught me a great deal, and I helped him with articles in *L'Initiation* and his books and we even travelled together to Russia to conjure the spirit of Alexander III. The prophecy proved correct – Tsar Nicholas was indeed overthrown by revolutionaries.'

He paused to take a swig of wine and to wipe his lips, which had been covered with a smear of the red sauce.

'We were very close, until one day we had a difference of opinion over the interpretation of a passage in an obscure Hebrew text. Of course, there were other things at play – namely that Papus thought that I was becoming more powerful than him and so he banished me from his order. I was rather fed up with his world and wanted to see something of other countries and so I volunteered to become part of an expedition to climb Pico de Orizaba in Mexico.

'It was there, standing on top of the world, that I had a vision of my life's work. I saw it all – everything appeared in a series of tableaux before me. I even glimpsed the face of the woman I was to marry, dear Jacqueline, and how she would die in childbirth. I saw our child being born and then the next image was that of a volcano, which I learnt was Teide. As the mist cleared I caught sight of a bleak barren landscape and, from the rocky soil of a barren crater, there appeared a small flower, a beautiful violet. That's how, when all this came to pass, when Jacqueline died giving birth, I knew straight away the baby had to be called Violet, a flower that blooms on Teide, even in the harshest of environments.'

Grenville had clearly enjoyed his little speech and was waiting for Violet to acknowledge him, but she did not raise her eyes from her plate. I was convinced that she knew something sinister about her father which she could be persuaded to share with me. But how on earth would I get her to myself?

Just as Grenville was about to launch into another long

speech about what he had seen on the top of that mountain, I set my knife and fork down on my plate and raised
the starched cotton napkin to my mouth.

'I wondered if you would excuse me?' I said, getting up
from the chair with a bolt. 'Violet, would you show me
where I could powder my nose?'

'Of course,' said the girl, rushing over to me. 'Are you
all right?'

'I'm just feeling a little off colour,' I said.

'I hope it wasn't our food,' said Grenville.

'No, not at all,' I said. 'Just my unpredictable stomach,
I'm afraid.'

Violet took my arm and led me out of the dining room
and down the corridor. Before I entered the room where
they had installed a primitive lavatory, I turned to her
and looked at her with a concerned expression. The look
prompted a spirited outburst that took me aback.

'What do you expect me to say?' she hissed. 'You heard
him in there. What a wonderful relationship we have, what
a fabulous father he is.'

'Violet, I know there's something bothering you,' I
whispered. 'If you have anything to tell me that relates
to your father or to Winniatt's murder, you must do so.
There's no point keeping this to yourself. I can see it's
eating away inside you, destroying you. Secrets like this
can be deadly.'

She looked frightened, haunted. 'What do you mean?'

'If you don't tell me what you know someone else
could be killed. First there was Douglas Greene, found
in that cave by Martiánez beach. And now Mr Winniatt,

murdered not far from this house. It's unlikely it's going to stop there.'

'It's not what you think,' she said.

'What is it then? You must tell me what's on your mind, as I can see that something is very wrong indeed.'

From down the corridor came the sound of the smash of a glass. 'Damn!' shouted Grenville from the dining room. 'Violet! Could you fetch something to clear up this mess? Violet, where the devil are you?'

'Coming,' she shouted back, before she whispered, 'Quickly, go in here.'

She pushed me in through the door and then turned back to the dining room where she could deal with the demands of her father. In case she remained outside the door, listening, I poured some water from a jug down into the bowl of the lavatory. I used some more to splash into a basin and onto my face, which I wiped with an embroidered white towel. When I was ready and composed, I returned to the dining room to see Violet on her knees, sweeping up the remaining shards of glass from the floor.

'Feeling better, I hope, Mrs Christie?' said Grenville, standing behind my chair and gesturing for me to take my place at the table.

'Oh, yes, very much so. I'm so sorry about that,' I said, sitting down again.

'It's no trouble, no trouble at all,' he said, moving away towards a cabinet at the side of the room. 'And sorry about this mess. You see, I was searching for the remedy I was telling you about, the one that is a miracle cure for digestive problems such as yours. Just as I found it, I misplaced a glass and sent it flying onto the floor. Never mind, these things can't be helped. Anyway the main thing is I found the remedy for you.'

From the top of the cabinet he took hold of a small vial of colourless liquid and said with a sinister smile, 'I would strongly recommend you try it.'

'W-what is it?' I asked.

'No need to be so nervous, Mrs Christie. It's from my garden here at Mal Pais, made from the finest herb and plant essences.'

'May I ask which ones?'

'Well, let's see, there's lemon verbena, fennel seeds, orange peel and camomile, I believe. All very soothing and calming, for the body and the mind.'

It sounded like a very dubious mixture to me. He unscrewed the bottle and, using a small pipette, sucked up a line of the clear liquid. 'A couple of drops should do it,' he said, proffering the pipette towards my water glass.

'That's very kind of you, thank you,' I said, moving my glass towards him.

Violet kept her head directed towards the floor, even though I was sure she had swept up all the shards by now. In the dustpan by her hands lay a large sliver of glass. What would happen if she were to reach out, grab the sharp, pointed piece of glass and use it to slit Grenville's throat? An image flashed into my mind of the blood oozing out of his neck to form a sinister necklace. His frog-like eyes bulging at being surprised by the indignity of imminent death. His great bulk slumping into the tableware before falling lifeless onto the floor.

Grenville was about to release the first drop of liquid into my water when I raised my hand and placed it on top of the glass.

'Although I would love to try it, I'm afraid I've just remembered the prescription that Dr Trenkel gave me, and I'm afraid that the two might conflict with each other.'

'But it's only plant essences – they can't do you much harm,' he said.

'I'm afraid I couldn't risk it,' I said. 'But as I'm still feeling a little weak I wonder if you wouldn't mind if—'

'You'd like to stay here for the night?'

'Exactly. You read my mind, Mr Grenville.'

'I was about to suggest the same thing,' he said, squeezing the contents of the pipette back into the vial. 'We'd be delighted, wouldn't we, Violet?'

'Yes, Father,' said the girl, straightening her dress as she eased herself up from the floor.

'Here, let me take that from you, my dear,' said Grenville. 'I'll go and dispose of this glass. We wouldn't want it hanging around. As we know, it can be quite dangerous.' He gave me a knowing look as he picked up the dustpan and left the room.

There was a moment's silence before Violet stepped towards me and, in a whisper, said, 'Come to my room around two o'clock. It's the third door on the right down from yours.'

Chapter Twenty-seven

Violet and Grenville showed me to my quarters, a modest room painted white containing a single bed, a small desk and chair and a table with a bowl, a pitcher of water, and a couple of glasses.

Grenville said that in the morning, after breakfast, he would be keen to try some more experiments, this time with a pendulum and the *I Ching*. He also wanted to show me his collection of Guanche figures and artefacts. Helen Hart, he added, was a huge fan of Guanche sculpture; it was, he said, her ambition to move her work towards a greater state of primitivism. We parted on this and retired for the night.

In the room I washed my face then sat on the bed and waited for the house to go to sleep. As I did so I ran through the strange events of the night: the odd dynamic between Grenville and his daughter; his eagerness to give me some of that tincture, which he said would help cure my digestive ills; and the strange feeling I had that Grenville could read my thoughts. What was he planning?

I opened my handbag and looked at my collection of poisons. Of course, the deadly vials would provide no protection if Grenville got to me first. All it would take would be one drop of something fatal, perhaps in my morning tea or coffee, and my life would be snuffed out. He would know that there were certain poisons that would be quite difficult, sometimes impossible, to trace in the body. He could tell the police that I had been complaining of stomach cramps before I had gone to bed and that I must have died in my sleep. No doubt Violet would serve as witness; I would be buried, as was the custom here, within a couple of days, and in years to come, no one would come and visit my grave on this island that lay in the sea off Africa, many miles from England.

But I was not ready to be defeated by Grenville. After I thought that both he and Violet had gone to bed, I quietly opened the door and, with the candle that lay on my bedside table, stepped out of the room and along the corridor towards the study. In the dim light, the ghouls and demons in the woodcuts on the wall looked even more sinister. Steadying myself, I made my way over to Grenville's desk and took up one of the sheets of paper lying on the surface. Using the candle to illuminate its contents I realised that the words meant nothing to me. This was not a language I had ever seen before. Was it written in some kind of code or were these words just so obscure that I had never encountered them?

If Grenville had murdered Winniatt then he must be the one responsible for the removal of the missing journal. Of course, he could have already burnt it, but it was still

214

worth searching the house for any other clues. I started to work my way through the drawers of the desk, finding ink bottles, some containing ink the colour of blood, unusual-looking seals, receipts and papers relating to the house, and some travel documents, before I came across a set of notebooks. Each of the books was written in Grenville's flowing, theatrical hand. As I scanned quickly over the words, I could see they described in detail a range of rituals, rites and magic spells. A great deal of it was impossible to understand, as it was written in a highly technical form, but certain words and phrases jumped out at me: 'dark power', 'the evil within', 'the love of Satan', 'succubi', 'Golden Dawn', 'The unspoken, secret act', 'The delicious corruption of an innocent', 'the book of the dead' and – most significant of all – a section devoted to 'How to drain a body of blood'. I thought of Douglas Greene's body in that cave, his corpse leached of its lifeblood, his skin painted red. Surely there was enough evidence here for Inspector Núñez to investigate Grenville? There were letters relating to the future establishment of some kind of commune on the island and correspondence from occultists in Paris, London, Egypt and Greece.

There were other notebooks devoted to poisons, which related the symptoms, signs and antidotes to a range of toxic substances: aconitine, cyanide, eserine, hemlock, horned rye, monkshood, mushrooms, nux vomica, pilocarpine. The last chemical, sometimes used for the treatment of glaucoma, pricked my interest as I knew that while it could be a poison itself, it could also be used as an antidote to combat the effects of atropine, the toxin contained in henbane that I thought may have been given to Howard Winniatt.

I passed quickly over sections that dealt with what seemed like Grenville's extended sexual imaginings. I did not want to dwell on the thought of him involved in illicit acts. The very idea turned my stomach. As I handled the notebooks and read these entries I felt evil emanating off the page, a force that seemed to leak through the membrane of my skin. I took a few deep breaths and tried to imagine all that was good in the world. My mother, my daughter, Carlo, my dog Peter. I thought of Torquay and the lovely view out to Thatcher Rock. I imagined the feel of the seawater on my skin. The image of water brought back the sight of that young woman standing on the deck of the *Gelria*. Why couldn't I stop thinking of Gina Trevelyan? That was a case of suicide, pure and simple. She had had a history of mental disturbance. She had discovered that her husband was in love with another woman, someone she knew. That was more than enough to explain her sudden, dramatic death. And yet there was something not quite right about it, something I couldn't put my finger on. I felt certain of one thing, however: her death had nothing to do with Grenville, and so, at least for tonight, I would have to put it out of my mind. However, I was determined not to forget Gina Trevelyan.

Listening out for signs of Grenville, I made my way from the study downstairs to the library. As I walked my candle cast a series of long, strangely shaped shadows. How odd that Grenville knew that quote from *A Shadow Passes*. Even odder that he should know Phillpotts himself.

I moved the candle along the spines of the books, some of which had curious titles: *The Book of the Sacred Magic of Abramelin the Mage*; the *Alexandria Codex*; the *Book of Soyga*; *Dogme et Rituel de la Haute Magie*, and so on. I took one down from the shelf at random, an illustrated Arabian manuscript called the *Kitab al-Bulhan*, or *Book of Surprises*. I let the book fall open at a page that showed a creature that was half man, half devil; a pair of horns sprouted from its head and two fangs protruded from the corners of its mouth. I turned the page to see another grotesque hybrid, three animalistic heads on top of a black man's body. The illustrations were beautifully done, finely drawn and expertly coloured, but the contents unsettled me to such an extent that I was forced to close the book and place it back on the shelf.

I pushed my fingers between and behind the spines, looking for Winniatt's missing journal, but nothing was to be found. I checked the fireplace for traces of burnt paper. Although there were some charred fragments in the grate, on closer examination these turned out to be from a local Canarian newspaper. From there I walked over to Grenville's display of Guanche figures. In the candlelight, the small, primitive sculptures looked like totems of evil. Grenville had arranged his collection like objects in a museum: on labels beneath each of the figures he had scrawled the name of the artefact and where it had been found. The first one that caught my eye was one of Tibecena, similar to the one Davison had found in the cave overlooking Martiánez beach. Next to this stood a small representation of Guayota, the malign spirit that lived in Mount Teide. *What had Davison told me?* That, according to local legend, Guayota had kidnapped the sun in the form of Magec, which he shut up inside Teide, plunging the world into darkness. The human race prayed to Achaman – the father god and creator – who rescued Magec and then punished Guayota by imprisoning him inside the volcano. Greene had believed that Grenville wanted to free Guayota from the mountain, so as to usher in a new world order of evil.

Of course, this was nothing more than far-fetched, superstitious nonsense – I doubted such a thing could ever happen – but nevertheless Grenville's deluded beliefs could still result in yet more pain, misery and violence.

Just then I heard a clock strike two. It was time to go and speak to Violet. Using my candle to guide me, I made my way up the stairs to the first floor. As I turned to walk down the corridor I felt the soft breath of a night breeze on my face and my candle went out. It was then, immersed in the darkness, that I heard a strange, muffled noise coming from the other side of Violet's door. What on earth was happening inside there? I felt my way back to my room for the matches that lay on a table by the window. I recalled the moment in the cave where I had encountered that spectral figure, when my hands had been shaking so much that the matches had fallen through my fingers. The same fear returned now. As I searched for the box my hands felt the outlines of various items on the table – a glass paperweight, another candle holder, a book – before I came across the matches. The first one I tried to light burnt my finger, forcing me to drop it on the floor. The next one broke, sending a minute splinter of wood into my thumb. The third match illuminated a spot of blood beginning to bloom from my skin. I quickly relit the candle and made my way out of the room and back down the corridor. I stopped outside Violet's room, a sickness rising from my stomach. A part of me did not want to see what was on the other side of the door. Perhaps it would be for the best if I left Grenville's house and never returned. Did I really want to know the full extent of the evils of Mal Pais? But then I recalled Violet's haunted look and her request that I come to her room at two o'clock. There was something she wanted me to know, something she wanted me to see.

I placed my ear to the wood and heard a series of bestial grunts and asthmatic pants. I gently eased the door open and, in the dim light, at first could not take in what I saw. A candle from the bedside table cast a warm glow over a grotesque, terrible sight, something truly against nature. On the bed were two intertwined forms: Grenville, his naked, hairy back rising and falling over his pale-skinned daughter. My instinct was to run across the room and claw the monster off, but in that instant I met Violet's eyes, eyes that were full of tears, anger and hatred. As I took one step towards her she shook her head, warning me off. She did not want me to do anything, at least not at that moment. She had been unable to tell me the truth about her father because she knew the words were too terrible to say. And so she had led me here to her room for me to see for myself.

I stepped out of the room, closing the door quietly behind me. As I entered my own room the sound of Grenville's heavy breathing stayed in my head, the memory of that vile act seared on my brain. Mal Pais was rotten to its very core, the evil emanating from the malignant personality of Grenville, a man who corrupted everything around him, even his own daughter.

What did Violet expect me to do? Did she want me to go to the police? Did she hope that this would lead to an investigation of his other crimes? Was she using me as a conduit through which to speak to Inspector Núñez? The shame that came with the act was all too real and I could imagine how hard it would be for her to talk about, especially to Núñez, a man who had shown feelings for her. I presumed she had never told Edmund Ffosse of the perverted attentions of her father; he would be the last person she would have wanted to find out. The next day I would have to make sure I could get Violet alone so I could ask her some of these questions.

The discovery also made me examine the comments made by Grenville about Phillpotts and his daughter, Adelaide. Surely he wasn't suggesting something untoward in that relationship too? Phillpotts was such a decent, honourable man. Was there nothing that this monster did not want to besmirch with his unholy filth? What else was he capable of?

Although the door to my bedroom had a lock, I couldn't find a key. And so I moved the chair from behind the desk to in front of the door. If he chose to come into my room I knew it would not stop him, but at least the sound of it being moved would give me a little notice. What I would then do I had no idea.

The more I thought about Grenville the more angry I became. As I sat there on my bed, in the light of a flickering candle, I had to do everything in my power to restrain myself from going back into Violet's room. I was afraid of what I might do. Although I lay down, I could not sleep. Instead, when I closed my eyes, I thought of my poisons and imagined Grenville suffering a long and excruciatingly painful death.

Chapter Twenty-eight

The night passed without any further incident. Grenville made no attempt to come into my room, but that hardly mattered, as the memory of what I had seen poisoned the air. I did not sleep, or if I did, it was for short spells only, brief lapses in consciousness haunted by terrible visions of Grenville and his daughter.

At half past eight I heard a knock at the door.

'Mrs Christie? Agatha?' The voice was weak, barely there. 'It's me, Violet.'

I stood up from my bed, walked across the room and removed the chair from its position. I opened the door to see Violet's weary face. Misery and pain seemed to ooze out of every pore, and as she looked at me her eyes started to fill with tears.

'You poor thing,' I said, reaching out to her. 'Come in here, quickly, and we can talk about last night.'

Violet took a step back and removed my hand from her arm. 'Last night? What on earth can you mean?'

'About what I saw in your room. With your father.'

'I'm sorry, but I haven't got a clue what you're talking about.'

The statement took my voice away. I opened my mouth to repeat myself, but the words would not form themselves on my lips.

'I was just asking to see whether you felt any better this morning,' she said.

'Yes, I'm perfectly well, thank you.'

'Because last night you were very ill indeed. Don't you remember?'

I felt my brows creasing with bewilderment and disbelief. 'But that was all a pretence. You know it was. We talked about it before I went into the lavatory. You told me to come to your room at two o'clock, which I did. And that's where I saw you, w-with your father.'

'I'm afraid you must have been suffering the effects of your illness. Your food poisoning. Father says sometimes one can have funny dreams and suchlike.'

'But Violet, this was no dream. I saw you with him. With your father. In bed.'

'I don't know what on earth you are suggesting,' she said, as she turned to go. 'I enjoyed the most restful sleep, as did Father. He told me so this morning.' She looked back at me with a concerned air. 'Perhaps you'll feel better after some breakfast. If not, we may have to call the doctor to take a look at you.'

'Violet, stop this now,' I said, feeling the anger begin to fire my cheeks. 'You know what you said. You know what I saw. I can understand that it's hard for you to accept, but it's something that I promise I will help you with. We can tell the Inspector together. You can trust me to be with you through all of this.'

'I don't know what is the problem, but it does seem as though the balance of your mind has been affected. Father told me that he'd read in the newspapers about you having some kind of breakdown back in England. Perhaps you're still suffering from an imbalance of mind.' Violet's voice was gentle, like that of a nurse trying to soothe a fevered patient. She reached out and placed a soft hand on my forehead to see whether I was running a temperature. 'You must rest now. Please go back to bed and I'll ask Father to call Dr Trenkel.'

With this, she gave me a hard push, slamming the door and locking it from the outside. I turned the handle, but the door would not open. I banged on the wood with some force.

'Violet! Violet! Let me out. I must talk to you. I know what's going on here. It's dangerous if you continue to live here. Your father is . . .'

I felt my voice fade away with each retreating footstep. Again I banged on the door with a fury. But there was no response. I walked over to the window, which was covered by *rejas*, a crisscross of bars, and which looked out towards Grenville's poison garden. I considered shouting out the window, but nobody other than Violet and Grenville would hear me. I unzipped my handbag and searched through it for anything that might help open the door, but there was nothing. I took some comfort in the note I had left for Carlo telling her of my whereabouts. If I had not turned up at the hotel by teatime she would start to get concerned; she might possibly tell Inspector Núñez.

What on earth had happened overnight to change Violet's mind? Had she told her father about what I had seen? If so, he could have threatened her with violence – or even worse things. I doubted that she intended to send for Dr Trenkel. But what did Grenville have planned for me? Surely he wasn't considering harming me in any way? He would know that he could never get away with it. A death on his premises could not be so easily explained. Or perhaps he was so sick in the brain that he no longer cared about what happened to him? Was this going to be his final crime? The one where he allowed himself to express his evil mind in all his ghoulish glory? I thought back over the last two murders. A body, partly mummified, in a cave, the corpse drained of blood. Another man dead of head injuries, his eye spiked with a bird-of-paradise flower. What would he do with me? Poison me and then do something to my body? Show me off in some grotesque way or sacrifice me to a heathen god of his imagining?

Thinking along these lines would not help me. I splashed cold water over my face and tidied myself. I sat on the bed and thought about how best to proceed, arranging a few items that I thought might prove helpful. Half an hour later, I heard a key turning in the lock. Instead of rushing to the door I remained seated on the bed and looked up to see Grenville's great bulk.

'Violet tells me you're still feeling unwell,' he said.

'Yes, that's right,' I said, thinking it best to play along with his sinister game.

'I'm very sorry to hear that, Mrs Christie. She also

tells me that you seem to be running a temperature and suffering from delirium.'

'I believe I was a little feverish in the night, yes.'

'I'm sure there's something we can do to help,' he said. As his large frame filled the small room he looked like some kind of giant trying to squeeze itself into a doll's house. From the pocket of his jacket he took out a vial of clear liquid. 'This is the essence I mentioned last night. Do you remember?'

'Yes,' I said. 'Perhaps it will do me some good after all.' The compliant words seemed to unsettle him slightly, as though he had not expected to encounter such an easy, submissive prey.

'Now, where's your water glass?'

'Here it is,' I said, picking up the tumbler from my bed-side table and holding it out. I readied myself for what I was about to do. Before Grenville had appeared at the door I had decanted some of my liquid smelling salts into the glass. I just had to wait until the right moment when I had Grenville within range.

He stepped towards me and proceeded to release a few drops of what he told me was the herbal essence into the water. He watched my every movement as I took up the glass and placed it near my lips.

'It will make you feel better in no time,' he said. 'After all, we wouldn't want you to suffer from any more confusion. Most exhausting, delirium, don't you find?'

My fingers tensed around the glass.

'Yes, I'm feeling very weak still,' I said. 'I would do anything for a few hours' sleep.'

Another second or so and I would have his eyes in a direct line.

"'To sleep, perchance to dream ...'" he said, quoting Hamlet. "'For in that sleep of death what dreams may come ...'"

I had no intention of shuffling off my mortal coil, at least not yet, and certainly not at Grenville's hands. As I pretended to sip the water the overpowering stench of the smelling salts filled my nostrils. But it would have a more devastating effect on Grenville when I threw the liquid into his eyes. Hopefully, the solution would blind him, albeit temporarily, which would give me the opportunity to escape.

'Are you drinking that? Now, you must swallow it,' he said, watching my lips. 'You'll begin to feel the benefits almost immediately.'

The atmosphere in the room seemed heightened, as if the air were charged with electricity. Grenville's dark eyes burned with a strange intensity. There was a hypnotic quality to them that seemed to cloud my mind. My hand felt numb, paralysed.

'I can see that you are feeling very tired,' he said, softly. 'Drink, and you can rest. I know the troubles you have been through. Close your eyes.'

My eyelids felt heavy, my brain almost stupefied. I felt so tempted to lie back on the bed and go to sleep, forget everything. I wouldn't have to think about Greene in that cave, about Winniatt with the bird-of-paradise flower sticking out of his eye. I could stop worrying about my unfinished novel. I would never have to think about Archie

227

again. I need never concern myself with the horrors that Violet had had to endure. But then the image of the poor girl on that bed and the terrible sadness in her eyes came into my mind. No, what Grenville had done could never be forgotten, neither could his behaviour be forgiven. Although I felt a renewed surge of energy rush through my system, I gave Grenville the impression that his hypnotic voice had worked its sinister power on my brain.

'That's right. Any moment now you will feel the warmth begin to wash over you,' he said, almost in a whisper. 'Now, take a sip of the water and then you can sleep for as long as you like.'

I opened my eyes to see him staring at me with a kind of morbid fascination, almost as though he was viewing me not so much as a person but as a mere object. Was he already imagining me dead? My fingers gripped the glass with such a force that I feared I might shatter it. In that instant, he realised that he no longer had control of me, possibly never had, and I saw a spark of fear in his eyes. I lowered the glass from my lips, and just as I was about to throw the ammonia into his face, I heard a commotion from downstairs.

'I'm afraid she's still ill in bed, she's asleep,' I heard Violet shouting, her voice full of panic. 'No, please, you cannot—'

'Agatha! Agatha!' It was Carlo, dear Carlo, who had come to my rescue.

'Carlo, I'm here, upstairs,' I called. I was answered by the sound of fast-approaching footsteps.

Grenville's face flushed with anger. 'If you don't want

my treatment, you won't have it,' he said, grabbing the glass out of my hand and smashing it against the wall. The smell of the ammonia began to leach out into the room. 'What the hell is that?' He looked at me with amazement, soon followed by disappointment and then undisguised disgust.

I grabbed my bag and ran out of the room and into Carlo's arms. 'I was beginning to get worried,' she said. 'Violet said you were feeling unwell. How are you now?'

'Much better, but I do believe it's time to get back to the hotel. I'm sure Rosalind must be missing me.' Despite the horrors of what I had encountered in Mal Pais, I still found it difficult to be uncivil. I knew that Violet would not have the strength to endure a public humiliation.

I turned to see Grenville stumbling along the passage, a handkerchief over his mouth, his face reddening, his breathing turning asthmatic. The noise reminded me of the sound of his panting in that bedroom. The memory of that grotesque squirming form on the bed brought back a wave of nausea. 'Goodbye, Mr Grenville. I'm sure I will see you soon.' I grabbed Carlo's hand and pulled her down the passage and towards the stairs, where Violet was standing.

'You're so pale,' Carlo whispered. 'What's happened?'

'We need to leave – quickly,' I said so only she could hear. 'That man is a monster.'

Her eyes acknowledged the danger. 'Thank you, Mr Grenville, Miss Grenville,' said Carlo, as we walked hand in hand towards the girl. 'I'm sure I can look after Mrs Christie now. But thank you for all your concerns and your kindness.'

As I passed Violet I stopped and placed my hand on her arm. She could not meet my eye. 'You need to get away from here,' I said quietly. 'It's not safe.'

'Goodbye, Mrs Christie,' she said coldly, moving her arm away from my touch. 'I do hope you make a full recovery.'

'Violet—'

My words of warning were cut off by Grenville, who had followed us, with a huge, manic grin on his face.

'Keep walking,' I whispered to Carlo.

'It's a shame you are leaving us so soon, Mrs Christie,' he said, and he reached the top of the stairs. 'There are so many things left to discuss. I suspected you of harbouring certain talents, but you've surprised me. Your resourcefulness is really quite extraordinary.'

When we descended the stairs and passed into the courtyard I kept my head bent forwards so as not to look up towards Grenville. As we stepped out of Mal Pais I heard Grenville's shouts begin to ring around the house, soon followed by the pitiful cries of his daughter.

Chapter Twenty-nine

'What on earth were you thinking?' said Carlo, as soon as we were at a safe distance from the house.

'I know, I'm sorry, but I couldn't see any other way of trying to find some proof.'

'Proof about what?'

'That Grenville is the killer, of course.'

The comment stopped Carlo in her tracks. She turned to me with a look of horror on her face.

'So you went in there, into that house, knowing, or at least suspecting, that that man was a murderer?'

'Yes, but—'

'Thank goodness you left me a note. Do you really want to make Rosalind an orphan?' she said harshly, the anger intensifying her Scottish accent. 'Is that what you want?'

'No, of course not, but the police have nothing to go on. I had to try to find out a little more about Grenville and his so-called dark arts.'

'And what did you discover?'

ANDREW WILSON

'More than I bargained for,' I said. As we walked I went on to tell her something of the terrible things I had seen in Mal Pais: the depraved contents of Grenville's notebooks, the man's seemingly unquenchable appetite for perversity, the array of titles about magic and demons and poisons on his shelves. I told her too of my suspicion of his intention to try and poison me with his 'herbal essence', the one he promised had restorative qualities. 'When you arrived he smashed the glass against the wall, no doubt afraid I could take it away and have it tested,' I added.

I did not, however, mention anything about how I had planned to escape nor anything about my secret collection of poisons. I left out all details that might link Grenville to the death of Douglas Greene, as Carlo had to remain ignorant of the true reason I had travelled to the island and my work for the Secret Intelligence Service.

'The worst thing was when, after Violet told me to call at her room at two o'clock, I saw Grenville in – in bed with his own daughter.'

Carlo looked as though she might retch into the dusty ground. 'You can't mean that—'

'Yes, I'm afraid I do,' I said, before I told her of how the girl had tried to make out that my illness had caused an attack of delirium and that I had suffered from hallucinatory dreams that had warped my perception.

'So when you spoke to Violet this morning, she denied all knowledge of it?'

'Yes, but only because she's afraid of what her father might do to her. I think if I got her alone again, I could persuade her. In the meantime, every single minute she

232

spends in that rotten place she is in danger. When we get back to the hotel I'm going straight to the Inspector to tell him everything I know.'

'Do you think that's wise?' asked Carlo.

'What other choice do I have? I can't let that girl suffer as she is at the moment. Every day, each night, must be like a little hell for her.'

'But what if she continues to deny it?'

I couldn't answer her.

'And despite the sinister nature of his library and the contents of his journals, as I understand it there's nothing concrete that you've found to show that Grenville is a murderer.'

The suggestion raised my hackles and I felt a rash of anger begin to prick the skin around my neck.

'But everything fits, don't you see? His interest and knowledge of poisons, particularly henbane. The location of the murder, near his house but out of sight of other properties. The bird-of-paradise flowers that grow in his garden. And his professed obsession with the occult.' I could have added something along the lines of his collection of Guanche sculptures, figures that linked him to what Davison and I had discovered under Greene's body in the cave by Martiánez beach.

I could tell that Carlo remained unconvinced by my argument. 'If you had looked into his eyes as I have done, then you would be in no doubt of his guilt,' I said.

As we walked over the bridge that led across the *rambla* where Winniatt's body had been found we fell silent for a moment. I had to admit to myself that Carlo was right.

233

'Even though I can't give Núñez definitive proof that Grenville was responsible for the murder of Howard Winniatt I can at least tell him about the other crime that is going on under that wicked roof. Hopefully Núñez might think that if Grenville can do that, to his own daughter, then he would be capable of other things too.'

'As long as you know what you're doing,' said Carlo.

'What do you mean?'

'It might open a very nasty can of worms, that's all.'

'But I can't just remain silent on the subject.'

'Perhaps not,' she said. 'All I'm saying is that we don't know how certain people will react. How will Violet take this kind of exposure?'

'I'm hardly going to shout about it now, am I?' I felt my voice rising, my cheek flushing. 'I hope you think I'm a little more sensitive than that.'

'Of course,' said Carlo, taking my hand and trying to calm me. 'It's just that I'm worried. I'm anxious not only about Violet but also about you. I promised that I would look after you. I don't want to see you upset like this, getting involved in other people's grubby lives. We don't want a repetition of what happened last year.'

There was nothing I could say on the subject. According to the version of the truth that Carlo knew, I had suffered a breakdown caused by the death of my mother, an episode of writer's block and my discovery that Archie had been having an affair. She believed the doctors' diagnosis that, when I had disappeared to Harrogate, I had been in the grip of a prolonged attack of amnesia. She could know nothing of the sinister Dr Kurs or my secret work for Davison.

'Yes, perhaps you're right,' I said, trying to appease her. 'Before I do anything, I promise to think it over.' I wanted to change the subject and so I asked her about what Rosalind had been doing. We talked of my daughter and her continuing obsession with her teddy bear, before we moved on to chat about some of the fellow guests at the hotel. Mrs Brendel continued to declaim her never-ending monologue about the *Titanic* to anyone who would listen. Professor Wilbor and Rupert Mabey had dined at the hotel the previous evening, where the conversation continued to centre around the death of Mr Winniatt. Daisy had still not appeared in public since the discovery of her husband's body. She had remained in her room, under the care of Dr Trenkel. Helen Hart and Guy Trevelyan had not been seen at the Taoro.

'No doubt they were busy with preparations for the party on Valentine's Day,' I said. 'It's not really my kind of affair,' I added, thinking of Helen and Guy's insatiable appetite for alcohol. 'But I promised to make an appearance. I suppose it will be interesting to see her studio and her work. Why don't you come?'

'You know me, I hate parties even more than you do,' said Carlo, smiling. 'No, I'd much rather stay at the hotel with Rosalind and a good book.'

We found Rosalind in the garden with her friend Raymond, watched over by his French governess, a woman with light auburn hair and sad eyes who was sitting on a bench reading in the shade of a palm tree. The two children were playing with their teddies, when suddenly the little boy grabbed hold of Rosalind's and ran off with it.

ANDREW WILSON

My daughter looked down at her empty hands and burst into tears.

'Darling, what's wrong?' I said, running up to her and wrapping her in my arms, closely followed by Carlo.

For a moment she could not speak and then she cried, in a pitiful voice, 'B-Blue Teddy – Raymond has taken Blue Teddy.'

'I'm sure he didn't mean to,' I said, wiping the tears from her face. 'Let's see where he's gone to . . . Is that lady over there Raymond's governess?' Rosalind nodded. 'Well, I'm sure she will be able to help.'

Carlo introduced the sad-eyed lady as Madame Giroux and asked her whether she had seen the altercation between the two children. She had not, she told us, as she had been reading, but when she heard what had passed between them she immediately took to fussing over Rosalind as if her own daughter had been hurt.

'That's right, *ma petite*, dry your tears,' she said, in her French accent, before standing up and turning to us. 'Raymond can be naughty at times, but I think it's because of what happened in the past, losing his brother. Of course, that doesn't excuse his behaviour.'

She suggested we walk towards the back of one of the glasshouses where she knew Raymond liked to play. We found him there, sitting on the ground with his legs crossed, holding both teddies.

'Raymond, I think you owe your friend an explanation, don't you?' said Madame Giroux, as she approached the boy. Raymond did not look up from his game. She knelt down and spoke to him softly, before he looked up and gestured for Rosalind.

'You can have your teddy back,' he said.

'Go on, darling,' I said, giving her a little push of encouragement. 'He's trying to be nice.'

Rosalind smiled as she walked awkwardly towards her friend. She reached out to take her teddy, but as she did so Raymond smacked her hand away.

'That's not yours, he's mine!' he shouted.

Rosalind immediately burst into tears and ran back into my arms.

'Raymond, what on earth has come over you?' Madame Giroux said to her charge in French. 'I just cannot understand why you are being so naughty.'

'But she tried to take the wrong one again!' shouted Raymond, his face flushing with anger. 'Can't you see? She's been doing it all day!'

'Oh mummy, why is he being so horrid?' pleaded Rosalind. 'Why won't he give me Blue Teddy back?'

'Now, now,' I said. 'I'm sure there's a simple explanation for all of this. Come on, let's go and talk to him.'

Although Rosalind resisted, I managed to persuade her to walk with me over to the boy.

'Hello, Raymond, I'm Rosalind's mother,' I said in a soft, gentle voice. 'There seems to be a misunderstanding. Can you tell me what's wrong?'

'I'm not being naughty, I'm not!' he said.

'I'm not here to scold you,' I said. 'Now which one is which?'

'You see this one here?' he said, lifting up the teddy that Rosalind had just tried to take from him, 'This is George, my teddy.' Had Carlo not mentioned that the boy's dead brother had been called George? 'You can see it's George because he's missing an eye. But this one here, this is Rosalind's.' He passed the toy to my daughter, who clutched it tightly to her chest.

'I see, it's because they both look the same from behind,' said Madame Giroux.

'Yes, but Rosalind kept taking the wrong one and I got cross and—'

'Never mind,' said Madame Giroux. 'But I think you owe dear Rosalind an apology. What do you say, Raymond?'

After Raymond, with a slight protruding underlip, said the obligatory 'Sorry', the two children ran off, as if nothing had happened. Carlo and I thanked Madame Giroux for her help in the arbitration between the two – we joked that she had resolved what could have turned into a nasty diplomatic incident – but she said it was nothing, adding that she would be delighted to continue watching over the two children. We thanked her again and accompanied her to the entrance of the hotel, before we parted on the steps.

Just as we walked into the Taoro, Gustavo came over and, after some pleasantries, he handed me an envelope. It was a note from Inspector Núñez asking me to call at his suite at my earliest convenience. There was, he added, some matter that required my assistance. Perhaps he had unearthed some information relating to Grenville which he wanted to ask me about. Had Dr Trenkel's tests finally proved that Winniatt had been poisoned? The doctor may have told the Inspector about my specialist knowledge of certain toxic substances and their effects on the body. Perhaps Núñez had realised that my help could be invaluable in this case?

'The Inspector wants to see me,' I said to Carlo, as I turned to make sure that Rosalind was playing happily with Raymond. My head was full of memories of my dear daughter, the smooth feel of her cheek against mine, the chirrup of her laughter. I recalled the threats that Kurs had made, and how I had been prepared to do God knows what to protect her. But poor Violet had no mother to look after her. If she had, perhaps Grenville would never have been able to defile his daughter. I realised I had no choice. When I saw Núñez I would tell him the awful truth of what I had seen. 'So perhaps fate has taken the decision out of my hands.'

I left Carlo and walked up the stairs and along the corridors to Núñez's suite. I knocked on the door and a moment later a tall man with a groomed moustache, one of Núñez's assistants, ushered me in. The Inspector sat at his desk frowning. I was about to launch into my narrative of the unholy goings-on at Mal Pais when he looked up from his desk, darkness clouding his eyes.

'Sit down, please, Mrs Christie,' he said.

'Thank you, I'm so grateful you called for me because I've got something important to tell you. A very serious matter indeed, which could change your view of the whole case. You see, last night—'

'I'm afraid I'm going to have to stop you, Mrs Christie,' he said sternly, holding up his right hand. 'There's something I need to ask you before you say anything else. And please think very carefully before you answer.'

'What is it?'

Núñez paused for effect, stood up and said, 'Did you steal a set of pearls belonging to Mrs Winniatt?'

Chapter Thirty

'I won't repeat myself,' Núñez said, looking at me with barely disguised contempt.

'No, of *course* I didn't steal Mrs Winniatt's pearls,' I said dismissively. 'Now, if you'd just listen to me. Last night I—'

'Mrs Winniatt was preparing herself for the forthcoming funeral of her husband. She went to her jewellery box for the pearls, apparently highly valuable and passed down through her family. But she could not find them. She looked everywhere, throughout her luggage, she searched her room, but to no avail. Obviously it's a very distressing time for her. But what she discovered only compounded her distress – the only conclusion she could come to was that someone must have stolen into her room and taken them. What kind of cold-hearted person could do such a thing? Now I will ask you a different question. Do you know anything about the theft of Mrs Winniatt's pearls?'

I could feel his eyes watching me. Should I tell him about

what I had seen from the confines of that wardrobe? That it was Dr Trenkel who had taken them.

'Well, I—' I said, before stopping myself. Something prevented me from saying anything more. I had a feeling that it would be wiser to keep this information back from the Inspector.

'Yes? You were saying?'

'No, I don't know anything, I'm afraid.'

Núñez's eyes narrowed as he looked at me. 'You know I don't like to play games, Mrs Christie,' he said, walking over to me. 'I don't like to be made a fool of. I know that in the world of crime fiction, it is highly fashionable to make fun of the police. We are all – what is it you English say? – blockheads. We have no brains. No aptitude for the job. Yes, the amateur detective is all the rage. Or men who have retired from the force. But let me tell you that in my world, the real world, an amateur would not stand a chance.' He stood so close now that I could feel his breath on my face. 'You may have a talent for writing books about murder, but that doesn't mean you can extend your abilities outside the cosy world of the written word.'

What exactly did he know about me? Had he heard something about my secret work with Davison? Why did I feel that I didn't want to share what I had seen in Daisy Winniatt's room?

'Is there anything you want to tell me?'

I shook my head.

'Then how do you explain the fact that we have some-one who insists they saw you coming out of Mrs Winniatt's room at just after eleven o'clock on Saturday night?'

'I suppose they must be mistaken,' I said, trying to control my nerves and deciding to bluff my way out of the situation.

'Mistaken?'

'Yes, after all there must be many women of roughly my age and colouring who are staying at the Taoro.'

'Is that so?'

'I can think of no other explanation.'

'You can't?'

'No, I'm sorry, Inspector Núñez, but whoever claims they saw me must have mixed me up with another woman.'

His eyes were steely now, cold and dismissive. 'And you have nothing more to say on the matter?'

'No, but I do have something I want to tell you about what I witnessed last night. I went to stay with Gerard Grenville and—'

'And no more news on the mysterious Mr Blake?' interrupted Núñez. 'He seems to have disappeared. You wouldn't have happened to have heard from him, would you?'

This time I could tell the truth. 'No, nothing at all. But getting back to what I saw at Grenville's house. I—'

Núñez turned his back to me, walked towards his desk, and called to his assistant with the manicured moustache who stood in the corner of the room. 'Borges, could you show Mrs Christie out, please?'

'But, you don't understand, I have a—'

'There's nothing left to say. Good day, Mrs Christie.'

I felt a light touch on my arm. Borges gestured towards the door. It seemed I had little choice but to leave.

'Could I make another appointment to come and see you?' I asked as I stood by the door.

Núñez did not bother to look up from his desk as he said, 'Only if you are willing to tell me the truth about the pearls. I'm not interested in anything else you have to say.'

What a stupid, ignorant man, I thought to myself as I stormed back down the corridor towards my room. No wonder the investigation into Winniatt's death was going nowhere. He seemed to be wilfully blind to what was staring him in the face.

'Is everything all right?' asked Carlo as I entered our suite of rooms. She was in the middle of pouring tea from a tray on the table. 'How did he take the news?'

'I didn't get the chance to tell him,' I said. 'The buffoon didn't want to hear it.' I couldn't go into the details about what Núñez really wanted to know.

'Perhaps that's for the best,' said Carlo. 'Would you like a cup?'

'Yes, please,' I said distractedly. 'But how can it be for the best when that poor girl is living with a father who does, well, who does those unspeakable things to her?'

'I suppose the Inspector's got his hands full with the investigation into Winniatt's death.'

'Yes, you're right – as usual,' I said, taking the china cup that Carlo passed to me. 'They do know how to make tea here. With water that is actually boiling and good quality tea leaves, not like some of the places on the continent.'

'A drink that bears little resemblance to what we would call tea,' said Carlo, sipping from her teacup. 'By the way, I didn't tell you the awful news about Mrs Winniatt?'

I knew what she was about to say. 'What news?'

'Apparently on Saturday, on the same day that she heard about her husband's murder, someone stole into her room and took a string of extremely valuable pearls. Can you imagine!'

'Terrible, such a heartless thing to do.'

'They think that the person took advantage of the fact that Mrs Winniatt had been sedated. The rumour is that the Inspector is looking for a pair of jewel thieves, a man and a woman who check into smart hotels and then proceed to rob their fellow guests. It caused such a stir among the ladies last night. Did the Inspector not mention any of this to you?'

'No, he didn't,' I lied.

'How curious,' said Carlo. 'Anyway, you should have seen Mrs Brendel. She was in her element.'

'I'm sure she was,' I said. 'Carlo. Can I ask you a question? Have you met anyone here, someone trustworthy, who can speak Spanish?'

'There's Miss Hart – I believe she speaks Spanish.'

I thought of Helen with her bright blue, flashing eyes and rather cynical manner. 'I don't think she would be quite right. No, I'm thinking of someone who is outside our immediate social circle.'

She looked at me with suspicion. 'What do you need a Spanish speaker for?'

'Just a little translation work. Of course, I'd be very happy to pay for it.'

'What is it that you need to be translated? It's nothing to do what's been going on here, is it? Nothing to do with—?'

I had to think of something to throw Carlo off track. 'Oh, no, nothing along those lines at all. I'm taking your advice and staying out of it. I was thinking about an idea for a short story.' It was an idea that had been fermenting at the back of my mind since I had arrived on the island. 'Something about a man who drowned off Martiánez beach some years back and the effect his death has on those left behind. I wanted to ask some questions, but I realise that the locals who know the most about it probably can't speak English.'

The answer seemed to satisfy her. Indeed, it could well form the basis of an atmospheric short story. I saw it all in my mind: a woman dressed in widow's weeds, living in that house up by La Paz; the rage of the sea below; a figure standing on the edge of the plateau thinking about throwing himself over the cliff and into the ocean.

'Well, I've heard Madame Giroux speak what sounds like very fluent Spanish.'

I thought of the woman who had been so kind to my daughter. 'Wonderful,' I said, taking my friend's hand in mine. 'Carlo, what would I do without you?'

Chapter Thirty-one

Carlo left me to go in search of Raymond's governess. After a few minutes Madame Giroux approached me from the terrace. We took a seat in the gardens of the Taoro as a warm breeze danced through the leaves of the palm trees, serving as a whispered counterpoint to our conversation. We spoke in French of the children, the silly incident with the teddy bears, the hotel, the volcano, the climate, before I switched to English.

'This is a very delicate matter, Madame Giroux, but one I hope you may be able to help me with,' I said. 'If you choose not to I will understand, of course, but please be assured that it is a matter of the utmost seriousness. It's nothing that will put you in danger, of that I promise. But if you do help me your involvement could save a life.'

I talked a little of the murder of Mr Winniatt and about how I had come into a piece of information that pointed to one particular person: José, the son of Consuela, who had worked at Mal Pais. He was not a suspect in any crime, but he might be able to provide some background on his former employer, Gerard Grenville. There were, I told her, certain rumours circulating about Grenville's behaviour, particularly his obsession with the occult, and I needed to know whether these stories had any basis in fact.

'So you see, it is a very pressing matter indeed,' I said.

'If it is so serious, why is the Inspector not dealing with this?' asked Madame Giroux.

'You're quite right, Madame. He should be. But Inspector Núñez seems blinkered, unable to see what is right in front of him.'

She bowed her head and then took off one black glove and then the other. She revealed hands that were nothing more than a mass of scars. Tears formed in her eyes as the fingers of her right hand caressed the battleground of skin of her ring finger.

'How did you know?'

'Dear Mme Giroux, I promise I know nothing about you. I simply asked Carlo if she knew anyone who spoke Spanish.'

'Well, then it's meant to be,' she said softly. 'You see, some years ago I was married. I knew Albert was too good for me, too good-looking for my plain appearance. But I fooled myself that I could make him happy so we married.' I felt a pang of recognition deep within me. I too had married a man who I thought was too dazzlingly handsome. And look where that had ended. 'I turned a blind eye to his drinking, the fits of temper, the violence. But then, one night, we had a terrible row. I don't know what I said to him to inflame his temper, but he took a knife from the kitchen and did – did this.'

She opened her palms to reveal more scars, rivulets

of red lines that criss-crossed her skin. 'Not only on my hands, but here,' she said, pointing to her stomach, 'and here too,' she added, her fingers moving up to her chest.

'Oh, Mme Giroux, I—'

'Albert left the apartment that night. We were living in Perpignan, and although the police tried to find him, he escaped. Perhaps to America, I don't know. Once I had recovered from my surgery – oh, how painful were those operations, all those stitches, all those bandages – I pleaded with his mother and sister to tell me of his whereabouts. I am sure that they knew, but they didn't want anything to do with me and they started to spread rumours in the town that I was a woman of ill repute. I had to leave Perpignan and make a way for myself in the world. Both my parents, my French father and my Spanish mother, had died and so I travelled to Paris. Earlier this year, a kind American couple, the Murrays, took pity on me and offered me a job. Mrs Murray needed someone to help with Raymond after the death of her other son, George.'

As she pushed her fingers back into her gloves Madame Giroux's mouth set itself in a fixed smile as though the action caused her some degree of pain. 'When you asked if I could help I was a little frightened, but now I under-stand,' she continued. 'If I can assist in any way, of course I will. Men like Albert, men who escape justice, they need to be caught. Just tell me what you'd like me to do.'

I was impressed by Mme Giroux's speech, and her bravery. I outlined how first I needed to find José. The best way to do that was through his mother, Consuela, who worked as a cook at Grenville's house. I told her that when she was making inquiries she could say that she was working on behalf of the English lady, a writer, who had been a guest at Mr Grenville's the previous night. But on no account was she to mention me to anybody at Mal Pais but Consuela herself. Obviously, I was persona non grata to Violet and her father now. She was to say that I had been so impressed by her cooking that I was keen to talk to her about the food of the Canary Islands for an article I would like to write for a British magazine. Although I promised to pay Mme Giroux handsomely for her work, she steadfastly refused the money. She told me that she would take a walk down to the town later that day when she knew that she had a few hours off from looking after Raymond. After I thanked her and we said our goodbyes, I walked back into the hotel and up the staircase towards my room.

As I made my way to the suite I saw a woman dressed in black at the far end of the corridor. It was Daisy. She looked as small and fragile as a half-dead bird. When she saw me she seemed to freeze, as if my very existence sucked what little life she had left out of her. I walked towards her, but as I did so she turned her pale face away from mine.

'Daisy, I know that you've—'

'I thought you were my friend,' she hissed. As she said this, I caught a glimpse of the hatred in her eyes.

'I am. If you only knew what I'm trying to—'

'How could you do such a thing? My pearls, my beautiful pearls, given to me by my mother on my wedding day.' Tears spilled from her reddened eyes down her face.

'If you let me explain, I can tell you what—'

'What? How you waited until I was asleep before you stole into my room and took them? And then you had the cheek to come back the next day and try to console me?'

I was tempted to tell her the truth about Dr Trenkel, but I still felt it unwise to do so. 'Daisy, I know what it must look like to you, but—'

'It's all in the hands of the Inspector now. I've got nothing left to say to you.' With that she turned from me and started to walk down the corridor, then stopped. 'And by the way, I'd rather you didn't come to the funeral.' The words hurt me, hitting me like a bullet, forcing me against the wall. My eyes smarted with tears. But who were they for? Certainly not for Winniatt, whom I had never liked. Daisy? Perhaps a little, as I knew the kind of grief that she was suffering. Mme Giroux, whose horrific story I had just heard? Yes, of course. And Violet too, whose ordeal was just too awful to comprehend. But mostly I was crying for myself and for the way first Núñez and now Daisy looked at me with contempt in their eyes. I felt alone, frustrated and angry, unable to tell the Inspector my fears, mute against the accusations levelled at me by Daisy. If only Davison had been here, at least then I would be able to vent my feelings to him, safe in the knowledge that the information would be understood.

I had to face it. It was up to me to try and solve this – this puzzle. No, it was too complex, too evil for that. I didn't even have a word for it. However, I knew that if I didn't dig out its dark heart I could hardly begin to imagine the terrible things that might happen next.

251

Chapter Thirty-two

The bird-of-paradise flower skewered through Winniatt's eyeball haunted my every waking moment. A simple death, the snuffing out of a life was not enough for this killer. This theatrical touch was a sign, I was sure, of the murderer's desire to punish the writer for something he had seen. And I still needed to establish a motive for the murder.

Over the course of the next day or so I started to ask questions relating to Winniatt's time on the island in order to build up a picture of exactly what he had witnessed and whom he had spoken to at any given hour. I tried to approach these encounters not as formal interviews, but something more gentle and leisurely. I chatted to Gustavo, some of the porters, a chambermaid who could speak only a smattering of English words, a waiter, and the tennis instructor. I transcribed all the details – what time Winniatt had woken up, what he had eaten for breakfast, whom he had talked to and when – into my notebook. I went on to speak to Mrs Brendel, Helen Hart and Guy

Trevelyan, Professor Wilbor and even the cold and distant Rupert Mabey, but none of them mentioned Winniatt in relation to Grenville and, as a result, nothing they told me seemed especially relevant. Of course, I could no longer approach Daisy, which was unfortunate. I thought of the way she had looked at her bedside drawer when I had asked her about whether the police had taken all of her husband's notebooks. Núñez already suspected me of taking Daisy's pearls, and I knew trying to gain entry into her room to search through her possessions would be too risky.

Just as I was thinking that I needed to put Winniatt's murder aside for the time being and get back to my initial inquiries relating to the death of Douglas Greene, whose uneasy spirit I felt guilty of neglecting, I received a visit from Mme Giroux. She had successfully located Consuela living in a house down by the harbour and had made an appointment for me to see the woman at two o'clock the next day. Apparently, the servant, or *criada*, had the day off, as Grenville and his daughter had made plans to visit some friends up in a village in the hills. When I heard this, part of me was tempted to break into Grenville's house, but I realised that by now, aware that I was on his trail, he would have destroyed any evidence that linked him to the deaths. Or perhaps he had just told Consuela that he and Violet would not be at home in the hope that I might try and search Mal Pais. The story could be a trap to lure me to his home. I could just imagine the look of sadistic pleasure that would spread across his ugly face when he saw me step into the courtyard.

As I walked down the hill from the Taoro towards the cluster of white houses by the harbour, I was conscious that I needed to prepare for my talk with Consuela and so I asked Mme Giroux about the basics of traditional cooking in Tenerife. Of course, since arriving in Orotava I had sampled some of the 'delights' of the island, but she took me through a typical Canarian menu containing such dishes as *papas arrugadas con mojo* (the wrinkled potatoes with red and green spicy sauces that I had tried at Grenville's house), *pimientos de Padron, croquetas caseras, escaldon de Gofio* (an unappetising-sounding casserole made from toasted grain flour and fish stock that had been apparently eaten by the Guanches), *queso asado,* and *carne fiesta.*

The whitewashed house was a traditional fisherman's cottage perched right on the edge of a promontory overlooking the sea. Mme Giroux knocked on the door and a moment later Consuela appeared, a smile lighting up her weather-beaten, careworn face. She looked at me with warm recognition and gestured for us to step inside. A smell of cooking fish lingered in the air, an aroma that had undoubtedly been absorbed into the walls over the generations. Although it was obvious that this was not a well-off household, Consuela kept her home clean and tidy.

I asked Mme Giroux to thank Consuela for her kindness and for the delicious dishes I had tasted at Mr Grenville's. When Mme Giroux spoke the words Consuela's tired eyes brightened with joy. She had always thought her cooking was nothing special. Señor Grenville never complained, but all she was doing, she said, was serving up hearty dishes, ones that her mother and grandmother had prepared before her. She was astounded that anyone would be interested in them. We talked of the importance of good ingredients, her husband's *huerta* or vegetable patch, the rich resources of land and sea. Standing by the open fire in her kitchen, over which she cooked her family's food, Consuela told me of her own secret recipes, ones of which she was most proud. From this, I turned the conversation to families in general, how I missed my late mother and how I adored my small daughter.

'I too have my joys and my sorrows,' she said. 'But I can't complain.'

'Often those we love the most are the ones who can cause us the most pain,' I said.

The old woman's hands, dark-skinned and wrinkled, twisted about her waist as she began to speak of José. 'My son has given me many worries,' she sighed. 'Each of these lines on my face is because of him. Each week another girl. Always getting into fights. Never staying for very long in any job. Too much drinking. I worry so about him, but my husband says I am being foolish, as this is the nature of boys.'

'Mr Grenville mentioned that José used to work for him at Mal Pais.'

Consuela's eyes clouded and she turned away from us. 'Yes, that is true. But that's all in the past now. He's got a job as a waiter at the bar on the seafront.'

'Are you happy at Mal Pais? Working for Mr Grenville?' I asked.

'I have a job, that's enough for me,' she said, now

looking with suspicion at both Mme Giroux and me. 'And what's this got to do with cooking?'

'Sorry, I'm too curious, one of my character faults,' I said, smiling.

By necessity I asked a dozen more questions about the many varieties of fish; the uses of olive oil, coriander, garlic; and the technique of making a batter for frying squid. Then I finally brought the interview to an end. I thanked her graciously and promised that I would send her the article from the magazine, care of Mr Grenville.

'Thank you for translating for me,' I said to Mme Giroux as we walked along the promenade. 'And I certainly know what to cook if a Spanish family ever came to visit me in England. At least I now know where José works.' I fell silent as I considered how best to approach the young man. The various scenarios playing through my mind were scattered by the sudden sound of violent shouting, soon followed by the expulsion of a dark-haired man from a bar.

'*De puta madre!*' he screamed, his black eyes full of hatred as he fell onto the ground.

'What is he saying?' I whispered to Mme Giroux.

'It's best if you don't know. Let's just say he's not happy.'

An older, more muscular man, with a mouth missing several teeth and a scar down the side of his left cheek, came to stand over the younger fellow. A tirade of guttural Spanish words spewed from his lips, along with a good deal of spittle, as well as the name José. It seemed as though Consuela's son had just lost another job. The older man was about to land a punch on José's head when he became aware of our eyes on him. With an emphatic nod of the head and a final kick at the younger man, he retreated back inside the bar.

'Can I help you?' asked Mme Giroux in Spanish, as she approached the man on the ground. Although he was handsome, I noticed that he had dark shadows under his eyes. 'Are you all right?'

'*Estoy bien, no pasa nada,*' José said in reply.

I didn't understand the exact meaning of the interchange between them, but after a few minutes Mme Giroux said something to make José smile. She helped him to his feet and proceeded to introduce me. I apologised, through her, for not being able to converse in Spanish. She then said something to him that included the words 'Señor Grenville', and his face darkened.

'He wants to know how you know Grenville?' asked Mme Giroux.

'What have you said to him already?'

'Just that you are aware that he used to work for him and that you are keen to ask him some questions.'

I knew there was no love lost between José and Grenville. 'Let's tell him the truth,' I said. 'Say to him that I suspect Grenville first of the murder of Douglas Greene and now the death of Howard Winniatt.'

The revelation produced an immediate, almost physical, reaction. As José started to shake his head violently his voice became louder and more rambling and his eyes looked wild and full of panic. Mme Giroux repeatedly tried to make him slow down and finally, through snippets of her translation, I began to understand.

'It started out as nothing but a silly rumour,' José told Mme Giroux. 'I had lost my job, I was in a foul mood. My head was full of stupid thoughts. Violet was not being friendly. And so I began to talk to people in the bars around town of the things that went on up at Mal Pais.'

'What kind of things?'

'It started as a joke. To begin with I told the truth, more or less. About Grenville and his interest in the Guanches and the occult. Then I started to exaggerate a little. I wanted my revenge, I suppose. The old fool! I had tried to be nice to his daughter, show her a little attention. She was starved of male company, what with that cripple – what's his name, Edmund? – what could he ever do for her? How could he ever please her? No wonder Grenville did not want his daughter to marry him!'

'And what about Greene? What did you say to him?'

'One night in a bar I got talking to Douglas Greene. I knew of him from when I was a boy, although he was a little older than me. He went away to school, I think back to England, and then returned to the island, but his Spanish was perfect. He was a bastard, you know – sorry, illegitimate. Anyway, he started to ask me what I had been doing and I told him that I had been working at Mal Pais. He seemed keen for me to tell him all the things that Grenville did and so I told him all I knew, and more – about how Grenville wanted to release the evil spirit of Guayota from Teide. He promised me that there were people in his country, England, who wanted to stop men like Grenville from practising their dark arts. He promised he would give me some money. He wrote some things down, I thought I was doing something to help. I didn't expect anything bad to happen. I felt sick when I heard that Greene had died. And in that cave, in that state. I started to drink more to try to forget about it. And now there is another man dead! I promise I will never touch another drink. I'll never say another bad word. Do you think I might be next? Oh God.'

By this point José was nearly wild with fear and Mme Giroux had to order a brandy from the bar to help calm him down. When she returned and gave him the glass, José quickly knocked back the dark brown liquid, immediately reneging on his promise never to touch another drop of alcohol.

'José, it's very important that you are telling the truth,' I said, looking him straight in the eyes. 'It's too dangerous to have any more falsehoods.'

'I'm sorry,' he said, whimpering like a small boy. 'It's lies, all lies.'

When I had recovered from the impact of what José had said – the revelation left me almost physically winded – I questioned him again and again to establish the truth. José's stories had started out as a slight exaggeration but, after repeated retellings and the ingestion of an excess of alcohol, had ended up as a complete fabrication. Grenville had never said any of those things about wanting to release the spirit of evil from Teide.

The implications of José's statement rippled through my mind, sweeping away certain aspects of the case that I had constructed – my preconceptions, theories and what I had regarded as facts – in a great swell of dirty floodwater. Everything I had assumed to be true had to be dismissed. I had to start to build up the case again from scratch.

I knew, from the evidence of my own eyes, that Grenville was an evil man. But was he the man behind the murders of Douglas Greene and Howard Winniatt? Surely he had to be, I told myself. Who else was there on the island who possessed that kind of degenerate mind? Grenville had the disposition – I knew him to be immoral or amoral, the difference did not matter to me – as well as the knowledge and the means to kill. Even if he did not intend to go through with his ridiculous plan to release the devil from the volcano, or whatever superstitious nonsense it was, in reality that is what he had already achieved. What else were those two deaths but a concrete manifestation of evil? And yet ... there was something not right about this. Out of the corner of my eye, I saw the vague outline of a shadow, an enigmatic figure. The more I willed it to come into view, the more it seemed to fade out of focus and step back into the darkness. I was sure there that was something I had seen, or heard, that would make sense of all of this. *What was it*? Scenes from the recent past flashed through my brain, snippets of dinner-party conversation and seemingly insignificant asides. But it was too chaotic – the fragments of memories began to blur into one and the conversations mutated into meaningless babbles of noise.

After leaving José, I returned with Mme Giroux to the hotel, too distracted to talk. She tried to help, but I had no choice but to carry the heavy burden of information on my shoulders. I would have to work this out for myself.

On our arrival at the Taoro, I thanked her once more and returned to my room, where I took out my notebook and looked through the pages relating to the murders of Greene and Winniatt. At the desk I worked with a kind of fury, reconstructing the crimes from the bare facts. And although it was difficult, I tried to reimagine how they had been committed without Grenville as the main suspect. If someone had heard the rumours spread by José about Grenville then that person could have taken advantage of these slurs to commit the crimes, knowing that the occultist would be the most likely suspect. Had I fallen into a trap? If so, who had laid this for me? Had someone deliberately set out to deceive me? From now on, I realised, I would have to keep an open mind both about the deaths and those responsible for them.

I thought back to my encounters with Grenville, reassessing his pronouncements and judgements. At the time I had interpreted his words through my belief that he was a murderer. What if he was only – only! – a pervert, a man who submitted his daughter to the worst kind of suffering? Had he really been innocent of any intention to harm me? Was that herbal draught nothing more than a harmless essence of plant extracts and not, as I believed, a poison designed to kill me? Had I got all of that wrong? I thought back to my behaviour, when I had been prepared to throw that glass of ammonia into his eyes. No wonder he had looked at me with astonishment and surprise and, as I remembered it now, a degree of hurt and betrayal. I had been the one ready to commit a crime. The thought of what I had been tempted to do turned my stomach, a feeling of nausea that lingered and made me late in getting ready for dinner.

As I sat down for supper that night I smiled at my companions already assembled around the table: Professor Wilbor and Rupert Mabey, who had decided to eat at the hotel again; Mrs Brendel and Dr Trenkel; and Helen Hart and Guy Trevelyan, who were regaling us with their plans for the dinner and party on Valentine's Day. But behind my seemingly gay smile lay something darker: shame, suspicion and raw fear. Talk turned to the funeral of Howard Winniatt the next day and inquiries as to who was attending. Everyone nodded their heads in agreement – they would all be going apart from Dr Trenkel, who had a number of appointments he could not change.

I tried to eat but the food – creamy croquettes full of cheese sauce, an onion soup, beautifully steamed white fish, a rich meaty stew, a cold rice pudding – lay mostly untouched; the few mouthfuls I managed to force into my mouth tasted foul. From the occasional sidelong glance, I could tell that some people had heard the rumour about my possible involvement in the theft of Daisy Winniatt's pearls. I could almost hear the thought worming its way through their minds: *although she looks like a nice enough woman, there is no smoke without fire.* Halfway through dinner, as Dr Trenkel stepped away from the table for a moment, I excused myself too.

'Dr Trenkel, I wonder if you have discovered anything more – about Mr Winniatt?'

The doctor looked embarrassed, and coughed into his

hand. 'I'm afraid I've already said too much about that,' he said, increasing the speed with which he walked across the dining room.

'What do you mean?'

'Mrs Christie, you know I shouldn't have said anything to you regarding Mr Winniatt. Inspector Núñez feels that it's only right and proper we keep the findings within a small group of people.' He tapped a finger against his nose. 'Discretion and all that. I'm sure you understand.'

'I see,' I said, trying not to blurt out what I knew of him. 'Of course, quite right.'

When I took my place back at the table I ran through each of the diners in turn, rehearsing possible criminal motives and murderous scenarios. When I found myself trying to invent reasons why poor Mrs Brendel might be involved in the murder of Howard Winniatt I put my napkin on the table and told everyone that I was feeling off-colour and was retiring to bed for the night. If this had been one of my books, one of my detective figures would have had all the suspects lined up in his head. He would have access to information such as alibis, the exact time of death and a wide range of witness statements. He would be able to conclude who had committed the murders through the precise sifting of evidence and the application of logic. For my part, I had no such inside information: Davison, who might be able to help me in certain matters, could not be contacted; Inspector Núñez suspected me of a crime I had not committed; Dr Trenkel was no longer willing to share his findings about the post-mortem, and one of the most important witnesses, Daisy Winniatt, would no longer speak to me.

In my suite all was quiet. Carlo and Rosalind were already asleep in the room behind the connecting doors. I walked over to the window and gazed out at the moon, which cast its soft glow onto the slopes of Mount Teide. The following day Howard Winniatt would be buried in the English Cemetery down by the sea. Daisy had made her wishes plain: I was not invited to the service, nor presumably to the small reception at the hotel afterwards. However, there was a way I might be able to use this to my advantage.

I tried to sleep, but was woken by a horrible dream about Rosalind and Blue Teddy. She had taken Raymond's toy by mistake and the boy had been so furious with her that he, in a fit of spiteful childish rage, had pushed my dear daughter off a cliff. I saw her falling through the air and then struggling in the waters, trying to swim before she drowned beneath the waves. I woke up in a cold sweat and it took me some minutes to steady my nerves. Even though I knew it to be quite irrational, I stole out of bed and quietly opened the double doors to check if Rosalind was safe. She was, of course she was, but as I fetched myself a glass of water something still troubled me. I took one of my notebooks back to bed with me. Taking up a pen, I wrote a series of names that would have seemed nonsensical to anyone but me: 'Gina Trevelyan. Blue Teddy. Rosalind and Raymond', closely followed by a sentence: 'If Gerard Grenville was not the man responsible for the deaths of Douglas Greene and Howard Winniatt: who was it?'

Chapter Thirty-three

From a window in one of the corridors at the top of the hotel, I watched the parade of mourners leave the Taoro. At the front of the group was Daisy, her head shrouded in black lace; around her neck, where her precious pearls should have been, there was nothing. Among the group of mourners, I made out the sombrely dressed figures of Professor Wilbor, Rupert Mabey, Mrs Brendel, Guy Trevelyan, Helen Hart, Inspector Núñez and, at the very tail end, Gerard and Violet Grenville, who was pushing Edmund Ffosse in his wheeled chair.

After arranging for Carlo to look after Rosalind and Raymond, I sent a note to Mme Giroux asking for her help. She was due to meet me on the terrace at ten o'clock. By the time I had taken my place at the table outside, the sun had clouded over and a mist had started to descend from the mountains. Although it was far from cold, the air felt a little damp and so I draped the shawl Flora Kurs had given me around my shoulders. I remembered that I had been wearing it that morning Gina Trevelyan had thrown herself off the *Gelria*. The memory of the young woman's death made me shudder, but something else about what I had seen also bothered me. I pictured the girl standing at the very edge of the ship, her arms in the air as if she was going to fly. Just like Howard Winniatt standing on that bridge overlooking the dry river bed.

An idea formed in my mind, but I had to stop myself from rushing ahead. I had already made one serious mistake in assuming that Grenville was the killer. I couldn't afford to make another dangerous supposition.

What I needed was some sort of evidence. I wasn't exactly sure what this would be, but I knew that Dr Trenkel was hiding something. Mme Giroux was only too willing to help – after all, the plan did not put her in any danger whatsoever – and by the end of our talk she seemed to understand perfectly what I was asking her to do.

After making an appointment to see the doctor later that morning, I walked with Mme Giroux towards the house that Professor Wilbor shared with his assistant, Rupert Mabey. The route took us out of the hotel, through the terraced gardens and down towards the sea. Instead of veering right to La Paz, we turned left along the track that led down to an old fort. The Professor had told me that his house was quite distinctive: it was painted pink and was situated on a hillock overlooking the bay. As we approached the sea the mist began to clear a little and we saw the house in the distance, standing above a curve of black sand.

As we walked closer I realised that the house was in a state of disrepair. Weeds grew out of the paving slabs on the terrace, the paint on the outside walls was flaking off like great swathes of skin, and large patches of damp crept up from the ground towards the windows. I knocked on the front door a couple of times to make sure there was nobody at home – although it didn't look like it, perhaps the men had a maid who helped with the cleaning – before I turned the handle. It was locked. The frame looked rotten and I was certain that if I pushed my finger into it the wood would turn to dust. However, I didn't want to draw attention to the fact that we had been here. The Inspector would no doubt realise that I had been one of the few people not to attend Winniatt's funeral and if I broke into the house then this would only give him more grounds to be suspicious of me. I walked around the house and peered through one of the grimy windows, while Mme Giroux waited by the front door.

Although the light was dim, I could just make out the shape of a few objects: a pile of books on a table, a shelf displaying shards of unwashed pottery, and a sink full of dirty dishes. If nothing else, the two men were in desperate need of a woman's touch. Part of me wanted to roll up my sleeves, get hold of a brush and some soap and hot water and give the place a thorough clean.

'There's nobody in and no way of getting in,' I said to Mme Giroux when I arrived back at the front door. 'So it's back to the hotel. At least I'll be in plenty of time for my appointment with the doctor.'

'Could you slip in through a window?' asked Mme Giroux.

'If I ever was able to slip in through a window, then I'm afraid those days are long gone,' I said.

The comment made Mme Giroux smile, and her eyes sparkled for the first time since we had met. 'You've probably guessed that since what happened with Albert, I haven't had the most enjoyable of lives,' she said. 'My existence has been one of duty and responsibility, looking after dear Raymond, soothing his brow after his bad dreams. I was so grateful to Mr and Mrs Murray that I couldn't complain. I didn't ask for anything more. But since arriving at the Taoro, since meeting you, I feel a certain *joie de vivre* returning. I know it's probably wrong of me to enjoy this kind of work, stealing around houses, going into bars to talk to men.'

As I told her of what I had planned next a smile spread across her face. 'You are a wicked lady, Mrs Christie,' she laughed. 'I haven't read any of your books yet, but I'm looking forward to it. If the novels are anything like, well like *this*, then I'm sure I will be entertained.'

We walked back to the hotel slowly, taking the opportunity to stop at various points and catch our breath. We talked as we went, a leisurely conversation that covered Raymond and the death of his brother, the Murrays, the other guests staying at the Taoro, before finally, as we reached the hotel's gardens, Mme Giroux stopped me and placed a gentle hand on my arm.

'You do know that there are some unkind rumours going around about you?'

'Oh, yes, this ridiculous idea that I'm some kind of jewel thief.'

'I know you didn't do it, although I wouldn't care if you had,' she whispered as a couple of disapproving

Germanic-looking women passed us on the terrace. 'But I think you know who did take them, don't you?'

I hesitated for a moment before I said, 'Your instincts are quite right, madame. I do know who stole Mrs Winniatt's jewels.'

'Then why don't you tell the Inspector? Put a stop to all these silly stories about you?'

'I have my reasons,' I said.

'Which are?'

'I'm not quite sure yet,' I replied truthfully as we sat down at a table on the terrace. 'All I know is that the person who took them is not who you'd expect. They are not short of money, or at least they don't seem to be. I can't say any more just now, I'm sure you understand, madame.'

'Of course,' she said. We passed the time of day quite pleasantly, and to fellow guests at the Taoro we would have seemed like two middle-aged ladies with very little to do, leisured types who spent their days gossiping, playing bridge, drinking endless cups of tea and talking about the weather. I knew never to trust appearances. Having said that, I had to reprimand myself for the serious mistakes I had made with Grenville. I had assumed that because he was an occultist, because of his interest in poisons, because he was a far from pleasant man, because he inflicted a terrible suffering on his daughter, he must therefore be a murderer. Of course, he could still be the one responsible for the deaths of Douglas Greene and Howard Winniatt, but I had my doubts. I must not let myself be blinkered again.

'I suppose it must be almost eleven, nearly time for my appointment with the doctor.' I said. 'How are you feeling? Weak?'

'Now that you mention it, I am feeling a little dizzy,' she said, her hand rising theatrically to her head.

'Good,' I said. 'I'll see you after . . . after you've made a full "recovery".'

I left Mme Giroux and made my way towards Trenkel's office. I said good morning to the nurse and told her that I had an appointment at eleven o'clock. After a few moments, Trenkel came out and, with a fixed expression, ushered me into his office.

'What can we do for you today, Mrs Christie?' he said, not looking up from his desk.

'It's the same trouble, I'm afraid,' I said, working my fingers into an anxious state. 'I'm having trouble sleeping. I have the most terrible bad dreams. I can't seem to forget about what I saw.' I took out a handkerchief from my handbag and started to dab away the tears that I had forced to form in my eyes. 'I know you said take plenty of rest and exercise and I have. I go to bed early, but I feel so restless, so nervy. I keep thinking about what kind of person did that to poor Mr Winniatt and what he might do next. Every little sound makes me jump. You must have noticed that I could hardly touch my food at dinner.'

Trenkel looked at me with suspicion. What was going through his mind? No doubt he would have heard, either from Núñez or from another guest at the Taoro, of my alleged involvement in the theft of Mrs Winniatt's pearls.

A witness, most probably one of the hotel's many chamber-maids, had seen me slink out of the widow's room. Was he wondering whether I had seen him take the jewels? Was he musing over the possibility of placing something in my room or on my person that would link me to the theft? Perhaps he was thinking that, if he played this right, it might work to his advantage.

'Yes, I did notice that you seemed a little distracted,' he said. 'Is there anything else worrying you at the moment? Anything you've done that is causing you anxiety?'

'I don't understand,' I said.

'There are some nervous conditions that lead to acts of irrationality. Some people, for example, sleepwalk and have no memory of doing so. Other people may behave quite oddly for no clear reason, do things they would never dream of doing normally. The unconscious, you see, is a very powerful force, one that is only just beginning to be recognised.'

'Do you think that's what might be wrong with me?'

'It could be. But a study and diagnosis of such a thing can take many months, sometimes years. You may want to consult a doctor at home, in London. But it seems highly feasible that the discovery of Mr Winniatt's body could have dealt a terrible shock to your system. The sight may have stirred up old memories, difficult memories that you haven't thought about since your childhood. It could indeed have forced you to do certain things, things of which you have no conscious memory today.'

By planting this seed in my mind, Dr Trenkel was laying

271

the ground for his masterplan: he wanted me to think that somehow I was guilty of the theft. No doubt he would place the pearls in my room and then suggest to Núñez that my suite be searched. Yes, he was clever all right. But not quite clever enough. I looked at the clock on the wall. It was time.

Chapter Thirty-four

'Doctor! Doctor!' It was the nurse. 'Please come! It's an emergency!'

'What?' shouted Trenkel as he pushed himself out of the chair and ran to the door. 'What's the problem?'

'It's a lady in the courtyard. She's been taken ill.'

Trenkel turned to me and paused. Just as he was about to open his mouth to say something the nurse called for him again, with rising panic in her voice. 'A guest says he thinks the woman might be having some kind of fit. Quick, Doctor. Quick!'

'You'd better come with me then,' he said to the nurse, grabbing his medical bag.

As soon as he left the room, I closed the door behind him and locked it from the inside. I needed to work quickly. The first thing I wanted to find was the post-mortem report on Howard Winniatt. But after looking through the papers in Trenkel's filing cabinet and desk, I concluded that the doctor must have sent it on to Núñez.

Although this was a disappointment, I still had some time, time that I could put to good use.

I wasn't quite sure what I should be searching for, but I had an idea that Trenkel's office contained something that would help me make sense of the stolen pearls, and perhaps of the murders too. If I found evidence of an outstanding debt then perhaps I could understand why Trenkel had taken the necklace. Or was he a compulsive thief, a human magpie who could not resist taking the shiny baubles of his patients? Had there been other cases of theft at the hotel or was this the first one? I made a mental note to ask Gustavo about this later, not that the Taoro's trusted employee would want to give anything away that might sully the hotel's good reputation.

I went back to the drawers in Trenkel's desk and started sifting through receipts, old newspaper cuttings, a few medical journals written in German and English, but found nothing relating directly to the doctor's finances. The more I searched, the more frustrated I became, as there was nothing that seemed to suggest he was anything but a respectable doctor. As I worked through papers, books and records I began to doubt myself.

Perhaps it would be better if I told Davison that, from now on, I would just concentrate on writing about crimes rather than trying to solve them. Despite what Davison had said, I was obviously not suited for this kind of professional intelligence work. As I started to compose a letter in my head to Davison, the image of Violet's tortured face pressed underneath her father's bulk flashed into my mind. This was soon followed by more horrific memories: the sight of the bloody mess on the rocks and the bird-of-paradise flower sticking out of Winniatt's eye socket. I thought back to the cave by Martiánez beach where Greene's body had been found and the sadness that emanated from Davison when he had told me about his friendship with the dead man. If I gave up now what would I have accomplished? I would retire back to a comfortable life in England knowing that the murderer or murderers had escaped punishment. Justice would not have been done. Evil would have been allowed to triumph.

I thought too of the looks of contempt that Daisy Winniatt and Inspector Núñez had given me. If I stopped now then these two people would continue to believe that I had been involved in the theft of a widow's jewels. There was always the possibility that – if, as I suspected, Trenkel went ahead with a plan to plant the jewels in my room – I might actually be arrested for the crime. Even though I would protest my innocence, the authorities would know about the very public scandal that had been reported in newspapers back in England. My doctors had issued the statement that I had been suffering from an attack of serious amnesia. This would be used in my defence – miti-gating circumstances and all that – but it would also seal my fate. They would say that, although the lady writer had no memory of the crime, in all probability the balance of her mind was still disturbed. I would return home in shame and Rosalind would be known as the daughter of a criminal.

No, I could not allow that to happen.

I looked at the clock. I did not know how much time I

had left before Trenkel returned. I went back over to the filing cabinet where he kept the records of his patients. The system was an orderly one, with the names separated according to sections of the alphabet: A–G, H–N, O–T, U–Z. I looked for Mabey's file, but there wasn't one. Next I flicked through the papers hoping to find a record for Gerard and Violet Grenville and again there was nothing. It would be in character for the occultist to treat himself and when the poor girl was ill she was no doubt prescribed a dose of her father's 'herbal essences'. The thought sent a shiver down my spine.

My fingers traced their way over the top of the files before they came to rest on the fourth and last section. The image of a man with wild hair and gooseberry eyes came into my mind: Professor Wilbor. He seemed so nice and friendly, but I knew that an appearance of geniality often covered a multitude of sins. I took out the file and, although it was difficult to read, I could make out certain words such as: 'indigestion', 'corpulent form', 'high blood pressure', 'at risk of diabetes' and a list of further details regarding the man's treatment. But there was nothing of any real significance.

Just as I was about to close the file and place it back in the cabinet I stopped and looked again. Not at the contents of the report, but at the way it was written. It was in a messy hand, the kind I normally associated with doctors. I pulled out another file at random, that of a middle-aged woman suffering from bronchitis. That too was composed of pages all written in an untidy hand. I selected another, that of a tubercular patient, and then another, belonging to an asthmatic, both of which had been written in the same scrawl. There was something wrong here, something very wrong indeed.

At that moment I heard footsteps approaching and then the sound of voices.

I knew what I had seen was important, but I needed to double-check. I quickly pulled Edmund Ffosse's file out of the cabinet and stole a look inside. The handwriting was neat and legible, almost as if it had been written by someone else. Had Ffosse seen another doctor in the past, a man who had then had his report sent over to Trenkel? I turned the page, but there, sitting at the bottom of the manuscript, was Trenkel's signature.

'Yes, indeed,' I heard Trenkel say, as he walked down the corridor. 'It could have been very much worse. Thank you, nurse.'

I shoved a few pages of these notes into my handbag, replaced the file, quickly unlocked the door and, just as the doctor came into the office, positioned myself on the chair where he had left me.

'I'm sorry about that, Mrs Christie.'

'I hope nothing serious?'

'No,' he said, his eyes looking shiftily around the room. 'A fuss over nothing, really. But I do believe she is a woman of your acquaintance.'

'Someone I know?' I said, pretending to start in my chair.

'Yes, Mme Giroux, but there's no need to worry,' he said, gesturing for me not to move. 'She's perfectly fine. A simple case, a fainting spell.'

'I thought the nurse said she was having a fit?'

'A misinterpretation of the symptoms.'

'So she's all right now? I—'

'Yes, she's made a full recovery.'

'I'm so pleased to hear that.'

'Yes, I'm sure you are,' he said. Had Trenkel's voice taken on a knowing tone? 'Now, where were we? Yes, that's right. We were talking about your nerves.'

As the doctor continued to talk, about hidden aspects of the unconscious and certain types of irrational behaviour, I found myself thinking about the handwriting in the files. *How curious*, I thought to myself. A theory began to form in my mind, one so elaborate and strange that I could hardly believe it. Of course I would need some proof, evidence that could be very difficult to find. It could be done, but it would involve a certain element of risk. And yet I could see no other way forwards.

'I'm not sure about all this – about talking about one's past, about one's childhood,' I said. 'In fact, I had an idyllically happy time as a girl.'

'Well, perhaps that's something to think about in the future,' said Trenkel. 'Firstly, let's deal with the here and now. From your symptoms it seems that you could be suffering from neurasthenia. So I would recommend a tonic to relax you, something like Clay and Paget's Glycolactophos, but I wouldn't rule out the kind of talking cure I've outlined.'

'Could you write down the name of the tonic? I'm afraid I didn't quite catch it.'

'Of course, quite a mouthful,' he said, scribbling the

name across a piece of paper with his fountain pen. 'Take two teaspoonfuls two or three times a day. It's important that you blend the powder with water into a paste first. Then you can add water or milk, or you could even take it with cocoa or beef tea.'

As he passed me the scrap of paper I noticed that the words, like the ones in all of his reports bar one, had been written in a loose, far from precise hand.

'Or, I can always make you something up myself,' he said.

'I think I'll try this one first,' I said, standing up.

'I'm sorry I couldn't say anything more about exactly what happened to Mr Winniatt,' said Trenkel, referring to the awkwardness at supper. 'Inspector's orders and all that.'

'I understand,' I said. 'It's a very difficult situation.'

'By the sound of it, I think it's best if you try and forget all that business. You've been under a lot of strain. The last thing you need is more worry and anxiety.'

'Yes, you're right.'

'Would you like to make another appointment with the nurse on your way out? Perhaps the day after tomorrow?'

'As soon as that?'

'It's best to nip these things in the bud.' With that he made a gesture with his fingers as though pinching off a flower bud that had been infected with a nasty attack of blackfly. 'And, in the meantime, if you do need to discuss anything else, please don't hesitate to contact me. As you know only too well, the mind can play funny tricks, particularly when we least expect it.'

279

Chapter Thirty-five

I had promised Mrs Brendel some time ago that I would accompany her on a group visit to picnic beneath the giant Dragon Tree in Icod de los Vinos. When she told me what time I should meet her the next morning I initially hesitated. No doubt it would be foolish to risk travelling to the town, knowing that there was a slight chance that my fellow guests would spot me talking to Davison. But there was something I needed to ask him, something that he needed to do which I thought outweighed that risk. All I needed to find was an excuse to slip away from the group for half an hour or so.

In addition to the practical considerations, it was important for me to behave as though everything was perfectly normal. Even though people suspected me of the theft of Mrs Winniatt's pearls, I had to appear blameless. I had to pretend that I could not smell the stench of evil breathing down the back of my neck.

After breakfast our little group – Mrs Brendel, Professor Wilbor, Rupert Mabey, Helen Hart, Guy

Trevelyan, Carlo, Rosalind and I – met on the front steps of the hotel. We travelled in two taxis – the women and my daughter in one, and the three men in the other – along the coast road, past banana plantations and disused onion seed farms. After Rosalind had gone to sleep on my lap, the talk turned to Howard Winniatt's funeral. Daisy had borne her grief with fortitude and the service, conducted by an English vicar who lived in the parsonage not far from the Taoro, had been simple but dignified. My absence from the service had attracted no comments, but as Mrs Brendel discussed the finer points of Psalm 23 – the same one that I had recited to myself as I had made my way to Grenville's house – I saw Helen Hart looking at me with a curious expression, as though I held the answer to some secret.

Her blue eyes seemed to ask the unspoken question that everyone wanted to know: was this lady writer really capable of stealing a string of pearls from a recently widowed woman? If not, what exactly had she been doing in Daisy Winniatt's room? Helen Hart was the one person with enough guile to ask me outright, and the prospect of dealing with this question created a bird of panic to flutter in my chest.

'Enough of this talk of death,' said Helen, placing a hand on Mrs Brendel's knee. 'I'm so looking forward to the party on Monday, aren't you, Mrs Brendel?'

'Well, yes, of course, my dear, but—'

'But nothing. It's important that we get on with life, don't you agree, Mrs Christie?'

'Yes, I do,' I said. 'But I'm sure Mrs Brendel only wanted to—'

'I know, I know. But it's so morbid. You are all coming, aren't you?'

All of us said we were looking forward to it, apart from Carlo. 'I think I'll stay at the hotel and look after Rosalind,' she said, from the front seat of the car.

'But why don't you bring Rosalind along?' asked Helen.

Carlo looked at me pleadingly. I could tell that the idea of attending a party, especially one hosted by a woman such as Miss Hart, was her idea of hell.

'As you can see, she has been rather overdoing it lately,' I said, looking down at my sleeping daughter. 'I think it wise if she stays with Carlo.'

'Very well,' Miss Hart said, before addressing Carlo. 'But it's a shame you won't be able to see the new sculpture I've been working on.'

'What is it?' I asked.

'I'm not going to say a thing. I want people to come to it completely fresh. But it's something I've been making, on and off, for the last couple of years. I had to leave it here in my studio on my last visit just as it was nearly ready – it was so frustrating not to have the time to complete it – but since I've been back I've been adding the finishing touches.'

'It sounds intriguing,' I said.

'I hope so,' she said, her blue eyes sparkling. 'Now, what are you working on, Mrs Christie?'

'As Carlo knows only too well, I'm having difficulty finishing my latest book,' I said, sighing. The thought of it was like a lead weight around my shoulders. I felt a sinking feeling in my stomach. 'I've rather neglected it of late, but I must get back to it.'

'What's it called again?' asked Miss Hart.

'*The Mystery of the Blue Train*,' I replied.

'Fancy that you, a writer of detective novels, should get yourself mixed up in all this trouble here! It seems, I don't know, almost too perfect for words.'

I tried not to sound too cynical. 'Really?'

'It's like one of your books,' she said, voicing an observation that seemed to please her.

'I wouldn't say that,' I said.

'No, I suppose I shouldn't be so presumptuous. As I told you, I haven't read your novels, but am I right in thinking that by now your clever detective would be tying all the loose ends together, so as to expose the dastardly murderer?'

I did not answer. Miss Hart, however, was in no mood to bring the conversation to a close.

'Doesn't writing about murder and crime depress you?'

'I never think of it like that,' I said. 'It started out as a hobby, a challenge really, to see if I could do it. It's true I've had a little success with writing, but now I can't think about it too much. I just have to get on and do it. Now that I have no husband to support me it's the way I will have to earn my living.'

'I see,' she said. 'And tell me, have you any theory about who did it? Who killed Mr Winniatt?'

I could have said something then, but I thought it best not to respond. 'No, but I'm sure the Inspector will get to the bottom of it all.'

'Do you think so? I don't know about you, but I don't think much of Núñez. I wouldn't be surprised if it ends up as one of these unsolved crimes, like—'

'And who's being morbid now?' interrupted Mrs Brendel. 'Fine talk indeed in front of a child, even a sleeping one.'

'Yes, you're quite right, Mrs Brendel, I'm sorry,' said Miss Hart, who did not look in the least bit apologetic. 'Let's talk about – I don't know – about the view from the car. No? What about the weather then!' Her voice took on a sarcastic tone. 'Yes, that's always a good subject if in doubt.'

Helen Hart was a fascinating creature, a woman who seemed full of contradictions. She was the kind of person who often said one thing but meant something completely different. I looked back at her strange behaviour on the *Gelria*, and the way she had reacted to the death of Gina Trevelyan. One moment she had been wracked with guilt, the next she seemed so light and gay, as if her greatest worry in the world was which dress to wear to her next party. I knew that she had a liking for alcohol, but I was beginning to suspect that she might be fond of other substances too.

'Let's hope we don't have another misty day like yesterday,' I said, smiling at her.

Just as she was about to reply, I caught a flash of contempt in her eyes. The effect was so subtle as to be almost undetectable, but there was no doubting what I had seen. Helen Hart knew that I had noticed it because, a split second later, her face radiated with an over-compensatory smile and her blue eyes twinkled.

'I couldn't agree more,' she said.

'I am so looking forward to seeing the famous Dragon Tree,' I said. 'People say it's more than a thousand years old. I wonder if it's true?'

'Who knows? But it's certainly a beautiful specimen.'

'I've always loved trees,' I said. 'In fact, it may sound odd, but one of my first imaginary friends was called, quite simply, Tree.'

'Really?' said Helen. 'How delightful.'

'I didn't know that,' said Carlo.

'I suppose it's because we had so many lovely ones at Ashfield,' I said, turning to Helen Hart to explain. 'That's the house where I grew up in Torquay.'

'They make for wonderful sculptural forms.'

'Yes, I believe I saw some of them in your last exhibition in London,' I said.

'What kind of trees did you have in your garden, when you were a child?' I knew Helen Hart was only asking this to try and be polite. She didn't give a fig for the answer.

As I told her something of the magnificent trees of Ashfield, and how I still dreamt of them, her eyes glazed over. 'How very fascinating,' said Helen. There was a certain false brightness to her face, as if she were forcing herself to be interested in what I had to say. I didn't blame her: this was deathly dull stuff, not her usual conversational fare of parties, gossip, drink and sex. 'Look, your daughter is waking up.'

I leant forwards and saw Rosalind's eyes begin to open. As I placed my hand on her head she asked whether we were nearly there and before long was telling us all how much she wished we could have taken an excursion to the volcano instead. We could see the snow-capped Teide on the left-hand side of the car, and we discussed the practicalities of such a visit before finally discounting it as too dangerous. The decision put Rosalind into a sulk, and Carlo tried to cheer her up by the promise of certain treats to be had at the picnic.

'Could you look after her for half an hour?' I whispered to Carlo, as the taxi pulled into Icod. 'I'd like to get her a present, something to surprise her with.' Although my daughter's dark mood gave me the perfect excuse to slip away to meet Davison, I felt guilty at using her in this way.

'Of course,' said Carlo, smiling.

'I'll meet you at the tree. I'm sure it can't be difficult to find.'

I stepped down from the car into a grand square shaded by a large fig tree, and planted with laurels and hibiscus bushes. The other taxi had arrived in front of us. As I passed by Guy Trevelyan and Professor Wilbor the men tipped their hats, while Rupert Mabey turned his back and pretended he had not seen me. I remembered the directions Davison had given me. I walked up a white stone staircase, past the church of San Marcos, and onto Calle San Sebastián, before I turned off onto Calle San Agustín. Instead of stepping into Davison's small *hostal* straight away, I walked up the street, past the convent of Espíritu Santo and around the block to make sure nobody was following me. By the time I arrived back at the *hostal* I was convinced that it was safe to enter.

I pushed open the door and stepped into a hallway full of shadows. The front shutters were closed, and the only light allowed into the gloomy interior came from a partially open door that led onto an inner courtyard. Gradually, as my eyes adjusted to the gloom, I saw that the walls of the hall had been covered by a series of religious icons – figures of saints and images of Christ on the cross, bloodied of brow and wearing a crown of thorns. The smell of incense hung in the air. I wondered, for a moment, whether I had stumbled into a small, private chapel, and I was about to step back into the street again when I heard a deep voice say something incomprehensible. The noise came from a tiny, shrivelled old woman, dressed in black, sitting in an armchair.

'I'm sorry, I don't speak Spanish,' I said, knowing that I sounded like an imbecile.

She repeated another sentence, quick and garbled, a mouthful of hisses and exotic-sounding vowels that I didn't understand.

'Is this the *hostal* Espíritu?' I asked.

'*Si, si,*' she said, nodding her head, her black eyes shining in the darkness. '*Necesita usted una habitación?*'

'I am looking for Mr Arthur Jones, is he here?' The question was met with silence and so I repeated the name, slowly. 'Mr Arthur Jones?'

'*Si, Señor Jones. Le conozco. Un caballero. Pero desafortunadamente Señor Jones no está aquí.*'

Finally, after a great deal of repetition and sign language, I understood from the elderly woman that Davison, although a guest at the *hostal*, had gone out. I took out a piece of paper from my handbag and proceeded to write him a short note, telling him of my presence in Icod and that I would be picnicking with the group from the Taoro under the Dragon Tree. I outlined what I needed him to do – there was a piece of information from England that I wanted him to obtain – adding that this was a matter of urgency, as I was afraid that I would soon be arrested for the theft of Daisy Winniatt's pearls. I didn't have time to tell him about my latest thoughts regarding Grenville, or the horrors I had seen at Mal Pais, but I related how I believed I had made a fundamental error that had skewed my judgement and given rise to some false assumptions. I placed the letter inside an envelope from my bag, addressed it to Arthur Jones, and left it in the claw-like hands of the widow of Espíritu.

When I walked back out, the sudden brightness of the day blinded me and for a moment I had to steady myself by the wall of the *hostal*. Avoiding the main shopping street, I managed to find a *pastelería* that was just on the point of closing for lunch. I went in and bought a selection of small biscuits for Rosalind and asked for directions to the Dragon Tree. Although the pale-faced girl behind the counter could not directly communicate with me, she did go to the trouble of drawing a make-shift map on the back of a paper napkin. With this, I made my way through the network of streets, towards the west side of the square and down another series of alleys until finally I stepped into a clearing that led to the tree. The sight of it stopped me in my tracks. Not only was it enormous – it must have been well over forty feet tall – but it had an immense grace and nobility, like a sleeping giant. The group from the Taoro sat on rugs beneath the wide shade of its canopy.

'Mummy!' shouted Rosalind as she spotted me. 'I told them we should have waited for you before we started eating, but the men said they were starving and couldn't hold off any longer.'

'Quite right,' I said, as I joined the party.

'Now, what would you like, my dear?' asked Mrs Brendel. 'The Taoro has done us proud. There's some pâté, a flan, plenty of bread, and I believe there's even some chicken left.'

'Oh, a little of the pâté and, yes, some bread would be very nice, thank you,' I said.

Rosalind made a space for me next to her and Mrs Brendel and I savoured the moment under the shade of the tree, eating a plate of simple food in the company of my daughter and Carlo. I felt the warm breeze on my skin, my eyes taking in the pleasing vista of lush terraces and vine-yards that ran all the way down to the sea. The talk was of the Dragon Tree, its history, mythology, and medicinal uses.

'Apparently, there used to be an even larger one than this,' said Professor Wilbor. 'The explorer Alexander von Humboldt saw it when he visited the island in 1799, and it was supposed to be over sixty feet tall, and forty-five feet in circumference. Even though I find it hard to believe, it was said to be six thousand years old, and that the Guanches hollowed out its trunk to make a kind of altar or sanctuary.'

'What happened to it?' asked Helen.

'It was destroyed after the terrible floods of 1898.'

'I can't imagine there being floods here,' said Mrs Brendel.

'Oh, yes, in fact the island has had quite a few,' the Professor replied. 'Back in 1826, the image of the Virgin of Candelaria was lost during one particularly bad flood. It seems as though a huge wave came in from the ocean and swept the statue into the sea, most probably caused by an earthquake out in the Atlantic.'

'How awful,' said Mrs Brendel. 'I, for one, know the devastating power of water. When I—'

Helen Hart cut her off. 'Is that the same statue that was supposed to have been discovered by two Guanche goat herders after it was washed up?'

Professor Wilbor smiled as he began to tell the story. 'Yes, and according to legend when one of these young men threw a stone at it his arm became paralysed. And then, when the other shepherd tried to attack it with a knife he ended up stabbing himself.'

A wave of light laughter rippled through the group. Just at that moment, I felt something wet on my face. Then I saw a drop of blood splatter onto my white dress. Rosalind caught the look of horror in my eyes and screamed at the top of her voice, soon followed by Mrs Brendel. Nerves were understandably frayed after the murders of Douglas Greene and Howard Winniatt. I strained my neck to look up into the tree, half expecting to see something horrific sitting in the branches. But there was nothing.

'Don't worry,' said the Professor, easing his large form up from the floor. 'It's just the tree. It's dragon's blood, nothing more than that.'

I took my napkin and, after wiping the sticky red liquid from my face, started to calm Rosalind. The Professor pointed out to us the section of bark that had peeled back and had started to bleed. Guy Trevelyan and Rupert Mabey helped move the blanket and picnic things – plates, bowls, dishes and glasses – to a safer spot.

'Has the tree had an accident?' asked Rosalind. 'Does it hurt?'

'No, my dear, that's just its way,' said Carlo, taking her hand. 'Nothing to worry your pretty head about.'

As I tried to work the stain out of my dress with a damp napkin, the rest of the group continued to stare into the umbrella-like canopy of the tree.

'The first time I saw this dragon's blood, splattered on a white marble pavement down by La Paz, I thought something terrible must have happened,' said Helen Hart. 'It was only when my friend told me to look up that I saw that it had come from a dragon tree overhead.'

I thought of Davison's description of Douglas Greene's desiccated corpse covered in the red sheen of dragon's blood.

'Were you with Mr Trevelyan?' I asked.

The question seemed to take her by surprise. 'No, someone altogether different,' she said, casting a concerned look towards Guy, who continued to busy himself with the picnic things. It was obvious that she wanted to change the subject. 'I think we deserve a little wine after that shock, don't you?' she said. 'Professor, can we have some of the wine that you mentioned to me earlier?'

'A very good idea,' said the Professor, taking two bottles of wine out of one of the satchel bags that lay on the ground. He passed a few glasses of the lethal-looking dark red liquid to brave individuals such as Helen Hart, Guy Trevelyan, and Mrs Brendel. 'I don't know what it's like,' he said. 'I was given it to try by Gerard Grenville.'

At the mere mention of the name Mrs Brendel, who was at just that moment taking a small sip from the glass, wrinkled her nose in disgust. 'Oh, it's ghastly,' said the elderly woman. 'If I wasn't in company I would spit it out onto the ground.'

'Don't mind us, my dear Mrs Brendel,' said the Professor. 'We're among friends.'

Helen cast the two grey-haired individuals a withering look. 'Well, although I wouldn't say it was up there with vintage Burgundy, I don't think it's that bad.'

Mrs Brendel took her napkin and used it to cover her lips as she leant to one side and spat out the remaining contents of her mouth onto the dry soil by the enormous roots of the Dragon Tree. 'Please excuse me,' she said, wiping her lips. 'If I'd known it had come from him I would never have taken a sip.'

'Why ever not?' asked the Professor. 'He's perfectly harmless.'

'Harmless?' Mrs Brendel's voice rose in disbelief. 'I wouldn't quite use that word to describe him.'

'What on earth do you mean?' asked Miss Hart. 'Surely you don't believe those silly rumours? Everyone knows that those stories were made up. I'm sure Mrs Christie can testify to his character.'

I was taken aback by her comment. What did she know about my visit to Mal Pais? 'I'm sorry, I don't understand you.'

'I hear you've become quite friendly with him since you arrived at the Taoro,' she said, with mischief playing in her blue eyes. 'Well, with both him and his daughter.'

I did not respond. I heard Carlo whispering to Rosalind, hoping to distract her from our conversation.

'How did you find Violet?' asked Miss Hart, taking a gulp of wine. 'I hope you were able to cheer her up. She's been so sad of late. Of course, one would be if one's fiancé did not have long to live. I wouldn't be surprised if she does something silly one of these days. There's even been talk that as soon as Edmund dies she will . . .' Out of consideration for Rosalind she lowered her voice at this point. 'She will end her life, the poor soul.'

'I wouldn't have thought so,' I said. 'People who talk about doing such things very rarely follow through. It's always the quiet ones you have to watch out for. They can often be the most dangerous.'

'Darling,' said Miss Hart, taking hold of Guy Trevelyan's knee and holding out an empty glass. 'Would you pour me another glass of that rough wine? I seem to have developed rather a taste for it.'

Guy Trevelyan did not immediately respond to his lover's request, but continued talking to the Professor and Mr Mabey about the formation of the volcano.

'Yes, it is interesting, it seems the Cañadas were formed

around 170,000 years ago when a huge landslide resulted in the disappearance of the top of the island.'

'Guy, could you—'

'And the landslide left behind a huge depression that was open to the sea, and covered the ocean floor with a—

'Please, Guy—'

'And subsequently, the reactivation of volcanic activity caused the Teide and Pico Viejo volcanoes to emerge in the interior of Las Cañ—'

'For God's sake, Guy!' screamed Helen, standing up.

Guy looked at her in amazement.

'It's so boring, don't you realise? *You're* so boring!' She spat the words out in a kind of manic fury. Her pale face had turned red now, her eyes wild like those of a rabid dog.

The group fell silent as Miss Hart reached over for the wine and, with a shaky hand, poured herself another glass. Realising the scene she had caused, she ruffled Guy's dark hair and, with a voice now tinged with artificial affection, said with a bright smile, 'You and your bloody rocks!' As she took a large sip of wine she smoothed her blonde hair and tried to regain her composure. 'The way you go on, sometimes people might think you love those rocks more than you love me!'

It was clear that Miss Hart wanted to pass off what we had just witnessed as a joke, but none of us were so easily fooled and, for a few seconds, the air seemed thick and heavy with embarrassment.

'Talking of rocks, Guy,' said Mrs Brendel, trying to bring an air of civility back to the conversation. 'I suppose you'll want to carry a great many specimens back with you to Britain?'

Guy looked confused, as though he did not grasp the meaning of Mrs Brendel's question. 'I'm not sure I under-stand you,' he said.

'It must be lovely travelling around the world, going to all these interesting places, picking up various rocks which you can then send back home,' she said. 'And knowing you have all that space. If I had an empty trunk with me, I would fill it with the finest samples of lacework and other fabrics. I know when I was on the *Titanic*—'

'Indeed,' he said, the words freezing on his lips. His eyes, which focused on a point beyond Mrs Brendel, seemed to lose their spark. I turned my head and looked up the path-way to see the figure of Núñez, flanked by two men. And so they had come to get me. Some evidence had been found to charge me with the theft of the pearls.

Rosalind did not deserve this. She should not be forced to witness her mother being taken away by the police. I whispered in Carlo's ear, stood up and excused myself from the group. The red bloom had spread across my skirt, a red badge of guilt if ever there was one.

'I'll come with you, but please can we do this quietly, discreetly,' I said to Núñez. 'For my daughter's sake.'

But Núñez was in no mood to allow me any dignity and said in a loud voice so that everyone seated under the Dragon Tree could hear, 'Mrs Agatha Christie, you are hereby suspected of the theft of a string of extremely valu-able pearls from the room of Mrs Daisy Winniatt.'

I heard a collective gasp of surprise from the group

sitting under the tree, soon followed by the cries of Rosalind.

He signalled for one of his men to seize my arm. 'I have to inform you that you are under arrest.'

The words set off an alarm call of raised voices.

'Don't be so ridiculous,' said Mrs Brendel. 'Mrs Christie would never do such a thing.'

'How extraordinary, most peculiar,' bellowed Professor Wilbor.

Carlo dashed up and ran towards me, panic freezing her face. 'There must be some misunderstanding,' she said. 'I'm sure there is an explanation.'

'Look here, Inspector,' said Guy Trevelyan. 'Can we just—'

But all I could hear was the startled cries of my daughter, who had followed Carlo and now clung to my skirt. 'Mummy,' she sobbed. 'Don't let the man take you.'

'Please, stand back,' said Núñez. 'We need to take Mrs Christie back to Orotava for questioning.' He nodded to his man to try and manoeuvre me towards his car. 'The quicker we get her back the quicker this can all be sorted out.' That sounded reasonable enough, but I doubted at this stage whether Núñez, once he had me under arrest, had any plans to release me.

'But, but . . .' I said, unable to articulate the words that stuck in my dry throat. If my theory proved correct, it would best to remain quiet about what I knew about Dr Trenkel for a while longer. The only problem was that if Núñez placed me under arrest there was little chance of me gathering the final pieces of evidence I needed to solve the case. I felt an increased pressure on my arm and I was directed towards the car.

'Mummy, don't go,' said Rosalind, her eyes a mass of tears. 'Please ... don't ...'

'I'm sure I will be able to sort this out – it's just a silly mix-up. Don't worry, darling,' I said, stroking her hair. 'I will see you back at the hotel. Carlo will look after you.' I gave my friend an imploring look and then turned my back on the ugly scene. I was fearful that if I looked at my daughter for a second longer I would completely break down. The last thing the poor girl needed was to see her mother reduced to an emotional wreck. 'Very well, Inspector Núñez. I'm ready.'

Núñez nodded with satisfaction and pride – the same kind of expression I had once glimpsed on the face of a big game hunter in South Africa who had just killed a lioness – and he led me towards the open door of his car. But as I was about to step into the vehicle, I heard a high-pitched scream crack the air.

'Mummy! Mummy!' The words disintegrated, soon replaced by the sound of sobbing.

I could not look back, knowing that to do so would break my heart.

Chapter Thirty-six

The journey back to Orotava was a miserable affair. Haunted by images of Rosalind's grief-stricken face I fell into a depressed silence. I caught Núñez eyeing the stain on my dress with suspicion. And did he really think that I was the kind of person who could rob a recently widowed woman of her pearls? Yet he was only being guided by the information presented to him – the sighting of me leaving Daisy Winniatt's suite and now, presumably, the tip-off from Trenkel that had resulted in the discovery of the pearls in my room. I wondered how the doctor had arranged it so that the jewels had been found there. It wouldn't have been hard for him to sweet-talk one of the chambermaids into letting him in to my room under the guise of leaving some medicine for me.

'Did you think you'd get away with it?' asked Núñez.

'Forgive me, but I have no idea what you're talking about.'

'The pearls. It was only a matter of time before we found them.'

I did not respond.

'Dr Trenkel told me that you've been suffering from nervous strain. He asked me to show you some special consideration.'

That was rich coming from him, I thought to myself. 'The doctor is a very attentive man,' I said. 'I'm grateful for his concerns.'

'Perhaps you can tell me why you did it? Did you need the money? Or were you driven by the thrill of it all? I've read about such cases, women so out of their minds with boredom that they turn to crime as a form of entertainment.'

'I'm afraid that sounds like the plot of a bad thriller, Inspector,' I said.

Núñez looked at me with scorn. 'Don't try and make fun of me, Mrs Christie. I think the time for such games is over, don't you?'

I fell into silence once more and looked out of the car at the stretch of blue sea and the clearly defined horizon in the distance. I remembered the interrupted view from the porthole of the *Gelria*, the ship that had brought me from the cold of an English winter to this paradise island in the sun. I recalled the feel of Flora Kurs's shawl as I stepped out of the door and onto the deck that early morning. The sound of Gina Trevelyan's cries echoed in my ears. The sight of her ready to leap off the side of the ship, her hands rising into the sky like a bird about to fly off to warmer climes.

The drive from Icod seemed to take an eternity, but when we arrived back in Orotava, Núñez took me not to the hotel, but to an official building on the harbour front. The smell of rotting fish filled my nostrils. He led me through a doorway, across a courtyard and into a bare, whitewashed room with bars at the window.

'Please, sit,' he said, gesturing towards a wooden chair as he took a seat behind a desk. 'As you can see, this is a world away from the comforts of the Taoro. I would rather we didn't have to bring a woman of your position to such a place, but I'm afraid you have given me no choice.'

'Can I ask who says they saw me leaving Mrs Winniatt's room?'

'I'm afraid I'm not at liberty to tell you.'

'What would you say if I told you that it was all done in the name of research?'

'So you admit taking the pearls?'

'If I did admit taking them – which I do not – how would you view the situation if I told you that I needed to do it for a scene in my novel?'

'I would be inclined not to believe you.'

'I see,' I said. 'Now, that is a shame.' I thought about what to say next. 'The thing is, I didn't steal the pearls, but I do know who did.'

Núñez looked at me with scepticism. 'Is that so? I'm afraid, Mrs Christie, that you've told too many stories, too many – how do you say? – tall tales. Anything you say, I have to question.'

'You've got to believe me this time, Inspector. It's connected to the murder of Mr Winniatt, and before him Douglas Greene.'

'How do you mean?'

'I can't tell you the details, precisely because I don't

know them all yet. But it's vitally important you let me go so I can find out the truth. I'm almost there, on the cusp of it, if you like. There is one piece of information I need before I can put together the final pieces of the puzzle.'

'What do you take me for?' asked Núñez, his face reddening with anger. 'I'm not a character in one of your books, I'm not a bumbling policeman or incompetent investigator. It's not going to be so easy, I'm afraid.'

'I can understand your difficulties. But, Inspector Núñez, you must see that if you keep me locked up we may never find out who was responsible for the murders of—'

'I think you'll find that solving crime is my job, and it really is not the preserve of a lady novelist.' He pronounced the last two words as though he had just tasted something particularly disgusting. 'Now, why don't you tell me the truth?'

What option did I have? I was hoping to keep back the information about Trenkel, which I was sure played a part in the larger picture. But now it seemed as though I had no choice but to reveal it.

'Very well,' I said, smoothing down my skirt. 'I know it may sound highly unlikely, but please take seriously what I am about to tell you.'

Núñez leant forwards in his chair. He took up a pen and was poised to take down my statement.

'You're right. I was in Daisy Winniatt's room the night the pearls went missing.'

With a self-congratulatory nod of the head, he began to write down my words.

'I was in her room looking for a clue, hoping to find Mr

Winniatt's missing journal. I knew that Daisy had been sedated and that this would give me the opportunity to look around.'

'I see. Go on.'

'When I was in there, I saw the handle of the door open and so, in a panic, I hid in the wardrobe. As you know the wardrobes in the rooms at the Taoro are very spacious indeed.'

'Yes, that's so. And?'

'And then, it was while I was inside the wardrobe that I saw someone come into the room and take Mrs Winniatt's pearls from her jewellery box. It was Dr Trenkel.'

As I said the name the Inspector threw down his pen onto the table.

'How can you expect me to believe this?' he exclaimed, his face wrinkling in disgust. 'Dr Trenkel? He's been a trusted member of the Taoro's staff for many years, he has helped dozens – no, hundreds – of sick men and women. And you expect me to believe that he is a common jewel thief? Why would he risk his position at the Taoro? No, it's preposterous!'

'But there's something that lies behind it. You see—'

'I cannot listen to any more of this nonsense,' said Núñez, raising the palm of his hand to stop me. He pushed back his chair, took up his notes, and walked to the door. He called for one of his men, who promptly entered the room. He said something in Spanish that I did not understand. I felt a hand grip my arm, the pressure on my skin as tight as a vice.

'But can't you see, I'm telling the truth.'

The Inspector ignored me and left the room.

'Listen! You've got to help me!'

Núñez's henchman seized me and started to drag me out of the room, down a dark corridor that led to two cells.

'You don't understand. I'm here working on behalf of—'

But there was no point shouting into the shadows. Núñez had gone and it was obvious that his sidekick did not speak English. As we stood outside one of the cells, the guard tried to take my handbag from me. I kept hold of it with all my might and signalled to him that I needed it. I pointed to my bloodied skirt in the hope that this would embarrass him. The trick worked.

'*Entra,*' said the guard, opening a thick wooden door into a dank, foul-smelling room. I had no choice. I resisted fighting and, with my head bowed, stepped into the cell. I heard the slam of the door, the slide of a bolt. As my eyes adjusted to the darkness I made out a mattress on the floor in the far corner and a bucket, which I suspected as being the source of the rank smell. I tried to stop myself from crying – I thought of all the happy times I had enjoyed as a child, the feel of my mother's arms wrapping themselves around me, the delightful freedom I had experienced playing in the garden at Ashfield – but I could not hold off the tears. I stood against the wall and sobbed until my body ached. *How could I have been so stupid, so naive? What on earth was I thinking?* I should have stayed in England, at Abney, my sister's house in Cheshire. I should never have been tempted by Davison's offer. And yet I had felt I had to do something to make up for those deaths last year, for the loss of Una Crowe and Flora Kurs. Otherwise, what had been the point of it all?

In my mind I ran through the facts of the Tenerife case once more. The discovery of the partly mummified body of Douglas Greene in the cave. The statue of Tibicena that Davison and I had found under the earth. The way in which Howard Winniatt had been killed and that horrible, *grand guignol* flourish of the bird-of-paradise flower spiked through his eye. It was all so theatrical, so staged in a way. Yes, someone had wanted me to believe that Gerard Grenville had been responsible for the deaths and I had fallen for it. He had a bad reputation – he was an occultist who believed in magic; he possessed a collection of Guanche statues and figurines and he exhibited an interest in poisons. When I had discovered that he also harboured an unhealthy interest in his own daughter – a desire that found an unholy expression – then I had assumed that Grenville had to be the killer. But if someone knew those things about him, then of course Grenville would be cast as the perfect murderer. Someone had played me like a puppet, manipulating my strings from a distance. I had my suspicions about the identity of this faceless killer, but I did not yet have the proof. And if I remained locked up in this foul prison I doubted I would ever be able to find the evidence I needed. I had to get out of here.

I opened my handbag and took out the pouch containing my small vials of poisons. I ran my fingers over the tops of the glass bottles, reciting the names of the toxins under my breath like an incantation. I dared not risk using the tetrodotoxin – which could bring about a sleep that could be mistaken for death – in case the guard did not come and check on me. I did not want to wake up inside a coffin, hearing the sound of soil being thrown into my grave. In fact, ingesting any of the poisons was too risky. What if I were to suffer real pain or be confronted with the prospect of an agonising death? Who would hear me if I were to cry out? No doubt Núñez had given the guard strict instructions not to check on me until first thing the next morning. If I was to take a poison then it would have to be done just before dawn, which meant that I would have to endure a night in the stinking cell. The refrain passed down to me from my grandmother – *What can't be cured, must be endured* – now sounded through my head like something from a nightmare.

I went to sit down on the damp mattress. I did not want to inspect the cover too closely, and instead laid Flora's shawl across the bed and made myself as comfortable as possible. I closed my eyes and let thoughts drift across my mind like images from a disturbing dream. There was something at the back of my consciousness that unsettled me, something that I felt was of great importance. Was it a fragment of a conversation, or something that I had read? I had the impression of two pieces of a puzzle that would not fit together, as though one side were jagged, the other had a rounded edge. No matter how hard I tried to force them to join together the pieces resisted. Something did not tally.

It was too dark to look through my notebook – the only light was the faint glow from under the locked door – and so I tried to sleep. But the scene under the Dragon Tree continued to play in my mind. The feel of those drops, of what I first took to be blood, splashing down onto my face. The look of horror in Rosalind's eyes. My daughter's screams, and then the cries of Mrs Brendel. It was so easy to be dismissive of the elderly lady's endless chatter, so tempting to let one's attention drift away from what she was saying. And yet . . . I was sure there was something she had said that was important.

As I tried to recall our conversations I felt myself drowning in the ocean of words that had spewed forth from her mouth: the wickedness of Mr Grenville, her experience on board the *Titanic*, her jewels, her trunks.

Suddenly I sat up in bed, a revelation running through me like a fever. *Packing cases.* What had she said? That she was jealous of Guy Trevelyan's empty trunk. It seemed so insignificant somehow, utterly without any meaning. But had I not read something to suggest that, on the outward journey, Trevelyan's packing cases had been so heavy that, when the porters had first taken them onto the *Gelria*, the men's faces had turned beetroot red. Yes, I was sure that I had read that in Winniatt's journal, the one I had taken from the couple's room on the night I had seen Trenkel steal Daisy's pearls. How stupid I had been! It was all beginning to make sense now. But what a wicked, wicked plan.

The thrill of the realisation – I was a step closer to understanding how everything began to fit together – was cut short by the knowledge that, if I was right, Mrs Brendel's life was in danger. I jumped up from the mattress and, in the half light of dusk, ran over to the door.

'Let me out!' I called. 'There's going to be another murder. Help! Please, you must let me speak to Inspector Núñez.' I searched my brain for snatches of Spanish I had learnt. '*Por favor*! *Sangre. Muerte. Muerte!*'

I banged on the door, then gave it a sharp kick that bruised my foot. 'You must help! Inspector Núñez. I must speak to him. *Muerte.*'

I kept repeating the words, but my screams did nothing to rouse the attentions of the guard. I continued to bang and kick until I felt exhausted, drained of energy. My voice began to get hoarse, and then, with tears running down my face, I let myself slump down onto the floor. I had been screaming into an empty darkness.

Chapter Thirty-seven

My head jolted forwards, waking me from a half sleep. I heard the sound of footsteps and then the unlocking of the door. I steadied myself by the wall as I tried to stand, a bullet of pain shooting through my shoulder blades. I quickly ran a hand through my dishevelled hair and brushed the dust and dirt off my skirt, and a moment later Núñez stood before me.

'I see you did not have a very comfortable night, Mrs Christie,' he said.

'No, I've realised that someone is in grave danger – it's Mrs Brendel.' The words tripped out of my dry mouth too quickly, like someone deranged. 'I can't tell you everything now, to do that would take too long, but you must believe me that Mrs Brendel's life is in danger. You must get a police-man to her and take her away from here. I had been so slow, stupidly slow, not to see it before, but it was only when—'

'Please calm down,' said Núñez. 'Have you got a fever?'

'No, I feel perfectly well,' I lied. 'But you have to help me. You see—'

'I should have listened to Dr Trenkel – he told me that you were far from well. I should—'

'Dr Trenkel?' I spat out the name as if it were an unclean thing. 'What I told you about him is—'

'I hope you're not going to persist in telling me that story of yours about the doctor. There's no need. In fact, I would have thought that you are going to require his care more than ever now. Once you're released from here, I would advise you to go and see him straight away for some help with your nervous condition. I read about your experiences at the end of last year, but I didn't realise you were quite so ill. I'm sorry to have held you here, in this rather unpleasant cell, but I think you'll realise I did it for your own safety.'

I could hardly take in his words. 'You're letting me go?'

'Oh yes, you see we've arrested two people who have confessed to the theft of Mrs Winniatt's pearls.'

'Who?'

'A governess, staying with one of the families at the Taoro. A Mme Giroux. She is the same age as you, roughly, has remarkably similar colouring so I suppose it was easy for someone to mistake her for you.'

I hardly wanted to know the answer to the next question. 'And the other person?'

'Another of your acquaintances, Mr Alexander Blake – also known as John Davison. He returned to the Taoro last night, asked the manager where he could find me and simply handed himself in. Apparently, the two of them had been working in tandem. Had something of a routine going on between them, where they would check

309

into top-class hotels, and then take one or two items of extremely valuable jewellery.'

What was Davison playing at? 'So this chap was just pretending to be Mr Blake?'

'Yes, it seems so. He very nearly pinned the crime on you. You had a lucky escape.'

'I see. Well, I don't know what to say.'

'I hope you can go some way to forgive us for this . . .' he said, opening his arms and gesturing at the dirty cell. 'But perhaps you will one day be able to use it in one of your novels.'

'I doubt it,' I said, my confusion beginning to lift. Davison had obviously got my note, heard that I had been taken to the cell, and had been forced to improvise. 'And you say the couple have confessed to the crime?'

'After some persuasion, yes. It seems Mme Giroux, realising that someone had seen her leave Mrs Winniatt's room, took advantage of her resemblance to you and managed to hide the pearls in one of the drawers in your room. They wanted to frame you for the crime, you see.'

I had to go along with the scenario dreamt up by Davison. 'But how did Mme Giroux get into my room?'

'The finer details of the crime have yet to be understood,' he said. 'But what I cannot grasp is why you told us all those silly stories.'

'As you say, my imagination can sometimes get the better of me,' I said.

'Indeed,' he said. 'I think it's best if your interest in crime remains confined within the covers of a novel.'

'I'm sure you are quite right, Inspector,' I said, with a

simpering smile. I needed to get out of the cell and back to the Taoro as quickly as possible. 'But I do have some concerns for Mrs Brendel. I believe that the person who was behind the deaths of Douglas Greene and Howard Winniatt may now try to kill her.'

'If I'm right we have that very man in custody at the moment,' replied Núñez. 'It's my guess that John Davison realised that both Douglas Greene and Howard Winniatt had discovered something about him that threatened his exposure, either as a jewel thief or a—'

I felt like shouting at the top of my voice. But I did not have time to argue with the Inspector, or explain the real reason why Davison was on the island. 'I am feeling very tired now,' I said. 'I would like to take a hot bath at the hotel – as you can see I'm hardly looking my best.'

'Yes, of course, I'll fetch a car for you now,' he said, accompanying me out of the cell and down the corridor. 'I can only apologise for your treatment – for your unpleasant stay – but as I said it could all have been avoided if only you had told us the truth, instead of making up those rather elaborate stories.'

'I don't know what came over me,' I said, my mouth forming itself into a fixed grin.

'Well, let's not say any more about it,' he said as he opened the door to the car and told the driver to take me to the Taoro. 'I hope we can put all of this behind us. And please don't worry about Mrs Brendel. I'm sure we've got our man.'

As soon as Núñez closed the door and the car set off I felt the muscles around my mouth tighten and I was sure

311

that my face looked like a mask worn in a Greek tragedy. Thoughts of Mrs Brendel's casual remark at the picnic ran through my mind. How curious that those carefree words, spoken in innocence, could serve as her death sentence. But I was certain that, if overheard, they had the power to finish her off just as surely as she had taken a dose of cyanide or arsenic. With each turn of the car's wheels I willed her not to be dead. *Please, please, please God*, I said to myself, *please save her.* I could not look out of the window, but simply stared down at the red stain on my skirt. As soon as the car arrived at the front entrance of the Taoro, I opened the door and ran up the steps of the hotel. I caught the eye of some fellow guests who looked at me with astonishment, if not horror, as though I were a mad-woman who had escaped from the confines of an asylum.

'Gustavo, please, do you know where Mrs Brendel is?' I gasped as I approached the front desk.

'Let me see,' he said. 'I know she tends to rise quite late, but I don't believe we've seen her for breakfast yet. Is something wrong?' He too cast a disapproving eye over my appearance.

'It's a matter of the utmost urgency,' I said. 'Mrs Brendel's life could be in danger.'

'Well, let me send a boy to her room.' He raised his arm to call one of the bellboys.

I feared what the young boy might find. 'Would you mind very much if you went to check? I do think it would be better.'

'Very well,' said Gustavo, calling over one of his assistants to take his place at the desk.

312

I followed him across the lobby and up the grand stair-case in silence, like a shadow. When we reached Mrs Brendel's room he knocked on the door. There was no answer. He knocked again and again we were met by no response. I felt fear begin to constrict my throat.

'Most unusual,' said Gustavo, looking at his watch.

'Mrs Brendel!' I shouted. 'Mrs Brendel – are you there? Please open the door.'

From down the corridor we heard the sound of someone pushing an invalid in a wheeled chair. Gustavo knocked once more, but again there was nothing.

'No, this is not right, not right at all,' said Gustavo, taking a key out of his pocket. 'Please, wait here. I will see if there's a problem.'

Gustavo knocked once again before he turned the lock and pushed open the door. I could not bear to stand outside and so followed him into the darkened room. There was no smell except for the faint scent of rose soap. The bed was empty. I asked Gustavo to check the wardrobe. I took a handkerchief and placed it over my mouth, fully prepared to see the elderly woman's body slumped inside, perhaps with her throat cut. The shock of seeing nothing but a rack of the lady's clothes made me gasp out loud. As Gustavo continued to check the room, I walked over to the bathroom and slowly opened the door. The noise of something caught between the bottom of the door and the marble floor made me take a step backwards, but then, after steadying myself, I took a deep breath and entered.

The wet floor was covered in pearls – one of the jewels

must have become trapped beneath the door. I remembered Mrs Brendel's pearl necklace which she always wore. I knew what I would find, but I continued to walk slowly towards the bath tub. There, in the water, lay the body of Mrs Brendel, fully clothed, her skin ghastly pale, her eyes open. I thought of Winniatt's quotation from *The Tempest*, when we had all been sailing on the *Gelria* bound for Tenerife: 'Those are pearls that were his eyes.' Now two of those people at dinner that night were dead.

'Gustavo!' I called, feeling my legs give way from under me. 'She's here.'

'Oh no,' cried Gustavo as he entered the bathroom.

'I was too late,' I said, stifling my sobs with my handkerchief. 'She's been murdered.'

'Murdered? What do you mean? Who would do such a thing?'

I did not respond.

'Was it a robbery that went wrong?' asked Gustavo, looking at the loose pearls that shimmered on the floor. 'Was it something to do with the theft of Mrs Winniatt's jewels? I had hoped to keep it quiet, but I suppose it will all have to come out into the open now.'

'What do you mean?' I asked.

'Last year, a lady mislaid an emerald brooch and the year before, another widow said she had lost a diamond and sapphire bracelet. We put it down to nothing more than carelessness, absent-mindedness.'

'Please go and find Inspector Núñez.'

'The Inspector told me that he had found the people responsible for the theft. Who would have thought guests of the Taoro, Mme Giroux and the man – what was his name – Mr Blake, could be jewel thieves? The strange thing is that I'm sure that they had never stayed with us on previous occasions. Perhaps they were in disguise when those other jewels were stolen. That or they crept into the hotel and took the brooch and the bracelet during the dead of night. After he had arrested Mme Giroux and Mr Blake, Inspector Núñez reassured me that we had nothing more to worry about. But now this.'

He looked down at Mrs Brendel in the water, the strands of her hair curling around her head like a halo of seaweed. The skin of her neck bore the red marks of where some-one had wrenched the necklace from her in a struggle. It seemed that, after that fight, Mrs Brendel's murderer had strangled her and, to make certain she was dead, he or she had then filled the bath with water and drowned her.

'Poor Mrs Brendel,' I said. The elderly woman had told me that after her experiences on board the *Titanic*, she had feared water. It seemed so cruel, so terribly pathetic, for her life to end like this, in a foot or so of bathwater.

'I hope she didn't suffer,' said Gustavo, as he left the room.

I could not bring myself to reply, because in those last frantic few seconds before her life had been snuffed out, Mrs Brendel must have suffered a very great deal indeed.

Chapter Thirty-eight

As Carlo opened the door to the room I fell into her arms.

'Oh my goodness,' she said. 'What on earth happened?'

At that moment, Rosalind came running through the door to the adjoining room. 'Mummy! Are you all right?' Her little hands pulled at my skirts.

'Yes, I am. But I feel much better for seeing you both, I can tell you. It was a terrible misunderstanding. The Inspector took me for a jewel thief, can you believe that?'

'Silly man!' exclaimed Rosalind.

'You're right, darling,' I said, forcing a smile. 'A very silly man indeed.'

I felt a soft touch on my arm. Carlo, I knew, would not be so easily fooled and she could tell there was something terribly wrong.

'Why don't you go and put Blue Teddy to bed now, dear,' she said to Rosalind. 'Your mother and I need to talk for a moment.'

'Oh, but do I have to? Blue Teddy says he has only just got up.'

'Yes, come on, none of that nonsense,' said Carlo.

'Very well, but I can tell you now that he won't go to sleep,' murmured Rosalind as she carried her favourite toy into the next room.

'You look awful,' said Carlo, closing the connecting door so my daughter couldn't hear our conversation. 'Now, what's been going on?'

'I'm not surprised I look awful, I spent the night in a horrible cell down by the harbour,' I said as I collapsed onto the edge of the bed.

'So the Inspector really thought that you were responsible for the theft of Mrs Winniatt's pearls?'

'Yes, it seems so.'

'And why did he let you go?'

I was tired of Carlo's questions, but she deserved some answers, even though I couldn't tell her the whole truth. 'Inspector Núñez has found who he thinks was behind the crime,' I said.

'There's something else, isn't there? Something else you're not telling me.'

I felt guilty keeping secrets from Carlo; in addition to serving as secretary and part-time governess, she was one of my dearest friends. But she could not know about my secret intelligence work with Davison, or the real reason why I had travelled to Tenerife.

'Yes, I'm afraid there is,' I said. 'It's Mrs Brendel. She's dead.'

Although Carlo did not know the elderly woman well, I knew that she had become quite fond of her quirks and eccentric nature.

'What happened?' she said, tears in her eyes. 'It's not another—'

'Yes, she was found drowned in her bath. There's no mistaking it – it was murder.'

'How awful. But why?'

'I think she saw or overheard something, something she regarded as insignificant, but which if it were known would be incriminating evidence against a dangerous criminal.'

'What do you mean?'

'It will all come to light shortly,' I said in a deliberately vague fashion.

'You promised me you wouldn't get involved in anything like this,' said Carlo. 'You said that you were just here to rest.'

'And I was – I am. I can hardly help it if a fellow guest, or guests, get themselves murdered.' I didn't mean the words to sound cruel – after all, I was trying to put Carlo off the scent – but cruel they sounded. 'Listen,' I said, taking Carlo's hand. 'I know I promised you that I would try and relax, but I think I know, or I am on the point of knowing, who was behind the murders.'

'So you're going to tell everything you know to the Inspector?'

'I'm afraid I tried that approach, but it was far from successful. He chose not to believe me.'

'So you still think it's that monster Grenville?'

'He may be a monster, but I don't believe he is the murderer.'

'You don't? Then who is?'

'Please be patient, Carlo,' I said, squeezing her hand. 'I know it's frustrating and I realise my behaviour must be quite maddening, but there are just a few more pieces of evidence I need before everything slots into place.'

She looked at me with a concerned expression. 'And you're not going to put yourself in danger?'

I didn't answer the question. 'Now, what I would like is a steaming hot bath and a few hours' sleep.'

'But—'

'Then later I'll order lunch – I couldn't eat a thing at the moment, not after the smell I encountered in that cell.'

'Why won't you answer me?'

The image of Mrs Brendel's body floating in that bath flashed into my mind. 'This has got to stop, Carlo. It can't be allowed to carry on. The Inspector has shown little insight so far and I doubt if he will show any in the future. Yes, a horrible series of crimes have been allowed to happen. And it seems people have been powerless to prevent them. But now that is all going to change.'

'You said that you wouldn't—'

'What I said is all immaterial now,' I said, my face flushing. It was all beginning to come together. 'There's a nest of vipers that needs to be destroyed. It can't be allowed to continue.'

'You're beginning to scare me now.'

'Well, it's a very frightening prospect. Evil breeds evil, don't you see?'

'Here, let me help you out of those clothes,' said Carlo, evidently trying to change the subject. 'I fear that we'll never be able to get that stain out of your skirt.'

It was the stains on the soul that worried me, an observation I chose not to share with Carlo in case it alarmed her even more.

'Oh, a telegram came for you first thing this morning,' she said. 'I hope it's not more bad news.'

'A telegram?'

'The terrible news of Mrs Brendel made me forget about it, I'm sorry,' she said, as she handed me the envelope from my dressing table.

I ripped open the paper and read the message. It had been sent from a man in Hartford's office – the headquarters of the Secret Intelligence Service – back in London. Davison must have managed to send over the request for the information – asking for it to be forwarded directly to me at the Taoro – before he had handed himself in to Núñez. The telegram listed the names and occupations of three young women who had gone missing in England in the week before the *Gelria* sailed from Southampton. One name – that of Susan Saunders – stood out, not because it held any special significance, but because of the two words that came after it. *Occupation: dancer.* This was a crucial part of the evidence I needed to make my case. Everything was beginning to fall into place. Poor Susan Saunders was another victim in this terrible cycle of death.

Chapter Thirty-nine

After bathing and dressing I heard a knock at the door. The news of Mrs Brendel's death had brought Inspector Núñez back to me. He looked terrible – the shock had left him ashen-faced.

'I just don't know how to explain it,' he said, as Carlo ushered him into the room. 'I'm at a complete loss. I thought I had it all worked out, that Mr Blake was responsible for the murders of Douglas Greene and of Howard Winniatt, who had somehow uncovered incriminating details about his career as a jewel thief and perhaps threatened to expose him. But it seems Mrs Brendel was killed at some point last night after I had taken Mr Blake and Mme Giroux into custody.' His words trailed off and his head dropped in defeat.

'Would you care for a glass of water?' I asked.

'Yes, that's very kind, thank you,' he said, as he took the glass of iced water I had poured for him from a jug on the table. 'Forgive me, Mrs Christie. I believe I've been dismissive of your observations. I know in the cell – that terrible place, how could I ever have taken you there? – you told me that you thought Mrs Brendel's life was in danger. But I swept aside all your concerns with a rudeness for which I am truly ashamed.'

I did not correct him.

'What I want to ask, if you will forgive me for my earlier indiscretions, is what led you to that conclusion?'

'Well, Inspector, it is a very curious case. Please sit down, as it may take some time to explain.'

I sent Carlo and Rosalind out of the room and started to outline the series of seemingly unconnected events that had taken place so far. The incident of Gina Trevelyan throwing herself off the side of the ship on the passage over. My initial suspicions of Gerard Grenville (I did not tell him what I knew of the true nature of the relationship between father and daughter) and the conversation I had had with José regarding the rumours he had spread about his former employer. Because Mr Winniatt and Mrs Brendel had noticed a small, seemingly insignificant detail about Guy Trevelyan's trunk – how it had been full and heavy when it had been loaded onto the *Gelria* back in England, but empty and light by the time it had arrived in the Canary Islands – and now the pair were dead.

'I'm right in saying that if you had known about this tiny detail – about the empty trunk – you would have had your suspicions about Guy Trevelyan?'

The Inspector nodded. There was a certain blankness to his expression.

'You would, no doubt, have started to investigate and perhaps asked some questions about what had been in that trunk,' I continued. 'And perhaps Mr Trevelyan might have given himself away. But I suppose nothing would have prompted you to start making enquiries back in England, as to certain missing women. Of course, one mustn't forget the use of atropine. Yes, that really is one of the keys to the case.'

Inspector Núñez was blinking with incomprehension. 'I'm afraid I don't understand,' he said.

'Sorry, I'm running ahead of myself,' I said, standing up. 'But there isn't really time for me to go into it all here as there is another thing I really must check. It is rather complicated, Inspector, but the motive for all the murders is linked and I'm still putting the pieces together.'

'What happens now?' he said, looking like a little boy who had just lost his mother. 'I can't see how—'

'We carry on as normal,' I said. 'Of course, there will be another funeral. It remains to be seen whether Helen Hart will have her party at her house tomorrow night. Knowing her, I'm sure she will. After all, she's never let a death stand in the way of her having a good time.'

'And should I arrest Guy Trevelyan?'

'Oh no, not just yet,' I said. 'It's a great deal more complicated than that, I'm afraid.'

'It is?'

'Oh, yes. It's like some kind of rotten onion. Peel away one layer of evil and there's another layer beneath. A different kind of evil. What we need to do is get to the very centre of it. The nasty, rank core of it all.'

'Perhaps we could go through this one more time. I'm still don't quite understand the—'

323

'Yes, of course,' I said. 'But before we do, I'm afraid you will have to do one thing for me.'

'Anything at all. I'm still feeling terrible for what I put you through. No lady should have to endure a night in that cell, least of all—'

'You must release Mr Blake and Mme Giroux.'

'Do what?'

'They have nothing to do with the theft of Mrs Winniatt's pearls. Please, Inspector Núñez, you must trust me.'

'But Mr Blake himself confessed to the crime. How do you—'

'He did that to try to ensure my release. I can guarantee that neither Mr Blake nor Mme Giroux had anything to do with the theft of those pearls. I know who did it, you see. I saw him with my own eyes.'

'But it cannot be Dr Trenkel. Why would he risk everything for the sake of a string of pearls?'

'Why, indeed – yes, a very good question. I'm sorry, there's a great deal I'm afraid I cannot tell you at the moment, but it will come to light shortly. It's all connected, you see. The suicide of Gina Trevelyan on the ship. The death of Douglas Greene whose body was found in the cave. Mr Winniatt's murder and now the strangulation and drowning of poor Mrs Brendel. The theft of the jewels is a small piece in a much larger puzzle. And hopefully I'm close to finding the very last clue – or couple of clues, I should say – which should explain everything.'

'I'm not sure, what if my superiors discover that—'

'Your superiors will be most displeased if they realise

you have failed to prevent yet another murder on the island.'

'What do you mean? Another murder?' said the Inspector, looking very worried.

'It won't stop here, I'm afraid.'

'It won't?' The Inspector's hand had started to shake slightly, the ice in his glass clinking against the side of the crystal. 'And who will be the next victim?'

I tidied an unruly strand of hair that had fallen over my face. 'Oh, there's no doubt about it. The next person to be murdered will be me.'

Chapter Forty

After a great deal of persuasion, Inspector Núñez finally agreed to free Davison and Mme Giroux. He had been proved wrong too many times, he said, and admitted that his career would be over if he failed to prevent another murder. However, he made me promise that the couple would not leave Puerto Orotava and told me that he was giving me forty-eight hours to solve the case. In return, he would do everything in his power to protect me. It seemed like a reasonable exchange and so, later that day, at five in the afternoon, I took a taxi down to the harbour to wait for the release of my two friends – for how else could I describe these two dear souls who had been prepared to go to prison for my sake? Both of them emerged looking tired and a little dirty, but that did not stop me from embracing both of them.

'My God, the conditions in there,' said Davison. 'I can't believe you had to endure a night in that stinking cell.'

'I know, simply awful,' I said. 'But let's not dwell on that now. Mme Giroux, how can I ever thank you enough?'

'I knew you had not stolen those pearls,' said Mme Giroux, holding both my hands. 'From the very first moment I could tell you were a good and honest lady, one who had – like me – been treated badly by a man whom she had loved. So when your friend Mr Blake came with the proposal to admit to the theft – in order to give you the time you needed to solve the murders – I was more than willing to help.'

'But you risked your reputation, your job . . .' I felt words beginning to fail me.

'It was the right thing to do,' she said. 'I'm sure everyone will understand when they know the truth.'

'Thank you,' I said. 'Unfortunately I was too late to prevent the murder of Mrs Brendel. I was so stupid not to pick up the clues earlier. They were there all right, but I was too blind to see them.'

'There's nothing you can do about that now, so let's get back to the Taoro,' said Davison, opening the door to the taxi for Mme Giroux and me. He tipped his hat to the two policemen in the car next to ours, men assigned by Núñez to protect me.

'The Inspector said that we've got only two days to solve the case, but it's not going to be easy,' I said, clearing my throat. 'In fact, it may well prove to be extremely dangerous.' I had to pull myself together. I had to try and pretend to myself, and to those around me, that I was strong. When I thought about it all, what I was risking – not only my life, but the prospect of never seeing Rosalind grow up, never holding my grandchildren – I felt like hiding away in my room or taking the first boat back to England. But

ANDREW WILSON

that was not an option any more. 'First, I'd like to check something before we return to the hotel. Please drop me at the English Library.'

Davison looked concerned. 'We can't take any risks, not after Mrs Brendel,' he said, lowering his voice. 'The Inspector told me all about it. You know the danger you are in. And I'm not going to let you out of my sight for a moment. Not after—'

'You're right,' I said. I knew he was thinking of Una. 'Even though the Inspector said that he would have two of his men follow me, I'd rather know that you were watching over me.'

'That's probably the nicest thing you've ever said to me,' said Davison, smiling. 'What is it you want to check at the library?' Before I could answer, his face darkened. 'Aren't you forgetting something? It's a Sunday – the building will be closed.'

'Yes, but I thought that perhaps we could ask Núñez's men to open it for me – surely they can find a key?'

Davison explained in Spanish our difficulty to the Inspector's assistants and the request was met by a series of encouraging nods and fast-flowing talk.

'What are they saying?' I asked.

'They say they know where to get the key – a spare is held by the caretaker – and that it should not be a problem,' Davison replied.

After calling by the caretaker's home, a modest building set within the Taoro grounds, the car dropped Davison and me at the English Library, before it carried Mme Giroux back to the hotel. The two junior policemen

328

walked behind us like our shadows as we made our way down a path flanked by palm trees to the simple, single-storey building. As we stepped inside we were met by the sight of hundreds of books all neatly displayed on shelves ranged around a series of rooms.

What a delight for the English community who lived in Orotava, having a little bit of their own culture to draw on. To think of the many different worlds captured within the pages of these books! For a few minutes, as I wandered into the large and airy central room, I forgot about the distressing events of the last few weeks. How many times, in moments of difficulty, had I escaped into the pages of a novel? I thought of the books I had read as a girl. How I had devoured *The Prisoner of Zenda*. How I had adored the works of Jules Verne, which I had read in French. And I had been addicted to L.T. Meade's books for girls, as well as the romances of Stanley Weyman and the historical adventures of G. A. Henty. Yes, they might have been silly, but they offered a chance to see the world from another point of view. And through empathy came understanding. If I had been able to be more articulate about it, I would have been able to explain some of this to Howard Winniatt. Instead, I had become all flustered and tongue-tied and now he was dead. I doubted very much that history would look kindly on the work of Mr Winniatt. Yet he had not deserved to be murdered. I wondered about the character of the person who could kill in such cold blood. Douglas Greene, Howard Winniatt, Mrs Brendel, their lives taken without conscience. Surely a person who could murder like this was not the kind who could settle down and enjoy a novel?

'By the way, did Hartford send you the information you were looking for – about girls who had gone missing back in Britain?' asked Davison, interrupting my reverie.

'Yes, and it proved extremely helpful,' I said. Even though the building was empty, we talked in whispers.

'I still don't understand how that could have anything to do with what's been going on out here.'

'I know it seems odd,' I said, 'but one missing girl – she's called Susan Saunders, by the way – is a crucial part of this chain of murders. I think there are quite a few things that if seen individually make no sense. It's only when you put the pieces together and stand back that you can see the larger picture.'

'I'm still none the wiser,' said Davison. 'And to think that I once thought of myself as your mentor. *L'élève a dépassé le maître.*'

The expression about how I had become his teacher made me smile. Indeed, I had come a long way since the time Davison had first met me on that cold December morning near my club on Hyde Park Corner, when I had been on the point of nervous collapse.

'I sincerely doubt it,' I said. 'I'll fill you in later on what happened while you were away in Icod. I wonder if they have any medical books here?'

'Why? What are you looking for?'

'It's something I saw in Dr Trenkel's office. Something that doesn't make sense.'

'How is it connected to what's happened?'

I did not answer his question. 'I'm looking for a book that contains information on the diagnosis and treatment of tuberculosis.'

'I would have thought that this would be quite a popular subject – look here,' said Davison, pointing out a selection of books in the reference section.

I ran my fingers ran along the shelves and pulled out a number of titles, including *Orotava as a Health Resort* by George Victor Pérez, *The Canaries for Consumptives* by E. Paget Thurstan and *A Handbook of Climatic Treatment* by William R. Huggard. I read about the health-giving properties of sun baths and the invigorating benefits of the trade winds. I learnt how medics believed that in areas between 5000 and 7000 feet above sea level the population was free of consumption. This area in Tenerife was so special because it had no excessive heat in summer and no cold in winter. There were no heavy dews, no frosts, no siroccos and no chill at sunset. Palms grew to a height of 120 feet, with one commentator proclaiming, 'Plants are witnesses that cannot lie'. Unfortunately, I thought to myself, one could not say the same about their human counterparts. Some men and women would do almost anything to further themselves in the world, men and women such as . . .

'What about this one?' asked Davison, proffering a book entitled *A Clinical System of Tuberculosis: Describing All Forms of the Disease* by Dr B. Bandelier and Dr O. Roepke. 'Dry as hell, but it might help you. If you'd only tell me what it is exactly you were looking for then I might actually—'

'Yes, this book might prove very helpful indeed. I'm sorry, Davison, I promise I'll tell you when we get back to the Taoro. It's just that when—'

As I turned the pages of the medical text book, which was written in language that only doctors or specialist practitioners could properly understand, I fell silent. Something on one of the pages, a section that dealt with symptoms relating to the circulatory organs, had caught my eye. My training as a nurse during the war came in useful as I read the following paragraphs:

Emaciation, fever and deficient blood circulation tend, in the later stages of phthisis, to atrophy and fatty degeneration of the heart muscle. A soft, blowing, functional murmur over the arterial apertures is often a sign that the heart is exhausted and beginning to fail.

In the chronic fibroid form of phthisis, in which the area of the pulmonary circulation is progressively diminished, hypertrophy of the right ventricle succeeded by dilation may be detected . . .

The pronounced condition is easy to recognise by the accentuation of the second pulmonary sound, the increase of cardiac dullness to the right, by epigastric pulsation, and by a systolic murmur over the tricuspid area. Under increased demands compensation fails, so that congestion of the liver, kidneys or extremities, and later phlebitis and venous thrombosis appear. There may be cyanosis of the visible mucous membranes, or asthmatical attacks on account of the respiratory deficiency.

I pulled out a couple of sheets of paper from my handbag. Phrases jumped out at me like bullets. 'Later stages of phthisis, atrophy and fatty degeneration of the heart muscle', 'congestion of the liver and kidneys', and 'cyanosis of the visible mucous membranes'.

The words matched exactly what I had just read. The doctor had simply copied out the words from a book. Perhaps that was why Dr Trenkel's handwriting appeared so neat on this report in contrast to the rest of his patients' records.

At that point, I could have handed over everything I had discovered to Inspector Núñez, and hoped that the police would be able to make a case. I could have left it in the hands of the authorities and, after giving my statement, retired back to England where I might have read about the brutal murders in Orotava in a paragraph or two in *The Times* or the *Daily Mail*. But to do so would have deprived me – and others whose lives had been destroyed – of seeing justice done. There was also a possibility that the person – a murderer who was clever, calculating and manipulative – would twist the evidence and try to shift the blame and, in doing so, escape punishment. I wasn't ready to step aside from this just yet. Davison had brought me here to this lush paradise to help solve this crime and solve it I would.

It was time to draw the killer out of the shadows.

Chapter Forty-one

As I had expected, Helen Hart decided to go ahead with her party, but with some last-minute changes. She sent word around that she had decided to turn it into an event to celebrate some of Mrs Brendel's achievements. The Spanish, she added, did not subscribe to the English custom of the wake and she believed that a little get-together of Mrs Brendel's friends in advance of the funeral would be more appropriate. 'It was what Edith would have wanted,' she added.

Davison and I had spent the day on a plan we hoped would work. But, as I had outlined to him, this was not like the denouement in a detective novel – in which the author would tie up all the loose ends – but messy and dangerous real life in which anything might happen. I made an effort to look the part, choosing an emerald green silk dress, which Davison complimented me on when I joined him in the bar of the Taoro.

'Una would have called it a dress to die for,' he said, taking a sip of his dry Martini.

'Or a dress to die in,' I said, smiling.

'Agatha, please don't joke about such things,' he said.

'I'm sorry, but you know I've no intention of letting anyone kill me.'

'I hope not,' he said, looking at me with concern. 'But are you absolutely sure you want to go ahead with this? It's not too late to change your mind. We have almost enough for Núñez to make an arrest as it is.'

'Almost is never good enough,' I said.

'And you won't have a drink? Not even to steady your nerves?'

'No. And I think we should be going – it's nearly half past seven.'

Davison drained the contents of his glass, offered me his arm and we walked out of the bar to the front of the hotel where a taxi was waiting for us. On the journey out of town and past La Paz we talked trivialities – vague travel plans, what we missed about dear old England, the overuse of garlic in Spanish food – until we arrived at Helen Hart's cliff-top house. Torches and candles lit the entrance, casting surreal shadows into the garden. As we passed down a line of tall date palms, breathing in the night air thick with the sickly sweet smell of exotic blooms, I could make out the shape of sculptures positioned around the garden. A Spanish maid greeted us at the door and showed us towards a large drawing room which was alive with the sound of conversation.

'Mrs Christie – I'm so pleased you could make it,' said Helen when she saw me. She was dressed in an elegant, pale blue dress and a matching jacket with big pockets. 'And you've brought your enigmatic friend along too. Forgive me, what was the name again?'

'Blake – Mr Alexander Blake,' said Davison, removing his hat.

'What can I get you – a cocktail? Guy – cocktails over here.'

I let Guy Trevelyan hand me a glass of clear-looking liquid that I had no intention of drinking. Davison took one too, and pretended to take a sip from it.

'I think you know everyone here,' Miss Hart said, her blue eyes flashing brightly. She was obviously in her element.

'Yes, I think so,' I said. I looked around the room. Dr Trenkel was in the corner talking to Professor Wilbor; with them were Rupert Mabey and a pale-looking Edmund Ffosse in his wheeled chair.

'Gerard and Violet Grenville are expected at any moment,' said Helen Hart. 'I know Edith was not a great fan of Grenville, but I'd already invited them before she died, and it seemed churlish to banish them from the party as I know Violet was looking forward to seeing Edmund. Also, I'm afraid Mrs Winniatt said she was still too upset to venture out. Talking of Mrs Winniatt, and taking advantage of her absence, you must tell us all about what happened, Mrs Christie. I couldn't believe it when the Inspector turned up at the picnic like that and took you away.'

'Oh, it was nothing but a silly misunderstanding,' I said.

'A misunderstanding?' exclaimed Helen, sipping her cocktail. 'If I had been locked in a cell overnight I think I would call it more than that. What do you say, Guy?'

'Well, yes, indeed,' he said, blinking bloodshot eyes.

'And Mr Blake, I hear that you were taken in by the police too?'

'Just to help the Inspector with his enquiries, that's all,' said Davison.

'Of course, we never suspected you were guilty for a moment – did we, Guy?' said Miss Hart. 'But I wonder who was responsible for the theft of those pearls? Obviously that pales into insignificance when compared to the murder of poor Howard. And now Edith. It must have been awful to find her like that – in the bath.'

'Yes, it was a terrible shock,' I said.

'She was a great friend and I know that Guy has taken her death particularly badly. You've been quite shaken up, haven't you, darling?'

Guy didn't respond, but turned from Helen towards the cocktail trolley and began to mix some more drinks.

'As I said in my note I thought we should mark her passing in some way, even if it is just raising a glass in her honour. Or, after dinner, if anyone here wanted to say anything – any memories they wanted to share. I know I've got a few light stories I could start with if everyone thought that was a good idea. But first, as promised, a tour of the studio and my latest work.'

The plan was met with solemn nods and murmurings of approval.

'I still can't believe that Mrs Brendel is dead,' said Professor Wilbor. 'Of course, I only met her when she arrived in Orotava, but she seemed a kind and decent lady.'

'Yes, why would anyone would want to kill her is beyond me,' said Dr Trenkel.

'Did you examine the body, doctor?' asked the Professor.

'Yes, there were signs of asphyxiation, but it was death by drowning, I'm afraid,' he replied. 'The Inspector thinks that whoever did it might have been trying to steal Mrs Brendel's jewellery. The signs of injury indicated that the killer wrenched the pearls from her neck in the struggle. Nothing was taken, so Núñez thinks the murderer might have fled the scene because he was interrupted and didn't have time to pick up the scattered pearls from the floor.'

'How awful,' said the Professor. 'I'm sure the Inspector will get his man.'

After Guy Trevelyan had topped up everyone's drinks, Helen Hart led the way out of the drawing room, down a corridor and towards the back of the house that over-looked the sea. The studio was an impressive structure, featuring enormous floor-to-ceiling windows that looked out towards utter darkness. Outside, you could hear the crash of the waves on the rocks below.

'Obviously, this is very different during the day,' said Miss Hart. 'It's filled with light. It can be quite dazzling at times.'

As she said this, I remembered the line from *The Duchess of Malfi*: 'Cover her face; mine eyes dazzle: she died young.' I now realised why I had first thought of those words and how they applied to Gina Trevelyan. I had been blinded and deceived from the very beginning.

'Here are a few of my most recent pieces,' said Helen, taking up a small chisel that was lying on one of the benches. 'This is a toad carved from green onyx and a snake I sculpted from a single piece of marble.'

338

There was no denying Helen Hart's talents as a sculptress. She invested her sculptures – some of which were abstract – with a raw, elemental power.

'As you can see, I'm trying to capture the essence of a thing, not the surface reality,' she said, pointing the chisel at a portrayal of a seated boy made from anhydrite stone. 'It can be quite difficult for some people to grasp at first. But the emotional reaction is really what is important. I want people to feel things very strongly when they see my work. For instance, Mrs Christie, what do you feel – not think about – when you see this?' she asked, directing her chisel towards a squat, flat-faced figure fashioned from African blackwood. 'It's also one my new pieces of work, something I'm rather proud of, in fact.'

It took me a moment to gather my thoughts. Although I was nowhere near as skilled as Helen Hart, I had, at least, had some training in sculpture. 'Forgive me if I'm wrong, but is it a representation of a kind of primitive woman?'

The interpretation seemed to take Helen Hart rather aback. 'Well – yes, that's very good. I wonder how you knew? She's my version of Eve – well, a savage Eve.'

I could have said more, but held back. There was time for that later.

'But what do you feel about it?' she persisted.

'Well . . . I suppose a sense of power. Yes, a great deal of energy. It seems more than a little frightening.'

'And Mr Blake – you strike me as an unusually sensitive man. What do you make of this? I've just finished it and thought it would be appropriate to show it on Valentine's Day.' She pointed her chisel towards a plinth that contained a large sculpture, in alabaster, of a pair of intertwined figures.

'I'm afraid the world of the arts is quite beyond me,' said Davison, keeping in character as the insurance salesman from Southampton. 'I simply do not have the vocabulary to express myself adequately. Perhaps it would be better to ask someone else.'

Helen Hart looked around the group and settled on Edmund Ffosse, who gazed up from his wheeled chair in astonishment.

'Well, I . . .' said Ffosse, blushing.

'Don't be shy, Mr Ffosse. It's the sexual union. I call it *The Joy of Congress*.'

'Now, Helen, darling, there's no need to embarrass Mr Ffosse,' said Guy, placing a hand on her arm.

Helen's eyes flashed with something – passion, anger, hatred – and she looked as though she was about to say something cruel or even lash out with the chisel, but instead she placed the instrument in a pocket of her jacket and smiled in an artificial manner.

'Perhaps you can tell our friends here something of your inspiration,' said Guy, trying to smooth over the situation.

'I don't know if anyone has heard of Ursula Edgcumbe or Elsie Henderson?' Helen asked.

The question was met by blank faces all round. 'Henry Moore and Jacob Epstein?'

'Oh, yes, we know them,' came the general reply.

'It's interesting, isn't it, how the names of male sculptors are household names. But there are many women who are just as talented, just as skilled.'

I was reminded of the Kipling poem that Guy Trevelyan had quoted on the *Gelria*. A cobra. A Himalayan she-bear. A squaw from the Huron or Choctaws.

'What about Barbara Hepworth?' asked Rupert Mabey.

'At last – one name people know,' she said. 'I could tell you a few things about that lady, in fact—'

At that moment, the maid appeared at the door of the studio to announce that Grenville and his daughter had arrived.

'Very well, let's go and greet them,' said Helen, leading the group out of the studio. 'What I want to say is that I'm trying to invest my work with an exciting feminine energy that I believe is missing from a great deal of sculpture. Anyway, I can tell I've bored all of you quite enough.'

'Not at all,' said the Professor. 'I find it all fascinating. As you know, Guanche sculpture often celebrates the feminine form.'

The Professor and Helen Hart led the group out of the studio and back into the house. Davison and I deliberately held back so we could talk in private.

'Did you see the way she was brandishing that chisel around?' whispered Davison. 'And the expression in her eyes?'

'She does seem balanced on a very sharp knife edge,' I said.

'A very savage Eve, indeed.' He paused. 'Are you truly certain you want to go ahead?'

'Yes, I am. As I told you in the bar at the Taoro, I've never been more certain of anything in my life.'

Chapter Forty-two

When Miss Hart's maid had announced that Grenville and Violet had arrived I was dreading the encounter, but they both greeted me as though my visit to Mal Pais had passed without incident. I knew I would never be able to forget that horrible image of the hulking form of Grenville pressing down on top of Violet. Perhaps Violet had not told her father what I had witnessed and she had chosen to try to erase the knowledge from her mind. I suppose that was one of the ways she had coped with the ghastly situation. Wasn't there anything I could do to help her? Perhaps when all this was over, I could confront Grenville. I dreaded doing so, but the only other option was to go to the police. And that would be distressing for all concerned, particularly poor Violet.

'I'm so sorry we missed the tour of the studio,' said Grenville. 'I had a problem with Consuela again.'

'Not her son, I hope?' asked Helen, leading us into the dining room. She did not wait to hear Grenville's answer to her question. 'Anyway, you've seen my work dozens of times before. All except for my new piece, which I'll show you after dinner if you like.'

Helen directed us to a large, rectangular dining table, which she said was imported from England. It was set with a beautifully worked lace cloth, the kind I remembered Mrs Brendel saying she wanted to take back home. She would never get the chance now. I thought of her body in that bath in the Taoro, the red marks on her neck, the pearls strewn across the marble floor. I felt a sense of anger rising within me, a physical feeling that manifested itself in a slight flush of my cheeks.

'We're very informal tonight, please sit anywhere you like, but I do hope you appreciate the flowers,' said Miss Hart, gesturing to the overladen vases of red roses that decorated the table. 'I got them from the gardener at the Taoro.' She turned to me and asked whether I had received any Valentine's Day cards. When I replied that I had not she gave me a smile of pity. 'Never mind,' she said, glancing at Davison.

As we began to take our seats, Dr Trenkel wheeled Edmund Ffosse into an empty place at the table. Violet came to sit by him and so I chose to sit on his right. Davison sat across from me, between Professor Wilbor and Rupert Mabey, Dr Trenkel took a place opposite Gerard Grenville, while Helen Hart and Guy Trevelyan sat at either end of the table.

'We haven't had a proper chance to talk since you arrived in Orotava, Mrs Christie,' said Edmund Ffosse as I opened out the linen napkin and spread it across my skirt.

'Yes, I've been rather busy,' I said. 'I was afraid that when I first arrived I wouldn't find the island particularly interesting, but in fact it's proved the opposite.'

'Indeed,' he said. 'And how is your writing going?'

'Slowly, I'm afraid. I need to get down to some serious work when—'

'When . . . ?'

'When I can find the time,' I said.

'Ah, yes, time – the one thing I no longer have,' he said wistfully. Violet reached towards him and clutched his hand, pain etched into her face.

I wondered as he said these words whether he knew what might happen next. Of course, Edmund Ffosse might simply have been referring to his medical condition, but still . . .

'"To every thing there is a season, and a time to every purpose under the heaven",' I said, quoting from *Ecclesiastes*.

'A time to be born, and a time to die; a time to plant, and a time to pluck up that which is planted,' Edmund continued.

I carried on with the passage in my head. *A time to kill, and a time to heal; a time to break down, and a time to build up . . . A time to keep silence, and a time to speak.* Soon it would be a time to tell everyone the truth.

'Are you a religious person?' asked Edmund.

'I believe faith can provide one with a certain degree of comfort in times of difficulty,' I replied. 'And what about you, Mr Ffosse?'

'Yes, I too find it a great solace,' he said. 'But there are other sources of comfort to be found, aren't there?' He looked at Violet, who gazed on him with utmost devotion. 'I'm sure you've heard about our difficulties,' he said, turning back to me. 'I just wish I had met Violet a few years earlier, then perhaps we might have been able to enjoy some time together before this wretched illness started to do its damage.'

The maid began to serve the soup, a light consommé.

'Where did you live before you came to Tenerife?' I asked.

'London,' he said. 'But doctors advised me to leave because of my condition. They told me to find somewhere with a warmer climate. And so I came here.'

'But it didn't help?'

'It did at first – in fact I thought Dr Trenkel had gone some way to curing me, but then I suffered another attack and this time ... well, it turned out to be much more serious.'

'I'm sorry to hear that,' I said.

'But we haven't given up hope,' said Violet, perhaps a little too brightly. 'There are other doctors besides Dr Trenkel. I thought we'd try Switzerland or America. I've heard of some successes in both places.'

'Perhaps, my dear, perhaps,' said Edmund, clutching her hand again.

From down the table I caught Grenville casting a disapproving look at his daughter. I wondered if the occultist had divined a sense of what I knew.

'Aren't you eating, Mrs Christie?' asked Helen from the head of the table. I hadn't touched my soup, not because I feared it to be poisoned – the maid had served the consommé from a large tureen – but because the prospect of what I had to do had taken away my appetite.

'I'm feeling a little off-colour,' I said. 'I'm sorry. Since the discovery of poor Mrs Brendel, I haven't quite been myself.'

'Of course, you must be feeling dreadful,' said Edmund.

'I hope it's not a resurgence of the same illness you had while staying at Mal Pais?' said Grenville. There was a barely disguised touch of malice in his voice. 'The English constitution is quite a delicate one.'

I signalled to Davison – we had agreed earlier that I would lift my right hand to my left earlobe as a sign – and set the plan in motion. He was to improvise so as to bring about some kind of diversion or disruption. Davison excelled himself by standing up and tipping the hot consommé into the lap of Rupert Mabey.

'Oh my —!' Mabey shouted.

'I'm so careless,' said Davison as he reached out and tried to dab the soup away with his napkin.

'Get your hands off me, you—' Mabey snarled before stopping himself. So perhaps he did know something of the nature of his brother's friendship with Davison. 'I can do it myself, thank you very much.'

All eyes were directed to the scene. Helen Hart jumped up from her place and rushed to help. In that moment – when attention and been diverted away from me – I opened my handbag and extracted what I needed. A second or so later I reached under the table and jabbed a needle into Edmund Ffosse's thigh. He cried out not so much in pain as in astonishment. With his hands on the table he tried to raise himself up – although his body was emaciated his arms were strong – but as the drug raced through his system he found it difficult to move. He opened his mouth to say something but couldn't speak, a realisation that brought a look of horror to his face.

As I moved to stand up I felt something grip me. Edmund's hand had clasped itself around my left wrist. I tried to free myself from him – the drug should have started to work by now – but he held on to me, with fury burning in his eyes. With my right hand I started to claw at his fingers, but he remained as fixed as a limpet on a rock. As the cutlery fell to the floor the guests turned their attention away from Mabey and Davison to the other side of the table.

'What on earth is going on?' shouted Helen.

'Mrs Christie – is something the matter?' asked Guy as he stood up.

I took a deep breath. 'I'm afraid to have to tell you that I've killed Mr Ffosse,' I said, feeling the man's grip on me weaken. 'I tried to think of another way, but in the end it was the only solution.'

Everybody fell silent and looked at me with astonishment.

'You have done what?' screamed Helen, the first person to speak.

'I have given him an injection of morphine.' As the drug began to work its way through his system Ffosse's arm dropped away and his head fell forwards. I stepped back from the table and held up the small syringe and the vial of the drug. I put on the calm nurse's voice I had learnt from my time with the VAD during the war. 'The effects will be fatal. His lips and fingernails will start to turn blue. He may soon start to vomit, have difficulty breathing and could possibly have a seizure. He will then no doubt fall into a coma and although death will inevitably follow, it will be pain free.'

Sets of eyes stared at me with a mix of bewilderment and fear. One of the servant girls dashed from the room, no doubt to fetch help. I hoped Núñez would be waiting near the house as we had agreed.

'I don't understand,' whispered Violet, deep in shock. 'Are you the one responsible for all these deaths? For the murders?' Her face looked frozen, almost as if it no longer belonged to her.

'I'm sorry, Violet,' I said softly. 'But it was the only way.' I reached out to touch her hand.

I braced myself for what was to come. Instead of lashing out at me, as I had expected, Violet did not stir and she sat there at the table like one of the porcelain dolls of my childhood. It looked as though the life had been drained from her. From across the room came a noise, half human scream, half animal cry, which eventually formed itself into words.

'No!' screamed Helen. The look in her eyes was wild now, beyond the point of control. 'Edmund! No!'

She ran towards me, pushing the others out of the way. 'What have you done?' she demanded.

I repeated what I had said earlier, in as calm a manner as I could. Helen bent down and cradled Edmund's head in her arms, dabbing his mouth with a napkin.

'Dr Trenkel, Dr Trenkel,' she shouted. 'Can't you save him?'

Davison placed a hand on Trenkel's shoulder, and whispered something in his ear.

'What's going on? Why won't anybody help?' Helen hugged Edmund's limp body to hers, and for a moment the scene was as poignant and pitiful as a Pietà I had seen at one of the museums in Paris. 'He's dying – dying! My love – my dear love . . .'

At this, Guy roused himself. 'Helen?' He walked over and tried to ease Helen away from Edmund's limp body. 'Are you all right?'

'Don't touch me!' she screamed, the spittle spraying from her mouth as if she were some base creature.

Guy's response was stiff and awkward, as if he couldn't allow himself to talk freely. 'I know this is awful to witness – and I really can't understand what is going on here, why Mrs Christie has done this – but you seem to be in shock. You don't know what you're saying.'

'Of course I know what I'm saying – can't you see?'

'What?' His eyes were confused and beads of sweat had started to appear on his forehead.

Her laugh was loud, cruel. 'You've always been so obligingly dim, Guy. So easy to manipulate. So pliable.'

He reached out to touch her again, but she pushed him away with a force that was frightening.

'Calm down now, Helen,' he said, panicking. 'Take a deep breath. Have one of your little pills.' He turned to me. 'In the meantime, we must get Núñez over here right away. It looks as though the person who has been responsible for those crimes has just confessed.' He looked around the table at the fellow guests, who seemed confused and lost, like an audience which had stumbled by mistake into a theatre showing a horrifying gothic drama. 'I think everyone heard Mrs Christie, didn't they?'

At the mention of my name, Helen reared up like something possessed. Her eyes burned with a fury that was frightening. Then, a moment later, she launched herself towards me. Her hands – strong, powerful hands used to working with marble and stone – were around my throat. They pressed down on my neck with an almost supernatural power. I felt my face reddening, my eyes bulging. I couldn't breathe. I tried to open my mouth to speak, but words would not form themselves on my lips.

'You're going to die for what you did to him,' she screeched. I felt her hands pressing harder around my throat. 'You're not going to get away with this.'

Davison moved quickly forwards and was about to wrench Helen from me when, with her right hand, she whipped out the small chisel from the pocket of her jacket.

'If you touch me, she's dead,' she screamed, as she raised the chisel above my head. Its sharp edge glinted in the candlelight. With her left hand she continued to press down hard on my throat.

'Miss Hart – I have a gun,' said Davison, as calmly as he could. He took a pistol from the inside pocket of his jacket and pointed it at Helen. 'If you don't release Mrs Christie this moment I will have no choice but to shoot.'

In that moment my senses became heightened. I heard every little whisper, each intake of breath.

'What?' said Guy. 'No, please God, no.'

'This is terrible – what on earth is happening?' cried the Professor.

'Is Mrs Christie – surely she can't be—' asked Violet again, bewildered.

'Yes, I see – it's beginning to make sense at last,' said Gerard Grenville, slowly.

'Stand away, I said,' Davison repeated, his voice deep and authoritative. 'I will not tell you again, Miss Hart.'

Davison and I had talked about what he should do if such a situation arose. He was to aim for a shoulder or a leg, but I knew that, even though he reassured me that he was an expert with guns, such a shot would also put me at risk.

'Please! I must insist. Drop the chisel and step away. I'm going to count to three.'

Helen pressed down harder on my throat with her left hand and brought the chisel closer to my face. The look in her eyes was one of pure hatred.

'One . . . two,' said Davison.

I felt the cold blade dig into my skin.

'Three.'

'Helen!' shouted Guy.

In that moment, just before Davison fired the gun, I saw Guy rush across the room and throw himself over Helen. There was a scream, followed by a stream of blood, some of which splashed across my face. Davison grabbed me and pulled me out of the way, before he wrenched the chisel from Helen's hand. The relief of pressure from my neck was immense and I took in great gulps of air. Guy, holding his shoulder, collapsed onto the floor, while Helen fell back from the scene, the ugliness of it all hitting her suddenly.

'I did it all for you, Helen,' gasped Guy, his eyes squeezing tight with pain. Blood started to spread across his white shirt. 'If it hadn't have been for you, I wouldn't have done any of it. First Gina, then that girl on the ship. Oh, Helen, I wish—'

'Stop talking, you stupid man!' spat Helen, as she saw Núñez and two of his colleagues rush into the room.

'I wish we'd never started it,' said Guy, panting. 'None of this would have happened. But you said it would be simple. First of all, you said we should put poor Gina out of her misery. She was in a desperate state. It could be seen as an act of charity, you said. But then it all went wrong. It got so messy. We would need to put people off the scent, you said. We needed another woman, someone who could stand in for Gina.'

Everybody looked confused. It was not surprising. They had all been told that Gina had jumped off the ship. It was time for me to do some explaining.

'And that's exactly what you found, didn't you, Mr Trevelyan?' I said, slowly recovering my voice. The words grated across my throat, each one a nasty little stab of pain. Davison passed me a glass of water, but drinking did little to ease the discomfort. Yet I had to speak. 'It wasn't Gina who jumped off the ship, was it? The girl who you killed had a name. She was called Susan Saunders. You were very clever in choosing someone who had the same heavy build as Gina. I wonder how you found her? Perhaps you waited outside cheap revue shows in Soho, hoping to spot a suitable subject. And one day you saw Susan. It was easy to charm her, I suspect. You bought her a few drinks, said you were sweet on her. Of course, she fell for your good looks and fine breeding. Did you promise her something? She had always harboured hopes that one day she might become a ballet dancer – every little girl's dream, I suppose – even though she was far too overweight for that. Whatever the case, I'm sure she had a bright future ahead of her, a future you and Miss Hart cut short.'

'I'm sorry ... I'm—' Guy clenched his eyes shut as the pain and humiliation coursed through his body. 'Doctor ... please help. I'm bleeding.'

Davison whispered something to Trenkel, who with a guilty expression knelt down by Guy's side and examined him. He pulled back his shirt and revealed a gunshot wound to his right shoulder. 'He is losing a lot of blood, the bullet will need to come out, but the wound is not fatal,' he said. 'I can give him something for the pain.'

'I think we need a little more information from him first,' said Davison.

'All this is ridiculous,' said Helen, trying to recover her composure. She looked nervously at Núñez who was at the back of the room. 'He's out of his mind. He's talking nonsense.'

'Far from it,' I said. 'He's telling the truth – probably for the first time in a long while.'

Helen Hart looked as though she might launch herself at me again. However, she ran her fingers through her blonde hair and remained still, fixed to the spot. At that moment, I think she realised she had played her last hand. There was no place to go. But she was not the type to throw herself at the feet of the Inspector and beg for mercy.

'And what do you know of being a woman?' she spat at me. They were cruel words, ones that she knew would sting me. 'Standing there, all high and mighty, without a true or deep feeling in your body. No wonder you have nobody to love you, apart from your "friend" here.' She gestured towards Davison in an effeminate fashion. She had gone too far now.

'Well, at least my one true love isn't dead,' I said, using a napkin to wipe the blood from my face. 'It's tragic, really. Guy admits he was willing to commit murder for you, but you never really loved him. Isn't that right?' The time had come for me to reveal a secret Helen had kept from Guy. 'You only ever loved one man – Edmund Ffosse.'

At these words Guy opened his eyes wide. 'Ffosse? But he's a cripple. Or I should say, *was*.'

'Well, he is much more of a man dead than you will ever be alive,' said Helen, looking at Guy.

'What are you saying?' asked Guy. 'Helen? You can't mean that it's true? I was prepared to die for you. What about our plans?'

The question was met by a cruel laugh. 'Plans! What, to live happily ever after together? With you! It was just a pantomime. A farce from the very beginning.'

'But—' The realisation hit Guy harder than the bullet in his body, draining whatever colour he had left in his face.

'There's little point in covering up anything, now that—' She looked down at Edmund's lifeless body in his wheeled chair. 'Yes, of course I would have married you, as agreed,' she said, addressing Guy. 'But then, after a year or so, once everything had settled down, we planned to do away with you, just like we had done away with those others, so we would then be free to marry.'

'Th-the others?' The words seemed to choke him. 'What others?'

'Howard Winniatt and Mrs Brendel.'

'Edith?' The name stuck in his throat. 'My God. You killed Edith? How could you? And Howard?'

'Yes!' she said triumphantly. 'And there's no point in trying to make me feel guilty, you hypocrite. You knew it would have to be done.'

'But you said that you would get some thug from the port to do that.'

'I did think about it,' said Helen to Guy. 'But I realised that after we killed Gina back in London and then the business with that girl on the ship . . . well, I suppose I got quite a thrill out of it all. And Edmund was a very good teacher.'

Guy looked at Helen now not with adoration, but with disgust and horror. 'You make me sick,' he said. 'So all along you just wanted Gina's fortune. All of – of *this* just for money?' He tried to pull himself up – no doubt to try and finish Helen off – but the pain shot through his body again and left him in a crumpled heap.

'What do you mean, Edmund was a good teacher?' I asked. 'Of what?' I knew what she was going to say.

'Murder, of course,' Helen replied. She said the words as if this sentiment was the most natural thing in the whole world. In the corner stood Núñez, with a horrified

355

expression, taking everything down in a notebook. 'It was Edmund's idea, all of it. From the very beginning. He planned everything, thought of every little detail. He had a brilliant mind. He even starved himself so as to appear as though he was dying. But he had plenty of other appetites. He was a fabulous lover. Oh yes, that too, as you can see from *The Joy of Congress*, a sculpture that poor Guy always believed honoured his lovemaking abilities.'

'But ... I thought that ... how – it can't be – no—' Violet suddenly spoke. But she was was so utterly confused, and paralysed by shock, that she could express herself only in fragments.

'You poor girl,' said Helen, turning to her. 'Did you really think that Edmund loved you? The reality was that he pitied you. You proved useful, I'll say that. What was it he called you? The decoy? Yes, that was it.'

Violet's eyes filled with tears. Finally a sentence came fully formed from her lips. 'I don't understand ... you were going to marry? You and Edmund?'

'Yes, how many more times do I need to tell you?' snapped Helen. 'We would do away with Guy and I would have his fortune. Then Edmund and I would run away. We thought a little island in the Caribbean, perhaps, or one of those exotic-sounding places like Zanzibar or Tanganyika. Far from here, anyway.'

'Did you really think you would be able to get away with it?' I asked.

Her blue eyes flashed at me, a look full of strange contradictions. She stood before us with the countenance of a headstrong young girl accused of some minor misdemeanour of which she was secretly quite proud.

'Don't think you're anything special,' she said to me petulantly. 'I'm not going to give you any credit for uncovering the truth. In fact, I feel sorry for you. Having your head stuck in a book. Always living your life through other people. It must feel like a second-hand life, not really yours.'

'That's out of order,' said Davison, coming to my defence.

'No, let her have her say,' I said.

'I thought one of the chief skills one needed to be a writer was to be observant,' she continued. 'If that's the case, you must surely count yourself a failure.'

'Yes, you're right,' I said, clearing my throat. I found it a little easier to talk now. 'There were some clues that I failed to pick up on.' I repeated the line from *The Duchess of Malfi*. 'To begin with, I too was dazzled. You staged that scene on the ship like a play. It took me a long while to understand that it was not Gina Trevelyan who jumped off the *Gelria*.'

All eyes were on me now and a hush descended on the room. 'Something went wrong with your original plan to murder Gina, didn't it? You wanted Gina's death to look like a suicide, but she had fought back. Guy is right to describe it as "messy" – you knew that if the police found her body then he would be suspected of the murder. And you needed him – or rather, the fortune that would come to him from his wife – to make your plan work. You had to dispose of Gina's body, but of course without a corpse then there would be no money – at least not for some time. And so you came up with this idea – oh yes, a very clever idea, of finding someone to play the part of Gina.' I thought of the silly argument I had witnessed between Rosalind and Raymond, the two children squabbling over their teddies that looked so alike. It had been that scene – and the subsequent distressing dream I had about it afterwards – that had helped me piece all of this together. 'So you then recruited poor Susan Saunders to stand in for Gina on the ship. Of course the advantage of this plan was that you didn't need a body – you knew that her corpse would most likely never be recovered from the sea. And I presume it was atropine you gave the girl? It made her believe that she could fly.'

'Aren't you the clever one?' said Helen sharply. 'Yes, Edmund had given me the drug, told me how it worked and what I might be able to do with it. I gave some to that girl – whatever she was called, Susan, did you say? – that morning. The fat little thing had been cooped up, bound and gagged, in that trunk with nothing to eat since leaving England and I suppose the drug must have got to work pretty quickly. I led her out of the hold, up onto the deck and whispered into her ear that she was a prima ballerina, that she was going to dance her way across the stage in the company of the Royal Ballet, that all the great and the good had come to see her. It was pathetic, but she really did believe me, I think.'

'And that's when you screamed and I came running to try and help,' I said. 'Although you didn't need a body, what you did need was an independent witness to her death.'

358

'A part played so wonderfully by you, Mrs Christie,' said Helen with a note of sarcasm in her voice.

'But I don't understand – how is Douglas Greene connected with all of this?' asked Núñez, looking up from scribbling in his notebook.

'Do you want to try and explain, Mrs Christie?' enquired Helen, with the kind of nonchalance a person might adopt if asking an acquaintance to outline the rules of bridge. 'You seem to know the story better than I do.'

'I'm not yet sure about the details,' I said, 'but my guess is that Douglas Greene discovered the truth about Edmund Ffosse.' I had the attention of the whole room now, a feeling that made me distinctly uncomfortable.

'And what was the truth, Mrs Christie?' asked Núñez.

I hesitated, wishing that I could have broken the news to Violet in private. But I had no choice but to continue.

'That although he had once contracted a mild form of tuberculosis, his case was far from fatal.'

'But he was under the care of Dr Trenkel,' whispered Violet. 'He said that there was little hope. Edmund told me so himself.'

'I'm afraid there's been another deception there, hasn't there, Doctor?' I asked him to step forward to explain his actions.

'I'm afraid it's true,' said Trenkel. 'Edmund was not going to die, at least not anytime soon.'

'But, I don't understand . . .' Violet was becoming quite agitated now. 'It was a matter of months, weeks even. So we could have married after all?'

'Let the doctor speak, dear,' said Grenville, trying to calm his daughter.

'I didn't think any harm would come of it,' said the doctor. 'I got myself in a bit of a fix, I'm afraid. Mr Ffosse had a hold over me. He had a certain piece of information that meant he could blackmail me. When he asked me to provide him with a more serious diagnosis in exchange for keeping something away from the owners of the Taoro I thought it a good idea to agree with him. He wasn't asking for money or a cut, simply a diagnosis of a fatal case of tuberculosis. He said it was to put someone off the scent, a woman who was pursuing him. He wanted to let her down gently. How could I argue with that?'

'And that certain piece of information?' asked Núñez. 'You may as well admit it now, Doctor.'

'Very well – Edmund knew that I was responsible for the theft of some jewels from the Taoro.'

'Including Mrs Winniatt's pearls?' the Inspector persisted.

'Yes, and an emerald brooch and a diamond and sapphire bracelet,' said the doctor. 'You see, I had over-stretched myself, certain gambling debts that mounted up over the years and—'

'We can come to that in good time, Trenkel,' said the Inspector. 'So, Mrs Christie, you were right about Dr Trenkel and the pearls. I'm sorry I didn't believe you. But how did you know there was a connection between the doctor here and Mr Ffosse? And how does that fit in with Douglas Greene?'

'I can perfectly understand why you wouldn't believe me at first, Inspector,' I said. 'After all, the doctor was a trusted member of the Taoro staff, responsible as you said for saving many lives. But as I cannot stress enough, appearances should never be taken at face value. One always has to question, to wonder what lies beneath the surface of even the most respectable person. Now, as to Dr Trenkel and Edmund Ffosse – I knew there was something amiss when I discovered that Mr Ffosse's medical record was written in a hand unlike that on the rest of the doctor's reports. It was written neatly, so very different from the doctor's usual, quite messy style. After I checked a book in the library – a book I am certain the doctor must own too – I saw that he had simply copied out a few lines from this volume. A silly mistake, but an important detail. Isn't that right, Doctor?'

Trenkel nodded his head. 'If I had known that the action would have such consequences, I would of course never have got involved. If you can only let me explain—'

Núñez cut him off again. 'Later, Trenkel,' he said. 'We need to get to the heart of the matter. Mrs Christie? Please tell us about Douglas Greene.'

'Yes, well, although I haven't got the proof yet, my assumption is that Douglas Greene probably discovered that Edmund did not have a fatal illness. Greene was working on the island as a secret agent, you see, and it was his job to look into individuals suspected of subversive tendencies. During the course of his investigations, Greene turned up the fact of Ffosse's pseudo-illness. He no doubt questioned Ffosse about it and, in doing so, sealed his fate. Ffosse murdered him and then took him, most probably at night, to that cave beneath his house where he made it look as though the death had some kind of ritual or occult element. He started a process of mummification, covered the body in dragon's blood and planted a small figure of Tibecena. This was done to cast suspicion on Gerard Grenville.'

'I see now why you acted so strangely when you came to see me,' said Grenville, a look of revelation on his face.

I couldn't look at him. In my eyes he was still a monster, if not responsible for a murder then for something nearly as bad.

'And, of course, Ffosse had a use for the blood that he drained from Greene's body,' I continued. 'As someone pretending to suffer from tuberculosis he needed a ready supply to daub on his handkerchiefs to make it look as though he was coughing up blood. I wouldn't be surprised to find out that, when that supply ran out, he started to cut himself, using his own blood that he then transferred to a vial. Before he went out I assume he simply dipped a handkerchief into the blood. Oh yes, Ffosse played the part of an innocent very well indeed. After all, who would suspect a man in a wheeled chair?'

'And Howard Winniatt and Edith Brendel?' asked Núñez. 'Why did they have to die?'

'Some things seem so insignificant that we hardly notice them, or if we do, we discount them as trivial,' I said. 'We let these details – small snippets of conversation, an overheard phrase, something glimpsed from the corner of our eye – pass through our brains like clouds, drifting to the back of our minds. I too was guilty of this, not taking stock of something, not realising its true import, because I assumed it was nothing more than a minor detail.

'That sounds like I'm going off on a tangent, but I promise you I'm not. You see, this is how it was with Howard Winniatt. In his quest to document all that was around him, he observed that when Guy Trevelyan's trunk was loaded onto the ship in England, it was so heavy it caused the faces of the porters who carried it on board to turn beetroot red. Mr Trevelyan, a geologist, told everyone that he was carrying specimens of rocks and of course there was no reason to doubt him. But you see, when the same trunk was lifted off the ship at the port in Las Palmas we know it was empty. Something – or I should say someone – was in that luggage loaded in England: poor Susan Saunders, who had been sedated to keep her quiet. That first night at dinner at the Taoro, Mr Winniatt must have said something to Mr Trevelyan about the difference in the two weights of the trunk. I noticed Guy's change of demeanour at the table, but I put it down to Mr Winniatt's insensitivity, a comment he must have made about the woman everyone thought to be Gina and her suicide on the ship. Edith Brendel, although she did not realise its significance, also sealed her fate when, at the picnic under the Dragon Tree, she made a comment about Mr Trevelyan's luggage. She too would have to be got rid of. Isn't that right, Miss Hart?'

Helen Hart's composure had not changed since the first accusation had been levelled at her. She remained cool and unperturbed, her complexion flawless. 'She was nothing but an interfering old gossip,' she said. 'And going on and on about her jewels and the *Titanic* and the gilded life before the war.'

363

'But to drown her like that?' I asked. 'In her own bath?'

'I knew she was scared of water,' she said. 'I thought it would serve her right.'

My God, Helen Hart was an utter sadist. I had no pity for her.

'And what about Mr Winniatt?' asked Núñez. 'How did he die?'

Helen Hart looked at me and raised an eyebrow, as if she expected me to explain the details.

'Well, if you're not going to tell, I suppose I'd better,' she sighed. 'I still had some of the atropine left over that Edmund had given me for Susan. That morning, I met Winniatt while he was out walking. He looked hot and thirsty, so I offered him a sip of my flask. Soon after drinking the wine, he started to hallucinate. I told him that I would lead him to safety. I walked with him arm in arm to the bridge, where he stopped and climbed onto the wall. "I can fly," he said. And then he threw himself off into the *rambla* below. So you see, strictly speaking Howard killed himself.'

'And the bird-of-paradise flower skewered through the eye?' I asked.

'Oh that,' she said dismissively. 'Just a little joke. The trouble with Howard was that he was always spying on other people, always looking and watching and scribbling things down. Like you, Mrs Christie. But at least you have a modicum of talent, more than can be said for Howard. I stuck the flower into his eye as a punishment for all that snooping and spying.'

'And what were your plans for me?' I asked.

364

Helen was about to say something more when a deep moan came from Edmund. All eyes turned towards him.

'Look – oh Father! – his eyes are opening! Edmund, dear Edmund,' said Violet. After all she had heard, it seemed as though she still loved the man. 'He's not dead.'

'Don't go too close to him now, Violet,' warned Grenville, as Violet bent down to stroke his cheek.

'Helen . . .' Edmund mumbled.

Helen's hand went up to her mouth. For the first time since I had met her she seemed uncertain about what to say or do.

'Of course he's still alive,' I said. 'It wasn't really morphine that I injected, just a sedative, something to put him out for a while. I wasn't going to let him off that easily. He needs to stand trial for his crimes, as do you, Mr Trevelyan and, of course, you too, Miss Hart.'

Inspector Núñez moved in closer. Helen Hart had panic in her eyes now, the horrified panic of a hunted animal finally cornered. She looked around for anything she could use as a weapon, casting her eye over the chisel that lay on the floor, one of her marble sculptures – a bird with its wings spread wide set on a pedestal in an alcove – the gun still in Davison's hand, even the knives and forks on the table. Perhaps she contemplated making a run for it. But as the front door was guarded by Núñez's men, there was only one way out: through the back of the house to the studio and over the cliff that dropped down to the sharp rocks and sea below. Helen was too vain and too proud a woman for that kind of death.

'Take me,' she said, holding up her arms for Núñez's handcuffs. 'I'm ready.'

Just as Núñez locked the handcuffs and I was about to relax, Rupert Mabey strode across the room and, before anyone could stop him, he took a swipe at Edmund.

'That's for what you did to my brother,' spat Rupert. 'If I had a gun I would shoot you dead, you bastard. The way you left him, it was barbaric. When I went to see that place, where you—' He stopped and drew back his fist. Perhaps he had been the one I had surprised that day in the cave by Martiánez beach.

Edmund tried to raise his hand to protect himself but he did not have the strength. Rupert hit him again, splitting his lip.

'Stop, stop,' cried Violet. 'It's impossible, Edmund wouldn't do such a thing. He would never hurt another person. I don't believe a word that awful woman has told us,' she said, looking at me.

Núñez came over and placed a protective arm around the girl, but as he did so Violet reached into his jacket pocket and pulled out his gun.

'Get away from me,' she said, pointing the weapon at Núñez. 'You've never understood. I've never even liked you, never mind loved you. I love Edmund, I always will.'

'Violet – Miss Grenville, you don't know what you are doing,' said Núñez.

'Move back,' she said.

As the Inspector stepped away from her, Violet, her small hands shaking violently, swung the gun around and pointed it at Helen.

'You'll never do it,' said Helen, smirking. 'You haven't got it in you. Do you know what Edmund used to call you, besides "the decoy", that is? Shrinking Violet. Yes, that's right!' Helen laughed as she watched Violet's face crumple. 'We used to mock you behind your back, with your simpering ways and old-fashioned dresses. The way you used to worship Edmund, oh it gave us hours and hours of fun. Did you think that he would ever seriously contemplate loving you? You fool – Edmund always hated girls like you ...' she said, pausing for full effect. '*Virgins.*' She spat out the word as if she had tasted poison.

At this, Violet's face underwent a transformation. Her eyes, although still brimming with tears, hardened with hatred, hatred towards not just Helen Hart, but no doubt towards her father too. The toxic emotions of frustration, repression, anger and jealousy seemed to distil themselves into a moment of pure resolve. It was time for Violet to get her revenge. She took a deep breath and readied herself to pull the trigger. As Helen prepared to take the bullet she looked towards her murderer with an expression of triumph.

'Put the gun down, Violet,' shouted Davison, his gun trained on the girl. Violet did not look in his direction. 'I don't want to shoot, but I will. You must let the people who carried out these crimes stand trial for what they did. I'm in no doubt that they will be executed.'

'Edmund did nothing – it was all her fault,' said Violet. 'She is the one who has to die.'

Violet started to press the trigger of the gun, but then, just as she took aim to shoot Helen in the chest – just at the same moment as Davison was about to fire a bullet into the girl's shoulder or leg – the great bulk of Grenville crashed into his daughter. Inspired by Guy's attempt to save Helen, he brought the full force of his body in front of Violet to serve as a shield and to take the bullet fired from Davison's gun. What he had done to his daughter was beyond contempt, but there was no doubt that he loved her.

There was a cry of pain and a splatter of blood. Father and daughter collapsed onto the floor. Davison ran forwards and kicked the gun from Violet's hand and towards me, and, with Núñez's help, pushed the obese form of Grenville off the girl. His shirt and jacket were stained with blood and life was ebbing from his eyes.

'I'm sorry,' whispered Grenville. 'Violet – please forgive me.' They were his last words.

Chapter Forty-three

Davison opened the door to his suite at the Taoro. Sunlight streamed into the room, which looked out towards the sea, casting everything in a warm, golden glow.

'It's gorgeous weather, isn't it?' he said, as he gestured for me to sit down on the sofa by the window. 'The horizon is so crisp and sharp. A time of new beginnings if ever there was one.'

'And, for some, a time of endings,' I said. 'Have you heard any more from Núñez?'

'Yes, it seems as though Edmund Ffosse has finally made a full confession and admits to coming up with the whole plan. How could he not, though, after what Miss Hart said?'

'So the Inspector's got everything he needs now to charge all three of them?'

'Yes, it seems so,' said Davison, pouring me a cup of tea. 'Guy Trevelyan sang like the proverbial canary and has told Núñez how he disposed of his wife. The police are looking for her body, or what remains of it, in the Thames, down by the docks. Apparently he is full of regrets and remorse. I think I believe him.'

'I do too,' I said. 'Not that that will help him.' I thought back to the time on the *Gelria* when Guy made that outburst about the female being the deadlier of the species. 'I bet he wished he had never met Helen.'

'And I'm sure she wishes you had never been on that ship or out here in Orotava,' he said, taking a sip of tea.

'Perhaps, but Helen really was very clever,' I said. 'From the beginning she needed a witness to the death of the woman we were supposed to believe was Gina Trevelyan. Of course, it looked to me as though she was doing everything in her power to prevent a suicide. But, in effect, that sudden lurch that Helen made towards the fake Gina made the poor girl jump to her death. When I mentioned the possibility of recovering her body to the first officer, Helen let out a sob, which at the time I assumed was one of grief. Now I realise it was motivated by something else – fear of discovery. But, listen, I'm running ahead of myself.'

I paused to take breath. 'It was incredibly risky of her to attempt it, but I suppose Miss Hart is the type of woman who thrives on danger. You see, on the *Gelria* there was one person who would have recognised the real Gina Trevelyan – Mrs Brendel. She would have known that the fake Gina who Helen and Guy said had stowed away on the ship was not her at all. It must have been maddening for Helen and Guy to learn that Mrs Brendel had booked a last-minute passage on the ship. But they couldn't change their plan; it was too late for that. They knew that Mrs Brendel did not like to get up early, but to make sure she didn't see anything I wouldn't be surprised if they had slipped something into her drink the night before. Do you remember that Mrs Brendel said she had woken up feeling a little off-colour? Miss Hart also waited until bad weather set in as she knew that there would be a high likelihood of not recovering the body. When the ship passed through the Bay of Biscay, which was like a duck pond, she must have been beside herself. When would she be able to put her plan into action? But then, as we left Lisbon, the weather changed and a storm appeared on the horizon. Miss Hart seized her moment, soon after dawn.'

'How ingenious of her,' said Davison.

'And extremely wicked. Miss Hart also realised that if she presented herself as the guilty party then she would almost certainly not be believed. That's why she made that silly confession to the captain on the ship, claiming that she was the one responsible for Gina's death. It was all staged you see, like a tableau from a play, including a very touching scene I overheard later on the ferry. They must have known that I was listening. And she would have got away with it had it not been for a couple of careless throwaway remarks made first by Howard Winniatt and then Mrs Brendel,' I concluded.

'That evening at dinner, our first night here, Guy suddenly looked distressed and he explained the change in his mood and countenance by saying he had just been thinking about Gina. But of course, it wasn't that at all. Howard Winniatt must have said something to Guy about noticing the change in the weight of Guy's luggage between arrival and departure. Miss Hart was worried about whether other people at the table had heard. But Mrs Brendel, who had been sitting next to Mr Winniatt, actually had overheard something, even though she didn't realise its significance – how could she? But Guy and Helen knew that if this small detail got out, it could undermine their whole plan. Guy and Helen knew that Howard would have written this comment down and Helen, after killing him, must have stolen his notebook from his pocket and burnt it to destroy the evidence.'

'And all done for money? For Gina's fortune?' said Davison.

'That and love, of course. The love that Miss Hart felt for Edmund Ffosse.' I thought of the comment Helen Hart had made to me: about how love had the power to turn us all into criminals. 'Yes, a very toxic combination indeed.'

'And Grenville was innocent all along.'

'Well, innocent of murder,' I said, deciding not to elaborate. Since Edmund's arrest Violet had been talking about having nothing left to live for. Apparently, she was pleading with Núñez to charge her with the attempted murder of Helen Hart and the accidental death of her father, but the Inspector told her that he was sure it would not come to that. What would her future hold? Would she live to appreciate Núñez, the one man who truly loved her?

I hoped too that Mme Giroux would one day allow herself to trust another man. It would be difficult, as I had told her over breakfast earlier that morning, but not impossible. During that meeting I had shared with her some of the details regarding my so-called mental collapse of the year before. I told her of my grief following the death of my mother and the breakdown of my marriage to Archie: the awful rows, my dark feelings relating to his mistress Miss Neele, the jealousy that had eaten away at me, the belief that I would not be able to exist without my husband. But now, as I had told her, I felt able to imagine a life, a future, without Archie. Soon I might even feel ready to remove the wedding ring that still encircled my finger.

'Is something troubling you, Agatha?' asked Davison with a concerned expression.

Although I suspected Davison knew what I was thinking – he was that rare kind of man who seemed to divine a woman's innermost thoughts – I wasn't in the mood for that kind of intimate conversation. 'I was just wondering if there was any more news about Rupert Mabey?' I asked.

'He's not saying anything at present,' said Davison. 'But we have our ways and means. We're also waiting for some more information from the department about Mabey's links to Arcos, the All-Russian Co-operative Society. You remember when I first asked you to come out here to investigate the death of Greene? We suspected someone of feeding information to Arcos. Of course, we could never have imagined then that all these other crimes would happen. That reminds me, I received a telegram from Hartford this morning.'

'Oh yes?'

'He's got nothing but the highest praise for you. He wants you to go and see him when you return to England.'

'Really? Whatever for?'

'I expect he wants to thank you in person for what you did. As do I.'

Since the arrests, Núñez had received praise from his superiors; I was happy for him to take credit for solving the crimes. I asked for only one thing in return: that he destroy any incriminating evidence he had in his possession about Davison. The loss of Douglas Greene was bad enough for him. Now I couldn't bear the thought of Davison losing his reputation or his job.

'It was nothing compared with saving my life,' I said.

Davison smiled as he poured me some more tea. 'In addition to settling a decent amount of money on you, Hartford would like to pay for you to have a little holiday. It's the least the department can do.'

'You haven't got a destination in mind?'

'No, not this time,' he said, laughing.

'Well, I must say the Taoro is a lovely hotel, but I have got rather tired of the late-morning mists and the fact that it's more or less impossible to swim here.'

'What about Madeira? I've heard that there is—'

'I'm not sure,' I said. It was a place I had been supposed to visit with Archie on the Empire Tour. I had been stuck on the boat with seasickness. To go back there would make me too sad.

'Or Grand Canary? I know a delightful man in Las Palmas, a Dr Lucas.'

I gave him a quizzical expression. 'Not another doctor, please,' I said, thinking of Kurs and Trenkel, who was due to be charged with various counts of theft. 'I think I've had my fill of medical men for the time being.'

'Dr Lucas is nothing like them. It's a shame I couldn't introduce you when we first docked, but as you know we had our work to do here. He's something of a born healer and possibly the sweetest, most caring person I know. He might be just the thing you are looking for. He lives there very quietly with his wife, an Australian lady, and his sister, Mrs Meek. There won't be much of a social scene, but I can promise Dr Lucas will ensure you get lots of sleep, and there's also the possibility of some rather good swimming.'

'A change of scene is a very good idea and it would be a nice little holiday for Carlo and Rosalind,' I said. 'I feel like I'm coming down with a sore throat and I certainly could do with a rest.' I remembered the brutal way Helen Hart had pressed down on my neck and the vicious look in her eyes. I was convinced that she would have killed me if Davison had not threatened to shoot her. 'And the lack of a social life would be just the thing I need. I do have my novel to finish.'

So much had happened since I had witnessed that poor girl leap off the side of the *Gelria*. There had been so much unhappiness, so much death. In addition to Douglas Greene, there had been Howard Winniatt, Edith Brendel and Gerard Grenville. And next, no doubt, there would be the forthcoming trials and executions of Guy Trevelyan, Helen Hart and Edmund Ffosse. I hoped, now that evil had been rooted out, that this would that be the end of it. Yet I could not be certain.

After all, old sins do cast awfully long shadows.

The Facts

- After her much-publicised disappearance in December 1926 and the breakdown of her marriage to Archie, Agatha Christie was desperate to escape Britain. 'There could be no peace for me in England now after all I had gone through ... life in England was unbearable,' she wrote in her autobiography.

  On 23 January 1927, Agatha Christie set sail on the SS *Gelria* with her daughter, Rosalind, and her secretary, Carlo, bound for Las Palmas, Gran Canaria. She stayed at the Taoro Hotel, in Puerto de la Cruz, Tenerife, between 4 and 27 February.

  From Tenerife, Agatha journeyed back to Gran Canaria, arriving in Las Palmas with what she described as an ulcerated throat. There she met Dr Lucas, a man she thought of as a born healer, who told her, 'You've got plenty of strength and courage. You'll make a good thing out of life yet.'

- Agatha believed that her mother possessed psychic abilities and the writer had been interested in the occult for some time. By this point in her life, Agatha – in addition to her crime novels – had already written a number of supernatural-themed stories, including *The Woman Who Stole a Ghost* (later published as *The Last Séance*). These tales would be gathered together in the volume *The Hound of Death* (1933). While in Tenerife, she was also inspired to write the short story *The Man from the Sea*, which is set on the island and was subsequently published in the collection *The Mysterious Mr Quin* (1930).

- Arcos – the All Russian Co-operative Society – started trading in London in October 1920. The British secret service suspected that the organisation was being used as a front for subversive activities and on 12 May 1927, its headquarters at 49 Moorgate, London, was raided. In Parliament, the prime minister Stanley Baldwin read from a number of deciphered Soviet telegrams that he claimed proved that the Russians were guilty of espionage.

- While in the Canary Islands, Agatha finished her eighth novel, *The Mystery of the Blue Train*, published in 1928. 'Really, how that wretched book ever came to be written, I don't know,' she said. This was a turning point in Christie's life as she realised that, from now on, she would have to support herself by her writing. 'That was the moment when I changed from an amateur to a professional,' she wrote in her autobiography. Her divorce from Archie Christie was finalised in April 1928. She is still the bestselling novelist of all time.

Acknowledgments

Firstly, I must thank Agatha Christie herself, who has provided so many hours of pleasure to readers all around the world, including myself.

This is a work of the imagination, but during the research for the book I consulted a number of sources, which proved invaluable.

For life in Puerto de Orotava, as it was known then, I read the excellent *El turismo en la historia del Puerto de la Cruz* by Nicolás González Lemus and Melecio Hernández Pérez (Escuela Universitaria de Turismo Iriarte, 2010), *Tenerife, fin de trayecto* by Ana J. Hernández (Ediciones Idea, 1995) and *Misters: Británicos en Tenerife* by Austin Baillon (Ediciones Idea, 1995). For details on the Guanche civilisation and the process of mummification: *Guanches: Legend and Reality* by J. P. Camacho (Weston, 2012) and *Tierras de Momias: La técnica de eternizar en Egipto y Canarias* by Milagros Álvarez Sosa and Irene Morfini (Ediciones ad Aegyptum, 2014).

While doing my research in and around Puerto de la Cruz, in the north of Tenerife, I was helped enormously by Ana E. Castillo; Ramón Michán; Hortensia Hernández and the whole team at CIT who organise the biennial Agatha Christie festival.

For details about life on board ocean liners during the golden age of travel I consulted the books of the late John Maxtone-Graham, particularly *The Only Way to Cross* (Macmillan, 1978).

There are a great many people who work tirelessly behind the scenes to help bring a book to life, but I would like to single out the following.

I would like to thank my fabulous agent and friend, Clare Alexander, as well as the whole team at Aitken Alexander Associates, in particular Lisa Baker, Lesley Thorne, Leah Middleton, Nishta Hurry, Nicola Chang, Anna Watkins, and Ben Quarshie.

At Simon & Schuster in the UK I would like to acknowledge the brilliant Ian Chapman and my fantastic editor Suzanne Baboneau, both of whom have supported me throughout the writing of this series. In addition I would like to thank Jo Dickinson, Carla Josephson, Anne Perry, Maisie Lawrence, UK copy editor Sally Partington, Justine Gold and the marketing department, Emma Harrow, Jess Barratt, Harriett Collins, Gemma Conley-Smith and everyone in publicity, Gill Richardson, Claire Bennett, and Richard Hawton and the super-enthusiastic sales team. The cover was illustrated by Mark Smith and designed by Pip Watkins.

In the US I would like to thank the wonderful staff at Atria, particularly Judith Curr, my editor Peter Borland, Sean Delone and Daniella Wexler. Thanks too to production editor Isolde Sauer and to copy editor Nancy Inglis, Albert Tang for the cover design and illustrator Mark Smith for his evocative cover image.

Thanks too to all the Agatha fans, scholars and academics who have embraced the series, particularly Dr John Curran, Mike Linane, Dr Jamie Bernthal, Scott Wallace Baker, Tina Hodgkinson, Emily and Audrey at The Year of Agatha blog, and many more.

Lastly, I would like to thank all my family and friends and – most importantly of all – to my partner in crime and everything else, Marcus Field.

Turn the page to read an exclusive extract from
Andrew Wilson's next Agatha Christie adventure:

DEATH IN A
DESERT LAND

Prologue

Dearest Father,

I can hardly believe the words that I am about to set down. It sounds ridiculous, quite preposterous, but I fear for my life.

There have been many occasions where I have been forced to confront the prospect of death. The terrifying ascent and descent of the Finsteraarhorn, when I was convinced I was going to slip into a glacial crevice or, in the midst of a ferocious snow storm, be swept off the edge of a precipice and fall thousands of feet to my death.

I remember, too, the time when I travelled across the desert sands to Hayyil, a perilous journey that many had not survived. When I finally reached the feared city, I was taken prisoner. There I heard it said that in that place murder was considered so normal it was likened to the spilling of milk. There are those, many of whom were born in Arabia, who seemed offended by my spirit of adventure, as if I was an affront to the female sex. Indeed, in Hayyil I was told that a woman should only leave her house on three occasions: to marry her bridegroom, on the death of her parents and in the event of her own death.

And then there was that no man's land of the soul that I inhabited after Dick's death. I have never been so low as then, when it felt as though I had nothing left to live for, when I had been tempted to put an end to it all. The shock of the news of his shooting at Gallipoli almost stilled my heart. I was at a lunch party in London when one of the group, I can't remember who, casually mentioned how sad it was that Dick Doughty-Wylie had been killed in action. How were they to know of my attachment to him? Afraid that I was going to be sick, I excused myself from the lunch, my head reeling. I learned later that Dick had left his pistol behind on his boat and witnesses told me that he strode into village houses, which conceivably could have been packed to the rafters with Turkish soldiers, holding nothing more than his cane. As he reached the top of the hill, a swell of Hampshires, Dublins and Munsters behind him, he was shot in the head and buried where he fell. What a terribly sad end to a glorious life.

The only conclusion I can come to as to why Dick would advance unarmed is that he could not face the situation back at home: a wife who threatened to commit suicide if he were to leave her, a woman – me – whom he loved but knew he could never live with.

I must resist the urge to get swept back into the past. But there is a reason why I cite these occasions, moments when I have been faced with the possibility of non-existence.

I realise, and have done since I was a girl, that there is nothing that lies beyond the here and now. When I am gone I will know nothing, be nothing. I don't expect to meet dear Dick, or my darling brother Hugh, in some paradise of an afterlife.

So you see it is not death that frightens me. It is the thought – quite natural and justifiable – that someone may want to wrest my life away from me before I am quite ready. I have lived a good life, a great deal fuller and richer than many women on this earth, but am I ready to die yet? Of late, I have become weak, I have suffered from illness, but not to see that rare bloom of a daffodil in my garden in Baghdad? Not to walk through the date palms on a spring day or take a swim in the waters of the Tigris on a hot summer's evening? Not to sit under the shade of a tamarind tree and eat a ripe fig? Never again see the delights of my little museum that houses the treasures of the past? And this is nothing compared to the important work still to be done with King Faisal and the continuing improvements in an independent Iraq. No, I am not ready to go just yet.

It could be my fancy, but I have become convinced that someone wishes to do me harm. An uneasiness of spirit has come over me. I feel as though I am being watched, studied, but when I look up there is no one in the room. In the early hours, when I have been in bed reading, I have noticed how Tundra suddenly stirs, the dog's ears pricked, her bright eyes turning on some invisible enemy, a low growl beginning to form in the back of her throat. I have gone to the window, looked out into the purple night, but I have been unable to see or hear anything beyond the stirring of the palms in the breeze. I have taken to sleeping with my gun under my pillow. I need to be ready, prepared. As someone once told me, 'Every Arab in the desert fears the other.'

Ever, dearest, your affectionate daughter,
Gertrude

Dearest Father,

I cannot write very much because my hand is trembling so; I apologise if you cannot read my words.

Enclosed is a drawing that I received this morning. As you can see, it shows a grave at Ur, which has recently come to light during the dig overseen by Mr Woolley and his team. Next to a stick figure you will see a set of initials. They are my own: G.L.B.

If the missive's purpose was to unnerve me then it has worked. I feel shaken to the core. My hope is that this was the only function of the letter, that it was designed to unsteady me and nothing more.

In my previous letter, I spoke of my irrational fears that someone wants me dead; now I am afraid that this is indeed the case. You know that I do not have a melodramatic streak. I do not strive to create drama where there is none. I have always borne my miseries with fortitude. I am of a practical bent and not prone to fancies. I wish I did not have to set the words down; to see them written before me gives them a certain reality that makes me tremble. But set them down I must.

If I were to be found dead – and if there was an indication that my death was not due to the onset of some terminal illness – then it is safe to assume that I was murdered. And my murderer? I suggest you look no further than Ur.

Ever your affectionate daughter,
Gertrude

Chapter One

'So what do you make of it?' asked Davison, as he took the two letters from me.

I did not answer immediately. Too many questions were crowding my head. I took a sip of iced soda water and gazed across the terrace of the hotel to the Tigris below. A lonely boatman was singing a queer, discordant song that, despite not understanding its precise meaning, spoke to me of ghosts from the past.

'And the handwriting is definitely that of Gertrude Bell?'

'It seems so,' said Davison, peering at the scrawl again. 'Someone who knows about these kind of things has compared the letters to others she wrote to her father and stepmother and although it's difficult to say for certain, there are particular elements of style – such as the distinctive way she formed the letter "d", for instance, with a curious backwards slope – that suggest they were indeed written by Miss Bell.'

'I'd always understood that she had died of an illness, pneumonia or something bronchial,' I said, remembering the obituaries I had read of the famous adventurer and

Arabist when she died in July 1926. At that time I had been in the midst of my own troubles, drowning in a sea of grief after the death of my mother, valiantly trying to hold together a marriage that was threatening to come apart at the seams and battling a creative blockage that was driving me to the edge of reason.

'Yes, that was the story put out by the family,' said Davison. 'But according to the doctor who examined her, Miss Bell died from dial poisoning. A bottle of tablets was found by her bedside at her house here in Baghdad. Of course, no one wanted to draw attention to the fact that her death, or so it was thought, was a suicide.'

'And tell me again how these letters came to light.'

'It had been thought that her family had taken possession of the bulk of Miss Bell's archive, diaries, numerous photographs, documents relating to the archaeological museum she founded, letters and such like. Indeed, as I'm sure you know, her stepmother published two volumes of Gertrude's letters only last year. But then, just last month, these two letters were discovered in a tin box that served as a place to store seeds. It was only when one of her former servants, Ali, a gardener whom the family continued to employ, started to look for a particular type of seed that he came across the letters. Of course, he couldn't read the bulk of the documents – he's a local and Miss Bell was always proud of the fact that she communicated with her servants in Arabic – but Ali knew that they had been written in his mistress's hand. And he knew enough English to realise that the initials G.L.B. were those of Miss Bell. He did the right thing and took the letters to our man in Baghdad. Apparently, the drawing distressed him a great deal. He thought it represented some kind of curse.'

'I can imagine it would have that effect,' I said. Although I had missed the British Museum's 'Treasures of Ur' exhibition earlier in the year, I had seen a similar drawing of dozens of stick figures reproduced in the *Illustrated London News*. Reading about the discovery of the skeletons, which were thought to be victims of human sacrifice that dated to 2,500 years before the birth of Christ, had sent a chill through me. 'Do you know if Miss Bell had any enemies?'

As Davison smiled, his intelligent grey eyes sparkled mischievously. 'Plenty, I would have thought. She was hardly the easiest of women to get along with. Headstrong, independent if one wants to be polite, bloody infuriating if one is speaking plainly. Sorry, I—'

'Davison, you know I always prefer plain speaking. Did you know her well?'

'We only met a few times, once out here in Baghdad, another time in Egypt, and then, of course, in London.'

'And is there anything I should know about her background? Her work for you or for one of your secret government departments, for instance?'

Davison looked away from me, his gaze settling on a cluster of black rocks on the other side of the riverbank. 'Now, is that a sacred ibis down there?' He started to raise himself out of the wicker chair to take a closer look. 'I do believe it is. You know what, I've never seen one of those. Fascinating, of course, especially if you're interested in

Egyptian mythology. Venerated and mummified by the ancient Egyptians, you know, a representation of Thoth.'

I could feel my cheeks begin to colour with frustration.

'But, on closer inspection,' he said as he squinted down at the river, 'it could be a northern bald ibis, said to be one of the first birds that Noah released from his Ark, that bird being a representation of fertility. Anyway, whatever it was, it's gone now.'

As he turned his head to me, Davison assumed a pose of the utmost seriousness. He managed to freeze his features into a mask of implacability before the skin on his cheeks started to turn pink, his eyes sparkled once more and he burst into a loud fit of laughter.

'I'm sorry, Agatha,' he said, taking up a starched linen napkin to wipe the beads of sweat from above his upper lip. 'It was too good an opportunity to miss to tease you. I know it's not really a laughing matter, but you should have seen your face! You looked like you wanted to slap me – or at the very least walk out of the hotel and take the first Orient Express back to London.'

'You can laugh as much you like,' I said, fighting the urge to smile, 'but there was a time, not too far in the past, when you didn't trust me enough to provide me with all the information I needed to help you. Remember?'

'But Tenerife was different,' he said, lowering his voice to a near whisper. 'You know the reason why I was so reluctant to share certain details of my life with you.'

'That may be so,' I said. Although it would have been easy to do so, I decided not to embarrass Davison, and instead turned the conversation back to the matter in hand. 'Now that you've had a jolly laugh at my expense, why don't you tell me what you know?'

'Very well,' he said, as he crossed his legs. 'Yes, you're right. Miss Bell did work in secret intelligence during the war.'

'In what capacity?'

'She was stationed in Cairo, where it was her mission to provide us with evidence about the links between the Germans and the Turkish Empire, particularly in eastern and northern Arabia. Because she had done all this travelling, trekking across the desert, gossiping with sheikhs over strong coffee, she had an unparalleled insight into certain alliances which would otherwise have remained obscure. She wrote reports for the Arab Bulletin, which I'm sure you know provided the British government with a stream of very helpful secret information.'

I thought back to my own time in Cairo, where I had lived with my mother for three months during the winter of 1907. What a stupid girl I had been. At seventeen years old, I had only been interested in romance – endless flirtations with dashing men in the three or four regiments stationed out there – and my appearance.

'Miss Bell sounds like she was an exceptional woman,' I said, feeling distinctly unworthy in comparison. 'I'm right in remembering that she took a degree from Oxford?' My education could be described as patchy at best – for great swathes of my childhood I did not even go to school – and, the more I heard from Davison, the more I was beginning to feel envious of Miss Bell's extraordinary achievements.

'Yes, the first woman to take a first – and a brilliant one

at that – in Modern History. And in two years, instead of the usual three. She always seemed the most intelligent person in the room. That had its benefits, particularly for the department, but of course she was not the most subtle of individuals. I remember once, at some grand dinner, sitting opposite her and hearing her describe one of the diplomat's wives, in a dismissive voice, as a "nice little woman". That was always her insult of choice for women she deemed her inferior, which was the majority.'

In that instant, I felt a certain relief that Miss Bell was no longer with us – I doubted she would have liked me – and then, almost immediately, I felt ashamed for thinking ill of the dead. 'But why do you think she believed someone at Ur wanted to kill her? Did she know anyone there?'

Davison took out a couple of photographs from the inside pocket of his jacket and passed them over to me. 'This is Leonard Woolley, of whom you've no doubt heard, the man in charge of the dig down at Ur.' I studied the image of a man dressed in shorts and a jacket, a man with a puckish face, who was sitting cross-legged on the ground, peering intently at a clay slab in his hands. 'Woolley and Miss Bell knew each other during the war when he was head of intelligence at Port Said and she was stationed in Cairo. From all accounts, they seemed to get on well. The only thing we've managed to dig up is a possible suggestion that the two did not see eye to eye in regards to the dividing up of the treasures at Ur.'

'What do you mean?'

'Well, in Miss Bell's role as head of antiquities in Iraq, it was her duty to decide which objects she should set aside for her museum here in Baghdad, and which ones she allowed the team at Ur to transport back to Britain and America. Apparently, Woolley was upset that Miss Bell insisted on keeping an ancient plaque showing a milking scene. I've been told that Woolley valued it at around ten thousand pounds. She also managed to secure a gold scarab, which experts believe is worth one hundred thousand pounds.'

I could not disguise my astonishment. 'Really? As much as that?'

'Yes, and she won it on the toss of a rupee.'

'I can imagine Woolley would be annoyed. But surely nobody is suggesting that's the reason why he might want her dead?'

'We both know that murder has been done for an awful lot less.'

'Indeed we do,' I said, taking a moment to pause to look at the river, with its traffic of *ghufas* and other vessels. 'So what do you have in mind? You told me something of your plan before we left London, but I'm assuming there is something more specific you want me to do?'

'Yes, there is,' said Davison, all traces of his former joviality now erased from his face. 'We need to know for certain whether there is any truth in Miss Bell's suspicion that she was going to be murdered. For that, I'm asking you to travel down to Ur. I've already discerned that you would be welcome there. There is a Mrs Woolley who normally dislikes other women on site. She is the queen of the camp and likes to be treated as such. She cannot endure the prospect of competition from other members of the female sex, but I am told that for you she would make an exception. The reason why you are most suitable for this assignment, the reason why your name was mentioned to me by the head of the division, Hartford, was because of Mrs Woolley's enthusiasm for *The Murder of Roger Ackroyd*. Something of a literary snob by all accounts, but her passion for that book is—'

'I see,' I said, feeling uncomfortable with the prospect of further praise of my work. 'Can you tell me any more about Mrs Woolley?'

Davison did not say anything for a few seconds. As he began to form his thoughts, I noticed a pair of horizontal lines crease their way across his forehead, making him look a good deal older.

'Perhaps it's better if you forge your own opinion of her,' he said, draining the last of his brandy. He raised his hand to call over the waiter. 'But know this: Miss Bell told various acquaintances that she believed Mrs Woolley to be a "dangerous woman".'

'And is this her, in this photograph here?' I asked, gesturing towards an image of a woman who, although middle-aged, still possessed a certain striking beauty. The photograph showed her sitting on the desert floor examining a shard of an old pot.

'Yes, that's her, all right,' said Davison. 'From what I've heard of her, Katharine Woolley is a Jekyll and Hyde character, charming one moment, cold and cruel the next. There is also some mystery surrounding the death of her first husband, Lieutenant Colonel Bertram Keeling, whom she married at St. Martin in the Fields in March 1919. Six months later, Keeling, who was only thirty nine, shot himself at the foot of the Great Pyramid.'

'And did Keeling work in intelligence too?'

'As a matter of fact he did – during the war, in Cairo. But at the time of his death he was Director-General of the Survey of Egypt and President of the Cotton Research Board.'

'A good cover for espionage if ever I heard one. Do you know if he had any dealings with Miss Bell? Had they a history I should know about?'

'Not as far as we know. But the very nature of these things means that a great deal of what occurred during the war remains a secret.'

'But doesn't it seem odd to you that Keeling and Miss Bell, both of whom worked in Cairo in intelligence during the war, went on to die as supposed suicides?' I asked. 'What if someone wanted them dead and made the murders look like suicides?'

'It's a possibility, of course. But we've never thought about connecting the two cases because—'

'Because the suggestion is that your own government, or an agency acting on its behalf, may have something to do with their deaths?'

'I wouldn't put it quite in those terms,' Davison said dismissively.

'I'd rather know the whole truth, if you have access to it,' I said.

'Yes, of course, but I promise on this occasion there is nothing else I can tell you. I'll put out some feelers, see what I can come up with, but at the moment there really is nothing to link their deaths.'

'That's not quite true,' I said, taking up the photographs

of the archaeologist and his wife. 'There is something that links them together: the Woolleys.' I tried to picture a sequence of possible events, the scenes flashing through my mind like a series of imagined tableaux. 'Why would a man kill himself six months after getting married? That doesn't seem right to me, as he would surely still be in the first flush of romance. Of course, he may have realised that he had made a terrible mistake or he could have faced the prospect of ruin. Perhaps he had saddled himself with debt or had embroiled himself in an impending scandal in his personal life. Those need to be ruled out. With suicide, there are so many factors one needs to take into account, but there's something about that case that strikes me as odd. And then, seven years later, Miss Gertrude Bell, at the peak of her achievements, takes her own life by an overdose of barbiturates. That too doesn't ring true. And these letters written by her just before her death, there is something very queer about them. Why have they just turned up now?'

Davison was looking at me with a mix of admiration and bafflement. 'I'm at a loss to know what to say,' he said. 'I'm afraid I don't have any answers.'

'The "suicide" of Colonel Keeling, Katharine Woolley's first husband, in 1919,' I continued. 'The "suicide" of Miss Bell in 1926, whom we know had dealings with Leonard Woolley and who described Katharine as "dangerous". Then the recent discovery of these letters, letters written by Gertrude Bell in which she directs us to Ur to look for her killer. Could the murderer be either Leonard or Katharine Woolley?'

'But what could be their motive?'

'Something that is hidden out of sight and kept in the shadows, at least for the moment,' I said. 'It could be connected with their intelligence work – we know that Colonel Keeling, Miss Bell and Leonard Woolley all served in secret operations during the war. Perhaps that's something you can look into?'

Davison nodded and scribbled in his notebook. Although we were sitting in the shade of the terrace, the breeze had dropped and the heat was becoming unbearable. I shifted in my seat and took another sip of my soda water, which was now lukewarm. 'Of course, there is another possibility.'

'There is?'

'Oh yes,' I said, pausing for a moment. 'The Woolleys, the husband and the wife, could have been responsible for both murders.'

'What do you mean? As if they had some kind of pact?'

'Perhaps,' I said. 'People have done stranger things for love – or some warped version of it.' I thought back to the case in Tenerife and the mess Davison had got himself into over his feelings for a young man, whose partly mummified body had been found in a cave. And I thought of Archie and the scandal surrounding my disappearance at the end of 1926.

'Yes, indeed, but best not to dwell on that,' said Davison, as he noticed the cloud of melancholy that had started to steal over me. 'So, what do you think? Are you happy to travel down to Ur? To see what you can dig up? As I said, I'm certain you're the perfect person for this.'

As Davison continued to talk – about what an extraordinary job I had done in Tenerife, how I had brilliantly applied my skills as a novelist to the business of solving crimes – I thought of my old life as a conventional wife and mother. Archie's affair with Miss Neele, followed by the nasty rash of newspaper headlines that followed my disappearance, the ridiculous rumours that Archie was somehow responsible, the allegations that I had staged the whole thing as some cheap publicity stunt, had taken their inevitable toll. And then there was the interview I had been persuaded to give to the *Daily Mail* earlier in the year which was designed, in that dreadful phrase, to 'put the record straight'. Little did anyone know how much I had drawn on my skills as a novelist to answer their questions.

I often wondered, when I woke in the middle of the night and was unable to get back to sleep, whether I could have saved my marriage to Archie. If I had been more attentive to Archie . . . if I had been a better wife . . . if I had never taken up writing and had simply devoted myself to him and his concerns, and laughed at the inane jokes of his golfing friends and never had a complicated thought in my head. Would that have made any difference? Of course, it was all too late now. The divorce had gone through. We were no longer man and wife. But if I was no longer a wife, who was I? A mother, of course, yes always. An author? After that awful period of writer's block, following my mother's death, I had produced a couple of books of which I was not proud. But I hoped I was back on track now. After all, I had no option: writing was the way I earned my living. But what else?

'Agatha – are you all right?' It was Davison. 'Did you hear what I was saying?'

'Sorry, it's this heat,' I said, feeling a little dizzy. 'I'm not sure Baghdad entirely agrees with me.'

'Yes, you do look a little pale. I say, why don't I walk you back to your room?'

'That would be very kind, thank you,' I said, as Davison took my arm. 'I really do think it's best if I lie down.'

But I had no intention of taking a rest.

NEWPORT COMMUNITY
LEARNING & LIBRARIES

A TALENT FOR MURDER

ANDREW WILSON

'You, Mrs Christie, are going to commit a murder.
But before then you are going to disappear . . .'

London, December 1926: a station platform is thronged with
evening commuters. A train hurtles out of the blackness.
A waiting passenger falls forward towards the track only
to be pulled back at the last minute by a passing stranger.
The passenger is **Agatha Christie**, her guardian angel a
blackmailer of the most insidious, manipulative kind.

That seemingly chance encounter takes **Agatha** on a
terrifying course, her adversary determined to exploit her
genius for plotting murders to kill on his behalf.

She disappears from view for ten full days. Where did she go
and what did she do? In this tantalising novel, Andrew Wilson
weaves an utterly compelling story about this still unresolved
mystery surrounding the world's bestselling novelist.

'The queen of crime is the central character in this audacious
mystery, which reinvents the story of her mysterious
disappearance with thrilling results' *Guardian*

SIMON &
SCHUSTER